Praise

—5 star review from *Love Romance Passion* on *Her Wanton Wager*

"I found this to be an exceptional novel. I recommend it to anyone who wants to get lost in a good book, because I certainly was."—A Top Pick from *Night Owl Reviews*

"I thoroughly enjoyed this story. Grace Callaway is a remarkable writer."
—*Love Romance Passion* on *Her Prodigal Passion*

"A very enjoyable book with a wonderful heroine, a well written romance, an interesting side plot, and lots of really hot sex."—*Romance Reviews by Alice* on *Her Husband's Harlot*

"The depth of the characters was wonderful and I was immediately cheering for both of them."—*Buried Under Romance* on *The Widow Vanishes*

"Callaway is a talented writer and as skilled at creating a vivid sense of the Regency period as she is at writing some of the best, most sensual love scenes I've read in a long while. For readers who crave sexy, exciting Regency romance with a fresh plot and intriguing characters, I would highly recommend *Her Protector's Pleasure*."—*Night Owl Reviews*

"Grace Callaway is one of my favorite authors because of her fearlessness in writing love scenes that truly get the blood pumping."—*Juicy Reviews*

Books by Grace Callaway

HEART OF ENQUIRY
The Widow Vanishes
The Duke Who Knew Too Much
M is for Marquess
The Lady Who Came in from the Cold
The Viscount Always Knocks Twice
Never Say Never to an Earl
The Gentleman Who Loved Me

MAYHEM IN MAYFAIR
Her Husband's Harlot
Her Wanton Wager
Her Protector's Pleasure
Her Prodigal Passion

GAME OF DUKES
The Duke Identity (2018)

CHRONICLES OF ABIGAIL JONES
Abigail Jones
Abigail Jones and the Asylum of Secrets (2017)

THE GENTLEMAN

WHO LOVED ME

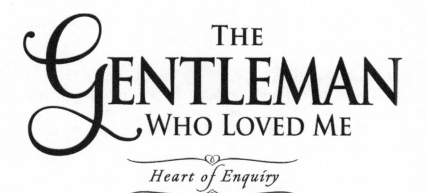

Heart of Enquiry

GRACE CALLAWAY

The Gentleman Who Loved Me is a work of fiction. Names, characters, places, and incidents are the products of the author's imagination and are used fictitiously. Any resemblance to actual events, locales, or persons, living or dead, is entirely coincidental.

Published in the United States

Cover design: © Seductive Musings Designs
Images: © Hot Damn Stock

Printed in the United States of America

Acknowledgements

For those who have been asking tirelessly for Andrew's story over the years—this one's for you!

I've been so touched and humbled by the support I've received from you, my lovely readers. From the bottom of my heart, thank you for reading my books, caring about my characters, and cheering me on during this wonderful—and sometimes challenging—journey of writing. I couldn't be doing this without you.

To the usual suspects: Tina, Diane, Brian, Brendan, all of my family, and the Montauk 8. Your support, expertise, love, and friendship make everything possible. Love always!

Prologue

1816

EASING FROM BENEATH the naked woman, Andrew Augustus Corbett left the bed. He froze, muscles bunching, as she stirred beneath the red satin sheets... still asleep—*Praise Jesus*. A widow twice his age, she'd put him through his paces. He had ample experience with the voracious ladies of the *ton* and hadn't been surprised by her appetite, but it had made him reconsider how he charged for his services.

As he tugged on trousers and boots, belting a dressing gown over his bare torso, he mused that he ought to be compensated for satisfaction given rather than time spent in a patron's company. After all, he'd brought the lady in question to climax a half-dozen times: no small feat by anyone's standards. Stamina was never a problem for him—by virtue of his hot-blooded nature and his expertise in his trade—but his expenditure of energy should count for something, shouldn't it?

He glanced at the bed: in her sleep, the widow stretched toward the place he'd vacated like a cat seeking a sunny spot. Another satisfied customer. Yes, he'd definitely talk to Kitty Barnes, his employer and lover, about upping his fees. Like any commodity, pleasure lost worth when it was sold too cheaply. At eighteen, he'd been in the business long enough to know that he had to make the most of his prime years.

And if I want to make it past my prime, he thought darkly, *I'd best secure us that extra blunt.*

Kitty had made some disastrous decisions in the past year. Despite his advice, she'd expanded her business with reckless abandonment. When her string of brothels failed, one after another like a line of dominoes, she'd compounded her error by betting on even riskier investments. Now she was up to her ears in debt to Bartholomew Black, a cutthroat not known for his patience.

Last week, a dove had appeared on her doorstep, a note tied to its snapped neck:

Pay—or face the consequences.

His chest clenching, Andrew closed the door behind him, his booted feet striding down the empty corridor. At this early hour, guests and employees of the bawdy house were sleeping, and he welcomed the stillness. The momentary solitude in which he didn't have to charm or cajole or be anything but what he was. A man with worries. A man who could no longer staunch his fears—for his lover, himself... and the girl in their care.

His gut knotted at the thought of Primrose. At four, the blonde tot was as bright as her namesake, her sweetness as unexpected as a flower springing up in the stew's dirty streets. Wherever she went, her charm and sweet songs made strangers smile; hell, she'd even wound her way into *his* jaded heart. She was the little sister he'd never had, and he was determined to protect her innocence—in and of itself a bloody miracle, given her murky origins.

Three years ago, Kitty had brought home the infant girl, surprising Andrew—his older lover wasn't what you'd call the maternal sort. Kitty's brisk explanation had cleared up any confusion: some rich cove was paying her to take care of his by-blow. Personally, Andrew thought a man could do better for his daughter (even if she was a bastard) than placing her with an infamous bawd, but who was he to judge?

He knew nothing about fathers. Self-deprecation twisted his lips as he treaded up the steps to Kitty's private suite. He'd neither met nor been acknowledged by his own putative sire; the only thing he had from the man was his middle name, which Kitty had fashioned into part of his *nom de plume*.

The world knew him as Augustus Longfellow. A better man might cringe at the crude moniker, but Andrew didn't fool himself: he was no gentleman. Honor and pride were luxuries he couldn't afford. He was a survivor, one who'd parlayed his every God-given asset—Longfellow wasn't false advertising—to make his way up in the world.

As his departed mama had put it, *If you have it, sell it.*

But it would take his less obvious gift—the one between his ears—to keep his ragtag clan of three safe. Over the years, he'd stashed away some savings, gifts and the like from grateful customers. He'd kept the money a secret from Kitty for pragmatic reasons. Whilst his paramour had many talents, fiscal responsibility wasn't one of them, and there was no use throwing good money after bad. He didn't have enough to clear her debts, but if he invested wisely, he might be able to appease Black with regular payments.

Thus, he'd been keeping his eyes and ears open for the right opportunity...

Shattering glass pierced his reverie. For a moment, he froze, staring at the projectile that had smashed through the window. A bottle—fire spewing from its rag wick.

"Bloody fuck!"

The words exploded from him as he sprinted to the window, yanking down a curtain, using it to beat down the flames spreading over the carpet and floorboards. He whacked at the fire as it strained hungrily toward the tinder all around. He fought off the conflagration—then heard more glass breaking, followed by terrible thumps, the whoosh of air being consumed.

Heart thudding, he spun around: the corridor—littered with flaming bottles.

Everything was ablaze.

Holy hell.

"Kitty!" he shouted. "Fire!"

The door at the end of the hall flew open, revealing a night rail-clad Kitty.

"Dear God." The inferno raged in her wild gaze. "It's Black, he's after us—"

"Sound the alarm, get everyone out!" Andrew was on the run, battling flames to reach the stairway at the other end of the hall. "I'll fetch Primrose and meet you outside!"

He raced up the spiraling steps to the garret room. At the top, he twisted the doorknob, cursing when it was locked, even though he'd been the one who'd lectured Primrose to keep it that way.

He pounded his fist against wood. "Primrose, wake up! There's a fire!"

No reply. He backed up, readying to break down the door when it squealed open. Primrose blinked drowsily up at him, her toes peeping beneath her nightgown. "Andrew?"

"Come with me. Now," he said urgently.

Without a word, she lifted her arms, and he scooped her up, heading back the way he'd come. Smoke thickened the air, stung his eyes. He came to a halt as waves of heat blasted into him: flames engulfed the floors, walls, ceiling. He jumped back as a beam collapsed in a shower of embers. No way to make it to the last flight of stairs. Against his chest, Primrose's small body wracked with gasping coughs, her arms tightening around his neck.

Cursing, he retraced his steps back up to the garret room. Slammed the door to shut out the choking smoke. Sprinting to the chamber's only window, he threw it open and pushed

Primrose's head through.

"Breathe, little chick," he said, his voice gritty from the smoke.

As she drew in great gulps of air, shouts and the clang of a fire bell came from the front of the building. Andrew took rapid stock of his options. Here, at the back of the house, there was only one way out: a twenty-five-foot drop to the empty alleyway. To climb down, he would need a rope…

He went over to the bed, yanking off the bedsheet. He tore it in half, twisting and knotting the pieces together. He tested the makeshift cord: strong but not long enough. Adding the curtain panels to extend the length, he secured the rope to the bedframe, tossing it out the window. The end dangled some fifteen feet above the cobblestones. Still not long enough—but a damned better option than being burned alive.

He crouched in front of Primrose. "I need you to do something for me."

"All right." Her trusting reply came readily, despite the fear in her wide jade eyes.

He placed a hand atop her sunny curls. "We're going to climb down that rope together, but I'll need both of my hands. That means you must hold onto me very tightly. You're not to let go under any circumstances, understand?"

"Yes, Andrew."

"Then up you go." He turned around, and she clambered onto his back, her arms circling his neck and her legs clamping his waist. He grabbed the makeshift rope and exited through the open window onto the narrow ledge of the roof. When the cord held after another testing tug, he readied to make the descent—and heard her frightened whimper.

"Trust me, sunshine," he said.

Her arms tightened around him; her curls brushed his neck as she nodded.

With a silent prayer, he stepped off the edge.

They swung in a dizzying arc before his boots hit the wall of the building. Bracing with his feet, he lowered them down the rope, fist over fist. He made the mistake of looking down: the cobblestones swam in his vision, miles away from where they hung, suspended, one false move away from certain death. Primrose's heart hammered against his back, and her face, buried against his neck, was slick with tears.

"Don't look, sweetheart," he panted. "We're almost there."

Trembling, she burrowed closer. His muscles bulged, straining as he climbed down foot by foot. He didn't have a plan for when they ran out of rope. He'd have to do a free fall for the last fifteen feet, to somehow cushion Primrose's body with his own—

"I'll be there in a minute!"

His head whirled in the direction of Kitty's voice, the clip-clop of hooves. Relief blasted through him at the sight of the wagon barreling down the alley, and he had a crazed desire to laugh. How could he have underestimated Kitty? If he could count on one thing, it was that she always landed on her feet—which meant, in this instance, that he and Primrose would too.

Strength renewed, he continued the hand-over-hand journey to the end of the rope, beneath which Kitty had now aligned the straw-filled cart, closing the gap to less than ten feet.

"Hold on," he told Primrose.

When she clutched him tighter, he let go of the rope. He twisted in the air, shielding her small body with his. His back hit the cart, the breath knocking out of him.

Primrose scrambled off of him and peered into his face.

"Andrew?" she said fretfully.

"I'm fine," he managed.

She burst into tears.

Gingerly, he sat up and patted her rumpled curls. "There,

my brave chick. No use crying after the fact, is there?"

"I w-wasn't brave. I was scared," she sobbed. "You s-saved me."

Survival had rid him of any capacity for self-delusion. He knew what he was, and it wasn't a hero, not by a longshot. Yet her words wended through him like dawn's first rays through the rookery's dark streets.

"Shut up, you stupid girl! Or I'll give you something to truly cry about."

Kitty's threat drew his eyes to the driver's bench. His lover's russet tresses were loose around her cloaked figure, her beautiful features hard with rage. Primrose instantly quieted, biting her lip, her breaths fitful as she tried to obey.

Andrew's gaze clashed with Kitty's.

She said defensively, "There's no time for bawling. Black's not done with us yet."

Bloody hell, she's right.

He tucked straw over Primrose, murmuring, "Close your eyes and try to sleep, all right?"

When she nodded, he vaulted into the seat next to Kitty.

He took up the reins. "Where to?"

"Somewhere far," Kitty said, her features feral. "Somewhere beyond the devil's reach."

Chapter One

1835

LOOKING LEFT AND right, Miss Primrose Kent (Rosie to intimates) ascended the stairs of the Hartefords' elegant townhouse. The Winter Masquerade—her Aunt Helena's annual January ball—was a crush, a fact that had helped Rosie to escape undetected. As she continued her stealthy mission, she held no illusions about herself, good or bad.

In terms of redeeming qualities, she was possessed of beauty and charm, which had fueled her popularity since her come-out four years ago. Since then, she'd been flocked by gentlemen, her dance card overflowing with names. And if the British Museum were to assemble an exhibit of Meaningless Courtship Artifacts, she could single-handedly furnish the entire collection.

She'd been given sonnets, compliments, and trinkets of every kind.

The one thing she'd not received? An honest proposal.

Which led to her faults. She was frivolous, scheming, and a flirt—and that was just scratching the surface. The list of her shortcomings was too exhausting to contemplate at the present juncture.

Reaching the top of the stairs, she peered furtively around the corner: the first floor corridor was empty, thank goodness. Although she wore a swan costume, the upper part of her face hidden by a feathered white demi-mask, the servants were bound to recognize her. After all, as the only niece of Lady Helena, the Marchioness of Harteford, Rosie had been given free rein of these halls all her life. Or, more accurately, since she'd been reunited with her family at the age of eight.

The earliest years of her childhood existed behind a curtain of fog—one that she wasn't certain she wanted to look behind, even if she could. Whenever her mind bumped up against that nebulous time, her hands would grow clammy, her pulse skittering. Moreover, her maid Odette (French and a true find) had told her that dwelling upon unpleasant things resulted in wrinkles on the brow and around the eyes, and that was the *last* thing Rosie needed.

She told herself it didn't matter that she couldn't remember her life before age five. Her mama, Marianne, had furnished her with the essential and disreputable details. Rosie was the product of her mother's youthful indiscretion with Aunt Helena's brother, Thomas, heir to the Earl of Northgate. Thomas had died in a riding accident, leaving Mama, unwed and in a delicate condition, with no choice but to wed Baron Draven, an evil man. After Mama had given birth, her new husband had taken Rosie from her... and here the facts grew hazy.

The first four years of Rosie's life took the form of shapeless, nameless shadows. Whenever she'd questioned Mama about it, the other evaded the subject or grew terrifyingly quiet, as if the mere mention of the topic elicited pain. All Mama would say was that, after a long search, she'd found Rosie with Sir Gerald Coyner, a childless gentleman who'd wanted a daughter of his own.

Rosie remembered Sir Coyner, of course: he'd been her guardian from age five to the time that she'd been reunited with Mama. She didn't like to think of Gerry—that was what he'd liked her to call him—because her memories were... confusing. On the one hand, she recalled that he'd been a doting, if oft absent, figure in her life. When he was around, he'd showered her with gifts, given her anything she'd set her heart upon.

On the other, she couldn't forget that terrifying night. The night when Gerry had almost killed Mama in order to keep Rosie for himself. If it hadn't been for the heroics of Rosie's adoptive papa Ambrose Kent—back then, he'd been a Thames River Policeman assisting Mama in her search for Rosie—all might have been lost. Papa had saved Mama and defeated Gerry, who'd died by his own knife.

Rosie fought off the shivers. Taking a breath, she composed herself with the help of a trick, one she'd used for as long as she could remember. She pictured one of the dolls in her collection: it didn't matter which one, they all had serene porcelain faces and pristine dresses. As the image of that perfect, impervious countenance expanded in her mind's eye, a girlish voice whispered soothingly, *Be pretty and charming, and nothing can hurt you.*

Her breathing calmed. The strategy was childish, she knew, but it worked and had helped her to carry on through the ghastliness of recent months with her chin up, a smile fixed in place. Yet, after four failed Seasons, she had to face up to the undeniable truth: with her infamous origins, there was no hope of her making a respectable match. Even the support of her influential aunt and well-connected family couldn't nullify the fact that Rosie was a bastard.

Fool that she'd been, she'd once mistaken popularity for acceptance, and she'd learned the hard way that the two were not the same. All along, the *ton* had been toying with her the way a cat does a mouse before enjoying it for supper. The years of male admiration had come to naught: those so-called gentlemen had only wanted one thing from her, and it wasn't marriage.

Mortification welled as she thought of the flirtations—

and, yes, a few stolen kisses—that she'd believed would win her a proper husband and coveted place in Society. In reality, all that had come of her dalliances had been more ugly gossip and scandal. Now she was a hussy *and* a by-blow. As if that weren't bad enough, her disgrace had been publicized by a gossip rag.

Last month, a vile publication called *The Prattler* had featured a poem entitled *The Plucked Rose*:

> *With hair as bright as sunlight,*
> *And eyes so fair and bucolic,*
> *Who'd have thought a miss like that,*
> *Would in dark gardens frolic*
>
> *With Lords H., M., N., and S.,*
> *And, lest one forgets, Misters R. and P.?*
> *Will this improper alphabet reach an end,*
> *Or stretch into perpetuity?*

Wordsworth it was not, but that didn't seem to matter. The poem caused a minor sensation: even though no names were named, everyone knew who it was about. Outraged, Papa had gone to *The Prattler*'s office to demand a retraction, only to find that the press had abruptly closed down (good riddance). Nonetheless, the damage had been done: her reputation now hung by a gossamer thread.

Never mind the past. You can still fix this, she told herself fiercely.

Desperation cemented her resolve. George Henry Theale, the sixth and newest Earl of Daltry, was the solution to her problems. Tonight, she *had* to convince him to propose.

Arriving at the appointed meeting place, she cast a swift glance around before slipping inside the room and closing the door behind her. The space was intimate, the light of a candelabrum gleaming off the Broadwood piano that took center stage. There was a grander music room downstairs, but Aunt Helena's husband had had this private atelier installed for his lady's pleasure. Rosie had spent many a happy hour here, listening to her aunt play and singing to the other's accompaniment.

At the thought of desecrating this place with an assignation, shame and guilt bubbled up. But she'd had no other choice. It hadn't been easy evading her chaperones, and this was the most convenient place to have a few private moments with the Earl of Daltry. Speaking of which... where was the blasted man?

She'd had a footman deliver a note to Daltry a quarter-hour ago, inviting him to meet her here. She'd been confident the earl would come. Not only had he paid marked attention to her in recent weeks, but he was in the market for a wife. In his early fifties, he'd recently and unexpectedly come into a distinguished earldom. Rich, titled, and never married, he was now faced with the duty of getting an heir.

Which made him perfect for Rosie's purposes. He needed a young wife; she needed a title with enough clout to restore her reputation. Given that it was January and the height of winter, London had a dearth of both, which meant that she and Daltry were the solutions to one another's problems. She had to clinch this deal whilst she had the advantage; when the Season started, fresh marriage-minded misses would flood Town, giving Daltry far too many options.

The door opened, a swell of sound invading the room. Despite her resolution, Rosie's heart thumped beneath her feather-trimmed bodice as the dark outline of a man appeared, the door sealing shut behind him. He stood outside the circle of the candelabrum's light, and she couldn't ascertain his identity.

She cleared her throat. "Is that you, Lord Daltry?"

Although she'd intended to sound worldly, her voice came out as more of a squeak.

"I'm not Daltry."

Her insides quivered at the deep masculine tone. Its faint rasp snagged in the far reaches of memory. Did she know this man? As he stepped out of the shadows, she didn't recognize him. If it hadn't been for the dimness, there was no way she would have mistaken him for the earl.

The stranger was far taller, for one thing, and his shoulders broader. Somewhere in his thirties, he was a male in his prime. He wore his thick, tawny hair a bit longer than the fashion; it brushed his collar at the back, giving him a leonine air. The rest of him exuded predatory grace as well. He wore no costume, and, like a lion's skin, his stark evening wear emphasized the virile power of what lay beneath. A black demi-mask hid the upper half of his face.

She couldn't discern the precise color of his dark and heavy-lidded eyes. His gaze seduced not with effort but with a lazy, just-out-of-bed sensuality. The lower half of his face was chiseled, his jaw strong and firm, an intriguing contrast to the fullness of his lips...

Why in heaven's name are you thinking about his lips? Or how recently he vacated a bed?

She shook off her daze. Even in his masked state, this male was undeniably striking—and definitely not a lord. Having memorized *Debrett's Peerage* and being an avid title watcher, she would have recognized him.

Botheration. She needed to be alone in a room with an attractive, untitled rake as much as she needed a run in her new silk stockings. She had to get rid of him.

"Who are you, sir?" she demanded.

"A friend."

"That would be impossible as we are not acquainted."

Something flitted through his eyes. It was gone in the next

instant, chased away by a sardonic gleam. "Nonetheless, I have your interests at heart, Miss Kent."

She frowned. "How do you know who I am?"

"Your brightness is difficult to conceal."

Oh, please. One more meaningless compliment to add to the heap. Stifling the urge to roll her eyes, she focused on getting him out of here before the earl arrived.

"Be that as it may, we cannot be alone," she said pointedly. "I am without a chaperone."

"That didn't stop you from arranging a meeting with Daltry, did it?"

Good God, how did he know?

When in doubt, brazen it out, her inner voice whispered.

"I'm sure I don't know what you mean," she said in lofty tones.

"And I'm quite certain that you do." Amusement deepened his voice. "Much as I hate to disappoint you, Miss Kent, the earl is not coming. I intercepted your note, you see."

Indignation made her forget her feigned innocence. "How *dare* you interfere with my affairs!"

"I wouldn't normally, but you left me no choice. It is one thing to flirt with disaster, Miss Kent, and another altogether to jump into bed with it."

She didn't know what offended her more: his arrogant meddling or plain-spoken wit. She squared her shoulders and went with the latter. "You oughtn't to mention a bed in a lady's presence!"

"Then act like a lady, and I won't have to."

In the next instant, he was prowling toward her, and she took an instinctive step back. But he passed her, going instead to the Broadwood. He ran a long finger over the ivory keys; beneath his controlled touch, the keys trembled but didn't make a sound.

It struck her that he seemed to know a lot about her, but

she didn't know a single thing about him. Which put her at a serious and dangerous disadvantage. If he circulated the fact that she'd set up a rendezvous with Daltry, she'd be utterly ruined. Her reputation was already a house of cards. The slightest waft of scandal and—*poof.* There would go her future.

Panic squeezed her lungs. She had to gain the upper hand and quickly.

Be pretty and charming and nothing can hurt you.

Summoning a conciliatory smile, she went over to the side of the instrument. "I thank you for your concern, sir," she said in dulcet tones, "and I'm sorry we got off on the wrong foot. I was, um, taken aback by your presence."

"Because you were expecting someone else."

"Because you claim to be a friend and yet I don't know your identity," she averred.

"My identity is irrelevant. I am here to talk about you. More precisely, about your behavior."

An ember of anger smoldering beneath her breastbone, she kept her tone light, even managed a dimple as she inquired, "What about my behavior, sir?"

His gaze met hers, and she had to quell a shiver at the shrewdness glinting in those dark depths. How could she have thought this man indolent in any way? He was a predator lying in wait.

"Let's start with the fact that you've been carrying on like a brazen flirt. Lords Thompson, Halper, Sandon, Millock, Templeby... the list goes on." His casual enumeration of her sins chipped at her composure and set her teeth on edge. "While I understand that your intention is to marry well," he went on, "you are not helping your cause by acting like a hussy. In sum, your behavior is not befitting of a lady—or worthy of you, Miss Kent."

No one had ever spoken to her in this fashion before—at least not to her *face.* The gall of the bounder! Heat pushed behind her eyes, and she pushed back.

"You have no right to address me in this manner," she said, her voice quavering.

"Believe me, I take no pleasure in doing so." His calmness added fuel to her fire. "But I take even less pleasure at the notion of harm befalling you, and it certainly will if you continue down your present path. Men like Daltry will not bring you happiness. You sell yourself too cheaply, Miss Kent, and you and I both know the *ton* has no desire for cut-rate goods."

Cut-rate goods. Blood roared in her ears. The ember in her chest became a conflagration, hot shame and fury melting away her composure.

"Better?" she said scathingly. "A man like you, I suppose? A *gentleman* who intrudes upon a lady without as much as an introduction and commences to lecture her on her behavior?"

For an instant, he regarded her, his expression unfathomable. Then his mouth took on a cynical bent. "I'm no gentleman, Miss Kent, nor do I claim to be one. And that is precisely my point."

"Other than insulting me, I wasn't aware you had one!"

"I regret that the truth offends. My point is merely that one ought to understand what one is and act accordingly." He rounded the corner of the piano, and she refused to back down when he stopped a foot away, towering over her. "I may not be a gentleman, but you *are* a lady."

"You don't know me," she said in a low voice.

I'm a bastard. At the core, I'm a wicked girl who'll do whatever it takes to get what she wants...

"I know that you come from a good family. Tell me, do you want to bring shame on their heads—worry to their hearts?"

His words tightened the screws of guilt. She knew that her behavior would disquiet her family, and they'd just gone through an ordeal with Mama's difficult birth. Fear surged through Rosie: why was it that this man could see through her, into the dark and shameful places that she wanted no one to see?

His brows raised. "Do you really want to act like a spoilt child?"

She reacted; her hand lifted, and she watched with horror as it flew toward his face. He caught it easily and then her other hand, too, when it went to join the other. In the next heartbeat, he had her trapped, his body caging hers against the curve of the piano, her arms immobile at her sides.

"Let me go, or I'll scream," she hissed.

"You won't. You can't risk getting caught with a man like me."

Damn his eyes. "You're a bastard!" she said in a furious whisper.

"I am," he acknowledged. "Now do we have an understanding, Miss Kent? Promise me you'll leave off Daltry. He's a libertine, and you deserve far better."

"Botheration, why do you care what I do?" she cried.

She renewed her struggles; he stepped forward at the same time. They collided, and she froze at the full-on contact with unyielding male power. She'd never been this close to any man—and definitely not one with such virile proportions. Each breath pushed her bosom against his hard chest, each heartbeat made her more aware of his muscular thigh wedged between hers. A strange heat unfurled in her belly, and her vision blurred... until he plucked away the feather drooping into her right eye.

"I just do, little chick," he said huskily.

Something stirred in the deepest recesses of her mind...

"Wh-what did you call me?" she stammered.

His eyes shuttered; he stepped back.

"'Twas nothing." His words were clipped. "Now do I have

your word that you'll steer clear of Daltry and his ilk and behave in a fashion that is worthy of you?"

His high-handedness snapped the gossamer connection, the uncanny awareness fading like a dream. Freed from his hold, she jerked away from the piano, dashing for the door and throwing it open.

Pivoting in the doorway, she saw that he hadn't chased after her. He remained where he was: an elegant masked stranger whose gaze seemed to see all too clearly through her.

"I'll do as I please." She lifted her chin. "And neither you nor anyone can stop me."

Having issued that bold decree, she fled on limbs that shook.

Chapter Two

THE SUDDEN SILENCE in the office percolated into Andrew's awareness, making him aware that he'd lost track of the conversation... yet again, devil take it.

He straightened in his chair. On the other side of the desk, the woman attired in grey silk was regarding him, her gaze slitting. Framed against the striped green walls of his office, she more resembled a proper matron on an afternoon call than a madam delivering a weekly report to her employer in his infamous pleasure house.

"Beg pardon, Fanny," he said curtly. "What were you saying?"

Fanny Argent's assessing gaze didn't waver. "It's not like you to woolgather, Corbett. Particularly when we are discussing profits."

That was Fanny: too perceptive by far. Then again, her keen mind was the reason Andrew had hired her on six years ago. At the time, his business had been undergoing rapid growth as he'd parlayed one brothel into a string of them—with Corbett's, his eponymous and exclusive club, being the jewel in his crown. Fanny had impressed him with her intuition and toughness, the core of steel beneath her petite brunette exterior.

It was rare to find a bawd who shared Andrew's own business philosophy: happy employees made for happy customers. Abbess Fanny (as she was known) managed five of his smaller clubs, and whilst she ruled with an iron fist, she also took care of her nuns. She, like he, had first-hand knowledge of working in the flesh trade, and they both understood its hardships. Thus, they took the welfare of their workers seriously.

That philosophy had allowed Andrew to attract the best in the business to work for him. He'd done that not through money alone, but through his commitment to the well-being of his employees from the wenches down to the chambermaids. Every employee of Corbett's could expect three square meals a day, medical attention when needed, and generous allowances for time off work. His novel approach had riled up his competitors, who raged against the "outlandish" wages and other benefits he offered—and he didn't give a damn.

Success allowed him to do things his way.

"I apologize, Fanny." He waved a hand. "Carry on."

Andrew set down the feather he'd been fiddling with and listened as the other continued reporting on revenue. Against the leather blotter, the white plume appeared feminine and fragile—reminding him of its owner. Primrose Kent seemed to have no idea about her own vulnerability.

He mused that his little chick had undoubtedly grown into a swan. His profession had made him a connoisseur of the opposite sex, and, by any objective standard, Primrose was a stunning beauty. She'd inherited her classic blond perfection from her mama, Marianne Kent, although her eyes—a rare shade of jade flecked with gold—were uniquely her own.

Andrew had met Mrs. Kent fourteen years ago, during the other's quest to find her daughter. Recalling Mrs. Kent's fierce determination, he surmised that strength of will must run in the bloodline. Despite Primrose's vulnerability, she was as headstrong as they came. If last night's fiasco was any indication, it was going to take more effort than he'd bargained for to protect the girl—*no, not girl any longer*, he reminded himself.

At the memory of her soft, womanly curves, his loins stirred... and he frowned. Bloody hell, what was wrong with him? Primrose was like his little sister. His reaction last night must have been a purely animal response—the result of not bedding a woman in... God, how many months had it been?

He'd ended the relationship with his on-again, off-again lover two years ago, and the only thing he regretted about that decision was that he hadn't done it sooner. Still, it had left him at loose ends when it came to his physical needs. He didn't relish the notion of paying for sex—yes, the height of irony— and while more than one of the wenches had offered their services gratis, he refused to take advantage of an employee. It also took more effort than he was willing to put forth to find a lover who was interested only in casual tupping when either of them felt the itch.

Besides, work was a demanding mistress and kept him busy.

Now there's an excuse, he thought with wry humor. *Next thing you know you'll be pleading a megrim, you bastard.*

The plain truth was that sex didn't hold the shine it once did for him. Perhaps it was because of his profession, the fact that he spent most of his waking hours surrounded by carnality. Perhaps it was because he'd been fucking since he was fourteen, and sex had lost its capacity to surprise or titillate. Or perhaps he was just getting older: at six-and-thirty, the idea of yet another meaningless encounter roused not excitement, but a strange and unwelcome malaise.

Still, it wasn't healthy to ignore his needs—especially when it led to unacceptable thoughts about the girl he'd once considered his younger sibling. He might not be a gentleman, but his motives toward Primrose were honorable and always had been. In fact, he wouldn't have shown himself last night, but her reckless actions had given him no choice but to personally intervene.

At least Primrose hadn't remembered him; for that, he was grateful. He had no business being around a lady like her. But he needed to keep her safe, to make up for the way he'd failed her all those years ago…

"Is my report boring you?"

Fanny's brusque words cut through his reverie. It wasn't the annoyed set of her features but the hurt in her eyes that gave him pause. If the bawd had one chink in her armor, it was that she hated when others underestimated her ability. He understood that—perhaps better than most.

"My apologies. Your work is of the highest caliber. My mind's just on other matters."

Looking slightly mollified, she said, "Care to talk about it—or, more precisely, *her*?"

He didn't bother to deny it. There was no point with Fanny.

"It's not what you think," he said.

Fanny smirked. "When it comes to treacle tarts, dearie," she drawled, reverting to their native Cockney slang, the marrow-deep language that no amount of elocution lessons could ever eradicate, "it ain't ever is."

"She's not my sweetheart," he said curtly.

"Surely you're not distracted by mere bed sport?"

"She's not that either."

Fanny's brows formed thin arches. "Pray tell, what is she, then?"

"She's none of your concern." Andrew rose to signal the end of that conversation. Striding over to the fireplace, he drummed his fingers on the mantel. "Now tell me of the progress with the Nursery House."

Genuine excitement entered the bawd's gaze. "Everything's on schedule," she said with clear satisfaction.

"We'll be moving the girls in by week's end."

With Fanny's help, he was launching an initiative to deal with one of his trade's biggest liabilities: pregnancy. Despite certain precautions he'd instituted at his clubs—vinegar sponges and rinses for his employees and, if the customer was willing, French letters provided on the house—conception was an unavoidable risk.

Being the bastard son of a whore, he ought to know.

Most pimps dealt with the matter by giving the wench a choice: get rid of the brat or be shown the door. It was a philosophy Andrew could not agree with—if for no other reason than that he valued his own existence. He couldn't call Maria Corbett an exceptional mother, but she'd given him life, and he'd loved her for it.

Of course, her decision hadn't been entirely selfless: she'd thought that she could exact payment for her bastard's care from her royal patron. But, as she'd recounted to Andrew bitterly whenever she got into her cups, the Prince Regent had never been one to pay his debts.

Andrew didn't know if his blood ran blue, but the rumor of his origins had given him a boost at the beginning of his career. High-kick ladies had enjoyed the novelty of bedding a blue-blooded gigolo. Aye, he'd fared better than most offspring of whores, a fact that had inspired him to build the Nursery House.

Located in nearby St. Giles, it was a place where his pregnant employees could pass their confinement and, afterward, where their children could be looked after if they chose to return to work. The Nursery House would provide lodging, food, and medical care for mother and child until they were ready to strike out on their own. As far as he was concerned, it would be a beneficial arrangement for all.

"The wenches are ready to move in?" he said.

"You can say that again. Sally Loverly's as big as a house."

Fanny paused. "Says she plans to name the babe after you, if he's a boy."

"Tell her that is unnecessary. She's a favorite amongst the patrons," he said in brusque tones, "and I'll be glad not to lose her."

Three knocks preempted Fanny's reply. Horace Grier, Andrew's right-hand man and the club's factotum, entered. A former seaman built like a warship, the gruff Scot kept Corbett's in shipshape and didn't suffer fools lightly.

Seeing the suspicious glance Grier shot at Fanny—and the hostile one she returned—Andrew stifled a sigh. For some reason, the factotum and bawd had locked horns from the day they met. Neither trusted the other, and both made sure their employer was aware of that fact.

"Time for the walk through, is it?" Andrew said.

Grier shifted his gaze from Fanny, whom he'd been watching the way a constable does a known thief. He bowed his grizzled head. "Yes, sir. Doors'll be openin' in less than an hour."

It was Andrew's custom to do a daily inspection of the club prior to opening. He would trust Grier with his life—indeed, he had once, which was why he was still breathing today. Nevertheless, he preferred to do a final check of the club himself.

Details were everything; he'd built Corbett's on that precept.

"Anything else to report?" he said to Fanny.

She'd already risen and was pulling on her gloves. Finger by finger, with a deliberateness that boded trouble.

"There is a list of extra expenses for the Nursery House that requires your approval… just a few items to make the girls more comfortable. Why, Grier," she said when the factotum (predictably) made a choked sound, "got something stuck in your craw?"

Her feigned innocence didn't fool anyone in the room. Seeing that Grier looked on the verge of an apoplectic fit, Andrew said sharply, "Send the list by. Good day, Fanny."

The bawd departed the room in a satisfied swish of grey skirts.

The moment the door closed behind her, Grier exploded.

"*Extra* expenses? Making the girls more *comfortable*?" The brawny Scot boomed in outrage. "Does that bluidy woman no' understand that you're already payin' too high a price for this venture—that 'tis your damned neck you're riskin'?"

As this was not a new argument, Andrew said mildly, "The idea for the Nursery House was not Mrs. Argent's but mine. She's just assisting me with the details."

"She's assisting all right—the way Eve did Adam," Grier said darkly. "With help like that, who needs enemies? And you with more than your share o' rivals already, and none o' them fond o' your latest venture. Trouble's brewin', mark my words."

Not the best news but also not unexpected.

"Let's talk whilst we make our rounds," Andrew said.

He and Grier headed to the front of the club. When he'd built Corbett's, he'd had passageways installed behind the walls, one running parallel to this hallway. It allowed him to keep an eye on everything that happened under his roof. Here, he was king of all he surveyed, and he never took that power for granted. Never forgot that he'd built this place out of nothing, that his blood and sweat soaked each brick and stone.

From the beginning, he'd known that quality attracted quality. Everything at Corbett's was first-rate, from the wenches to the food, gaming, and other entertainments. A gentleman who was allowed the privilege of a membership would find himself as much at home here as he would at Brooks's or White's—only it would cost him three times as much.

The waiting period for membership was now over a year long.

Andrew began his inspection in the foyer, a grand space that soared four stories high and ended with a stained glass dome depicting Aphrodite rising from the sea. A double-winged mahogany stairwell led to the floors above. Polished marble gleamed under his boots as he walked, Grier still ranting about the dangers of antagonizing the competition.

As if, Andrew thought wryly, the bastards weren't in a constant state of warfare.

Whoremongering was a dog-eat-dog business and not for the faint of heart.

"The situation is nothing new," he said as they moved into one of the card rooms. Seeing a stain on the buffet table linens, he waved over a liveried footman who stammered an apology and hurriedly set about changing it. "I don't tell the others how to run their business, and I sure as bloody hell won't allow them to tell me how to run mine."

"But how you're going about things impacts their profits." Grier dogged his heels as he headed into the adjoining chamber.

Outfitted with rosewood furnishings and Aubusson carpets, the high-ceilinged drawing room could have belonged in any grand Mayfair mansion and served as a place for clients to mingle with the wenches before selecting their partner—or partners—for the eve. From here, guests ascended to one of the upper floors, where private chambers boasted a number of exotic themes. For those willing to spend the extra coin, a custom room could be made up to fulfill the customer's wildest desires.

From a dungeon to a barn to a Sultan's seraglio, Corbett's offered up fantasies at their finest.

"The bastards were already up in arms 'bout the 'igh pay o' our wenches," the factotum insisted, "and don't get me started 'bout the bleedin' French letters. They blame ye for makin' the whores uppity and too expensive to 'ire. They're lookin' for any excuse to tear ye down—and you're 'andin' it to 'em on a silver platter with that bleedin' nursery."

"How I treat my employees is my prerogative," Andrew said shortly.

"Well keepin' ye alive is mine, and you're not makin' it easy."

"You've done a fine job of it so far, my friend."

"Aye, but Malcolm Todd weren't involved afore this."

The mention of his ruthless competitor gave him pause. "You've heard from Todd?"

"Not directly. It's just rumblings so far, but word is that he ain't pleased. And when Todd ain't pleased..."

The Scot didn't finish. Didn't have to. Everyone in London's Underworld knew the consequences of crossing Todd. The pieces of his enemies that surfaced in the Thames served as a frequent reminder.

"You've escaped 'is notice in the past because ye were small fish," Grier went on when Andrew remained silent. "But the bigger ye grow, the smaller the ocean becomes, and sooner or later, you're goin' to cross paths with a shark."

"I have my own set of teeth." In the early years, he'd settled the brawls at Corbett's with his own fists, and he still trained at a boxing club to stay in fighting shape. Even so, with success had come the need for added security; he now had over a dozen men on retainer for the purpose. "But, as to your point, I'll ask Mrs. Argent to proceed with more discretion on the project. Let's leave it at that."

The Scot opened his mouth... and closed it. It was one of the factotum's finer points that he knew when to hold his ground and when to stand down.

"Now onto the other matter I asked you to inquire into." Andrew raised his brows. "Any progress?"

"Aye," Grier said. "Dug up more on Daltry like ye asked."

Information was Andrew's stock-in-trade. The gossip that circulated in Corbett's was as prime as that of the St. James's clubs and worth its weight in gold. He kept files on anyone who stepped foot in his establishment (and some who hadn't). Daltry wasn't a regular, but he'd been in a few times, and Andrew had pegged him as an arrogant skinflint. He'd complained about the high prices while demanding the most exotic entertainments.

Andrew's gut knotted as he recalled Daltry's preference for young blondes. "Go on."

"To start, 'e's the black sheep o' the family, coming from a branch that made their fortune in trade. You know 'ow nobs frown upon that." Grier crossed his arms over his chest. "Well, 'is hoity-toity relations got a surprise when a bunch o' their own cocked up their toes, leaving Daltry to inherit the earldom. Now they've 'ad to change their tune about 'im. The dead earl's widow and one o' Daltry's aunts 'ost some 'igh-kick salon, and they've been singing 'is praises there. But, truth is, there's no love lost between Daltry and 'is kin."

"What about his personal affairs?"

"Never married. Three bastards by three different mistresses," Grier said, scratching his ear, "maybe more I 'aven't found. Daltry gave 'em all a 'undred pounds and washed 'is hands o' 'em."

Andrew's jaw tightened. "And his business dealings?"

"Owns a slew o' mills in Lancashire." Grier's face darkened. "Women and even bairns 'ave lost limbs and lives in 'is factories, but 'e hasn't done a thing about it. For 'is sort, it's all about profit—even if it's made on the backs o' others."

Andrew's hands curled. *Damnit, little chick. Why did you set your cap for this blackguard?*

As last night's encounter had proven, Primrose had grown into a surprisingly willful woman, and he knew that it would be no easy task to dissuade her from pursuing Daltry. To protect her from a disastrous course of action.

Somehow, he'd have to find a way. Because he wasn't going to let her down.

Not this time.

Chapter Three

"Oh, please, may I hold her next, Marianne?" Polly, the Countess of Revelstoke, begged.

Rosie's mama smiled from the chaise where she cradled Sophia Helena, the newest member of the Kent family, in her arms. "Of course you may, my dear."

Rosie tried not to sigh as Polly, her bosom companion, eagerly abandoned the settee—and the conversation they'd been having—to admire the babe. Since Polly's marriage several months ago, the girls hadn't spent as much time together, and Rosie missed the other dreadfully. She'd been looking forward to catching up before supper. But seeing Polly's aquamarine eyes light up, her face wreathed in smiles as she cuddled Sophie, Rosie knew that wouldn't be happening.

She supposed it was yet another flaw in her character that she didn't understand what all the fuss over the babe was about. Fastidious by nature, she had no urge to hold a small human who would drool on her new lavender satin frock and wreak havoc upon her coiffure (a pearl-studded coronet that had taken her maid over an hour to arrange). And what was so enticing about a creature who did nothing but sleep, slobber, and wet her nappy?

Shame followed in the wake of her uncharitable and, worse yet, *unsisterly* thoughts.

What's wrong with me? Why can't I be good—like the rest of the family?

She watched as Polly rocked the babe in her arms, clucking and making silly expressions with unselfconscious delight. She thought of Polly as her sister although, technically, the other was her aunt. The youngest of Papa's five siblings, Polly was the same age as Rosie, and they'd been bosom companions since the age of eight, when Papa had married Mama and adopted Rosie, officially making her a Kent.

In name only, came the unbidden and desolate thought.

Rosie considered honesty to be one of her chief virtues (and, let's face it, there weren't all that many to choose from). Hers was not the kind of honesty that involved telling the truth to others; one couldn't hope to survive in the *ton* with that sort of gauche earnestness. She had no compunction about using white lies to grease the social wheel: "Lady Fanglebottom, how I adore the little bird nests in your coiffure!" "*Did* you step on my toes during the waltz, Lord Kennelly? Why, I declare, I didn't feel a thing!"

Rosie could flirt, charm, and maneuver with the best of them.

Where her honesty came to bear was in regards to herself. She saw her faults with the same sort of cursed clarity with which the mythological Cassandra had seen the future. Rosie could portend personal disasters with painful acuity: she knew that the defects in her character would lead to trouble, and yet she seemed powerless to stop herself from making mistakes.

She had never been one to bemoan her fate, however—or take challenges lying down. She refused to allow the labels of "bastard" and "flirt" to prevent her from attaining her rightful place in the *beau monde*. She simply had to try harder and be smarter about it.

I'm going to win them all over, she vowed fiercely, *and nothing's going to stop me.*

Not even some outrageously attractive and virile masked

stranger.

Since the masquerade last week, he'd tracked her through her waking hours and even into her dreams. She was positive she'd never met him before—a man like that would be hard to forget—and yet she couldn't shake off a sense of *déjà vu*. As if she *did* know him… in some distant, twilight part of her mind that memory couldn't reach. When he'd called her "little chick," a bewildering warmth had burgeoned inside her…

Frustrated, she told herself to leave it be. Her mind was just playing tricks on her; if he was anyone worth knowing, she would know him. He was just some overbearing cad who had enjoyed amusing himself at her expense. The man had had some *gall* to intercept her note to Daltry: not only had he foiled her plans, he'd seen fit to lecture her on her behavior as well?

Righteous anger sparked, yet it was tempered by self-doubt. Her reputation must be in tatters indeed if some *nobody* thought he could meddle with her without consequences. Nothing could deter her from her plan to become the Countess of Daltry… but perhaps it wouldn't hurt to try some self-improvement? Not because she was heeding the stranger, of course, but because *she* wanted to turn over a new leaf.

At the very least, she decided, she could try to reform her less charitable thoughts. It could be one of her resolutions for the New Year. She would treat bad thoughts like sweets: limit them to no more than one a week…

"Goodness, Sophie's smiling at me," Polly gasped. "Rosie, come and see!"

Dutifully, she went over and peered at the infant. Unfocused amber eyes stared back. Tiny rosebud lips puckered.

"I think she is just passing gas," Rosie said.

"No, she was looking right at me and smiling—weren't you, precious?" Polly cooed.

The babe's gurgled response sent Polly into paroxysms of delight.

Rosie fought the upward impulse of her eyes. *One would think Sophie had just recited a sonnet—oh, botheration.* That was uncharitable thought Number Two already. She hadn't even made it to supper without exceeding her quota.

"Is something amiss, dearest?" her mama's soft contralto inquired.

Rosie schooled her expression before facing her mother. Neither age nor a difficult childbirth had dimmed Marianne Kent's celebrated beauty. Lustrous silver blonde locks were piled gracefully atop Mama's head, curls framing her famously sculpted features. She was as elegant as ever in an evening dress of cassis velvet, its cross-over bodice baring the top of her shoulders and emphasizing her newly svelte figure.

Confronted with her mama's shrewd emerald gaze, Rosie felt a mix of love and frustration. From the moment they'd been reunited, the two of them had shared an unbreakable bond, but of late tension had settled into their relationship. They had butted heads over the issue of Rosie's future: despite once ruling the *ton* herself, Mama could not seem to grasp Rosie's desire to secure a title. She disapproved of Rosie's husband-hunting tactics, which had resulted in endless rows between them.

In recent months, pregnancy and a new babe had prevented Mama from policing Rosie as keenly. The rift between them continued to widen, however, filling Rosie with nameless panic. She felt powerless to mend the breach with her mother because she couldn't give up on her goals—the acceptance she desperately craved.

Why, oh why, can't Mama understand?

She shaped her lips into a smile. "Nothing's amiss, Mama."

"You seem preoccupied. Care to share?"

"It's just a trifle. So inconsequential, in fact, that it's slipped my mind entirely."

"Hmm."

Rosie didn't like Mama's assessing gaze. For the other was beautiful *and* clever—which kept Rosie on her toes. Last week, she'd mentioned Lord Daltry in an off-handed manner, just to test the waters.

Mama's reply had been succinct: *"Daltry's an aging roué. You can do far better."*

But I can't. Rosie fought the rising despair. *Why doesn't anyone understand that?*

Scandals aside, she was fast approaching three-and-twenty and the dreaded shelf upon which unmarried ladies languished, stale and unpalatable. At this point, the only men sniffing at her heels were fortune hunters after her dowry, and even she hadn't quite stooped *that* low.

The door opened, a welcome distraction. Papa entered with his customary long-limbed stride, and the sight of his earnest features filled Rosie with love that equaled hers for Mama—minus the complications. From the moment Ambrose Kent had entered her life, she'd adored him. Reliable, honorable, and steady of character, Papa had always been her anchor in the storm.

He went to Mama, whose worldly demeanor slipped when he bent to kiss her cheek. The once scandalous widow looked as infatuated as a schoolgirl, Rosie thought with amusement.

"What are my girls up to?" he said.

His warm amber gaze included Rosie and made it easy for her to say lightly, "We were just waiting for you, Papa."

"And admiring Sophie," Polly added.

As if she knew she was the center of attention, the babe let out a wail from Polly's arms.

"I'll take her," Mama said.

"You've had her all day, my love. Mind if I have a go?"

Papa took Sophie from Polly, tucking the babe easily against his checkered waistcoat. "How is my little poppet?"

Rosie felt a queer pang in her bosom: "poppet" was his endearment for *her*.

You're being ridiculous. Stop it.

"Watch out for drool, Papa," she heard herself say. "It stains silk, you know."

"Does it?" He answered absently, his gaze never straying from his infant daughter.

Footsteps approached, and Rosie's brother Edward strolled in. At fourteen, he was a replica of Papa with his dark, unruly hair and lanky build, although his brilliant green eyes were a maternal inheritance. He was followed by Sinjin Pelham, the Earl of Revelstoke, and Rosie couldn't quell the surge of embarrassment at the sight of Polly's handsome new husband.

Not long ago, she'd made a cake of herself, setting her cap for the earl. She'd wanted him for the usual things: his title, wealth… and, let's be honest, his Adonis looks hadn't hurt either. Yet her heart had never been engaged, and she'd acted horribly—the memory scorched her cheeks—when she discovered the romance blooming between the brooding rake and her shy sister.

But what man *wouldn't* want Polly—who was good and sweet, so worthy of love? Polly, being Polly, had forgiven Rosie for being a petty brat, a fact that Rosie counted as one of her life's blessings. Because no man was worth losing Polly over. And seeing the newlyweds standing together now—Revelstoke's dark virility the perfect foil to Polly's wholesome, round-cheeked beauty—Rosie knew that the two were meant to be. As well-matched as a pair of bookends.

"What are we discussing?" Edward said without preamble.

Rosie loved her brother who, being a boy and an

adolescent, could also be a bit of a pest. He was regrettably brainy and hopeless when it came to matters of fashion (Rosie had to fight the urge to straighten his crooked cravat). Nonetheless, he'd been an unexpected ally since Sophie's arrival.

"We're on the topic of babies," Rosie said innocently.

"*Again?*" Heaving a sigh, Edward muttered, "No offense, Sophie."

Papa's dark brows rose. "What would you rather talk about, son?"

"Your work, for one," Edward said. "I was hoping to get some tips."

Papa was London's best investigator, and his firm, Kent and Associates, was in high demand. Edward had decided, along with his cousin Freddy, to follow in Papa's footsteps. Hence, the two fourteen-year-old boys were constantly underfoot, practicing their "detection" skills.

Papa gave a rueful shake of his head. "I'm sure such talk would bore present company."

"I would be interested," Edward protested, "and Revelstoke would be too, wouldn't you?"

"Actually,"—the earl cleared his throat—"Polly and I have some news to share. Sorry, Edward, old boy, but it's in the familial vein."

Seeing the bright glances exchanged between the newlyweds, Rosie gasped, "Polly... are you... are you *expecting?*"

Blushing, Polly nodded. "The babe will come next summer."

Gladness for her sister brimmed over in Rosie. As congratulations and calls for champagne filled the room, she rushed forward to clasp the other's hands.

"Oh, my dearest, I'm so happy for you," she breathed.

Polly squeezed her hands in return, their shared smiles

celebrating the joy of the moment.

After supper, the men retired to the study for cigars and brandy, and Mama headed up for an early night. Which left Rosie and Polly alone to finally have a cozy chat. As they had done so many times as girls, they curled up side by side on Rosie's bed.

"I can't believe you're going to be a mama," Rosie said in wonder.

Next to her, Polly relaxed against a mound of pillows, her blue skirts fanning over the coverlet. "Trust me, I haven't gotten used to the notion myself. Or even that of being married."

"Clearly, you've gotten the hang of *one* marital activity."

"*Primrose Kent.*" The other's attempt to appear severe was ruined by her giggles. "What do you know of such things?"

"Oh, *please*. Just because I'm a virgin doesn't mean I'm a ninny. But, dearest," Rosie said seriously, "you *are* happy? Marriage is everything you hoped for?"

"Everything and more." Pink-cheeked, Polly tucked a loose golden brown curl behind her ear. "But enough about me. I want to know what you've been up to."

At last. Oh, how Rosie had missed her confidante. Eagerly, she told the other about her plan to land Daltry and the mysterious masked stranger at the Harteford masquerade.

"Goodness," Polly said, round-eyed, "you have *no* idea who this stranger was?"

"None whatsoever. And you know I know everyone."

"But why would he care to intervene in your affairs?"

"I haven't the faintest notion. Perhaps he's just the arrogant, meddling sort."

"How strange." Polly bit her lip. "Rosie... you don't

suppose he had a point? Perhaps Lord Daltry isn't the best choice for you—"

"*Et tu*, Polly?" Rosie crossed her arms over her chest. "The last thing I need is another lecture."

"I promise I'm not lecturing," Polly said solemnly, "nor am I in any position to do so. I'm a middling class miss who married above her station, and I'm not an expert on the *ton* like you are."

Knowing Polly's old insecurities and all the obstacles she'd conquered to find her heart's desire, Rosie said fiercely, "Revelstoke is the luckiest man alive to have you, Pols. You deserve *every* happiness."

"As do you. And I can't help but note that when you speak of Daltry, you fail to mention what qualities of his will bring about that state for you."

"Of course I've mentioned his finer points." She had, hadn't she?

Polly arched her brows.

"Daltry has plenty to recommend him," Rosie said defensively. "He holds one of the oldest peerages in the land—"

"Qualities *other* than his title and money, if you please."

With a huff, Rosie left the bed, going over to the glass-fronted cabinet that housed her collection of dolls. Even though she knew she was too old for the hobby, she couldn't seem to relinquish it. She'd received her first doll from Sir Coyner, and now she had over a hundred of them, all preserved and sealed behind glass. She opened the doors and took out Calliope, whose calm porcelain face and pink satin ballgown were particularly soothing.

"Well, Daltry's two-and-fifty, so he's not utterly ancient. He has some of his hair and most of his teeth." She expertly retied the doll's cerise sash and turned triumphantly to her bosom companion. "And he is absolutely obsessed with the hounds."

"You detest the hunt!"

"But I adore Town, which is where I'll stay while he enjoys country pleasures. Amongst the *ton*, it's considered bourgeois for couples to live in each other's pockets."

"But I like spending time with Sinjin." Polly's brow furrowed. "Marianne and Ambrose are hardly apart. And the same goes for the rest of the family—"

"I'm aware of the Kent tradition." Melancholy tinged her words.

Papa's sisters had made brilliant matches: headstrong Emma had married a duke, gentle Thea a marquess, and even Violet, the incurable hoyden, had netted a Viscount. The irony was that, unlike Rosie, they'd chosen their spouses out of love rather than practical considerations. Kents were idealistic, uncovetous of worldly things, and morally good.

The opposite of me. The thought was depressing.

"What about love?" Polly persisted. "Isn't that important in a marriage?"

"Not for me." A lump rose in Rosie's throat. "I'm running out of time, Pols. Four seasons out, still unmarried, and a bastard tinged with scandal to boot. I don't have the luxury of waiting for a love match—and, moreover, one that comes with respectability. Because you know that's what I want." Her grip tightened on the doll. "What I've always wanted more than anything."

A rustling of skirts and Polly was there beside her, placing a hand on her shoulder. "After the way the *ton* has treated you, of course you want the security of a title. Of a marriage that would protect you."

Rosie nodded, her sister's words a balm to her spirit. She loosened her hold on Calliope, smoothing out the satin she'd crushed before returning the doll to the cabinet and closing the doors.

Facing her sister, she said tremulously, "Let me be happy in my own way, Pols. I know what I want. Please support me in following my own dreams."

"Of course I will. And I'll support you in any way you want me to."

When opportunity knocked, only a fool ignored it.

Rosie eyed the other. "*Any* way?"

"You know you can count on me," Polly said.

"Excellent. Because I have a plan,"—Rosie clutched her sister's hands—"and I *desperately* need your help."

Chapter Four

THE CHILL OF the January afternoon vanished as Rosie, accompanied by the Revelstokes, entered the bustling warmth of the Pantheon Bazaar two days later. She felt a kinship with this mecca of extravagant goods—and not only because she adored shopping. Once home to lavish assemblies for the *beau monde*, the grand building had gone through various iterations and owners, losing its reputation in the early part of the century. In recent months, however, it had undergone a radical transformation, reopening its doors to become a premier shopping destination.

Hope soared through Rosie. *Like the Pantheon, I, too, shall rise from the ashes of disgrace.*

Now everyone who was anyone flocked to the Pantheon's stalls. The finest goods could be found within the colonnaded grand atrium, which was decorated with plaster moldings and topped with a coffered dome. In addition to the shops, the Pantheon boasted a gallery of paintings on the upper floor and a glass-walled conservatory that housed a collection of exotic plants and beasts.

"Do you see Daltry?" Polly whispered.

Rosie, who'd been scanning the throng of well-dressed patrons, shook her head. "In my note, I said that I would be in the conservatory at two o'clock. There's still an hour to go."

"Are you certain you wish to do this?" The white silk lining of Polly's bonnet enhanced the clarity of her aquamarine eyes and their worried expression. "Because we can always—"

"This is what I want." Having heard the anxious litany on the carriage ride over, Rosie headed the other off at the pass. "Now onto more pressing matters: how do I look?"

Her question was prompted by pragmatism rather than vanity. Physical appearance being her main asset, she had to make the most of what she had. Moreover, conveying a proper, fashionable image was essential in battling the gossip about her.

No matter what anyone said about her, she would always *look* like a lady.

Thus, she'd worn a pink merino carriage dress with gigot sleeves and full skirts embroidered with black silk thread at the hem. A matching pink mantlet bordered with black velvet draped over her shoulders, a square-buckled ceinture cinching it all in at her waist. To top it all off, she sported a capote bonnet trimmed with pink ribbon and adorned with a clever mix of wax cherries and real hothouse blooms.

Although her corset made breathing a challenge and her bonnet required that she keep her head subtly tilted to offset the weight of the fruit, the effect was worth it. She was as perfectly turned out as any one of her dolls. She was ready to meet Daltry—and to land him.

"You look beautiful, as always." Polly nudged her husband. "Doesn't she, Sinjin?"

"You look very well, Miss Kent," Revelstoke said.

How he could make that assessment was anyone's guess since he had eyes for no one but Polly. Former rakes apparently not only made the best husbands, they were the most besotted ones, too.

Stifling her amusement, Rosie said, "Shall we make our rounds?"

The three of them spent the next half-hour meandering through the stalls. For once, the Pantheon's abundant delights failed to distract Rosie, her mind preoccupied by her bold plan. Daltry's new title was attracting unwed ladies like flies to honey, and she had to act whilst she still had an advantage. Thus, she'd sent Odette on a covert mission to deliver a note to him yesterday; the French maid had returned with an affirmative reply.

Now I must strike while the iron is hot...

"What do you think of this silver comb?" Polly asked.

With an expert eye, Rosie perused the tray of hair ornaments laid out by a stall keeper. "The silver filigree is pretty, but the gold comb would look ravishing with your coloring."

"Excellent choice, miss." The merchant beamed, no doubt at the prospect of the higher sale.

"We'll take both," Polly told him, "the silver for my sister and the gold for me."

As Revelstoke completed the transaction with the merchant, Rosie murmured, "You didn't have to do that, Pols."

"I know I didn't *have* to." Polly linked arms with her, their gowns swishing as they strolled on together. "But recall how whenever you went shopping, you always bought something for me too. I'm returning the favor."

"Back then I *had* to buy you things. For reasons I'll never comprehend, you chose charitable work with foundlings over shopping. But now look at you," Rosie said fondly. "You're a veritable fashion plate."

"I still prefer the foundlings," Polly admitted. "Sinjin chooses my wardrobe for me."

"No doubt he knows your measurements by heart."

"*Rosie.*"

Rosie laughed. "Oh, don't look so scandalized. Save it for when I tell you my good news about Daltry. Speaking of which—I'd best get on to the conservatory to meet him."

"At least let me accompany you—"

"I need privacy. But don't worry: Daltry and I are meeting in the section at the back where hardly anyone goes. And if anyone sees us, I'll pretend I lost you in the crowd, and Daltry was escorting me back to you."

Polly chewed on her lip. "If I don't see you back here in *exactly* fifteen minutes, I'm going to the conservatory to look for you."

"All right, mother hen." Rosie winked. "Wish me luck."

Rosie arrived at the conservatory a tad breathless. A new shipment of tea had arrived from China, and she'd had to make her way through a throng vying to get a sample of the fashionable brew. As a result, it was a few minutes past the appointed meeting time, and she saw that a uniformed man was cordoning off the entryway, shooing away would-be visitors.

"Oh dear," she said in dismay, "the conservatory isn't closed, is it?"

The man touched his hand to his cap, bowing. "For cleaning, miss."

Botheration. Had Daltry come and gone already? Should she wait here or go look for him...

"Beg pardon, but you wouldn't happen to be Miss Kent?"

She looked at the guard in surprise. "I am indeed."

"You're expected, miss." He untied the rope, granting her access. "In the rotunda at the back."

"Thank you." Flashing the man a relieved smile, she made her way in.

She'd never been inside the conservatory while it was empty, and, as she hurried through the long hall, she felt as if she were inside an enchanted garden. The greenhouse walls were composed of glass panes held together by a delicate grid of ironwork. Flowering vines climbed toward the vaulted ceiling, and a stone fountain gurgled merrily as she passed.

Here, she would have the privacy she needed to negotiate the future with Daltry, and things were working out even better than she planned… so why was she feeling uneasy? Why did she have a sudden impulse to turn around and run?

This is what you want. Don't lose your starch now.

She reached the end of the corridor, which opened into a rotunda shrouded with greenery. Citrus and gardenia perfumed the humid air, and she followed the maze-like path created by the tall potted plants toward the hidden heart of the room. At her arrival, she stopped short: an all-too-familiar tall, broad-shouldered figure was standing next to a basin filled with darting fish.

"Dash it all," she blurted. "What are *you* doing here?"

"I might ask you the same thing, Miss Kent," the stranger replied.

But he wasn't a stranger, was he? she fumed. This man was the same bounder who'd ruined her plans the last time! To her further annoyance, he looked even more attractive unmasked and in the daylight. Beneath the brim of his elegant hat, his hair gleamed like polished bronze.

His features were the sort that ought to be immortalized in marble: straight, strong, classically male. She saw that he was a tad older than she'd first assumed—in his mid-thirties, most likely. The fine lines around his eyes and mouth saved him from bland perfection and enhanced his aura of sensual experience.

And his eyes… the light revealed that they were a rich brown. Dark as chocolate and disturbingly knowing. As he bowed, she noted that his tailoring was undoubtedly superb, the azure double-breasted tailcoat, tan waistcoat, and buff trousers showcasing his long, sinewy form. His tall black boots, banded by brown leather at the top, hugged his muscular calves.

Stop gawking and gather your wits, you ninny.

She drew her shoulders up and skewered him with a glare. "What business is it of yours?"

"You made me a promise, and you didn't keep it," he said mildly.

"I made you no promise! You *assumed* that you could order me about," she snapped. "Now kindly make yourself scarce as I am expecting someone—"

"Daltry's not coming."

"How would you know?" She blinked. "What do you mean he's not coming?"

"He's having some problems with his carriage, I'm afraid."

Suspicions collided like carts on Covent Garden market day, words scattering from her.

"Did you *sabotage* Daltry's vehicle? That guard back there," she cried in outrage, "he's not even an employee of the Pantheon, is he? You set this all up!"

The stranger regarded her. "The man is a guard, actually. I bribed him."

"Of all the *nerve*." She marched up to him, jabbed a gloved finger at his chest. "For the last time: who in blazes are you, and why do you insist on ruining my future?"

"I told you: I'm a friend. My sole purpose is to protect you." His dark gaze was steady, mesmerizing in its intensity. "Daltry will cause you pain, my dear."

"He is an earl, possessed of one of the oldest titles in the peerage," she said acidly. "I'll take the torture, thank you very much."

"He has three by-blows. By three different mistresses. None of whom—mother or child—he treats with any degree of responsibility."

The revelations were made more shocking by the

emotionless tone in which they'd been uttered. Ruthlessly, Rosie pushed them aside to deal with later.

"It's easy to talk about a man's sins when he's not present," she scoffed.

"If you don't believe me, ask your mama. Or your father. He's an investigator, isn't he? I'm sure he can have the information verified."

"I'm not going to discuss Daltry's by-blows—*alleged* by-blows, I mean—with my parents!"

"Don't you think they'd want to know the character of their potential son-in-law?"

The *last* thing Rosie wanted was to place Daltry beneath the parental magnifying glass. Mama already thought he was a *roué*. Papa always agreed with Mama.

Switching tactics, she said, "If you're a friend, why won't you reveal your identity?"

Shadows ghosted through his eyes. "Because you shouldn't know a man like me." His jaw tightened. "And you wouldn't have to, if you would only behave."

Behave? Her head jerked at the insult. "I am not a witless child, sir, to be ordered about!"

"To the contrary, discipline is what you need. You've been given too much latitude, which has resulted in you running about pell-mell, courting disaster at every turn," he said grimly. "A young lady's reputation is her most precious and irreplaceable commodity, Miss Kent, and you are dangerously close to losing yours."

His words struck with the precision of a sniper's bullet, hitting the bull's-eye of all her failures. In a single stroke, he shattered her defenses, her pretty composure cracking like porcelain, shards slicing into her heart. Her wicked, ugly self was bared, and it snarled, fighting back against the exposing light.

"How dare you speak to me that way? I *despise* you." She

raised her fists.

He caught them. Panting, she struggled to free herself, but she was trapped by his superior strength. She fought and fought and still his hold on her wrists didn't budge. As her energy sapped, something else began to flow in its place. Something dark and terrifying, as if she'd been walking on the edge of a dormant volcano, and it was suddenly rumbling to life.

To her horror, humid heat surged against the back of her eyes.

She hadn't cried in ages. Not when she'd discovered that yet another gentleman had been dallying with her, not even when that literary "masterpiece" about her had been published for the world to see. Now, tears leaked down her cheeks, and she couldn't stop them.

His arms enveloped her, the comfort so absolute that she had no choice but to surrender. To bury her face into his solid strength. To allow her disappointments and humiliations to soak into the spice-tinged wool of his jacket.

After the jag ended, she felt lighter—but perhaps that was because she was no longer wearing her bonnet. It had tumbled to the ground, the sight of the scattered cherries bringing her back to reality. What had just happened? Why had she abandoned herself in the arms of a stranger—and *this* stranger, no less?

Why did she feel... safe with him?

Trembling, she drew back.

He didn't stop her, his arms falling to his sides.

"I—I don't know what came over me. I'm not normally a watering pot," she blurted.

"Without rain, nothing grows."

The understanding in his warm eyes made her heart thump against her ribs. The sense of familiarity unfurled inside her, awareness blossoming. *I know him, and he knows me.*

But how was that possible?

"Tell me your name," she whispered.

He cupped her cheek with his hand, his gloved thumb swiping away a stray tear. "It's better for you not to know. Just trust that I want what's best for you. That I'll be there for you when you need me."

Mesmerized by the husky intensity of his words, the tenderness of his touch, she said, "How can I trust you if I don't know who you are?"

"Listen to your instincts. What do they tell you?"

The answer surfaced from some inner abyss. Her hand lifted, closed over his, which was still cradling her cheek. Through their gloves, their heat mingled, her pulse racing at the rightness of it. Before she knew what she was doing, she rose on tiptoe and brushed a kiss against his jaw. She heard his sharp intake of breath; before her heels touched the ground, he had her face framed between his hands, his gaze holding hers intently.

You know this man… trust him.

A breath puffed from her lips. Her eyes closed, her head tipping back.

This is wrong. Don't do this.

As he beheld Primrose's loveliness, her head resting trustingly between his palms, her fresh floral scent filling his nostrils, the words pounded in his skull. They were as futile as a prisoner's fists against iron bars. His rationality had dissolved the moment she'd kissed him. One innocent, tentative kiss—and desire had roared to life inside him. Desire that was anything but brotherly. Desire that was unexpected, unwanted.

Undeniable.

Her upturned lips trembled, as did her lashes against her cheeks. Her offering was so vulnerable and sweet that he had to partake. Just one taste. One time. He bent his head, touched his mouth to hers—*ah, Christ*.

Her sweetness hit him like a right hook: his head reeled, thoughts scattered.

Only instinct remained.

His mouth sank into hers, a gentle fusion of honey and heat. A perfect fit. Before long, he *had* to delve deeper into the source of pleasure. His tongue slid against the seam of her mouth, and, after a brief hesitation, she yielded.

God, her taste. Fresh. Intoxicating.

Right.

Arousal blasted through him. His tongue foraged inside, and he felt her shivered response all the way in his balls. Angling her head back, he deepened the kiss, savoring her sugar and softness, the essence of who she was. When her tongue brushed shyly against his, a hot drop of pleasure slid down his spine, and he groaned against her lips.

"Rosie, are you in here?"

The distant, feminine voice snapped his head up. *Bloody fucking hell.*

He let go of Primrose, who stumbled back a step. Her gaze locked with his: he saw shock and innocence in those jade depths, the bright remnants of desire. A stray curl lay against her cheek like an upside-down question mark.

What the hell have you done, you bastard?

"Rosie, I'm coming in *right now*," the voice warned.

He lifted his hand toward her—and let it fall. Nothing to say, no time to say it. Without a word, he turned and left her... again.

Chapter Five

Past

"WHERE IN BLAZES have the two of you been?"

Kitty's voice reverberated through the cramped quarters they'd been occupying for the past week. The inn was a decrepit, vermin-infested place just beyond the outskirts of London, and it was still more than they could afford at the moment.

Andrew, who'd just passed through the door with Primrose, felt the little girl's hand tremble in his, her cheerful song dying in her throat. Her gaze bounced between him and Kitty. Crumbs of gingerbread—the first she'd tasted and which she'd joyfully inhaled—clung to her quivering chin.

"I told you I was taking Primrose to the mop fair," he said in even tones. "Since she's never seen one—"

"Why would the stupid brat need to see a hiring fair full o' clodhoppers?"

Hearing the slurred edge to Kitty's words, he surmised that the heightened color on her face didn't come from paint. Her chignon had unraveled, russet strands lying heavily upon her shoulders. Her gown was a field of stains.

When Kitty was in her altitudes, she was less than pleasant to be around, and since their escape from Black three months ago, she'd been in this state more and more often. Her bitter litany ran through his head: she hated being on the flit, hated being destitute... hated doing "charity work." For when it rained, it poured: despite Kitty's repeated letters to the man who was supposed to pay for Primrose's upkeep, the money had ceased to come.

Seeing the virulent flash in Kitty's eyes, Andrew felt his gut tighten. Best to get Primrose out of here while he dealt with the situation.

"Go play outside," he told the girl softly. "Don't wander far."

"Yes, Andrew."

She turned to go; Kitty's voice halted her.

"What have you got there?" the bawd snapped.

Primrose's throat worked above the plain collar of her frock. "G-got, Miss Kitty?"

"In your hand, you dimwit!" Before Andrew could stop her, Kitty marched over to the cowering girl, snatching the object from her hand. "Where did you get this?"

Primrose's lips, though trembling, remained pressed together. Despite her obvious fear, she didn't look in his direction. He felt a curious pang... of respect. The four-year-old showed more loyalty and backbone than most adults he knew.

"Answer me, or I'll box your ears! Who gave you this?" Kitty shook the cheap rag doll in Primrose's face.

"Leave her alone," Andrew said quietly. "I gave it to her."

Kitty spun around to face him, and he braced for the storm.

"You did *what*?" she screeched, flinging the doll across the room.

He jerked his head at Primrose. Getting the message, the tot dashed off the battlefield... but not before scooping up her doll, cradling it like a wounded soldier. Kitty, her anger now targeted at him, didn't notice.

"We are living like bleeding *paupers*," she shouted, "and you squander our coin on that worthless little leech?"

"Don't speak of her that way. She's a child, for God's sake." He hated when Kitty was in this state, hated how familiar it felt to be on the receiving end of a drunken tirade. "And it is not *our* coin which I spent but my own."

His private stash—which had taken years to save—was now nearly gone. Faced with the prospect of no food or shelter, he'd had no choice but to offer it up. The only reason he had any money left was because he'd managed to win a few card games here and there. He'd never liked gambling, but he was discovering that he had a knack for it. Not that he wanted to rely on capricious Lady Luck.

"Your pockets are as let as mine." Kitty's lips curled in derision. "You've but one skill worth anything, Corby, and *that* hasn't been in evidence,"—her gaze dropped to his groin—"in quite some time."

He hadn't tupped her since they'd been on the flit. Hadn't wanted to. Pointing out that fact didn't seem like the wisest course of action at present.

Instead, he ignored her dig and tried a different tactic. "On the topic of employable skills, that was why I went to the mop fair in the first place. To see what jobs were available."

Kitty stared at him—then threw back her head and laughed. "Oh, Corby, pull my other leg, eh? It's shorter."

"I'm not joking," he said curtly. "We need the money."

She sauntered up to him, trailed a finger down his chest. "You *do* know how one advertises one's trade at the mops, lover?"

Though he might have lived his whole life in London's underbelly, he wasn't an idiot. "One walks around with a tool from one's trade. You hold a mop if you haven't any specific skill, but you're willing to learn."

"Exactly," she drawled. "So how will it look for you to prance up and down the fair—waving that giant cock of yours about?"

His jaw clenched. "I can do honest work, Kitty."

"You say that because you've never done it before." She smirked. "Other than fucking, what are you good at, hmm? You're far too good-looking to be a field hand, and your skills don't qualify you to be even a second footman."

His face burned; he had no reply.

"Self-delusion is for the stupid and weak." She suddenly palmed his crotch, her rough squeeze driving a harsh breath from his lips. "Besides, can you imagine being in service day in and day out? And for what? Twenty-five pounds a year," she scoffed. "You've made four times that in a single night— and enjoyed yourself far more in the process. No, Corby, drudgery wasn't meant for the likes of us."

His mind knew she was right, yet something in him resisted.

He shoved her hand away. "Perhaps in your dotage," he drawled, knowing how much she hated any reference to her age, "you've given up hope for change, but I'm a young man. I've a whole future ahead of me."

"You're a whore," she said flatly. "A pretty one, to be sure, but your future lies between your legs, and don't you forget it."

Anger roiled; he held it ruthlessly in check. "My future is mine to decide."

"You wouldn't even have a future if it weren't for me. I *made* you, Corby: I gave you your manners, your clothes, your fine accent. Without me, you'd be nothing but a whore's bastard."

The reminder pitted his anger against his sense of loyalty—his greatest weakness. Because despite everything, he couldn't forget what Kitty had done for him. Where he might be now if it hadn't been for her.

Dead, probably.

"It's because of you that we have nothing." His hands

curled in frustration. "If you hadn't gotten mixed up with Black, we'd still have a roof over our heads, a thriving business—"

"We can have that again." In a blink, Kitty went from petulant to seductive. Manipulation was the tool of her trade, and even knowing that didn't make him impervious to the tears that glimmered in her fine grey eyes. To the hitch of remorse in her voice. "I know I've made mistakes, Corby, but I can fix this. I have plans to get us out of this mess."

He crossed his arms over his chest. "What plans?"

"London's still too close, clinging to us like a hangnail. We need to make a clean break—get farther into the countryside," she declared. "Shropshire, maybe. Or Dorset."

"Sheep and pigs," he said with a snort. "What in bloody hell are we going to do there?"

"Start another business. It doesn't have to be a bawdy house, although,"—she slid him a look—"that would be the obvious place to begin. Given our areas of expertise."

"Let us not forget those. I fuck for money, and you spend it as if it grew on trees."

"Sarcasm isn't going to get us anywhere."

He lifted a brow. "Was I being sarcastic?"

"Just think of the advantages we'll have over the local competition," she went on as if he hadn't spoken. "We'll bring panache, class, exotic tricks—"

"We?"

"To start. All hands on deck and all that. Oh, don't give me that look," she said crossly. "I was plying the trade whilst you were in your nappies. I suppose I still know how it's done."

"I suppose." He wondered if it ought to bother him that his lover planned to bed others... but he was no hypocrite. And, truthfully, he didn't give a damn.

Possessiveness wasn't part of his nature.

"There is one small problem, of course."

He didn't like the glint in Kitty's eyes. "What problem?"

"Primrose." As his gut chilled, she said, "Now that she longer pays for herself, we can't afford to keep her. To embark on my plan, we'll need to cut all unnecessary expenses—"

"Primrose stays."

"Be reasonable." Kitty trapped his face between her palms, her beautiful face pleading. "This is our future we're talking about."

"Where will she go? She's only four, for Christ's sake. You can't throw an innocent out on the street—"

"You and I are living proof that you can." Kitty dropped her hands, her steely gaze pinning him. "I thought you were smarter than this."

"I'll pay her way," he gritted out. "You don't have to lift a finger."

"Don't fool yourself. You're no hero, Corby."

"I know that," he snapped. "Just let her stay, and I'll do what it takes to make your bloody plan work, all right?"

Kitty studied him, his heart pounding out the seconds.

"All right," she said finally. "But if you can't manage her, she goes."

He gave a terse nod.

"Well, it seems we have a bargain. Best strike while the iron is hot."

"I don't follow."

"I spoke earlier to a fellow traveler. A widow staying at this very inn." Kitty smiled thinly. "As it turns out, she's in need of consolation this eve."

He knew then that he'd been had. From the start of the conversation, this was what Kitty had been angling for. But he couldn't turn back... not with Primrose's future hanging in the balance. And given how far down this path he'd gone, maybe the only choice was to soldier on.

What difference did it make anyway? Another customer, another fuck. He'd trained his body to go through the motions while his mind remained uninvolved. Detached. He could make a patron climax again and again while he planned for the day when he'd have his own club and determine his own future. When he shot his load, it would be to the ultimate fantasy: success.

So let them buy his cock, his hands, his mouth—his *mind* was his own.

"After the fuck, I'm not sleeping with her," he clipped out.

"I haven't forgotten your rule, lover." Now that she'd gotten her way, Kitty's manner turned conciliatory. "You never sleep with customers. I wouldn't expect you to."

"Widows can be clingy."

"For the twenty pounds she paid, I told her she'd get an hour of your time and no more."

He went to the battered washing stand and cleaned himself up. He did a final inspection in the cracked looking glass: the eyes that stared out of his youthful face were cool, flat. Ready.

Straightening his cravat, he turned to his bawd. "Take me to her."

Chapter Six

Heart hammering, she raced down the shadowy corridor.

She didn't know what she was running from, only that it was close, too close, and she needed to hide. She arrived at a dead end, three doors surrounding her: which one should she choose? She grabbed the closest handle, her clammy hands fumbling to get it open. Stumbling inside, she slammed the door shut.

Silence. Darkness. The carpet beneath her slippers was thick as a bog, slowing her clumsy steps toward a flickering in the distance. A fireplace? As she got closer, she saw the back of a massive wingchair. Someone was sitting there. Smoke rose in ghostly spirals, the distinct fruity scent churning her stomach.

A man's disembodied voice floated to her. "Come here, my little flower…"

Sweat leaked down her palms; on shaky legs, she ran from the room, through another door.

She found herself in a garret room, small, bare… at least no one was there. Her feet took her to the only window: through the glass, dawn's first rays spilled over the rooftops and streets below. She blinked as the light grew brighter and brighter, a strange orange glow glazing the buildings and blazing into the sky…

Then she smelled it. *Smoke*.

She whipped around: the room was aflame.

Fire swirled, advancing hungrily toward her. Terror seized her as flames rose higher and higher, thick black smoke choking her lungs. Only one way to escape. She turned, threw open the window, stepping out onto the ledge. Her belly lurched as the cobblestones spun dizzily in her vision, so far away…

The fire exploded, a fist of air punching her out the window, and she screamed as she plummeted backward through darkness…

"Open your eyes, little one."

Blinking, she found herself staring into the face of a god.

"Wh-where am I?" she stammered.

"You're safe now." His brown gaze was warm, his deep voice reassuring. "I've got you."

She was on a bed, she realized, and he was on his side next to her, a wall of masculine strength.

"Who are you?" she murmured.

"You know who I am."

"I don't…" Yet staring into his beautiful countenance, she felt recognition stir. Like an autumn wind, it swirled through the leaves of her memories: feelings without images, familiarity without facts. *I know you.* She reached up, her hand curling against his jawbone.

His eyes smoldered. He bent his head, and her eyes closed in anticipation.

His kiss was like coming home to a place she'd never been. The touch of his lips, soft yet firm, threw open the curtains, dazzling her. *So this is desire.* Longing flooded her. His taste made her crave more, the disciplined forays of his tongue making her shiver and shake. She arched closer—

"Rosie, darling, are you awake?"

Rosie's eyes flew open. Her heart thumped in her ears, and it took her a moment to recognize the chintz canopy and buttercup yellow walls, the cabinet of dolls. Her bedchamber.

She touched her still-tingling lips, the dream slow to recede, ethereal tendrils clinging to her mind.

Beneath her nightgown, her breasts surged, achy and full. The tips were stiff and throbbing, a syrupy warmth gathered between her legs. Shame and horror collided.

Dear Lord, what is the matter with me? Why did I have such a wanton dream… about him?

"Rosie?"

"Coming, Mama!" Jumping out of bed, she hurriedly donned a flannel wrapper, took a breath, and opened the door.

Mama stood there in a lilac promenade dress.

"Good morning, dear," she said pleasantly. "Odette said that you were not yet up, and I thought I'd check on you myself." She made her way inside, the dark-haired maid following in her wake. "You may set the tray down, Odette. I'll help my daughter with her ablutions this morning."

Odette bobbed a curtsy and left after drawing open the curtains.

Mama waved Rosie to the rosewood vanity.

Obediently, Rosie took a seat. "You're up early, aren't you?"

"I have Sophie to thank for that." Mama's smile was rueful as she poured steaming water from the ewer into the basin. "Libby brought her to me at dawn."

"You ought to hire a wet nurse like other fashionable ladies."

"I like nursing Sophie. I did the same for Edward and…"—Mama lined up the grooming implements with undue care—"as long as I could for you."

The reminder of their separation was there, always. Rosie knew it wasn't her mother's fault: Mama's late and unmourned husband, Baron Draven, had stolen Rosie from her. Nonetheless, Rosie couldn't squelch her bitterness at the infamous start to her life. Unlike her half-siblings, she'd been born on the wrong side of the blanket, *and* she'd been kidnapped by that bounder Draven, *and* God knows what else had happened in the period before Sir Gerald Coyner had become her guardian.

Darkness rose from the depths of her dream, bringing with it that nameless dread that made her pulse throb at the base of her throat. *Don't think about it. Shut it out.*

She washed her face with a towel and managed, "Is Papa out already?"

Mama nodded. "Since he was up helping with Sophie, he thought he might as well get an early start at the office."

Sophie *again*. "I'm surprised you're not with her now." The minute the words slipped out Rosie cringed at how petulant she sounded and hoped her parent didn't notice.

"Libby took her for her daily outing earlier than usual." Mama selected a silver-backed brush, running it through Rosie's hair. "I thought I could have some time with you. We've not had much of late, have we?"

Relieved, Rosie returned her mama's smile in the mirror. "No, we haven't."

"As a matter of fact, Helena paid a call yesterday while you were out shopping, and it made me realize that you and I have not discussed the Harteford masquerade."

Despite the soothing strokes of the brush, she tensed. Aunt Helena, the Marchioness of Harteford, was Mama's bosom friend, and the two were as thick as thieves. Had her aunt noticed her absence during the ball?

"There's not much to share," she said cautiously.

"Helena said that you were radiant in your swan costume." Mama set down the brush, placing her hands onto Rosie's shoulders. "Any prospects, dearest?"

Rosie contemplated confessing about the stranger (*not* that he was a prospect) and instantly rejected the notion. If her mother found out that she'd been unchaperoned in the presence of some mysterious man twice *and* she'd shared a kiss with him, she'd be subjected to a lifetime of sermons. Not to mention, she'd be kept under lock and key henceforth.

Fear of those consequences had led Rosie to withhold the truth even from Polly and Revelstoke. When they'd found her in the rotunda, she'd skimmed over the details of what had transpired, saying simply that Daltry hadn't showed. Although she'd sensed the couple's skepticism, she couldn't very well confess that she'd kissed a stranger in a public place. And that she'd experienced desire for the first time.

And that she was an utter trollop.

"No one of consequence," she forced herself to say lightly.

"Hmm."

She was unnerved by the astute gleam in Mama's eyes. "Hmm... what?"

"You know I only want the best for you, dearest."

The phrase that always preceded a lecture. Her jaw tensed. "But?"

"Well, Helena mentioned that Mr. Fellowes, a nice young man, asked you to dance and you refused—"

"Because he has no title and no position in Society," Rosie burst out. "He was only invited because his father does business with Lord Harteford. There was no point in encouraging him when marrying him won't help my situation at all!"

"There's no need for dramatics. Your situation, as you put it, isn't as dire as you believe—"

"Not dire?" Rosie shot up to face her mother. "After that poem, my reputation is hanging on by a thread. If I don't marry soon and *well*, I'll be an outcast, a nobody—"

"You're not a nobody," Mama said sharply. "Why does the *ton's* opinion matter so much?"

"Because it *does*." Her hands curled at her sides. "I want to belong, Mama. Why is that so dashed difficult for you to understand?"

"I do understand. I just don't agree. Rosie, my darling,"— Mama touched her arm, but she pulled away—"desperation doesn't become you. You are better than this."

She wasn't. Why couldn't anyone get it through their thick skulls?

"I am a *bastard*," she cried. "I was kidnapped, and no one even knows how I ended up in Gerry's care. I was damaged goods even before I got publicly branded a flirt!"

Pain—and awful guilt—seized Mama's features.

"Those are my failures," she said in a stilted voice, "not yours."

Ashamed and angry in equal parts, Rosie lifted her chin. "Regardless, *I* have to live with the consequences. I have to find some way to hold my head up. I have to prove that I'm just as good as other debutantes!"

"That's my point: you don't have to prove anything. You think I don't understand, but I do. I've experienced more of the world than you have. When I became Mrs. Ambrose Kent, the *ton* thought I'd married beneath me, and they could not have been more wrong. In that match, I was the lucky one. It was my great fortune to win your papa's love, and Society's opinion matters not a whit."

"Papa is a prince among men," Rosie said impatiently, "but you had the opportunity to make your choice to leave the *ton*—and that's where we're different. The *beau monde* won't let me in, and I want a place there, more than anything."

"More than love?" Mama frowned.

Who's going to love damaged goods? All those failed flirtations had made the truth clear. Rosie had lost her faith in romance long ago, and as for her foolish reaction toward the stranger—hadn't she learned anything? Like all the other men, he'd merely been dallying with her. Why, he'd taken off like a shot at the first sign of trouble. And that claptrap about protecting her?

Hah. Gentlemen were always chivalrous until they got what they wanted.

He said you were a hussy… and he proved it, didn't he?

Humiliation oozed through her. Her encounter with the bounder was proof positive that she needed the protection of a high connection: a marriage that would make her untouchable. A locked cabinet that put her out of the reach of gossip and rejection.

She returned her mother's direct gaze. "More than anything."

Mama sighed. "Sometimes I just don't understand you."

"I know." The panicky feeling returned. When the sounds of crying broke the taut silence, Rosie was relieved. "Sophie is back. You'd best see to her."

"I suppose I should." Mama paused in the doorway, turning. "By the by, your father and I were thinking that it might be nice to spend some time in Chudleigh Crest. Sophie's early arrival kept us here in Town, but I think we could all use a sojourn to the country."

"That's a *terrible* idea," Rosie said, aghast. "Chudleigh Crest has no society to speak of! This is my last chance to meet someone suitable—"

"Eligible bachelors are far and few between in Town at the moment. Like everyone else, they've gone to their country seat. I think a little rustication would do us all good."

"But *Mama*—"

Sophie's wails rose in volume.

"It'll be best for all of us. Trust me, dearest." With that gentle yet implacable decree, Mama left to tend to her other daughter.

"I am sure a bit of shopping will lift the spirits, Miss Primrose," Odette said the following afternoon as they alighted in front of the Bond Street shop.

A devotee of shopping, Rosie couldn't rouse even an iota of excitement as she and the maid approached Madame Diderot's atelier. The *ton* literally owed its fine feathers to the famed plumassier's art.

"What good will feathers do me in Chudleigh Crest?" Rosie's breath formed puffs of despair in the chilly air. "The only attention I'll attract there is that of the local inhabitants—the dashed grouse and pheasants who'll want their plumage back."

"I believe Madame Diderot's plumes come from more exotic game, mademoiselle." Looking as if she was trying not to smile, the dark-haired French maid opened the door, and Rosie went inside.

No matter the time of day, the plumasserie was dappled in shadow due to the strings of feathers festooned overhead. Plumage from every kind of bird and in a rainbow of glorious hues fluttered as the door closed. The scent of dyes, wax, and something earthier tickled Rosie's nostrils as the proprietress came from behind a counter.

"Mademoiselle Kent," she said with a curtsy, "what a lovely surprise to see you!"

Rosie wondered at the woman's high color. Usually Diderot was as pale as a ghost.

"Likewise, Madame. Odette convinced me to brave the cold to attain a replacement. I lost the white ostrich feather at a masquerade," she said apologetically.

"You are in luck. Today I received a special shipment which included several heron feathers."

At the mention of the prized species, Rosie perked up. "I should love to see them."

"They are in my specimen preparation room, which is a

bit cramped. You would not mind your maid waiting here?"

At the words "specimen preparation," Rosie's belly had lurched. Being fastidious by nature meant that she was rather squeamish. The image of bloody carcasses flashed in her head, and she said uneasily, "There aren't any specimens being, um, *prepared*, are there?"

"Not the animals, mademoiselle. Just the feathers."

"All right then," she said with relief. "I'll be back, Odette."

She followed the plumassier to a backroom. A large work table cluttered with specially shaped knives, scissors, and other implements of the trade dominated the space.

Diderot opened a door at the side of the room. "After you, Mademoiselle Kent."

Rosie stepped inside the small chamber—and froze.

"*You*," she said furiously.

Chapter Seven

THE SIGHT OF Primrose tore into him like a bullet of sunshine.

His rationality—all the reasons he'd given himself for arranging another meeting—bled away. Her impact on him went beyond that of her beauty. It was more than her corn-silk locks, her rare green-gold gaze, her figure so fetchingly displayed in a blue pelisse and gown edged in ermine.

It was *her*. The sum total of who'd she become. The transformation of his brave little chick into a passionate, willful woman devastated his senses: she affected him as no woman ever had. If the kiss at the Pantheon hadn't made him aware of the true nature of his feelings, then he was a fool. And a greater fool still if he gave into those yearnings.

He no longer saw Primrose as a sister; he had no right to desire her as a woman.

Which was why he'd arranged this meeting, he reminded himself. To make his apologies. To disentangle himself from a situation that, contrary to his intentions, was placing her reputation in greater jeopardy than ever before. Bad enough that she'd suffered for the inconstancies of her aristocratic admirers; imagine if it became known that she'd been kissed by a goddamned pimp.

For her own good, he had to retreat, to return to his strategy of protecting her from afar.

He gave a subtle nod to Madame Diderot. She discreetly closed the door, leaving them in the privacy of the stock room, a small space with boxes piled along one wall, a table tucked up against another. Drying feathers fluttered on clotheslines overhead.

"Good afternoon, Miss Kent," he said.

Her icy stare would have frozen a lesser man. "How did you know that I would be here? Did you bribe Madame Diderot?"

Tread carefully.

From the inner pocket of his jacket, he withdrew the ivory feather he'd taken from her at the masquerade and held it out. A peace offering. "I figured sooner or later you'd be in need of a replacement. And bribery was unnecessary in this instance. Madame owed me a favor."

Primrose snatched the feather from him. "Well, if you've come to lecture me on my behavior again, save your breath."

"Actually, it's my behavior I wished to discuss. I owe you an apology."

Her eyebrows winged.

"What happened at the Pantheon..." He cleared his throat. "I was entirely at fault."

"Without a doubt," she said coolly. "You ruined yet another opportunity for me to meet with Lord Daltry."

"Will you leave off Daltry for a bloody moment?" Taken aback by his own vehemence, he forced himself to say in calmer tones, "I wasn't referring to the earl but the kiss we shared."

He'd imagined how she might react to his apology. Profuse blushes. Stammering denials.

Her shoulders hitched in a careless shrug. "It was just a kiss."

"*Just* a kiss?" He had to check himself. Again. "How many times have you been kissed?"

"You ought to know. After all, you're the expert on my behavior." She wandered to the table. Her back to him, she lifted a magenta feather from its surface. "The advantage of being a hussy is that one doesn't fall into a swoon over something as inconsequential as a peck."

"It was more than a peck, and you know it," he said shortly. "And don't call yourself a hussy."

"I'm just quoting you. And, by the by, one must wonder at your familiarity with hussies."

"I beg your pardon?"

Her head angled in his direction, her smile as sharp and delicate as a scalpel. "You so readily identified me as one, so it speaks to your experience with the breed, does it not?"

"I do not discuss my personal affairs," he said stiffly.

"And that makes you a hypocrite, sir, since you seem to have no compunction meddling in mine." She set the feather down, looking bored. "Now is there anything else you wished to discuss? I have other appointments today."

He prided himself on his self-control, his ability to keep a cool head. He'd seen and done too much to let anything or anyone get under his skin. But he'd overestimated his forbearance—or underestimated Primrose. He'd embarked on this time-consuming, effort-intensive quest to protect an unspoiled girl; instead, he was confronted with this insouciant *brat*.

Irritation simmered. She didn't want his help? Then he'd wash his bloody hands of her.

"Don't let me keep you," he bit out.

"I shan't. This will be our last meeting, I hope?"

A scathing rejoinder was on the tip of his tongue. But then she turned, and the heightened sheen in her eyes slammed into him like a battering ram. His wall of anger crumbled, and he was moving toward her before he knew it.

She retreated a step, hissed, "Stay away from me!"

"I'm sorry," he said, his voice pitched low. "I meant no insult."

"I don't believe you. You're like the rest. You think that because of my reputation, you can treat me any way you wish." The hitch in her breath stabbed him like a blade. "That I'm a strumpet you can dally with and toss aside—"

"No, sweetheart," he said, "I think the opposite. You're a jewel."

"I don't believe you!"

"It's the truth. You're beautiful, but more than that, you've courage and spirit to spare. You light up any room you walk into. Any man would count himself blessed to have you by his side."

Something flickered in her face. "You're lying."

"I'm not. You're precious, Primrose," he said hoarsely. "Beyond words."

"If what you're saying is true,"—her voice quivered— "then why does no one want me?"

The naked vulnerability in her gaze tore down the remnants of his resistance. He closed the distance between them. At the whiff of her unique floral scent, need clawed his belly.

"*I* want you." His words were raw, guttural. "So goddamned much."

Her lips parted, her lashes fluttering.

He didn't know who made the first move, but in the next heartbeat she was in his arms, his mouth descending hungrily upon hers. She kissed him back with equal abandon. Her sweetness laid waste to his good intentions, and the kiss raged into a fever.

Rosie felt herself being lifted onto a table, her back propped up against a wall. Things fell—but the world could have come crashing down for all she noticed. Because there was only him.

This man who wanted her.

Who said she was *precious*.

Who made her feel treasured—and safe.

Fear's hold on her loosened. Guided by instinct, she kissed him with all the passion awakening inside her. Eagerness and inexperience made her a bit clumsy, but it didn't matter because he was in control. Masterfully so. No one had ever kissed her with such finesse before. With such care. His mouth courted hers with discipline and skill, and longing sizzled through her.

When he tossed aside her bonnet and crowded into the lee of her thighs, she shivered with primal delight. It felt right; *everything* about him did. His dark male taste, his spicy scent, his virile strength. Her hands clutched his hard shoulders, her knees bracketing his hips, and still she was desperate to get closer. When his mouth left hers, she made a sound of protest. His soft laugh heated her ear… then he drew the lobe *into* his mouth. Shock faded to bliss as he suckled the sensitive flesh. His tongue flicked back and forth, the caress hardening the tips of her breasts, causing a flutter between her thighs.

Desire made her dizzy. She could barely breathe.

And she wanted *more*.

As if he knew what she was feeling, his lips coasted over her jaw and neck, pleasure ruffling up her spine. His hand slid beneath her pelisse. She was wearing countless layers, but somehow he found where she was aching, his strong touch titillating the taut peaks of her breasts, rubbing them against the cage of stiffened fabric.

It was exquisite. Torturous.

Tension twisted her insides. Panting, squirming against the table, she didn't know how to get relief. But somehow she trusted that *he* did.

"Help me," she whispered. "Please."

The bright, desperate need in her eyes was his undoing. Hell, she needed to come—badly. And release was something he could so easily give her.

He kissed her, licking deeply into her sweetness. At the same time, he dragged up her skirts and petticoats, his hand clamping on her drawer-clad thigh. Beneath the fine linen, her sleek muscles trembled, and he continued upward, finding the slit in the cloth.

She tensed, her knees pressing against his hips.

"Don't hide, sweeting," he murmured. "You're so beautiful."

"I oughtn't—"

"Let me take care of you. I'll give you what you need. Trust me, Primrose."

Her golden lashes fanned upward. Gold swirled with green... and her legs slackened.

Pleasure shuddered through him at her trusting acquiescence... and that was before his finger passed through the slit. *Christ Almighty.* Her pussy was soft, wet, unbelievably lush; behind the placket of his trousers, his cock shot up as if injected with steel.

He reminded himself that this wasn't about his pleasure; it was about hers. He had a sudden flash of insight: with Primrose, the two could be one and the same. Sex could be an act of sharing rather than a mere exchange. Arousal pumped his blood, his erection jerking.

Reverently, he slid his finger up her plump crease, and she gasped when he found her pearl, rubbing it, painting it with her own dew. Watching her expressive face, he varied pace and pressure and stroke to maximize her pleasure. He'd never seen anything more beautiful than her sex-flushed cheeks, her bottom lip catching beneath her teeth as she approached her finish.

It didn't take long: she'd been on the edge from the start. When she went over, he claimed her mouth. Her cries reverberated through him, shaking his foundations.

As Rosie slowly floated down to earth, several facts entered her awareness. One, she'd just experienced earth-shattering pleasure—a kind that she'd never even known existed. Second, the gentleman responsible for her state was standing between her thighs, his face buried in her neck, his heavy breaths heating her ear. Third, she was disheveled: a fallen curl dangled in her eye, and she was wet between her thighs.

Surprisingly, she couldn't rouse herself enough to care. Embarrassment and shame—her constant companions—were conspicuously absent. In their place was a languor she'd never known before, a sense of rightness that made no sense... but there it was.

Trust me, Primrose.

Some deep instinct had told her that she could. And so she had. He might not be titled or rich or any of the things she'd been looking for in a husband—and *she didn't care*. For the first time, she wanted something more. Something that she'd felt in the presence of this man from their first meeting. Something so primal and absolute that she couldn't help but believe in it—and herself.

So this is what all the fuss is about. What Polly, Mama were trying to tell me...

Wonderingly, she touched his hair; the bronze waves slid through her fingers like rough silk. He lifted his head, and, staring into his coffee brown eyes, that gloriously handsome face, she was mesmerized by that pull of recognition. As if she were a dreamer trying to get back to the world she'd left behind.

"Tell me your name," she whispered. "I must know."

He hesitated. "Andrew."

Andrew…. Andrew… The name danced like joy through her. Why?

"How do you know me? Because you do," she said.

"Primrose, I…" He tucked a wayward curl behind her ear, her heart flip-flopping at the tender gesture. "It's better if you don't know."

His words sent a quiver of anxiety through her.

"But you'll have to tell me eventually. I mean, after what we… what just happened…" She trailed off at the harsh set of his features.

"I've acted unforgivably. Again." He pushed back from her, dragged a hand through his hair. "It was wrong, taking advantage of you as I did—"

"You told me I could trust you!" She jumped off the table, shoved her skirts into place. Panic hammered in her chest. *Please, please, please don't be like all the rest.* "Aren't you… aren't you going to do the honorable thing?"

Their gazes held, and her stomach plunged.

"Offering you marriage would not be the honorable thing to do," he said quietly. "Other than money, I have nothing to offer you. I don't have a title, and I don't come from a distinguished family—or a family of any sort, really—and my reputation… it's far from respectable."

"I don't care," she whispered, "about any of those things."

"But you do. Or you will, once you find yourself without the privileges of your world. At the moment, you're just blinded by desire—damn me to hell." He swore with startling fluency, his expression ravaged. "I deserve to be strung up for introducing you to such things—"

"Then why did you?" she cried. "It's because you think I'm a hussy, isn't it? Because I'm a tart who is so unworthy and low that even some... some *nobody* can dally with me and walk away without consequences!"

"That's not true. Like I said before, you're an angel, but I'm not worthy—"

"*It's not me, it's you?*" Rage entered the fray. "If you're going to lie, at least have the grace to do it with a modicum of originality."

"I'm not lying," he said tersely.

"Just answer one question: are you, or aren't you going to marry me?"

Slowly, he shook his head. "For your sake, I cannot."

"Then the devil take you!" Snatching up her bonnet, she marched to the exit. She heard him say her name an instant before she slammed the door behind her.

Chapter Eight

Past

"YOU'RE... YOU'RE REALLY leaving, Andrew?"

Primrose stood in the doorway of his shabby room in yet another shabby inn. In one hand, she gripped the rag doll he'd bought her months ago at the fair. She and the doll were rarely parted, and both were bedraggled from weeks on the flit. Primrose's blond hair hung in limp, unwashed plaits, the doll's yarn locks similarly dulled by dirt. Threads unraveled from both of them.

The trembling in Primrose's voice, coupled with the brightness of her eyes, constricted his chest. But he'd made his decision; after the fight with Kitty last night, there was no turning back.

"It's for the best," he said.

He continued packing his possessions into a battered valise. There wasn't much. Not after the fiasco of Kitty's plan had taken the rest of his savings and nearly both their lives. As it turned out, those who dealt in pleasure in the countryside were as lethal as their city counterparts. The local brothel owners had made it clear that no upstart bawd from London was going to poach on their territory.

Now, after months of selling himself to countrified matrons and traveling ladies in search of a night's companionship, he had no money and no prospects.

Primrose came closer. "But why?"

Because I'm a whore. I can't take care of you. I can barely take care of myself.

"Kitty and I are parting ways," he said.

"Because of me?"

Unable to bear the pain shimmering in her wide eyes, he crouched. Tipped her little chin up. "No, little chick. It is a grown-up matter that has naught to do with you."

"Kitty says I'm too..."—her cherubic features tensed in concentration—"'spensive."

The ache in his chest intensified into a burn. Parting with Kitty wasn't easy—their history was a long and knotty rope— but leaving Primrose to an uncertain fate was the most difficult thing he'd ever done. This was the demon he wrestled with. The one that crawled beneath his skin by day and injected venom into his dreams by night. The one that had delayed the inevitable dissolution of his partnership with Kitty.

"It's not you, Primrose," he said firmly.

She grabbed his hand just as he was pulling back. "Then take me with you. *Please.* I don't want to stay with Kitty; I want to go with you!"

Her plea lashed him like a cat-o'-nine-tails. He stood abruptly. "I can't take you."

"Wh-why?"

"Because... I just can't."

If you take Primrose, I'll send the constables after you. Kitty's enraged vow rang in his head. *Imagine what that will look like— a male whore stealing a young girl. You'll be strung up by the mob before they get you to the gallows. I'm her guardian, and I've got the papers to prove it. I decide her fate—not you. If you don't like the fact that I'm going to find her a nice home with some rich nobs, then take your bloody arse off. I don't give a damn. But just try to take Primrose—and I'll guarantee that's the last thing you do.*

He knew Kitty meant every word—and that she was right.

He had no legal standing to take Primrose. Not only that, he had no money, no means to look after a little girl.

"I won't be any trouble. I promise, Andrew! *Please.*"

His hands curled in helpless frustration; he wanted to punch something.

"I know you won't. But where I'm going…"—he refused to dwell on his own grim future—"it's no place for little girls."

"I don't care! I don't want to be with Kitty. I hate her, I hate her!"

Primrose flung herself at his knees, sobbing. She'd never before voiced her feelings about her guardian. Or, indeed, said a negative word or showed any sign of temper. She was always a biddable, sunny child, and now he realized that she'd been too afraid to be anything else.

The recognition ravaged him, but what could he do?

Kitty has papers. And she's right: you're just a whore. His teeth ground together. *What authority will entrust Primrose to you, even if you could take care of her?*

He placed a hand on the weeping girl's head and managed a soothing tone. "There now. It won't be so bad. You'll miss me a bit, and then you'll meet new friends."

As he said the words, fear shadowed his heart. He didn't know for certain what lay in Primrose's future. Kitty was steadfast in her resolution to sell the girl. The bawd had claimed that she would find a good home for Primrose, one where she would be well cared for.

But he knew Kitty, knew that she was moved by money more than sentiment. And he feared that she would sell Primrose to the highest bidder rather than the one best for the child's welfare. While he would give anything to believe that some rich, childless couple would end up adopting Primrose, he couldn't ignore the grim possibilities. The ones who hunted in the streets of the Seven Dials, using sweets and coins to coax crossing sweeps and flower girls into dark alleys.

The ones who he, himself, had learned to evade as a boy.

Looking into Primrose's upturned face, he was haunted by the possibilities. His gut twisted with guilt, rage, and hopeless despair. Yet what choice did he have? He could make a run for it with Primrose... but even if he could somehow evade the authorities, what sort of life could he offer her? One filled with pimps and whores, lechers and degenerates. She wouldn't be any safer. And who'd take care of her while he was off fucking just to keep some leaky, crumbling roof over their heads?

At least with Kitty's plan, Primrose had a chance at a happy ending.

"I don't want new fr-friends. I want you," Primrose said tearfully.

He let out a breath and cupped one of her cheeks, its wetness soaking his palm. "You're a bantling yet, and you'll forget me in time," he said. "But I will always remember you. And I'd prefer to remember our parting as one of smiles rather than tears."

"I'm not going to smile!" Primrose stamped her foot, flung the doll at him. "I h-hate you, and I'm glad I won't ever see you again!"

She raced out of the room.

Slowly, he bent to pick up the grubby toy. He traced a fingertip over the dye-drawn smile, already fading. He thought of leaving it for Primrose—but she'd be better off without reminders of him.

He tucked the doll on top of his belongings, closed the case, and made his way out.

Chapter Nine

CLAD IN A dressing gown, Andrew sat at the side of his bed, looking at the object he held in his hands. Years hadn't been kind to his little rag companion. Her expression had faded, her button eyes chipped, and she'd lost some of her yellow yarn locks. She'd accompanied him on countless journeys, had been there during his darkest hours and rise to success, and he'd never been able to let her go. She was a reminder of all the roads he'd traveled to get where he was; just looking at her caused emotions to swirl up in him like sediment in disturbed waters.

Right now, holding her in his palm, he felt… guilty.

What the bloody hell was I thinking?

The truth was he hadn't been thinking. From his encounter with Primrose at the masquerade to the debacle at the plumassier's a week ago, he'd been driven by a force that had nothing to do with rationality. It didn't matter that his desire for her was intense, inexplicable, and irresistible: he had *no* excuse treating her like he had.

As if it weren't bad enough that he'd abandoned her when she was a girl, he'd now done it to her again—and Primrose deserved better. Hell, she deserved everything.

Everything that you can't give her.

Telling himself that he'd left her for her own good didn't ease his frustration. Nor did he find consolation in the fact that he would continue to protect her from afar as he'd done in the months preceding his disastrous intervention at the masquerade. Now that he'd held Primrose, kissed her, touched her... his gut clenched, his groin burgeoning with heat.

He'd had sex with countless women, for profit and for pleasure; never *once* had he felt the way he had with Primrose. Never had he been so absorbed by another, body and mind. Never had another's pleasure been so inexorably twined with his own.

She's not for you. Let her go.

He yanked open the drawer of his bedside table, his touch gentling as he returned the doll to its rightful place. He got up, pacing the confines of his large and luxurious bedchamber. He'd purchased this grand house in Mayfair three years ago, and being in this room with its white marble fireplace, Aubusson carpets, and carved mahogany furnishings usually settled him. Reminded him of how far he'd come. He was no longer a whore living hand to mouth but a man who had businesses, properties, investments—everything he'd once dreamed of.

For the first time, he wondered, *Is it enough?*

"What the devil is the matter with me?" His muttered words echoed in the empty room.

He dragged a hand through his hair. Then he rang for his valet.

A while later, hot water lapped against his skin as he leaned back in a large copper tub. He'd spent far too many years surrounded by grime and dirt, and bathing was one of his favorite rituals. Equipped with the latest plumbing innovations, the room had hot water piped directly to the brass taps on the side of the tub. Marble imported from Italy lined the walls and floor, and a fireplace kept the room steamy even as wind and rain blustered outside the window. Here in his sanctuary, he was protected from the winter storm... but not from his own inner tempest.

He wasn't fit for Primrose. He didn't have a title or family; his reputation couldn't be more notorious. There was not one respectable thing about him.

I don't care about any of those things. Her words haunted him.

He rubbed his hands over his face. If she knew what he'd been—what he was—she'd undoubtedly be singing a different tune. Yet he couldn't keep the devil from whispering in his ear: *what if... what if...?*

The notion was unthinkable. She needed a husband whose status could protect her, give her the security she needed—the kind she hadn't had for the first four years of her life. He wondered if she understood the origins of her fears. If she recalled any of those roaming childhood days, no anchor to safety, people floating in and out of her life... including him.

The coward who'd left her behind.

The old knots of guilt tightened; he shoved the thought from his head.

Instead, he reached for the bar of translucent soap that he'd had his valet pick up for him. He brought it to his nose, sniffing. He'd recognized the distinctive garden scent of Pears soap on Primrose. In truth, he'd smelled the soap on too many ladies to count and never taken a particular liking to it—except on Primrose. On her, its fragrance mingled with the subtle feminine musk of her skin to form a rare and potent aphrodisiac.

Beneath the water, he went hard.

He ran the bar over his damp chest, the turgid muscles twitching at the slippery sensation. Perhaps his self-imposed celibacy was feeding into his inappropriate desire for Primrose. Since ending his last relationship two years ago, he hadn't bedded anyone. Hadn't wanted to. Being alone had seemed right somehow. His focus had been on work, success—making something of himself.

Whenever the urge had arisen, he'd simply taken matters into his own hands. Looking back, he hadn't frigged himself in weeks; perhaps he needed a release. Something to take the edge off. He fisted his cock, running the tight grip from root to tip.

The fantasy he'd fought to suppress rose in his mind's eye, and, this time, he let himself go back to the plumassier's. Closing his eyes, he inhaled the fragrant skin of Primrose's arched neck as he fondled her pussy. God, she was wet, her passion natural and generous. When he rubbed her bold little pearl, she gasped his name. He swallowed the breathless cries of her climax as his fingers delved deeper into her lushness.

His biceps flexed, the sound of the rippling water transforming into the silken rustle of skirts being raised. He imagined himself going down on one knee—only right to worship such a treasure. He pictured what he had touched: slender, curved legs topped by a silky blonde nest. With his thumbs, he parted her cunny and swiped his tongue up her sweet pink slit.

His chest surged, his fist jerking. He'd always enjoyed a woman's pleasure, and the idea of eating Primrose's pussy made his heart pound in his cock. He searched out her love-knot with his tongue, tickling it, egged on by her breathy pleas. Her fingers slid into his hair, holding him close as her cunny gushed honey into his ravenous mouth.

He found her entrance with his middle finger, the tight little hole resisting as he eased in just the tip. Her lush passage squeezed his digit, his grip tightening on his cock to mimic that delight. He'd never had a virgin before, never thought he wanted one. Yet the idea of being Primrose's first—her *only*—made him shudder with lust.

His bollocks burgeoned, and he palmed them with his other hand. Water sloshed against the tub as he frigged himself harder, faster, fantasy blurring into animal need. He climaxed, releasing his seed in hot, rapid spurts.

Panting, he rested his head against the tub's edge and closed his eyes. He was sated but not satisfied. A part of him wondered if it would always be this way.

"I think that does it, sir." Kendrick, Andrew's valet, stepped back, waiting for his approval.

Andrew inspected himself in the cheval looking glass. He'd lured Kendrick away from a penurious viscount; as far as he was concerned, the valet was worth his weight in gold. As fastidious as the famed Beau Brummell, Kendrick ascribed to strict principles of simplicity and elegance. The navy frockcoat, shawl-collared waistcoat, and grey trousers fitted to Andrew's form with nary a wrinkle. Beneath his cleanly shaven chin, the cravat was tied in a perfect Mathematical.

"Yes, that will do—" At the knock, Andrew frowned and bade entry.

A footman entered the dressing room. "Pardon the interruption, sir, but there is a young woman here to see you."

Andrew's heart bumped against his ribs. "What is her name?"

"She wouldn't give it, sir, but she said that she is here on an urgent matter and that you told her to seek you out."

Would Primrose abandon all propriety... to see me?

Joy, raw and ungoverned, jolted him into action. Before he knew it, he was striding out of his suite and down the steps to the drawing room. He entered... and stopped short.

The woman standing by the window wasn't Primrose.

"Odette." Reining in his disappointment, he frowned at his employee. "What are you doing here? I gave you specific instructions to stay with Miss Kent at all times..."

He trailed off as premonition hit him like an icy fist.

"A calamity has befallen, sir," the French maid blurted. "Miss Kent—she has eloped!"

Chapter Ten

STARING OUT THE window into the dark, pelting rain, Rosie thought, *Did I make a mistake?*

It wasn't the first time she'd questioned her decision during the last three days. She'd had her share of misgivings since embarking on the wild elopement with Daltry... and now it was too late.

The firelight glinted off the gold band on her ring finger. Its selection, like everything about her marriage—from the travel arrangements to the ceremony over the anvil to the obtaining of present lodgings—had been conducted in a rush. The adage about marrying in haste entered her head; she shoved it out.

What's done is done. The bargain is sealed... or very nearly.

As her gaze went to the door adjoining her and her new husband's rooms, her apprehension surged higher. She missed her family with an acute ache, her price to pay for eloping. She'd never felt more alone than right now, in this room at a strange inn, waiting for her bridegroom to arrive. The way other debutantes talked about it, consummation was a necessary evil. Like tight-lacing a corset, one had to endure the pain in order to get the desired results.

She knew, of course, that what went on the marital bower after the first time wouldn't be all bad. In her family, she was surrounded by couples who clearly didn't mind retiring together. And there were her own recent experiences of passion... her reckless interludes with Andrew butted into her thoughts. The way he'd kissed her, that shocking, ravishing pleasure she'd known in his arms... try as she might, she couldn't forget those memories.

So she used them to bolster her present resolve.

Despite all the travails she'd endured—being a bastard, being dallied with and labelled a trollop, even being immortalized in that poem—*nothing* had hurt the way Andrew's rejection had. His refusal to be with her had cut into a place so tender and deep that she knew she'd forever bear the scar. It made no sense why he could wound her so... but he had.

Trust me, Primrose, he'd said.

Her heart clenched. Andrew was like all the beaux in her past, only he'd treated her *far worse.* He'd raised her hopes, made her trust him, and for the first time, she'd wanted ... oh, how she'd wanted...

The one thing you'll never have.

Because she was a shameless wicked girl. And she deserved to be tossed aside.

In short, Andrew had proved what she'd known all along: love wasn't for her.

Her vision blurred, but she refused to let the tears fall. Having reached the lowest rung of her existence, she had nothing left to lose. To hell with Andrew and his ilk. Though Daltry might not be the man of her dreams, his position meant that she could spit on men like Andrew from her new perch at the top of the social ladder.

I'm a countess now, she thought fiercely.

Why didn't she find any consolation in the fact?

After the rough journey—she and Daltry had driven straight through, pausing only to change horses at coaching stops—they'd arrived in Gretna in the afternoon. After the blacksmith had married them, they'd ended up at the present inn. She'd promptly fallen into an exhausted sleep and awakened to find Daltry gone. Knowing her reprieve would be temporary, she'd stiffened her spine and forged ahead.

She'd had a bath brought in. Without the assistance of a maid, she'd performed all twelve steps of her ablutions with the meticulousness of a warrior preparing for battle. Then she'd donned a night rail edged in lace and brushed her hair the requisite one hundred strokes before winding it into a single plait. The looking glass had reflected her crisply perfect ensemble, her porcelain-smooth countenance, her lifeless eyes.

That had been two hours ago, and her groom still had not shown. Boisterous rumbling came from the tavern below. Was Daltry amongst the merry crowd? The innkeep had claimed that it was a local tradition for the bridegroom to purchase rounds for local revelers. The more drinks he bought, the more luck he'd supposedly bring to his new marriage—and the more he'd line the proprietor's pockets, Rosie thought dryly. What fustian. Unfortunately, she couldn't go downstairs unaccompanied to check if Daltry had fallen prey to such silly superstitions.

With nothing better to do, she went over to the table by the fire. A cold collation had been laid out, yet her stomach was too knotted to eat. Instead, she poured herself a glass of wine... which tasted surprisingly good. So good, in fact, that she refilled her glass. A third glass settled her nerves, and she curled up on a chair, tucking her feet beneath her.

Lightheaded, she raised her glass to the crackling fire. "Cheers to me: the new Lady Daltry."

The words echoed hollowly in the room. Time slowed as she sipped the wine and brooded into the flames. The door opened sometime later, startling her from her stupor.

"You're awake, m'dear," Daltry said.

From his slurred accents and the way he fumbled to close the door behind him, she guessed that he had, indeed, been cavorting in the tavern below. She rose—and had to steady herself against the table when she swayed.

"I've been waiting for you," she said.

"Eager for the proceedings, eh?" he leered. "What a good wife you are."

She decided not to disabuse him of the notion, especially since uncharitable thoughts had begun to play in her head again. She'd managed to keep them in check during their long journey—no easy feat. For one, the earl wasn't renowned for his wit or conversation. While his mind stayed well within the boundaries of convention, one couldn't say the same of his hands. It had taken no small amount of maneuvering on her part to finish the journey in the same intact state with which she'd started it.

Experience had given her insight into the workings of the male mind. As the saying went, no man would buy the cow when he could have the milk for free. (See? She had learned from her mistakes.) Ergo, she'd remained firm in her stance that there would be no preview before their wedding night.

Now that she was legally bound him, however, he had husbandly rights. Tipsy as she was, she saw her situation with sudden clarity. It was… disheartening. Daltry had never been the most prepossessing of men. Around her height, thinning on top, and protruding in the middle, he looked every day of his two-and-fifty years.

She told herself that his physical characteristics mattered not: his title was his redeeming attribute. Yet she couldn't help but wish that he would take a tad more care with his personal appearance. That he'd try to, well, *do better* with what Nature had seen fit to give him.

Instead, he seemed to have some aversion to personal hygiene. What hair he had lay in limp strands across his bald pate. His complexion was both florid and greasy, his light blue gaze bloodshot. His cravat was splotched with stains, and several buttons had popped off his waistcoat. As he closed in on her, it became obvious that he hadn't bothered to wash since their arrival. He reeked of sweat, dirt… and, Dear Lord, *vomit?*

Her stomach lurched.

His hand shot out, his stubby fingers grabbing her braid. "Always had a liking for blondes."

To avoid smelling him, she tried breathing through her mouth. "Thank you. I managed best as I could without a maid."

"Good thing you didn't bring one. Only get in the way, eh?"

Tamping down nausea, she said, "I had a nice bath after my nap. Perhaps you'd care to—"

"No need." He let go of her hair, began shrugging out of his coat. "Not when I'm 'bout to get dirty again."

Her belly quivered at his coarseness. Daltry had never been a refined man; now that they were married, he was apparently going to drop any pretense of being a gentleman.

"Perhaps we ought to have a glass of wine first," she said faintly.

"Don't play coy with me, young lady." He fumbled with buttons, managing to divest himself of his waistcoat. "The fact that you're a shameless doxy is why I married you in the first place."

Her cheeks flamed. "I'm not—"

"I ain't deaf; I've heard the rumors about you. And you approached me, brazen as can be, making me an offer I couldn't refuse. What does that make you, if not a trollop?" He smirked, his hands on his waistband. "But worry not: I like a hot-blooded wench in bed. And it'll amuse me to watch those uppity relations of mine swallow their spleen when I parade you in front of them."

He'd married her to annoy his family? The revelation was

unsettling, to say the least. Especially given the social influence wielded by the dowager countess, Lady Charlotte Daltry, and Mrs. Antonia James, Daltry's formidable aunt. The ladies hosted a salon so exclusive that it made getting vouchers to Almack's seem easy by comparison. If Rosie wished to have the *ton* at her feet, she would need the dowager and Mrs. James as allies not enemies.

Tentatively, she said, "Perhaps our marriage will help mend fences—"

"To hell with those bleeding hypocrites!" Daltry's words boomed with drunken belligerence. "Treated me like dirt 'til I got the title. The smell of trade offends them, but that don't stop 'em from asking for handouts. Well, they ain't as lily-white as they seem. Got mud on their shoes like everyone else, and I know that first-hand. Know *all* their dirty secrets." His lips stretched into a satisfied smile. "Now they'll have to kowtow not only to a merchant—but to his trollopy bastard of a bride as well. Hah!"

Rosie cringed—and that was before Daltry shed the rest of his clothing.

Dear God. Even the hazy focus of wine didn't improve her first view of a naked male body. Then he turned, giving her a full view of his backside. *Eww.* She'd had no idea that a man was that hirsute... *all over.*

With shaking hands, she reached for her wine glass and polished it off.

"Enough delay. Time to pay up, young lady."

"Could we... dim the lights?" she whispered.

"I told you to dispense with those virginal sensibilities—"

"I *am* a virgin," she burst out.

"We'll find out if that's true soon enough. Not that I'm particular—as long as you're a fine breeder, eh? But all right," he muttered, "just this once. Off with those clothes and into the bed, you hear?"

He went to douse the lamps, stumbling along the way. The moment darkness blanketed the room, Rosie disrobed with unsteady hands and rushed to the bed, jumping under the covers. She lay against the cold sheets, her heart thumping.

You made this bed, the unsympathetic voice in her head said. *Now you have to lie in it.*

The bed creaked in protest, the mattress sagging beside her.

Near dawn, Andrew strode into the inn, removing his hat and shaking off the rain. Vicious storms had delayed his journey by half a day, forcing him to take shelter at inns on the way to Gretna Green. He'd barely slept the past three days, catching a few minutes here and there in the carriage, always awakened by a sense of pounding urgency.

Where the devil are you, Primrose?

He'd arrived at Gretna three hours ago—after the closing of the blacksmith shops. He could only hope that the inclement weather had delayed Primrose and Daltry's journey, and they hadn't yet had their anvil wedding. He'd gone through the inns one by one, knowing that if the pair had arrived, they would need a place to stay the night. His gut tightened, his boots taking him to the innkeep's desk, where he rang the bell.

A few minutes later, a bleary-eyed man shuffled to the desk, wearing a dressing gown and sleeping cap. Taking quick stock of Andrew's garb and bearing, he perked up. "Coming in a bit late, are you, sir? Never fear, I 'appen to 'ave a braw set o' the rooms suited to a gentleman such as yourself. The name's Alfred McCready, owner and proprietor o' the Galloway Arms, where we offer the finest in Scottish 'ospitality—"

"I'm looking for a couple," Andrew said impatiently. "An older man and a young lady. Have you seen them?"

McCready's wary expression betrayed that he'd likely been confronted with this scenario before—no surprise since eloping couples formed the backbone of Gretna's economy. "'Fraid I won't be much help, sir. It's been a busy few days on account o' the weather—"

"Perhaps this will jog your memory." Andrew dropped a coin purse on the counter. "His name is Daltry; the lady is Miss Kent."

The innkeep weighed the purse, which quickly disappeared into a drawer. He opened his registry, running a finger down the lines of ink. "No, sir. I don't see those names."

"He's in his fifties, short, balding. She's blonde—beautiful," he said tightly.

"Come to think o' it, that does fit the description of Mr. and Mrs. Jones, sir. They arrived just after noon today and booked the newlywed suite."

The knot in Andrew's chest tightened. "Show me to their rooms."

"Now ye ken I don't want any trouble—"

"If you do not show me the way immediately, I will bring a wrath down upon this place such as you've never seen nor will you see again," Andrew vowed grimly.

"Yes, sir." McCready grabbed a metal ring of keys and a lamp and scurried from behind the counter. "Right this way, sir."

Andrew followed the proprietor up a narrow flight of stairs to the first floor, the latter's candle casting ghostly shadows over the dark wood interior.

"Their suite is at the end of the hall—" McCready began.

A scream shattered the night.

Chapter Eleven

Panic propelled another scream from her throat.

"Shh, love, it's all right." Hands gripped her shoulders. "Are you hurt?"

Her mind wouldn't function. Numbly, she stared up at the face whose lines were achingly familiar in the moonlight. "A-Andrew?" she said uncomprehendingly.

"Yes, sunshine. What's happened? I heard you scream..."

He trailed off, his gaze suddenly shifting to the figure beside her on the bed. The unmoving form whose blank eyes had greeted her when she'd suddenly come awake. A buffle-headed feeling swathed her. Perhaps this was all a dream... oh, please, please, *please*...

"What's amiss, sir?" A man wearing a sleeping cap—the innkeeper, she recognized—peered around Andrew, his lamp casting a bright glow. "Holy Mother of God, is he—"

"What happened, Primrose? Tell me," Andrew commanded.

This wasn't a dream, then. Nausea surged, and she swallowed thickly.

"I don't know. When I w-woke up a few minutes ago, he was like this." She was so cold... and shaking. She couldn't seem to stop. "H-he was fine when I f-fell asleep..."

"I understand." Andrew removed his jacket, placed it over her shoulders. "I'll take care of everything."

She drew the warm, spice-scented wool closer around her.

Gathered her wits enough to ask, "Wh-what are you doing here? H-how did you find me?"

"I'll explain everything later." He turned to the innkeeper. "McCready, send for a maid to escort Miss Kent to a new room. Have food and brandy brought as well." His mouth was a grim line. "It's going to be a long night."

Later that morning, he found Primrose in her new suite. Fully dressed, she sat in a chair by the window, her arms hugging her raised knees. A pang struck his chest: as a little girl, she'd often curled up just that way. A posture both innocent and guarded. Her head turned as he approached, and there was no mistaking that she was a woman now. The eyes that met his held too much worldly knowledge.

Pain that he was powerless to erase.

Insides clenching, he noted the untouched glass next to her. "You didn't have the brandy."

"I didn't want any. I'm muddled enough as it is." She lowered her feet to the ground, sitting up straight. "What did you do with Daltry?"

"The undertaker is preparing his remains. I've arranged transport of the body back to London."

"Thank you," she whispered.

He gave a gruff nod. "How are you faring?"

"It feels like a dream... a nightmare. This cannot possibly be happening." She rose, pulling her shawl tightly around her shoulders. "We weren't even married for a full day."

"I know." He'd gotten all the details from the innkeeper. In fact, he'd gotten more than he'd bargained for.

I've seen it before, the innkeeper had confided. *Older gent elopes with a young thing, thinks he's won the prize. But then the business proceeds and the sod's old ticker can't handle the excitement.*

Mark my word, sir: wedding nights can be dangerous.

"And now Daltry's dead. I'm a *widow*." Her voice hitched.

Swiftly, he went to her. Held her as the tears began. The shock was wearing off, reality wracking her slim body with sobs. He stroked her hair, murmuring soothing nonsense until she calmed. Her fragrance curled into his nostrils: Pears soap, feminine sweetness, temptation itself. He was acutely aware of how well she fit against him. The perfection of her curves nestling against his own hard edges... which were getting harder by the moment.

It was wrong, of course. Yet of their own accord, his fingers tangled in her silken tresses.

"Once we return to London," he said hoarsely, "your family can get you an annulment."

She stilled. A heartbeat later, she pushed at him.

It took everything he had to let her go.

"Why would I want one?" Her voice quivered, her gaze remaining steady.

"Because..." He caught himself in time. "Because you were only married a matter of hours. You could argue that the consummation didn't take place. You would be a free woman."

"And why would I want to be free?"

He couldn't look away from the vulnerable gold swirling in those pure green depths. His lungs strained. He knew what she was asking.

What you can't give her, you bastard.

"Because you are young and have a whole life ahead of you," he forced himself to say.

Her bottom lip trembled. "What place do you have in this plan for my lifelong happiness?"

"I want what's best for you, Primrose."

"And that is not you?"

"No." A single syllable—and it killed him to say it.

She drew herself up. "Well, then, thank you for your help. I can take things from here."

"Don't be ridiculous," he said shortly. "I'm escorting you home."

"If you don't want me, why won't you just leave me be?" she cried.

"What I want is irrelevant,"—he shoved a hand through his hair—"because I cannot give you what you need. Hell, I can't even keep you out of trouble."

"I'm not your relation, pet, or property, sir, and, therefore, not your responsibility." In a blink, she transformed from vulnerable girl to outraged siren. Her eyes glinted like gilded emeralds, her full bosom surging with passion. "What I do—and who I do it with—are not your concern. But it does beg the question: how did you find me?"

He reckoned this wasn't the time to tell her that Odette worked for him. "I have contacts."

"What are you—some kind of a spy?" she said with derision.

"No. But in my business I have access to a great deal of information." Not a lie, certainly.

"What business are you in?" When he didn't answer immediately, she folded her arms over her chest. "Let me guess: it's better for me not to know."

"You're catching on," he muttered.

"And you're insufferable, do you know that?" She looked ready to stomp her foot in frustration, and his lips twitched despite his bleak mood. Her next words, however, chased away all traces of humor. "Well, Mr. Andrew Whoever-You-Are, I want you to stay out of my life from here on in. As the Countess of Daltry, I do not need the services of some stranger who fancies himself a knight-errant."

"Are you the Countess of Daltry?" he said curtly.

After a moment, her chin angled up. "Yes."

The affirmation punched him in the gut. After the undertaker had removed the earl's body, Andrew had checked the sheets. No blood—but that didn't necessarily mean anything. As a pimp, he had an insider's knowledge of just how fragile virginity could be. Horseback riding, for instance, could divest a female of her maidenhead. And the reverse was also true: he knew wenches who'd managed to successfully auction off their virginity half a dozen times.

But hearing Primrose admit the truth stirred a myriad of emotions. Jealousy, possessiveness... anger at himself for being a bloody fool.

"I see," he said quietly.

"I see, *my lady*."

Irritation joined the fray. "Then I suggest you pack up, my lady," he said coolly, "and we head on our way. No doubt your family will be beside themselves. Having lost you once before, your mama—"

"What did you just say?" Her eyes widened.

Instantly, he recognized his mistake.

"How do you know that my mama *lost* me? Only my family knows that," she said in low tones. "Everyone else thinks Mama placed me with country folk until she married Papa and he adopted me."

Faced with her scrutiny, he faltered. "I meant only that your parents must be worried—"

"That is not what you said." He could almost see the gears turning in her head. "We knew each other in the past, didn't we? That's why you've always seemed... familiar."

He didn't want to lie to her. Nor did he want to tell her the sordid truth. "Primrose, I—"

The rapid approach of footsteps made him whip around. A fist pounded on the door.

"Rosie, are you in there?" a man's voice bellowed. "Open this door at once!"

"*Papa*," she breathed.

She dashed over to the door, threw it open. Two men stormed in, and she flung herself into the arms of the first. "Oh, Papa!"

"Poppet—*thank God*. We've been looking all over for you!" Ambrose Kent enfolded his daughter in a fierce embrace. "Are you all right?"

The second man looked over at Andrew.

"By Jove," the Earl of Revelstoke said. "What the devil are you doing here, Corbett?"

Chapter Twelve

As THE CARRIAGE bounced over the roads the next day, the storm eased, sunlight slanting through the fogged windows. Maybe the heavens had temporarily run out of rain—the way Papa had of words. Rosie's ears were still burning from his latest lecture. His relief at finding her unharmed had swiftly transformed into parental wrath.

She knew she deserved it. Papa's reprimands didn't make her feel as ashamed as how weary he looked. Sitting across the carriage, his handsome face was haggard, shadows betraying his lack of sleep. As he brooded out the window, light glinted off the spreading silver at his temples. He looked tired and worn, and she was the cause of it.

She swallowed, wanting to apologize again, knowing that it would make no difference. What was done was done. When she'd left her family a mere four days ago, she'd been a girl. Now she was the widowed Countess of Daltry. Some fathers might rejoice at the prospect of their daughter making a fine connection... but not hers.

She suppressed a sigh. Papa didn't give a jot about things like money and titles. The fact that Mama had been a wealthy baroness when he'd first met her had nearly *prevented* him from proposing. How, then, could he understand why his own daughter would choose status over love?

At the thought of love, her unruly heart skipped a beat. Her life was presently in chaos, yet all she could seem to think about was Andrew... Andrew *Corbett*. At least now she knew his true identity. Revelstoke's revelation had been startling, to say the least.

Last year, Polly and Revelstoke had been brought together by mayhem: accused of beating a whore named Nicoletta, the earl had sought Papa's help to clear his name. Nicoletta's employer (and owner of the club where the crime had supposedly occurred) had wanted to press charges—and that owner had been a Mr. Corbett.

It can't be a coincidence. Thus, it followed that if Andrew was *that* Mr. Corbett, then he was the proprietor of London's premier bawdy house. He was a procurer... a pimp.

She had difficulty reconciling his profession with what she knew of him. Not that she numbered many brothel owners amongst her acquaintances, but she would assume that such men would be evil and heartless. Despite the tumultuous state of affairs between her and Andrew, she knew he was neither of those things. He'd tried to protect her from Daltry—had pursued her all the way to *Gretna* to do so. There'd also been times when he'd understood her like no one else ever had, when he'd made her feel so safe...

In fact, she was beginning to wonder if he hadn't lied after all. If his refusal to marry her *was* indeed because he was trying to protect her—from himself.

You're an angel, but I'm not worthy, he'd once said.

Had he truly rejected her for her own good?

Whatever the reason, his rebuff had hurt like nothing else ever had. Her reaction confused her, but no more so than his inadvertent disclosure that he knew about her being kidnapped as a child. Outside of her family and those involved, *no one* knew about that fact.

Was Andrew a part of my past? The question festered. After Papa and Revelstoke's arrival, Andrew had met with them privately—she'd been barred from the proceedings (big surprise there)—and soon thereafter he'd departed. Without even saying goodbye.

Her frustration mounted. She *needed* to understand the truth. Her attraction to him went deeper than the physical. Somehow it was related to her history: the darkness that her family never discussed—that she, herself, had walled off.

Now the shadows were calling to her.

"Chin up, there."

At the deep murmur, her head swung toward Revelstoke, who shared the bench with her. The earl didn't usually pay her much attention. She suspected he didn't like her very much, and she didn't blame him: she'd acted like a spoilt brat when Revelstoke had declared his feelings for Polly rather than her. To this day, she was ashamed of her behavior.

At present, however, the earl's handsome visage appeared sympathetic. Rosie supposed this was Polly's doing. It was amazing how love had transformed the jaded rake into a man of sentiment.

"Thank you, my lord," she said hesitantly. "I'm afraid I deserve to hang my head."

"Been there myself. But, as Polly likes to remind me, to err is human."

"I suppose I'm *very* human then."

"That makes two of us." The earl's smile was rueful. "By the by, you should know that Polly is at home under protest. She would be here if I hadn't put my foot down."

"In her condition?" Rosie said, aghast. "Thank heavens you stopped her! I'd never forgive myself if anything happened to her."

"That's what I told her," Revelstoke said.

The unexpected camaraderie boosted Rosie's spirits—and her courage. She slid a glance at her father, who was still ruminating out the window.

Taking a breath, she said, "I was wondering something, my lord."

"Yes?"

"What is your opinion of Andrew Corbett?"

The ensuing silence boomed like a clap of thunder. Revelstoke looked to Papa, his lifted brows saying louder than words, *You can take it from here.*

"That is none of your concern, young lady," Papa said with a foreboding frown.

"It is. In recent weeks, Mr. Corbett has been,"—she chose her words carefully—"endeavoring to protect me from scandal. Yet never once did he let on about his identity. Now that I know he's, um, an acquaintance of Revelstoke's, I want to learn more about him."

"Now that you know who Corbett is," Papa said sternly, "you ought to know that he was right in keeping his identity from you. While I do not agree with his tactics, I do with his discretion. You will have no further contact with him, Rosie."

"Is he truly that wicked?" she said hesitantly.

Her father seemed to struggle with his response. *Interesting.*

"The world is rarely black and white," he said at length. "I cannot in good conscience defame Corbett's character, but he is not suitable company for you."

"But he's a part of my past, isn't he?"

Papa stilled, his amber eyes wary. "Is that what he told you?"

Her frustration spilled over. "He told me *nothing*, just as you are telling me nothing now! I am no longer a child. Why won't anyone tell me the truth?"

Trepidation prickled over her skin like thorny vines. What was so terrible about her past? Why did her parents think it necessary to keep it concealed?

"It's true that you're no longer a girl." Papa's chest heaved on a sigh. "As for Corbett, it is not for me to tell you about him. When we get home, you'll speak to Mama."

"Why bother? She never tells me anything," Rosie said sullenly.

"She wants only to protect you. She loves you, Poppet, more than you'll ever know. This time, however, there is no hiding from the past." Papa's troubled expression ramped up Rosie's guilt—and anxiety. "For either of you."

Two evenings later, Rosie sat in her mother's sitting room. As a girl, she'd always felt privileged to be permitted into this feminine sanctuary. Mama changed the décor from time to time, but the room was always a statement of her inimitable good taste. Presently, the walls were papered in pale lemon silk, the furnishings upholstered in eggshell velvet. The vase of hothouse peonies on the escritoire provided the only sign of cheer at the moment.

"How could you do such a thing, Rosie?" Her emerald dressing gown swirling around her slender form, Mama was pacing before the settee where Rosie sat. "This was beyond reckless. Beyond the *pale*."

"Have a care, my love." Papa watched the proceedings from the hearth, one arm braced on the marble mantel. "You've just recently regained your health—"

"I blame myself." Mama's famously sculpted cheekbones were pale. "If I hadn't been bedridden, I could have kept a better eye on her. Prevented this *catastrophe*. It is my fault."

With throbbing remorse, Rosie watched as Papa crossed over to Mama, enfolding her in his arms. He whispered to her, his hand moving over her loose silver blonde tresses in a soothing stroke. Witnessing the love between her parents had always made Rosie feel safe, but now a host of other emotions swelled in her.

Longing to have what they had. Determination to

understand her own history.

And sudden, inexplicable anger.

She stood. "I am sorry that I have caused you both worry. But I am not a child, to be discussed as if I am not present."

Mama lifted her head from Papa's shoulder. "If you are not a child, then why have you acted like one? Eloping with a blackguard... on some petty *whim*..."

"It was not a whim." Rosie was proud of how steady she sounded. "It was the logical solution to my problems."

"Marrying a lecherous old peer solved your problems?"

"I took a leaf from your book."

She saw the stunned look on Mama's face—and was too angry to care.

"Primrose Kent," Papa said severely, "you will apologize to your mother this instant."

"I'm sorry, Papa, but I will not apologize for the truth." Swallowing, she said, "I'm four years older than Mama was when she married Baron Draven; I'm perfectly capable of making my own decisions. If we're to talk, I wish to be treated as an adult."

Papa looked ready to argue, but Mama put a staying hand on his arm. "I think it'd be best for me to speak to her alone, Ambrose."

"If you're certain, my love." At Mama's nod, he left, sending Rosie a warning glance.

Mama said quietly, "The last thing I want is for you to make the same mistakes that I have, Rosie. Marrying Draven remains the biggest single regret of my life."

"More than having a bastard?" The words left before she could stop them.

"How could I regret having you, my darling?" Mama came to her, tipped her chin up. "From the moment you were born, you were my reason for living. When Draven took you from me, I vowed that I would do anything to get you back.

That I would never stop looking until you were in my arms once more."

Seeing the shimmer in her mother's eyes, Rosie felt heat push behind her own. The truth left her. "I hate being a bastard."

"I know you do. And I am sorry," Mama whispered.

When her mother reached for her, Rosie took a step back. "I'm not saying that to make you feel guilty. I *know* you've done everything in your power to be a good mother to me. I know you love me."

"I do, Rosie." Mama's voice broke. "So much."

"Then tell me the truth about my past." Fear lodged in her throat; she spoke around it. "Tell me about Andrew Corbett."

Mama drew the lapels of her dressing gown closer. "You are certain you must know? The past... it's ugly." Shadows darkened her eyes. "That is why I've always sheltered you from it."

"I want to know," Rosie said in a quivering voice. "Mr. Corbett—he knows me, doesn't he?"

Mama sank onto the settee, nodded slowly.

Shivering with anticipation, Rosie took the adjacent seat. "How? When?"

"It was during your early years. Before Coyner."

Whenever Mama referred to Gerry, her voice vibrated with hostility—understandable, given that Gerry had kidnapped and nearly killed her. On the rare occasions when Rosie thought of her former guardian, confusion bombarded her. How could she reconcile the doting, if oft-absent man she'd known with the villain that he'd become? Sometimes she even dreamed of that terrifying night when she'd helped Papa to rescue Mama and defeat Gerry.

Tamping down dread, she said, "I don't remember anything before Coyner."

"I had hoped it would remain that way." Mama let out a breath. "You know that after you were born, Draven took you from me. Used you as leverage to bend me to his will. After his death four years later, I ransacked his belongings for any clue to your whereabouts, and I found... a receipt." Her throat rippled. "He'd paid a woman by the name of Kitty Barnes to care for you."

"Kitty Barnes." As Rosie repeated the name, no face emerged in her mind's eye, yet a sense of apprehension swamped her. "I don't remember her."

"That is not surprising since you left her keeping when you were only four years old. After I learned of Barnes, it took me another four years to hunt her down. It was during this search that I met Andrew Corbett."

Rosie's pulse raced. "You know And—I mean, Mr. Corbett?"

"I met him briefly." For some reason, Mama's cheeks flushed. "The investigators I hired to find you had proved worthless, but they had dredged up one clue. Kitty Barnes had an associate and lover named Augustus Longfellow."

When Mama hesitated, seeming to struggle with her next words, Rosie pleaded, "Go on, Mama. Please."

"Longfellow was easier to track down than Barnes. He was using his real name, Andrew Corbett, by the time I found him working in a house of ill repute owned by a Mrs. Wilson."

Rosie blinked. "Working there? You mean as a footman?"

"As a prostitute," Mama said bluntly. "There are dens of iniquity which cater to women, my dear, and Mrs. Wilson's was the premier place of its time. Corbett was her star attraction. Rumors that he was one of the Prince Regent's by-blows boosted his popularity."

Rosie's mind whirled. Andrew had been a *prostitute*? And he might have *royal* blood? As she tried to absorb these staggering facts, she recalled his masterful lovemaking. How skillfully he'd brought her pleasure. And her cheeks burned.

"It was through Corbett that I located Barnes. Although he and she had parted ways some years ago, he told me that she'd gone into hiding because of her debts to Bartholomew Black, an infamous cutthroat." Mama paused. "Corbett's information allowed me to flush Barnes out and, eventually, to find you. He didn't have to help me, but he did. And he refused payment, too."

"Why did he help you?"

"Because he is a gentleman. Not in Society's eyes, of course, but in the true sense. I believe his honor prompted him to do the right thing." Mama's fingers knotted in her lap. "His honor... and you."

"Me?"

"He told me that Kitty had decided to... sell you. To the highest bidder," Mama said in a haunted whisper. "He parted ways with her because he could not condone her decision."

A sickening sensation gripped Rosie by the throat. She couldn't speak. Couldn't give voice to the vile, unthinkable question exploding in her brain.

"Gerry?" she managed.

"Nothing happened to you." Her mother grasped her hands, which had gone numb. "You must believe me. But when your father and I finally hunted down Coyner, we found evidence that he meant to... eventually..."

"What?" she said in an anguished whisper.

"Marry you. To make you... his child bride." Mama's eyes shone with unshed tears. "But *nothing* had happened as yet, Rosie. You were only eight when we found you, and he was waiting for you... to mature. To show the first signs of womanhood before he put his despicable plan into action."

She was going to be ill. Right here, on the pristine velvet cushions. She lurched to her feet, pulling free of her mother's grasp.

"Rosie?" Mama stood, reaching out.

"Don't touch me!" Rosie backed away, her arms wrapped around herself. "Why didn't you tell me all this before? Why have you and Papa been lying to me for *years*?"

"Don't blame your father. He wanted to tell you the truth," Mama said in a suffocated voice, "and I wouldn't let him. I couldn't bear the thought of you being burdened with this. You must believe me: Coyner never—"

"Why should I believe anything you say?" The words left her in a shout. "Why should I believe you ever again when you have lied to me my *entire life*?"

Moisture trickled down her mother's cheeks. Feeling her own tears well up with uncontrollable force, Rosie whirled around and ran from the room.

Chapter Thirteen

Past

ANDREW SAT ON his bed, elbows braced on his thighs. A half-finished bottle of whiskey sat on the bedside table. It was five in the morning, and he'd recently finished his shift. His hair was damp from the bath he'd taken, and, beneath his dressing gown, his skin was tingling from the scrubbing he'd given it.

It had been a long night, the kind that left you feeling dirty no matter how many baths you took. He'd serviced a trio of women, high-kick types who thought it would be a lark to share a piece of rookery meat. They'd all ogled him coyly through bejeweled masks.

Look at that cock! It's a wonder he can walk, one had giggled.

He's at least twice the size of my illustrious husband, the second had observed.

Size is all well and good, the third said, *but does he know how to use that monstrous asset?*

Did they think he was so ignorant that he didn't know how to fuck? Like a trick pony, he'd performed on command. He'd given the three what they wanted, and after he'd left them panting and satisfied, he realized that not once had any of them addressed him directly.

He was less than a servant whom one might call by name. Less than human.

He took a swig directly from the bottle, welcoming the

burn. If he couldn't feel clean, then at least he could feel nothing. He hated his present mood. Hated his weakness, his stupid desire for…

Don't be a fool like I was, my boy. His mama's last words flitted through his head. *Love ain't for the likes of us.*

He didn't want love. Just some bleeding respect.

It didn't help that tonight came on the heels of yet another argument with Kitty. Her plans to expand her business were failing and her debts to Bartholomew Black growing. She didn't like it when Andrew pointed out the facts. Today he'd committed the worse offense of all: he'd offered to help.

You—manage *one of my bawdy houses?* Her derisive laugh had made his face burn. *Don't delude yourself, luv, and keep to what you know. Got a trio of ladies booked tonight, all in need of a good swiving, and it'll be a test of even your God-given talents.*

He took another swig of whiskey to drive out the scornful voices.

Hinges creaked, and his head swung in the direction of the door. It had better not be Kitty. His temper simmered dangerously. *If she wants me to fuck another customer—or fuck her…*

"Andrew?" Primrose's head poked around the corner.

At the sight of her tear-stained face, his anger receded.

"What's the matter, little chick?" he said with concern. "Another nightmare?"

"Y-yes." Her voice hitched.

At three, the tot was having bad dreams with increasing regularity. He'd told Kitty that the girl needed a nanny to watch over her at night, to which Kitty had replied: *And I need a proper mansion in Mayfair, but neither of those things are going to happen.*

He patted the place next to him. "Do you want to tell me about it?"

Primrose dashed over pell-mell, scrambling onto the bed

and throwing her short little arms around his waist. "It was scary," she sobbed. "I was scared."

"Monsters again?" he said gently.

She nodded, her tears soaking through his robe. "*Big* monsters. Loud ones stomping through the house."

He cursed silently. A brothel was no place to raise a child.

"There are no such thing as monsters," he said.

Primrose looked up at him with glimmering jade eyes. "I s-saw some in the hall. *Three* monsters. So ugly they had to wear masks!"

He choked back a laugh. *Out of the mouths of babes…*

Lips twitching, he said, "You're safe in here. I won't let the monsters get you."

"I know." Her smile temporarily chased away his own demons. "Andrew?"

"Yes?"

"Are *you* ever scared?"

He hesitated. "Yes."

"What are you afraid of?"

He thought of the faceless customers, the perfumed hellholes, the poverty.

"That things will never change," he said quietly.

He'd never given voice to his worst fear before. Didn't know why he would do so in front of Primrose, a bantling who couldn't understand.

"I don't like change." Her bottom lip trembled. "I don't like new things."

"Some new things are good. Don't you want a new dress, a nicer house to live in?"

She shook her head—then surprised him by throwing her arms around him again. "I don't want anything but you."

With those words, she reached inside him and touched his heart. Unlike others in his life, she didn't try to take it or rip it out or mold it in any way. She just… held it. The way a child holds an injured bird, trying to coax it to fly.

His throat thickened. "You have me, little one."

"Promise?" Her head tipped back, her eyes searching his.

"Promise." He ruffled her bright curls. "Now time to get some sleep."

He got under the covers. She followed him, cuddling up close. He watched over her until her lashes lay still against her small cheeks, her breathing turning deep and even. Then his own eyelids grew heavy, and he followed her into sleep.

Chapter Fourteen

ROSIE STOOD IN the wood-paneled foyer of Daltry's townhouse, conferring with Mr. Horton, a junior solicitor in the firm that handled her late husband's affairs.

"The funeral procession is ready, my lady," Mr. Horton said in discreet tones. "Shall I give them leave to begin?"

"Please do," Rosie said wearily. "Thank you."

"It is my pleasure to assist." The young solicitor paused. "My firm extends its apologies again for Mr. Mayhew's absence. Rest assured he is doing his utmost to expedite his return to London."

Mr. Mayhew, Daltry's executor, was on the Continent on business.

"You are doing a fine job in his stead, Mr. Horton," she said gratefully.

With a bow, Mr. Horton left to orchestrate the transfer of the coffin from the drawing room to the conveyance waiting outside. The man was a godsend; she didn't know what she would have done without him. He'd made all the arrangements for the funeral, including setting up the vigil at Daltry's townhouse, which Rosie had never set foot in before today.

It was a testament to her wicked nature, she supposed, that she didn't even feel sad... just numb. When it came to her union with Daltry, she'd never harbored any illusions. Their marriage was like a business that had gone bankrupt on opening day. In her mind, sending him off in style was better than any false manifestations of grief on her part, so she'd instructed Mr. Horton to spare no expense on this final tribute to her husband.

A part of her couldn't help but wonder if she'd been born beneath some unlucky star. It was just so *typical* of her to fling herself out of the frying pan and into the dashed fire. After all the trouble she'd gone through to land Daltry and elope with him—not to mention the indignities of the wedding night (she ignored the uncertain flutter)—she was now worse off than when she'd started.

She was a countess, yes, but one whose marriage had started and ended with scandal. At the moment, her state of mourning put her in social limbo, but when that period ended, who knew what her fate would be? Would the *ton* accept her… or make her a pariah?

Her throat tightened. Why, oh why, had she run off with Daltry?

You know why.

Regret seeped painfully through the numbness. She'd neither seen nor heard from Andrew since his abrupt departure from Gretna, and she… missed him. Somehow, through the chaos of the past month, she'd grown to rely on their unexpected encounters. On the fact that he was watching out for her like some brooding guardian angel. Now that she knew more about their prior connection, she yearned to excavate the artifacts of their history…

Did he feel the same way? Was he staying away because he truly thought he wasn't good enough for her? Or had he realized that she was damaged goods and washed his hands of her?

A spasm gripped her heart. Regrets piled up like dirty laundry, *if onlys* joining the heap. If only she hadn't acted so recklessly and out of wounded pride. If only she'd tried to discover the truth about Andrew—why he wouldn't marry her, why he felt as *essential* to her as breathing—instead of eloping with another man. If only she hadn't acted like the flighty, wicked girl that she was.

"Rosie?"

She turned to see Polly coming down the corridor, followed by Aunt Helena, the Marchioness of Harteford. Like Rosie, both wore black. They had provided immeasurable support, staying by her side throughout the day as visitors had come to pay their final respects.

"Is everything all right?" A curvaceous brunette, Aunt Helena was sweetness itself, concern radiating from her hazel eyes.

"Yes... No." Sighing, Rosie stowed away thoughts of Andrew. "The procession's getting ready to leave."

The men—including Mr. Peter Theale, Daltry's heir, and Mr. Alastair James, the stepson of Daltry's aunt—would be accompanying the body to the churchyard. To give her lord his proper due, Rosie had asked Mr. Horton to arrange a stately night march that included a dozen black horses with feathered headdresses and professional funeral attendants to swell the ranks.

"That's just as well." Polly squeezed her hand. "It's been a long day for you, dear."

"I don't know how I would have survived it without the two of you. But it's not over yet." Lowering her voice, Rosie said, "What is the state of affairs in the drawing room?"

The look exchanged between Polly and Aunt Helena spoke louder than words.

Today had been Rosie's first official encounter with Daltry's relations. As a whole, they had not greeted her with what one would term enthusiasm. Peter Theale, Daltry's cousin and heir, had been the sole exception.

Ginger-haired and possessed of an awkward stammer, he had expressed his condolences and assured Rosie, "You n-need not worry about you future comforts, my dear."

She wasn't worried—not about money anyway. That had never been her reason for marrying Daltry. She knew her parents would continue to provide for her, and, moreover, she didn't want to receive handouts from the new earl.

Nonetheless, Mr. Theale's kindness had been comforting, especially compared to the coolness she'd sensed from her dead husband's female relatives. At present, four of them awaited her in the drawing room. Daltry's aunts—Mrs. Antonia James and Lady Charlotte Daltry, the dowager countess—had greeted her with a touch of frost, and his cousins, Misses Sybil and Eloisa Fossey, had taken their older relatives' lead.

"Mrs. James has been complaining about the, um, odor," Polly murmured. "The dowager countess, for her part, appears to have an issue with the lateness of the hour."

"Everyone knows night funerals are all the rage." Rosie's hopes sank even further. In order to have *any* hope of salvaging her reputation, she would need the support of her husband's formidable aunts. "And given that Daltry had to be brought back from Gretna, it was inevitable that he'd be a bit overripe. It's not my fault; I couldn't have done any better for him!"

"You've done your best," Aunt Helena said firmly. "Given the circumstances, the last thing you need is to fret over impressing his relations."

Rosie bit her lip. "But I need them, Aunt Helena. You know I do."

Her aunt sighed but didn't disagree. "Your mama would know what to do. You should really talk to her, Rosie. This rift between you two—it hurts Marianne dreadfully, you know."

Rosie did know, and her misery grew. Yet every time she thought of the past Mama had kept from her—of what Coyner had intended for her, even if he hadn't carried it out—her insides crawled. Walls sprang up in her mind; she just couldn't cope with it. Not yet. Not with everything else on her plate.

Thus, she had been avoiding her mother and had gone to stay with Polly. Today, during the funeral, she and Mama had exchanged a few awkward words, their interactions stiff. Her parent had eventually left to tend to Sophie.

"I'm not ready to talk to her," Rosie said, staring at her black slippers.

"Everything Marianne did, she did out of love." With a finger, Aunt Helena tipped up Rosie's chin. "You do know that, don't you?"

"I love her, too. I just can't…" To her horror, Rosie felt her voice crack.

"All right, my dear. One thing at a time." Her aunt took her hand and squeezed it. "For now, what do you say we face the dragons together?"

Rosie nodded. Accompanied by her aunt and Polly, she returned to the drawing room.

The coffin was gone, and servants had tidied up. Mrs. Antonia James, Daltry's dark-haired aunt, paced by the shrouded window, her tall, thin frame bristling with suppressed energy. In her forties, she was a striking woman with slashing cheekbones and feline features. In contrast, Lady Charlotte Daltry, whose husband had been the earl before Rosie's, was a plump, hen-like woman with feathery silver curls and shrewd eyes.

Flanking Lady Charlotte were her protégées, Misses Sybil and Eloisa Fossey. The dowager had no children of her own, and she'd taken her husband's orphaned nieces under her wing. The sisters were both unmarried. The younger sister, Miss Eloisa, was in her twenties and a beauty with chestnut hair, alabaster skin, and sapphire eyes. Miss Sybil, the older sister, was a spinster and muted version of her sibling. Her hair was a dirty blonde shade, and her skin had a sallow undertone. Her light blue gaze peered out timidly from beneath straight brows.

All eyes turned to Rosie: some wary, others hostile.

Daltry was right about his family, Rosie thought with an inward sigh. And if they hadn't respected *him* because of his connections in trade, what hope did she have that they would welcome his bastard bride of less than a day into their fold?

Yet she needed their support. If her late husband's relatives did not take her side, then her position would be more precarious now than before her elopement. They held the key to her social survival.

She summoned a smile. "Pardon my absence. I was making final arrangements for the procession. Shall I ring for refreshments?"

"I've already done so." Mrs. James' eyes glittered like jet beads. "Since I and my stepson Alastair—he was a great favorite of your late husband's—have been so much in this house, the servants naturally looked to me to play hostess. I hope you don't mind."

"Not at all, ma'am," Rosie said politely. "I wish only for your comfort."

In the stilted silence that followed, Aunt Helena came forward.

"Lady Daltry," she said pleasantly to the dowager, "it has been quite some time since we have met. I regret the circumstances, but may I say how well you are looking?"

"Thank you, Lady Harteford." The dowager inclined her head graciously. "I trust your husband and sons are well?"

"Very well. Thank you."

Aunt Helena took a seat, and others followed suit.

The ticking of the ormolu clock soon became deafening.

"I wanted to express my gratitude," Rosie said. "For your support today—"

"You misunderstand," Mrs. James said coldly. "We are not here to support you."

"Now Antonia—" the dowager began.

"You may choose to pretend that this is some cozy family affair, Charlotte, but I'll not." Mrs. James crossed her arms over her scant bosom, directing a livid glare at Rosie. "Not after this *chit* has brought scandal down on our heads. Why, she's made poor George a laughingstock—the punch line of a vulgar joke."

Heat scorched Rosie's cheeks.

"What happened wasn't Rosie's fault," Polly said staunchly.

"Perhaps your notion of wrongdoing and mine are different... Lady *Revelstoke.*"

Before his marriage, Polly's husband had been an infamous rake, his presence deemed unwelcome by certain sticklers. Mrs. James' snide emphasis reminded Polly of the fact.

Seeing Polly's bottom lip quiver, Rosie felt a rush of anger. "Speak to me any way you like, Mrs. James, but you will *not* speak to my sister that way."

The other's brows arched. "I've said nothing that isn't true."

"As I'm sure everyone is quite peaked," Aunt Helena intervened, "I think it best that we defer this conversation. Until everyone is in a better state of mind."

"I quite agree," Lady Charlotte said. "The funeral is no time to delve into family affairs."

"Are we certain we *are* discussing family affairs, Aunt Charlotte?" Miss Eloisa's delicate inquiry was girdled with steel.

"Hush, girl." Lady Charlotte clucked at her charge. "Mind your manners."

"But everyone is saying it," Miss Eloisa protested. "You

know they are, Aunt Charlotte. It is better for her sake that she knows."

"Eloisa," Miss Sybil said timidly, "perhaps this isn't the best time—"

"Did anyone ask for your opinion, Sybil?" her younger sister shot back.

Miss Sybil fell silent.

Rosie swallowed. "What are they saying?"

"How do I put it politely?" Miss Eloisa tapped her chin. "That your marriage is a sham."

A fist of panic pounded in Rosie's chest. "It isn't. I have papers—"

"Papers don't mean anything." Mrs. James stood.

Aunt Helena and the dowager rose as well.

"Now, Antonia, I must insist—" the latter said.

"Do you want to be recognized as a part of this family?" Mrs. James demanded.

"Yes," Rosie whispered. "I do."

"Do you wish to have our backing through the scandal that you've caused? To be lifted onto our shoulders rather than be fed to the wolves of ruination?"

Rosie gave a mute, desperate nod.

"Then you shall have to furnish proof."

"Of... what?"

The fires of judgement blazed in Mrs. James' gaze. "Consummation."

Chapter Fifteen

"WE'VE GOT A problem," Horace Grier declared.

A common refrain of late, Andrew thought wearily. The afternoon was his time to get work done before the club opened its doors to the usual mayhem. On his desk, he had a stack of ledgers that he'd intended to review, but Grier and Fanny had burst in, facing him across the desk, hostility crackling between them.

He set down his pen, his gaze taking in the pair. "What now?"

"Malcolm Todd, that's what," Grier said.

At the mention of his rival, Andrew's jaw clenched. "I just met with the bastard. Made it clear that Nursery House is no threat to his business."

Three days ago, he'd had a parley with Todd. He preferred to avoid bloodshed whenever possible, and thus he'd taken pains to quell any rumors concerning his venture. He'd informed the other of Nursery House's purpose—and that it posed no competition to Todd's brothel two blocks away.

"Todd didn't get the message, apparently. Got his men surveying that damned nursery of yours," Grier said. "He's spread the word that you're encroaching on his territory."

Andrew slammed his fist on the desk. "The lying bugger. He's been spoiling for a fight, and now he's using this as an excuse to start a war."

"Choose your battles," Grier advised. "This one ain't worth it."

"Surely you're not suggesting that he shut down the place to appease Todd?" Fanny crossed her arms beneath her bosom, which was generously displayed by her scarlet gown. She wore paint, and her lashes were sooted; on the nights she worked, she looked the part of Abbess Fanny. "Why should he kowtow to that bastard?"

"Because he wants to keep his head on his neck, that's why," the Scot growled.

"I thought it was your job to keep it there," she shot back. "Not up to the challenge?"

"I swear to God, woman, if you push me—"

"Devil take it, that's enough." Andrew rose, and the pair swung to face him. "You're both right. I have to choose my battles—but I'm not bloody going to back down, either. To do so would be a show of weakness. Once the bastards smell blood in the water, they'll all come circling."

"What do you want me to do, sir?" Grier said.

"Todd is powerful," Andrew said grimly, "but even he must tread carefully. He was part of the Accord, like the rest of us. He has no legitimate reason to strike out against me; any violence he incites violates the terms we all agreed to. He'll have to answer not only to me but to the King."

In recent years, the London Underworld had undergone a quiet revolution. The bloodshed had risen to a degree that benefited no one—and resulted in the most powerful men of the rookeries coming together to hammer out a solution. Both Andrew and Todd had been at the table when territories had been drawn, treaties negotiated. And Bartholomew Black, the most powerful of them all, had been crowned King of the Underworld, giving him the right to mediate and dispense justice as necessary.

In some ways, the system heralded back to old Arthur and his round table. Only the King was a certified cutthroat and the knights were men who made their living off the darkest trades of London.

"I don't see Todd quaking in his boots," Grier said with a snort, "seeing as how the King happens to be his father-in-law."

"Black may be ruthless, but he's fair." Andrew straightened the papers on his desk. "Moreover, he and Todd don't see eye to eye, and Todd won't dare risk Black's wrath. In the meantime, put an around-the-clock watch on the Nursery House. Tell the men not to engage but to report in immediately if there's any trouble."

Grumbling, Grier took off, but not before he snuck a glance at... Fanny's bosom?

Good God. Andrew headed for the whiskey decanter. Half-past three in the afternoon and he needed a drink. Not a good sign.

Fanny tagged at his heels. "You're not going to shut down Nursery House, are you? I've just finished settling in the girls and—"

"I'm not shutting it down." He downed a shot of whiskey.

The bawd studied him. "You look like hell. As hellish as an Adonis can look, at any rate."

"Is that a compliment or an insult?" He tossed back another shot.

"An observation. You look like you haven't slept in days."

He hadn't... because of Primrose. She'd featured nightly in his dreams, torturing him with what could never be. Now that she knew who and what he was, she would understand that no future was possible between them. That the one thing she craved—respectability—was the one thing he couldn't offer. As much as he told himself that this was all for the best, that he had no business being a part of her life, his spirits had plunged into an abyss.

"And you've been distracted since you returned from your trip." Fanny's brows formed thin arches. "Care to talk about...

her?"

A rap on the door prevented the necessity of a reply.

Tim, one of the footmen, appeared. "Sorry to disturb you, sir. But someone's here to see you."

"I'm not expecting visitors." Andrew frowned. "Did he give his name?"

"It's a lady. Came through the back and dressed in black, she is—and veiled like a bloody apparition." Tim shuddered. "Scared the bejesus out o' Cook and the kitchen maids."

Hope seized Andrew. *Don't be a fool. Primrose would never come here, would never want to see you again now that she knows who you are.*

"Send her in." The footman left, and Andrew said to Fanny, "We'll talk later."

The bawd took her sweet time gathering her things. The door opened, and Andrew forgot all about her as Primrose swept in, taking center stage. Her slender form was cloaked head to toe in black, lace veiling her face, yet he'd know her anywhere. She lifted the heavy veil, revealing the golden jade eyes that haunted his every waking and sleeping moment.

He strode over to her. Staring into her exquisite oval face, he thought he must be dreaming. He lifted a hand to touch her cheek—as smooth and silky as he remembered. Real.

"What are you doing here, sunshine?" he said hoarsely.

"I had to see you." Primrose's voice trembled.

A foreign emotion leapt in his chest. It took him an instant to recognize it as joy.

"Ahem."

The indiscreet throat clearing from behind him brought reality crashing back. Hell, he and Primrose weren't alone. He turned to Fanny, deliberately blocking Primrose from the other's view.

"You were just leaving," he said curtly.

"Was I?" Fanny inquired.

Before he could march the other out, Primrose peered around him. "Who's she?"

He would be damned if he introduced her to a madam. "No one to concern—"

"I am Mrs. Fanny Argent. I work with Corbett." The bawd gave Primrose a once-over, her brows lifting. "Who are you?"

Primrose stiffened. Before Andrew knew what was happening, the two women were facing one another, their expressions reflecting mutual animosity.

"I am a friend of Mr. Corbett's," Primrose said, her chin lifting. "Not that it is your place to inquire about his affairs as you are a mere... employee."

The glance she raked over the bawd's working attire made Andrew wince. Clearly, she'd jumped to the wrong conclusion and assumed Fanny was one of the wenches.

"Forgive me." The dangerous glitter in Fanny's eyes belied her apology. "Due to my *close* working relationship with Corbett here, I see so many of his hoity-toity friends that it can be difficult to sort out who is who."

Color flooded Primrose's cheeks.

Enough is enough. He said sharply, "Be off with you, Fanny."

The bawd smirked and sailed out. Andrew shut the door, locking it.

The instant he turned, Primrose burst out, "Who is she?"

"She works for me." He couldn't take his eyes off Primrose, couldn't believe that she was standing in front of him. In his club—wait. What the *hell* was she thinking? "You shouldn't be here. Your reputation—"

"Is she your lover?"

He blinked. "Who...you mean *Fanny?*"

Primrose gave a fierce little nod. She was... jealous? While, normally, he avoided possessive females like the plague, the idea of Primrose feeling that way about him filled him with tenderness.

He touched her cheek. "No, she isn't. She manages several of my clubs."

"You mean she's a... procurer?" Primrose's golden lashes swept up.

"Yes. Like me," he forced himself to add.

He waited for her response. He didn't know if her parents had told her about his past, but given that she'd found him at his brothel, she could have no illusions about who and what he was now.

"Well, I don't like her manner," Primrose said with a scowl.

Absurdly, he found himself fighting a smile. She was so damned adorable. At the same time, the rational part of his mind reminded him that she was taking an unacceptable risk.

"Sunshine, you shouldn't be here. If anyone were to see you—"

"I took precautions." She waved at her pinned-up veil. "And I came in through the back."

"Your parents..."

"I'm staying with my sister, and she thinks I'm out on an errand. *Please*, Andrew," she said, "don't send me away. You told me once that you would be there for me. So much has happened, and I need to talk to you." Her eyes beseeched him. "Only you can help me understand my past."

He had no defense against her pleas. It was only natural that she would want to know that which had been kept from her—and it was the one thing he could give her. So they would have this time together, he reasoned. He would tell her what she wanted to know.

Then he would let her go once and for all.

"Let's sit," he said quietly. He led her to the divan in front of the crackling fire, taking her cloak while she removed her bonnet. "Shall I ring for some refreshment?"

"All I want is the truth." With her hair glinting like spun gold and delicate chin lifted, she looked like a warrior princess. "Mama has been hiding it from me all these years, and I won't stand for it any longer. I *must* know about my past."

He sat next to her. "How much of it do you know?"

"Mama told me about you… and Kitty Barnes." Her cheeks turned pink. "And what your, um, trade was."

"I fucked women for a living." He refused to sugar-coat or be ashamed of the fact, even for her. "Kitty was my pimp. Occasionally my lover."

"That's what Mama said. But I don't remember anything of my life with the two of you."

Seeing the uncertainty in her gaze, he felt that familiar surge of protectiveness. Only now it was mingled with desire, the combination dangerously potent.

Stay in control.

"That's not surprising. You were only four when we parted," he said.

"What do you recall of those years? Of… me?"

Too much. Everything.

"You were a little chick, chirping away and making everyone around you smile. You were brave, too. Life wasn't easy, and we didn't stay in one place for long, yet you never complained. About anything."

"Were we friends?" Her gaze searched his.

"In a fashion. Given our age difference, I thought of you more as a little sister."

"Is that how you think of me now?" she said softly.

God help him, what kind of question was that?

He rubbed the back of his neck, muttering, "I should think the answer is obvious."

Her tremulous smile made him ache with something more

than desire. More than he'd ever felt for any female. "If I asked you something, would you tell me the truth?"

"I won't lie to you," he said.

Her gaze dropped to her lap, her knotted fingers. "What do you know about the man Kitty Barnes sold me to?"

His gut clenched. "Not much. Kitty and I had parted ways before then."

"Did you know what she planned to do with me?" Primrose raised eyes bright with anguish.

The years ripped away, and guilt bled like a fresh wound.

"I knew that she could no longer afford to keep you. She said that she meant to place you with rich folk who could take care of you. I tried to stop her," he said gruffly, "but I didn't have the means, the money or the power. You were her ward, not mine. In the end, I... left."

Self-disgust burned like acid in his chest. At least Primrose now knew the truth of his cowardice. He waited for her condemnation.

"I *hate* Kitty Barnes. She's a callous, calculating witch." Primrose's voice shook not with fear but rage. "Wherever she is, I hope she suffers the way she made me suffer."

It crossed his mind to tell her... and he couldn't bring himself to do it. He reasoned to himself that it didn't matter; true, whatever he'd had with Kitty had lasted far too long— but it was over and done with. It had no bearing on what was happening now between him and Primrose.

"You confused me," she said suddenly. "When you showed up out of nowhere at Aunt Helena's masquerade and started telling me what to do. Without even telling me who you were."

"My approach to you was wrong from the start," he admitted. "I kept my identity a secret because you shouldn't know a man like me. In truth, I should have just continued handling matters from afar—"

"Hold up." Her eyes narrowed at him. "What do you mean *handling matters from afar?*"

Right. He slanted her a glance, wondering how badly she was going to take this.

"For some months now," he said, testing the waters, "I've been keeping an eye on you."

"Define keeping an eye."

"When gossip about you and those men began to circulate, I squelched them," he said bluntly. "I couldn't stop the talk entirely, but I made sure the bastards in question kept their mouths shut."

Her jaw slackened. "How did you do that?"

"I have access to certain information about them. Between the various businesses I own, I also hold the vowels of half the men in London. It was easy enough to gain their compliance."

"You *blackmailed* them?" She stared at him. "For me?"

"I used what leverage I had to shut up a bunch of lying braggarts," he said flatly. "They dallied with you, not vice versa. If anyone deserves condemnation, it's them. The buggers are lucky I didn't call them out, but to do so would have only caused more scandal for you."

"That is what Mama said when Papa wanted to challenge them," she murmured. "She said it was better to let the business blow over. And it might have, if it hadn't been for that poem…" She froze, and he saw the instant that realization struck. "Oh my goodness—*The Prattler*. Did you blackmail the owner too?"

"No, I paid him off." Andrew shrugged. "He was happy to retire on the sum."

Her eyes were as round as saucers. "Is there anything else that you've done on my behalf?"

Might as well be hanged for a sheep as a lamb.

"Odette reports to me. That is how I found out about your rendezvous with Daltry in the Pantheon and your elopement."

He paused. "And that's it, I swear."

Primrose lowered her gaze to her lap, unusually quiet. What was she thinking? How was she taking the news of his interventions? To a sheltered miss, his actions likely seemed ruthless. He didn't give a damn: no one was going to bully or hurt her while he had the power to stop it.

"I did what had to be done," he said. "I have no regrets."

Her eyes lifted, and the shimmering gratitude in them stole his breath.

"Thank you," she said softly.

He gave a wordless nod.

"Do you know," she said after a heartbeat, "it wasn't your identity that confused me the most but how I *felt* about you. You were a stranger, and yet you made me feel safe. Protected. How could I trust someone I didn't even know?" Her eyes searched his. "Now I understand. You've always protected me, haven't you?"

"I've tried. Your happiness, Primrose,"—his voice roughened—"it matters to me."

Her shoulders straightened, and her chin jerked as if she'd come to some inner decision. "If that's the case… if I asked you to help me with a matter, would you do it?"

Yes. Anything. Name it, and it's done.

He'd lived long enough, however, to know the folly of his heart's reply.

"It depends," he said, "on what the matter is."

"Could you… that is *would* you… be as kind as to…"

"Yes?"

She drew in a breath. "Would you please relieve me of my virginity?"

Chapter Sixteen

SHE COULDN'T BELIEVE that she'd said the words aloud.

Instinct had brought her here tonight; Andrew's gruff admission that he'd been protecting her from afar confirmed that her decision had been the right one. The fact that he'd done all of that for *her*—she could scarcely fathom it. She owed him too much, and now she'd asked one more favor of him.

She trusted him to take care of her problem. And, given his worldly experience, he had to be the one man in London who wouldn't be shocked by her request. Judging from his dumbfounded expression, however, her assumption might have been wrong.

"Pardon?" he said.

"Please don't make me say it again." Embarrassment scalded her cheeks. "You heard me."

He stared at her, his dark brown eyes inscrutable. He stood abruptly. "I need a drink."

As he went to the decanter, she said, "I'd like one too, please."

"I'm afraid I don't stock ratafia or sherry in here."

"Whatever you're having is fine."

"I'm drinking whiskey." He swigged it like water.

Although she'd never had whiskey, the occasion might call for it. "I don't mind."

Wordlessly, he refilled his own glass and brought one over

for her. As he handed her the drink, their fingers touched. Awareness shot through her, tingling at her nerve endings.

His hand jerked back, and he prowled to the mantel like a restless lion. "Perhaps you'd care to explain your... request."

She took a sip of the amber liquid; it went down like fire. "Daltry's family wants proof that my marriage was consummated."

"In Gretna, you told me that it had been."

Discomfited by the intensity of his stare, she said, "What I *said* was that I'm the Countess of Daltry. Which I am. I have the marriage papers to prove it." She blew out a breath. "And I did, um, share a bed with Daltry."

"Did he tup you?"

"There's no need to be crude—"

"You're asking me to relieve you of your virginity. Given the topic, I think we'll call a spade a spade," he said flatly. "Did Daltry tup you?"

"Um... perhaps?"

"Bloody hell," he growled, "stop playing games. There is no *perhaps* about it. Either Daltry put his cock in you or he didn't."

Shivering at the lethal expression on Andrew's face—not to mention his carnal vocabulary—she said defensively, "I'm not playing games. I'm just not certain what happened. I'd had several glasses of wine, you see, and it was dark. Daltry came to bed, and he started to, um, touch me. You know... down there."

"What else did he do?" Andrew set his glass on the mantel, his knuckles white.

She strove to maintain an impervious façade. To preserve the veneer of her composure.

"He got on top of me. He was heavy, suffocating,"—panic fissured, too close to the surface, and she fought to keep her voice from cracking—"and I couldn't really tell what was happening. He fumbled about, and for an instant, I felt stretching... down there. But I don't know if it was his fingers... or his, um, you-know-what. But then he started cursing, saying this had never happened to him before, and it was all my fault—"

To her horror, her voice broke, her vision fracturing into liquid fragments.

An instant later, the glass was removed from her grasp. Male strength engulfed her, and she buried her head into the comfort. Into the sanctuary that was Andrew.

"It's all right. You don't have to say any more."

"I haven't told this to anyone—I'm so ashamed," she whispered into his waistcoat. "I don't know why I thought I could talk about it with you."

"Because you can, sunshine. You can tell me anything."

"Do you... hate me?"

"No, love. Never."

Soothed by the immediacy of his reply and his spicy, familiar scent, she sniffled. "I've made such a fool of myself. When you didn't want me, I got so angry that I went after Daltry."

"It was never a question of wanting. You know that now, don't you?"

"So the times you refused me," she said haltingly, "you truly did it to protect me?"

"Yes." His eyes told her this was the truth. "You want respectability; I can't give you that."

His honesty gave her the courage to make her own confession.

"I don't deserve respectability. The only reason men have shown any interest in me is because I'm pretty on the outside. But inside," she said in a small voice, "I'm frivolous and scheming. Wicked through and through."

A sound rumbled beneath her ear. He was... laughing at

her? When she'd just confessed her greatest flaw?

Wounded, she struggled to get away. "It's *not* amusing."

He kept her caged against him with one arm. Tipped her chin up with his other hand. "It is, actually. Imagine a little thing like you calling yourself wicked."

"I *am* wicked," she insisted. "I'm a flirt, and I eloped with a man I didn't even like."

"Why did you? Elope with Daltry, I mean."

"Because I'm shallow and flighty," she said hollowly. "I wanted to be the Countess of Daltry."

"Because it would make you rich?"

"No. I mean, money is nice, but I have everything I need from Mama and Papa. I didn't marry Daltry for that reason. What I want is the title—the position. I want to be called *my lady*, to be welcomed in the upper echelons, to have the *ton* acknowledge that I belong," she said with a touch of defiance. "See how awful I am?"

"No." He rubbed his thumb over her bottom lip, making her shiver. "I don't."

"You must be blind then," she said decisively.

Crinkles appeared around his eyes. "My vision is quite acute. In fact, I see you more clearly than you see yourself. And I know what you really want."

An arrogant statement, no doubt. Yet she couldn't help but ask, "What do you think I want?"

"To be free of fear." His knuckles skimmed along her cheekbone, his touch as mesmerizing as his words. "You've been running for so long, haven't you, sweetheart?"

His words resonated like music in a cathedral. Pure, soaring in their accuracy. Suddenly, she realized she *was* afraid—had been all her life. Images flashed: walking on shaky legs down that dark dock to where Sir Coyner waited, holding her mama at gunpoint; waiting by the window whenever Papa was late coming home from work, her small hands clenching the sill; hearing Mama's moans of pain during Sophie's birth...

A dark undertow sucked at her, threatening to pull her under.

Heart pounding, she fought to stay afloat. *You can't do anything about the past. Focus on what you can control. Your future—that is what matters.*

"I hate caring what Society thinks," she said in a suffocated voice, "but I do. If Daltry's family manages to annul the marriage, then I'll be ruined. I'll be the unwed harlot who eloped and spent the night with a man. I'll be a pariah."

He studied her, his hooded gaze giving nothing away.

"There is only one solution," she plunged on. "When the physician examines me, I can't be a virgin. You're the only one I trust to help me."

A muscle ticked in his jaw. Still, he said nothing.

"Andrew, would you please,"—she summoned all her courage—"take me to bed?"

He rose, a violent movement that rocked the cushion beneath her. Lines of tension slashed around his sensual mouth, his eyes no longer hooded but blazing with anger. His hands bracketed his lean hips.

"Why me?" he said.

She wetted her lips, her mind spinning with reasons. "Because you're a man of experience. You understand my situation—that I'm only asking for one night... I mean, I hope that was clear," she said in a rush, realizing she had not said this aloud and wondering if its omission was the cause of his sudden temper. "This would be done strictly as a favor to me. There would be no further obligation on your part afterward. I would hope, however, that we would part as friends."

"I see. Because that is what friends do. They fuck and then they leave."

His mockery cut like a razor through the last threads of

her composure.

She shot to her feet. "It was a mistake to come. I don't know why I did."

"You said so yourself: you needed a man of experience." He raised a brow. "Unless I seriously underestimated your boldness, I doubt you know any former prostitutes other than me."

"That's not what I meant," she cried. "By *experience*, I was referring to the fact that you're a man of the world, and nothing seems to rattle you. I sought you out because I believed you could understand my less than conventional request. Obviously, I was mistaken. I'm sorry to have bothered you."

She nearly made it to the door when an arm hooked her waist from behind. Her back met with a wall of rigid muscle.

"Don't go." His breath was harsh at her ear.

"I'm not going to stay and be ridiculed—"

"I'm sorry." His chest heaved against her spine. "I thought you came to me because of what I used to do. And I didn't like that."

When she pushed against his arm, he let go. Whirling around, she studied him—saw the sincerity etched across his hard features... and the shadows in his eyes. Understanding dawned that he had a past to run from as much as she did.

"It takes one to know one, doesn't it?" she said softly.

"Pardon?"

"What you said about me running from my fears. You've been running too, haven't you?"

His gaze didn't waver. "I'm not ashamed of my past. I did what I had to; it's made me who I am. But I'm no longer that man—and I won't be used in that fashion by you or anyone."

"I understand."

She really did. Due to her tarnished reputation, plenty of men thought they could get a kiss—or more—from her without consequence. Being seen as an object, a play thing, had made her feel dirty... like soiled goods.

Andrew had made the choice to use his assets as a means of survival, and he wasn't apologetic about it. Nor should he be. Even so, it couldn't be easy knowing that he'd once been bought and sold as a commodity of pleasure.

"The last thing I want is to use you, Andrew." She exhaled. "In truth, I owe you far too much already. I can never repay you for what you've done on my behalf."

"You don't owe me anything."

"I do." She touched his jaw gently. "I want us to part as friends."

When she tried to withdraw her hand, he covered it with his own, trapping it there.

"Why?" he said intently.

"Because..." *I care what you think. Your opinion of me matters... too much.*

"There's no need for us to be enemies," she finished lamely.

"Not that. I meant why *me*. Why do you want *me* to be the man who beds you, Primrose?"

Her heart grew wings, beating frantically against its cage. The easy words surfaced, hovering on her lips. But he deserved more, and she fought to give him the truth.

"I feel safe with you," she said. "When I'm in your arms, I know it's where I'm meant to be."

The throbbing in her ears was echoed by the ticking muscle beneath her palm.

Then the world spun, and, swept off her feet, she just managed to hold on, her arms wrapping around his neck as his lips claimed hers. His kiss roiled with hunger, and she kissed him back with equal ferocity. She didn't have to hide her passion for him, this man who didn't judge or condemn her— and the freedom was intoxicating.

When he set her down by the sofa, her legs wobbled. He held her securely as he suckled her earlobe, pleasure spreading through her like a fever. The tips of her breasts tightened into tingling points, a viscous warmth gathering in her belly. The sensations intensified as his lips glided along her jaw and down her neck, his skillful hands peeling off her layers.

When her chemise floated to the floor, leaving her in nothing but black garters and stockings, her wits suddenly returned. What must she look like sans her proper accoutrements? Was her coiffure mussed? Her panic flared as he sat on the sofa, pulling her onto his lap. She was acutely aware that she was in a disarray whilst he remained impeccably dressed.

Feeling exposed, she tried to cover herself.

He caught her chin, held her to his gaze. "Don't hide your loveliness. You never have to hide anything from me."

"But I'm not properly—"

"You're perfect as you are. Beautiful beyond compare," he said huskily. "No woman has ever affected me the way you do."

He sounded earnest. Even if she doubted the words, there was no denying the physical evidence supporting his claim: beneath her bottom, his arousal was a hard and heavy bar.

Her anxiety subsiding, she whispered achingly, "Make love to me, Andrew."

His eyes darkened, and he leaned in to kiss her. The gentle brushes of his mouth swept aside her worries, need spiraling through her. His hand closed over her breast, and this was *nothing* like Daltry's groping in the dark. Andrew cupped and molded her achy mounds, pinching the throbbing tips, and she moaned against his lips.

"You're so pretty here." His voice matched the brushed velvet of his eyes. "Pink and ripe like a berry. Do you taste as good as you look, I wonder?"

"Taste?" She blinked at him.

The slow, sensual curving of his lips made her belly flutter. He took one of her hands, bringing it to his mouth. Separating the index finger from the rest, he licked the tip, the wet swirl setting off a wild pulse between her legs. He guided her moistened fingertip to her nipple.

"Imagine me kissing you here," he murmured, using the damp point to simulate what he was describing. "Would you like that?"

Bold and brazen as she was, she couldn't bring herself to answer him. Her body, however, had no such reservations. To her mortification, moisture trickled from her womanly place, and she could feel it dampening the fabric of his trousers.

Out of nowhere, Daltry's voice assailed her: *You're a shameless doxy.*

She tried to get away, but Andrew kept her caged against him.

"Your response is lovely," he said, "just like you are."

"But I made your trousers..." Cheeks aflame, she couldn't finish.

"I want you wet for me. The wetter the better." His words were shocking, his eyes warm and steady. "It's your body's way of telling me you want me."

Once again, she felt a rush of gratitude for his experience and honesty. Relaxing, she allowed him to lay her back against the cushions while he knelt on the floor next to the sofa. Her respiration quickened as he kissed the slope of her breast. His lips explored, circling but not touching the straining peak.

She began to squirm, and, when she couldn't stand it any longer, she slid her hands into his thick bronze hair, urging him to go where she wanted him. *Needed* him. He laughed softly, and then his lips captured her nipple, bathing it in heat and wetness. Bliss.

Her legs moved restlessly, the throbbing between them

nigh unbearable as he lavished attention upon her breasts. Licking, flicking, driving her mad with wanting. She didn't know how to ask for what she needed; she didn't have to. His hand coasted over her rib cage, down the quivering valley of her belly, landing where her desire for him swelled, humid and pulsing.

"Your pussy is drenched, love." His nostrils flared, his eyes smoldering. "Do you know how much that arouses me?"

Shyly, she said, "How much?"

"I feel as needful as a lad with his first wench."

"Me too," she whispered. "Like a wench with her first lad, that is."

Amusement flashed across his chiseled features. "You *are*, you silly chit."

"I don't know that for certain—"

"I do."

His kiss cut her off. She couldn't have spoken anyway for he was rubbing that hidden bud just like that time at the plumassier's, and it melted her mind. Her hips bucked as he stroked her, faster and faster, winding the coil in her belly ever tighter. It suddenly sprung free, and she gasped his name as pleasure ricocheted inside her.

When she regained her senses, heart still thumping wildly, she saw that Andrew was watching her with an intense, heated gaze.

"Are you going to... bed me now?" she said bashfully.

His head canted, almost thoughtfully.

He said, "No."

Chapter Seventeen

"WHAT?" PRIMROSE JERKED into a sitting position on the sofa.

Refusing to plow a beautiful, naked woman wasn't high on Andrew's list of preferred activities, especially when he was kneeling between her thighs. He had a perfect view of temptation: her hair cascaded over her creamy shoulders, her full pink nipples playing peek-a-boo through the strands. His gaze dropped to her little blonde nest, dewy from his recent frigging. Even as his cock strained toward all that bounty, his brain reminded him that this wasn't just any woman.

This was Primrose.

She deserved better than a meaningless fuck.

And so, he realized, did he.

He didn't fool himself into thinking that a permanent future was possible for them. She'd been clear about the respectability she needed, and he knew the limits of what he could offer. Even so, he couldn't turn his mind from the possibility of them… together. Before, when she was unwed, he wouldn't have considered it, but things had changed. She was a widow now—and would have the title and status she so craved, once he helped her with her "problem."

She would also have freedom.

The notion roused both anticipation and unease. Undoubtedly, Primrose would soon have packs of men sniffing at her heels. Her origins and reputation might have rendered her ineligible as a wife in some men's eyes—but those same men would have no compunction pursuing her as a lover now that she was widowed and fair game. And with her youth and passionate nature, she'd eventually want companionship.

His muscles bunched at the idea of Primrose taking a lover. If anyone was going to make love to her, it was damned well going to be him. An affair wasn't what he wanted, but he would take what he could get.

He wanted Primrose. More than he'd ever wanted anything.

Which meant he had to play his cards right. He had full confidence in his ability to do so. If there was any game he knew how to play, it was that of seduction.

"But I thought you were going to help me!" she cried.

"I am." A plan unfolded in his head. To prevent her from rising, he clamped his hands on her thighs. The sight of the frilly black garters against her pale skin tested his resolve, but he said calmly, "I'm going to do it my way, however."

"And what way is that?" Her glorious eyes narrowed in suspicion.

"This way, love." His hands slid to her bottom, tipping her up, and he bent his head.

"What are you...?" she gasped, "No, you mustn't! That's not clean, that's—oh, *heavens*..."

His first taste of her pussy fired his blood. Sweet and feminine with a hint of salt, the reality of her was even better than his fantasies. He hid a smile as her protests melted into shapeless moans. As her superficial primness dissolved, revealing the hot, passionate woman within.

He ate her cunny with the hunger he'd suppressed for weeks. Spreading her petals, he tongued her slit up and down before circling her entrance. When she was moaning, her hands gripping the cushions, he slid the tip of his middle finger into her hole.

Goddamn, she was tight. Exquisitely so. But she was also slick from his licking and her earlier climax; when he saw no sign of pain from her, he pushed in until he was knuckle-deep.

She gasped his name.

"All right, love?"

"Yes... yes..." She looked dazed with desire.

He added another finger and stirred in a motion that would remove any flimsy barrier that might mark her as *virgo intacto*. He thrust firmly, simulating the fucking of a cock, sweat gathering beneath his collar as her pussy gripped his digits with lush insistence. Devil and damn, to feel that snug heat sheathed around his prick...

Her thighs trembled, her head lolling against the back of the sofa. He could feel her crisis approaching; it would be so easy to free his throbbing erection and bury himself inside her. To give in to the desire that raged between them. Lust warred with rationality: he reminded himself that, for her, desire had a purpose, a goal.

And that goal isn't you... not unless you convince her otherwise.

After one last thrust that pushed a moan from her lips, he pulled out.

Her head popped up, her cheeks flushed and breathing uneven. "Why did you..."

"That should take care of your maidenhead," he told her. "There's no bleeding, so I suspect yours might have already been dispatched by horse-riding or the like. That's common for young ladies, you know."

From her blank look, she didn't.

He rose, plucking up her chemise. "I'll help you get dressed. You've been here too long already."

"But don't you want to...finish?" She wetted her lips, looking so disappointed that he was sorely tempted to do just that. "I don't mind if you want to. That is, I came fully prepared to..."

"Lie with me?" he said mildly.

Her head bobbed, and damn if the little minx didn't sneak a look at his groin. To be fair, that part of his anatomy did command attention. The bulge strained the placket of his trousers, stretching the grey wool to dangerous proportions; only excellent tailoring—and steely self-control—held him in check.

"I know this was a favor for me," she said haltingly, "but I had assumed that you would gain some pleasure out of it too. Now it all seems rather... one-sided."

"Do you want me to make love to you, Primrose?" he said evenly.

She bit her lip. "I think... I do."

Her aching whisper almost undermined his resolve. Almost.

"Let me know when you are certain." Pulling her to her feet, he said casually, "Arms up, sweetheart." Looking adorably befuddled, she obeyed, and he pulled the chemise over her head. He followed with her corset, deftly tying the laces. "And let me be clear: there is only one circumstance under which I'll make love to you."

Her brow puckered. "What circumstance is that?"

"When I take you, it won't be a one-time affair. It won't be because you have to rid yourself of your virginity or because you're simply curious about being bedded. It won't even be because you trust me to make the experience good for you."

"Pray tell, what reason *would* move you?" she said with a touch of tartness.

"I'll make love to you when you want *me*," he said. "When you can't stop thinking about me kissing you, touching you, my cock filling your sweet pussy." He noted with satisfaction her deep blush and flaring pupils and gave her corset a final tug. "I'll make love to you when you admit I'm the only man who can give you what you need."

"Rather sure of yourself, aren't you?" Her voice had a breathy edge.

He buttoned up her gown and set her bonnet on her head. "I'm honest. When you're ready to be, send word to me." He twitched the veil in place over her astonished face. "Do us both a favor, sunshine: don't keep me waiting."

Chapter Eighteen

T WO DAYS LATER, Rosie descended the steps of the Revelstoke townhouse in a distinctly grumpy mood. She could have blamed it on the indignity of the physician's examination she'd endured that morning. At least he'd confirmed the consummation of her marriage. Mr. Mayhew, Daltry's executor, had returned to Town and set up a meeting tomorrow to finalize Daltry's affairs; she couldn't wait to put the grim business behind her.

Yet her surliness wasn't due to her marriage. She placed the blame for her mood squarely on the broad shoulders of Andrew Corbett. She couldn't get him out of her thoughts, and she had a sneaking suspicion that he'd done that on purpose.

You're mine. I'm the only man who can give you what you need.

He'd planted that notion, and it flourished in the jungle of her mind. Images of him proliferated, filling her every waking hour—and even when she wasn't awake. Her cheeks warmed. Who knew that dreams could be so depraved? He'd awakened some dormant need in her, and now she couldn't contain it.

Even now, her body simmered with awareness. With each step, her breasts pressed against her bodice, achy and full, the tips pulsing as she recalled how he'd suckled her. His mouth had felt so good there and lower… Goodness, had she really allowed him to do that? To kiss her… pussy? Just thinking the word liquefied her insides.

Botheration, she thought sourly. *Now not only do I need to guard against uncharitable thoughts, I have to watch out for* lewd *ones too.*

Thanks to Andrew, she couldn't get words like *cock* and *fuck* out of her head. They were wicked, coarse... and rather titillating.

Heavens above, she *was* a trollop.

She couldn't stop herself from imagining what it would be like to be in Andrew's bed. To hear his deep voice murmuring deliciously naughty things. To feel him *doing* those things. To have his cock inside her, filling her, making her forget everything but how right it felt to be with him...

Don't be a nitwit. Are you really going to throw away everything you've worked so hard for—to have an affair?

Frustrated at her own stupidity, she stomped through the foyer toward the drawing room. The door was open, and she stopped short at the sight of Polly... and Revelstoke. The earl had his wife pressed up against a wall, their profiles revealed to anyone who might walk in, but they were too absorbed in each other to notice.

Revelstoke had one hand braced on the wall by Polly's head. Polly's eyes were closed, her lips parted as he nuzzled the side of her neck. Tingles danced over Rosie's skin as she recalled Andrew kissing her there, along that sensitive slope, then sucking her earlobe the way Revelstoke was doing to his countess now. A sensual sigh escaped Polly—and that was when Rosie noticed that the other's stockinged legs were visible between the earl's booted stance. Polly's skirts were bunched at her waist, the fabric spilling over the sleeve of the earl's jacket, his blue gaze burning with possession as he watched his wife's face...

Unbearable longing flooded Rosie. What would it be like to have Andrew look at her that way? To allow herself to be possessed by him... to surrender to the desire blazing between them?

In that same instant, she realized she was standing there like a Peeping Tom, intruding upon a highly intimate moment. Mortified, she whipped around, rounding the doorway—and collided with the butler.

They rebounded off one another, she landing on her bottom, he reeling backward with a grunt, a tray flying from his hands. Tea and pastries rained through the air, and silverware clanged to the floor in a finale worthy of an orchestra.

Seconds later, Polly appeared, the earl behind her.

"What in heavens?" she exclaimed. "Are the two of you all right?"

"My apologies!" His face red and flustered, Harvey, the butler, rushed to help Rosie up—only to realize that the hand he'd extended was covered in clotted cream.

"I've got it, Harvey." Revelstoke hauled Rosie to her feet.

"I don't know how I could be so careless," Harvey began.

"It was my fault entirely," Rosie mumbled. "I was going too fast…"

She trailed off, catching the chagrinned look Polly cast at Revelstoke. For most of her life, Polly had possessed a unique gift for sensing other's emotions. Polly had always considered the extraordinary ability a plague and had been glad to be rid of it, yet her natural perspicacity remained. She'd obviously guessed the cause of Rosie's clumsy flight.

Not wanting to embarrass the other or herself further, Rosie muttered, "I'll, um, get changed."

A few minutes after she arrived in her room, a knock sounded. She went to the door.

Polly stood there, chewing on her lip. "I thought you could use some help."

"Thank you, dear." To hide her mortification, Rosie ushered the other in. Opening the wardrobe, she said lightly,

"What shall I wear—the black... or the black?"

A smile tucked in Polly's cheeks. "The black?"

"Excellent choice."

She took down the ebony taffeta and hung it on the dressing screen next to the chevalier glass.

Polly came over to help, keeping her eyes studiously on the buttons she was undoing. "I'm sorry about what you saw." Embarrassment quivered in her voice. "Sinjin and I—"

"Are newlyweds," Rosie said in a rush. "Truly, there's no need to apologize. You've both been so gracious whilst I've intruded on your privacy."

"Nonsense. Our home is your home. But what you must think of us—"

"I think you deserve every happiness, dearest. And the truth is... I've been thinking that I need a place of my own."

The idea had been percolating for the last week. As cordial as Polly and the earl had been, there was no denying the awkwardness of living with newlyweds; Rosie felt like a fifth wheel. She also didn't want to return to her parents' house. Not just because of the rift with her mother—which she was gathering the courage to address—but because she was beginning to see the truth: that was no longer her home.

She wasn't the innocent girl she'd once been. She was a widow, and as brief as her marriage had been, it had changed everything. She was now the Countess of Daltry, and she had to use that hard-earned status to carve out a future for herself.

"You can stay here as long as you want," Polly insisted.

"I know that, dear. I also know that I cannot live in limbo forever." Rosie bit her lip. "I've bungled things up so badly—with the elopement and my reckless behavior before that. I can't change the past, but I can take responsibility for my future. I'm an independent woman now; it's time I started to act like one."

"But moving into your own place?" Polly's eyes were

wide. "Won't you be lonely?"

"Solitude might do me good. Once the mourning period is over, I'll have social activities to keep me busy—especially if I can convince Daltry's aunts to sponsor me." At the reading of the will tomorrow, she would start her campaign to win the approval of Mrs. James and Lady Charlotte.

Polly's brow furrowed. "But where would you live? And how would you afford it?"

So there were a few details Rosie hadn't ironed out yet.

"I haven't the faintest how much a lease would cost," she admitted. "Do you know?"

Polly shook her head. "I could ask Sinjin. I'm sure he would know."

"I wouldn't need anything extravagant: a small cottage would do. I have my allowance from Mama and Papa. If they forbid my plans, then I... I'll simply sell my jewelry and gowns," Rosie said determinedly. "If I must, I'll find a way to finance my future."

"I doubt such drastic measures will be necessary." Her sister's voice was dry. "And speaking of your future, I was wondering..."

"Yes?"

Polly helped Rosie out of her stained dress and into a robe. "What about Mr. Corbett?"

Since returning from Gretna, Rosie had told Polly about all her interactions with Andrew—with the exception of her last visit. As much as she loved Polly, some things were just too difficult to share. Asking a gentleman to rid one of one's virginity topped the list.

"What about him?" she said cautiously.

Polly tugged her over to the bed, where they sat side by side. "Given what has transpired between the two of you, I wondered if he would be a part of your future plans."

Longing beat its wings... which were clipped by hurt as

she recalled his refusal to marry her. She understood now why he'd rebuffed her—and why, even during his more recent possessive (and rather thrilling) rhetoric, he had not once mentioned marriage. But just because she understood his reasoning didn't mean that she was eager to expose herself to more pain.

He was right: marriage *wasn't* possible between them. He couldn't give her respectability, and, if she were perfectly honest, she wasn't so certain what *she* had to offer *him*. With his looks and wealth, he would have no shortage of females willing to share his bed or his life. What was so special about her: an inexperienced semi-virgin who'd brought him naught but trouble?

Why pursue something that can't have a happy ending? Why open myself to torment?

"He can't be part of my future," she said dully.

"Why not?"

"He's a brothel owner so I can't marry him. And he's too good for me, anyway."

Polly blinked. "I think you'll have to explain."

Leaving out the fact that she'd asked Andrew to deflower her, Rosie confessed her visit to him—and her discovery of what he'd done on her behalf.

"Oh my goodness," Polly breathed when she was done. "If you don't marry him, I will!"

"Better not let your husband hear you say that." Rosie was only half-joking; the earl was more than a little possessive when it came to his bride.

"Why, Mr. Corbett is your knight-errant," Polly said, her eyes dreamy. "He's protected you all this time without your knowledge. And buying *The Prattler*? I cannot think of a more gallant and *romantic* gesture."

Her defenses crumbling, Rosie reinforced them by slapping on the plaster of common sense. "It doesn't matter. I can't get involved with him. Not now, when I finally have what I want."

Polly's brows rose. "Do you?"

"I have a title. Once I garner Mrs. James and Lady Daltry's support, I'll have a position in the *ton* too. No one can snub or reject me again," she said fiercely.

"I know acceptance is important to you, but I've always thought you deserved more."

"Love, you mean?" She shook her head. "That's for other people—"

"I believed the same thing once. When I wanted to settle for a loveless marriage, you told me I deserved better. Now I'm returning the favor." Polly took Rosie's hands, her expression earnest. "If I've learned anything, it's that *nothing* is as important as love."

"I didn't say I was in love with Andrew Corbett," she said quickly.

Perhaps *too* quickly because Polly gave her an acute look. "But you do have feelings for him?"

Heat rose into her cheeks. "I may be attracted to him, but it doesn't matter," she said a tad desperately, "because *he* has no intention of marrying me. In fact, I practically offered for him once, and he turned me down flat."

At least he's been consistent, she thought forlornly. *He's never pretended that marriage is possible between us. He probably wants a less troublesome wife and a woman who's good for more than just looking pretty.*

"Only because he thought he was doing the honorable thing," Polly argued. "If you told him that you don't care about what Society thinks—"

"But I *do*." Her hands balled; there was no solution to her conundrum. "I cannot compromise everything that I've worked for just to indulge some whim of passion. I won't prove the *ton* right by carrying on like the veriest trollop."

"Falling in love doesn't make you a trollop." Polly gently touched her arm. "When I was confused about Sinjin, when I didn't know what I ought to do, the truest guide was my heart. I hope you will listen to yours. And whatever you decide, know that I'll be here for you."

Rosie placed her hand atop her sister's, said gratefully, "What would I do without you?"

"You'll never have to find out, dearest."

Later that evening, Polly's maid was brushing her hair out after her bath when Sinjin entered through the door that connected their bedchambers. At the sight of her husband, Polly felt a tingle from head to toe. She still couldn't believe that this beautiful, loving man was all hers.

Dismissing her maid, he came to her, his big hands settling on her shoulders. His eyes, a rich sensual blue, met hers in the looking glass. "Ready for bed, kitten?" he murmured.

"I'm not tired," she said truthfully. Too much was brewing in her head.

"Capital." He picked her up, startling a giggle from her, and carried her to the bed. Making short work of her robe and his, he lay her down, crawling over her like a sleek, playful panther. "Now where were we before we were so rudely interrupted this afternoon?"

Desire warred with worry as she stared up at her gorgeous husband.

"What's the matter?" Concern lined his features. "Are you feeling unwell? Is it the babe—"

"It's not the babe," she said quickly.

"Do you wish to talk about it?"

It still amazed her how he could read her so easily. And

she loved him for being understanding, especially when it was clear that he had other plans. His massive erection pressed into her belly, but his gaze patiently searched hers.

"I'm worried about Rosie," she blurted.

Heaving a sigh, he rolled onto his side. "Tell me what happened."

Gratefully, she did, concluding, "I think Rosie's in love with Mr. Corbett, even though she won't admit it. I've never heard her talk about any gentleman with such emotion. Such *longing*."

"I thought your sister set her sights on gentlemen rather regularly," Sinjin said, his tone dry.

"Not in this way. Not with her heart involved," Polly said. "She may seem flighty, but when it comes down to it, she has a loyal and loving heart. I wish she would trust her own instincts."

"And her instincts are correct in leading her to Corbett?"

"After the way he's protected her? Of course." Polly slid a look at her husband. "There's also what you've told me about him."

Before their marriage, Sinjin had been accused of beating a prostitute named Nicoletta at Mr. Corbett's club. Mr. Corbett had been relentless in his pursuit of justice for his employee, making life difficult for Sinjin. When the truth had come to light, clearing Sinjin of the blame, the pimp had wasted no time in making amends, providing information that had led to the eventual capture of the true villain.

"Despite our initial differences, I respect Corbett," Sinjin said slowly. "He acted in what he believed to be the best interests of his employee. That's more than one can say for most pimps, I'd wager. And he apologized when he was wrong—which is more than one can say for most men. But, given his background, are you certain he is a suitable husband for your sister?"

"When it comes to marriage, you know that I don't hold strongly to conventions—"

"That's for certain." Sinjin ran his knuckles along her jaw. "You married me, after all."

"You're a rich earl. Not to mention an honorable and ridiculously attractive man," she said, casting her gaze heavenward. "I don't think I did too badly."

"But that's not all that I am. And you accept all of me."

Seeing his shadows emerge, she framed his hard, beautiful face in her palms. "Just as you accept me. I love you as you are, darling. You've made me so happy."

"Not half as happy as you've made me."

He kissed her hungrily, and she kissed him back with all the love in her heart. Passion blazed, and before it raged out of control, she broke away to gasp, "Do you think I did the right thing, advising Rosie to follow her heart?"

"That strategy worked well for us. Let's hope it'll do the same for her," Sinjin murmured. "Either way, we'll be there for her, kitten."

"Yes, I—" Her words melted into a moan. "I can't think when you do that, Sinjin!"

"Thinking is overrated. Isn't this much better... or this?"

It *was*... and he was right. No matter what, she'd be there for Rosie. She let go of her worries and, with a sigh of bliss, surrendered to her husband's loving.

Chapter Nineteen

"CHIN UP, POPPET," Papa murmured. "This'll be over soon."

They were in the waiting room outside the office of Arthur Mayhew, Daltry's executor. Daltry's family members were present as well. The greetings from Mrs. Antonia James and Miss Eloisa Fossey had been decidedly cool, but the warmer ones from Lady Charlotte and Miss Sybil had given Rosie hope.

As for the gentlemen, Mr. Peter Theale, Daltry's ginger-haired heir, had been his usual amiable self and Mr. Alastair James, Mrs. James' stepson, a trifle *too* friendly. A blond rakish sort, Mr. James had a rather high opinion of himself and seemed to believe that everyone shared in the delusion. Even now, he was smirking at her as he strutted about like a puffed-up peacock.

Rosie turned to her father. Somberly attired, his unruly hair neatly combed, he exuded dignity.

"Thank you for accompanying me, Papa," she said, ever grateful for his presence.

His amber eyes studied her. "Mama wanted to come too, you know."

With so much going on, she'd put off setting things right with her mother. "I'll speak to her soon, I promise," she said guiltily.

Papa looked as if he might say something, then the door to Mr. Mayhew's office opened, and everyone was ushered inside.

The dark paneling, drab green upholstery, and shuttered windows gave the solicitor's inner sanctum a gloomy feel. A heavy desk dominated the room, a semi-circle of chairs facing it. After everyone found seats, Mr. Mayhew, a stout fellow whose heavy jowls and wide-set eyes reminded Rosie of a bullfrog, addressed them from behind his desk.

"I'd like to begin by offering my sincere apologies for the delay," he said in deep, resonant tones. "It was unfortunate that I was detained abroad when Lord Daltry passed."

"*Quite* an inconvenience," Mrs. James said.

"My stepmama doesn't like waiting." Sprawled languidly in the chair next to Mrs. James, Alastair James added snidely, "Especially on the help."

Mr. Mayhew's eyes bulged, his face turning red.

Feeling sorry for the man, Rosie said quickly, "Thank you for sending Mr. Horton to assist during your absence. I don't know what I would have done without him."

The solicitor inclined his head at her. "You're welcome, my lady. I was gratified to hear from Mr. Horton that the funeral was a stately affair. George Theale was a long-time client of mine, and I consider it an honor to execute his last wishes. Thus, without further ado,"—he lifted a document from his desk—"ladies and gentlemen, this is the last will and testament of George Henry Theale, the fifth Earl of Daltry…"

Mayhew began with the letters patent, which dealt with the passing of the peerage and all its entailments to Peter Theale. As the solicitor droned on about estates and finances, Rosie's mind wandered back to Andrew. The talk with Polly yesterday had added fuel to her longing, and she'd spent a restless night fantasizing about a future with him.

Her practical nature had weighed in with a compromise. What if she allowed herself to explore her feelings for

Andrew... *without* the expectation of marriage? She was a widow now, and everyone knew widows played by a different set of rules. As long as she was discreet, she could take a lover—and the only one she wanted was Andrew.

I'll make love to you when you admit I'm the only man who can give you what you need.

Botheration. Having to capitulate to Andrew *would* be annoying... but a small price to pay to be in his arms. Even as excitement poured through her, she reminded herself of another caveat.

If she and Andrew were to have an affair, she *must* guard her heart.

She couldn't allow herself to hope for more than what was possible. Besides, being rejected by him once had been painful enough, and she didn't want to go through that again. Thus, she would present her terms to him: she'd be willing to have an affair as long as (a) there were with no strings attached, (b) it was done discreetly, and (c) it didn't threaten her ultimate goal of achieving social acceptance.

Feeling mature (and rather proud of herself) for working out a plan, she was reminded of her present objective and glanced at the dowager countess and Mrs. James, who were perched on the edge of their seats. As a first step, she would invite the ladies to luncheon. She'd plan a special menu and pour on the butter boat, if necessary. Maybe she'd be able to convince them to say something favorable about her at their popular Thursday Salon.

She warmed to her plan. The *crème de la crème* were like lemmings: just get one to change course and the others would follow. All she had to do was sway Lady Charlotte or Mrs. James...

At that instant, their gazes swung to her. She blinked and had a panicked thought: did they somehow catch wind of her machinations? But, no, it wasn't just them—*everyone* in the chamber was staring at her.

Uh oh. Her heart sped up. *What have I done now?*

"This is *unacceptable.*" Alastair James shot to his feet, all feigned lassitude gone. Rage flashed in his blue eyes. "I was Daltry's favorite. After all the time I spent with him, the bastard has *no right* to do this to me. To any of us!"

"On the contrary," Mr. Mayhew said, "Lord Daltry had every right to dispense with his personal fortune as he wished."

"B-but the estate." Peter Theale looked bewildered, the color of his face approaching that of his hair. "How the d-devil will I manage?"

"Outrageous," Mrs. James snapped. "There must be some mistake."

Completely lost, Rosie tried to piece together what she'd missed.

"There's no mistake." The solicitor's voice rang with authority. "Lord Daltry brought in two colleagues from his company to witness the signing of the will. They can and will attest to his sound state of mind and intentions."

"We are to rely on the word of *merchants*?" Fury accentuated the angularity of Mrs. James' features. "Well, I won't have it. I won't allow this *strumpet,*"—her black gaze honed in on Rosie—"to destroy the future of the Daltry lineage."

Papa rose, his expression lethal as a blade. "You will kindly show my daughter some respect."

Mrs. James stuck out her chin, the bodice of her black bombazine heaving.

"It is just a shock, you see." Lady Charlotte spoke up, exchanging glances with her wards. Miss Eloisa was thin-lipped, and Miss Sybil's gaze darted around the room like that of a frightened rabbit. "None of us was expecting this."

Rosie couldn't contain herself any longer. "Expecting

what? What is going on?"

Everyone stared at her as if she were a few cards short of a full deck.

Clearing his throat, Mr. Mayhew was the first to speak. "Your husband left the entirety of his fortune to you, Lady Daltry."

Shock percolated through her. She said faintly, "But I thought... I thought the estate would go to his heir."

"The estate, yes. But your husband's wealth did not come from the Daltry holdings. On the contrary, he was using his personal fortune—gained from his businesses and investments—to restore the earldom." The solicitor regarded her solemnly. "He's bequeathed that fortune to you."

She blinked. "He has?"

"Yes, my lady." Mr. Mayhew briefly surveyed Daltry's relations; when his gaze returned to her, it held a gleam of satisfaction. "To be precise, you've inherited a sum of one hundred thousand pounds."

Chapter Twenty

"KEEP AN EYE on Lord Michaels." Andrew shut the peephole, having seen enough of the drunken nob's belligerent swagger. "Water down his drinks, and post Tim by his room. If Lord Michaels so much as raises his voice at Lizzie, he's out on his arse."

The wall sconces cast shadows across Grier's rugged countenance. "I'll see to it."

It was midnight, and the two of them were carrying out the nightly rounds from the hidden corridors that ran through the club. Andrew had a vantage point into every room: the club was his domain, and he didn't take the responsibility lightly. Everyone who entered Corbett's knew the rules. Patrons unwise enough to abuse the wenches—or trespass in other ways—would be dealt with severely. Enforcing the rules was no easy task and kept Andrew on his toes.

Usually, he liked the challenge. Tonight, however, he was tired from lack of sleep and unabated arousal. The two days since he'd issued his ultimatum to Primrose felt like millennia.

Why hadn't she come to him? Had he overplayed his hand? Misjudged the situation?

"There's something else, sir."

Annoyed that he was moping like some lovelorn greenling, he said curtly, "Yes?"

Grier's look was grim. "One of the guards you have posted at the Nursery House reported in. There was another incident."

Andrew's shoulders tensed. "Malcolm Todd's men?"

"Aye, sir. They were attempting to block deliveries to the house. The grocer was scared witless by the time our boys noticed what was happening and chased off the buggers."

Devil take Todd. Andrew's hands fisted. "Request an audience with Bartholomew Black. We're sorting this business out once and for all."

Not much intimidated Grier, but at the mention of the King of the Underworld, he grimaced. "You ken what involving Black could lead to?"

"I'm not doing this dance with Todd. If he wants to challenge me, he'll have to do it in the open and with the King as his witness," Andrew declared. "If he still wants bloodshed, then by God I'll give it to him."

Grier's chin jerked in acknowledgement. "Anything else, sir?"

"Just keep an eye on Lord Michaels and Lizzie. I'll finish the rounds on my own."

The factotum exited to attend to his tasks, and Andrew continued on to the upper floors. He walked soundlessly behind the walls, stopping to make quick checks on the proceedings. Sex was happening in a variety of configurations: couples, *ménage à trois*, a rollicking orgy in the ever popular Sultan's Seraglio. It was business as usual, the mayhem controlled—which was more than he could say about the situation with Malcolm Todd.

If that matter wasn't handled carefully, damage could be severe on both sides.

He returned to the first floor, a commotion in the corridor beyond catching his attention. He heard one of the footmen inquire with heavy suspicion as to a guest's purpose.

"I assure you I was invited here by Mr. Corbett." The feminine voice sent his heartbeat into a gallop. "I was on my way to his office and got turned about—"

Andrew pressed a switch, the panel in the wall swinging open like a door. He stepped into the hallway, noting with relief that it was empty save for the footman and Primrose, the latter once again dressed in black and heavily veiled.

"I'll take it from here," he told the footman. "Have refreshments sent to my quarters." After the servant left to do his bidding, he crooked a finger at Primrose. "You—come with me."

She followed him into the passageway, and he closed the panel behind them.

The instant they were sealed in privacy, she whipped up her veil and breathed, "Is this a secret corridor? How exciting! Does it go all around—"

He silenced her by laying a finger upon her lips. Goddamn, her mouth was plush, silky and inviting. He couldn't resist stroking her bottom lip with his thumb and hid a smile when he heard her breath catch.

While risky, his move had paid off: she'd come to him at last.

"If you'd let me know of your plans," he said huskily, "I would've prepared a proper welcome."

"I wasn't *planning* to visit," she averred, "but I couldn't sleep. All I could think about was that I had to see you. The next thing I knew, I was sneaking out of Polly's house and hiring a hackney to come here."

"You took a hackney at night—by *yourself?*" He frowned, some of his satisfaction fading. "That is too dangerous by far."

"Something's happened. You're the only one I can talk to. It's a matter of *utmost* exigency."

Despite her flair for the dramatic, the urgency in her voice was real. Panic fleeted through her luminous eyes. His joy at her appearance was tempered with sudden foreboding.

"We'll talk in my suite," he said. "Follow me."

He led the way toward his private rooms, which were cloistered at the back of the building. The air grew sultrier as they walked, her clean feminine scent pervading his nostrils. The sounds of the club's activities hummed through the walls: rowdy conversation, scattered laughter… and the guttural resonance of sex.

He'd long grown immune to the noises, but Primrose's presence was like a lightning rod, amplifying his sensual awareness. The acoustics in the passageway seemed intensified, moans and groans surrounding him. Her perfume twined with memories of her taste, the sweet flavors of her mouth and pussy.

Just like that, he was stiff as a poker. He was not the only one affected; he noticed Primrose's high color and rapid respiration. She was also casting curious glances at the wooden slats placed at eye-level along the wall.

"What are those for?" she whispered.

"They're viewing holes. So I can stay apprised of all that goes on in my club." He said it matter-of-factly, wondering how she would react.

"Oh." Her golden lashes fluttered. "Does that mean you can see… um… your patrons?"

He nodded, noting with more than a little interest that the idea of voyeurism didn't elicit any sign of disgust from her. Rather, her eyes widened, her blush so vivid that he could see it in the dim flicker. When her tongue darted out to wet her lips, he had to bite back a groan.

Sex being his trade, he knew arousal when he saw it. Despite her innocence, Primrose was a hot-blooded thing. The notion of exploring what fanned the flames of her desire tightened his trousers to an excruciating degree.

He had the unholy urge to take her then and there. Up against the wall in this dark corridor, showing her what her lovely body was made to do. He wanted to bury his erection in her tight cunny until she screamed with pleasure—until they both came together.

Instead, he escorted her on. By the time they reached his suite, he was as randy as a sailor on shore leave, his hand shaking a little as he activated the release mechanism. The panel swung open, and he led Primrose into his private domain.

She looked as if she belonged there, her cameo-worthy profile perfectly set off by the blue-grey motif of the décor. Her slippered feet padded softly over the floral border of the Axminster carpet, woven in shades of azure, burgundy, and cream. Removing her gloves, she ran her fingertips along the back of the velvet settee and then his favorite studded leather wingchair, gazing around the room in surprise.

"Oh, but this is lovely," she breathed.

He smiled at her reverent tone. "Not what you expected of a pimp?"

"That's not what I meant." Her brows knitted. "Based on your style, I always assumed you had exquisite taste. I just didn't expect such lavish private quarters at your place of business."

"I have other houses," he said gruffly, "but I work a lot and keep late hours. Sometimes it's easier to sleep here."

The reality was he spent more time here than at any of his residences. The club was a demanding mistress—and it wasn't as if he had a wife or family to return to at the end of the day. While it hadn't bothered him before that he had only work in his life, now he had to push aside an uncomfortable pang.

A knock heralded the arrival of the refreshment. Dismissing the footman, Andrew rolled in the cart himself. It contained a cold collation and selection of pastries artfully arranged on tiered plates.

Primrose removed her bonnet, peering at the cart's offerings. "That looks fit for a king."

"A prince, actually. My pastry chef once worked in an Austrian royal household." He lifted the silver tongs. "What would you like?"

"Oh, nothing for me, thank you."

He caught the wistful way she eyed the desserts. Especially the slice of chocolate sponge layered with apricot jam and glazed with dark chocolate icing.

"Not even Chef Franz's special torte?" he said. "Some of the club members swear they come for it as much as for... the other entertainments."

He didn't know why he bothered with the euphemism. She knew the nature of his business. Her lack of aversion to being in a pimp's company was a constant source of surprise for him.

"I'm sure it is delicious," she said with a sigh, "but I cannot afford the indulgence."

He frowned. "You're as slender as a reed."

"*Because* I watch what I eat. At any rate, my dietary habits are inconsequential when *disaster*,"—her dramatic pause did not bode well—"has struck once again."

He set down the tongs. "Will I need whiskey for this?"

When her blonde curls bobbed vigorously, he went to pour drinks. He settled next to her on the sofa, his whiskey in one hand and a ratafia for her in the other. She took the glass from him, her gaze narrowing.

"Would you prefer something other than ratafia?" He'd assumed she would want the sweet peach-flavored liqueur, which was generally favored by ladies.

"Ratafia is fine, but as I recall you don't stock it in your office." Her mouth had a sulky curve. "Why do you have it here in your private suite?"

He must be nicked in the nob because he found her feminine possessiveness absurdly endearing. He chucked her beneath the chin. "Because I like to keep a well-stocked bar,

silly chit. Now what is this matter of life and death you wished
to speak about?"

She stopped pouting. Drew in a breath. "Daltry's will was
read yesterday."

"Indeed." Andrew took a swallow of whiskey, wondering
how on earth she managed to make mourning look so damned
sensual. The way the black crepe clung to her nubile curves
ought to be a sin. "Did he leave you anything of interest?"

"I suppose. If you would call one hundred thousand
pounds interesting."

He coughed. "Pardon?"

"You heard me. What in heaven's name am I supposed to
do?" she cried.

He could think of a lot one could do with that
astronomical sum. He also understood the tangled workings
of her mind. "You feel guilty taking the money," he guessed.

"I don't want it," she said, setting down the glass with a
fierce *clink*, "not a single penny! But I can't refuse it either—
not without stirring up suspicion as to why. And I refuse to
give up respectability now that it's finally within my reach."

"That is a dilemma." His mouth twitched; he couldn't
help it.

Truly, the chit was her own worst enemy.

"You're *amused*?"

"You must admit the irony of the situation. First, you
wanted to establish the legitimacy of your marriage. Now
you're wanting to dissolve it. But only a part of it." He lifted
his shoulders. "As the adage goes, my dear, you cannot have
your cake and eat it too."

"Well, you're no help." She scowled at him. "I don't know
why I came to you."

"Don't you? We'll get to that in a moment," he
murmured. "Now you want my advice on your quandary?"

Her nod was so grudging that he almost smiled.

"Take the money," he said.

"I can't possibly take Daltry's money—"

"Why not? He left it to you, didn't he?"

She nodded, again reluctantly. "Apparently, he met with his solicitor before we eloped and specified that, in the event of his passing, his personal property was to go to me... and any children we might have."

"He left nothing to his family members?"

"They're in line to inherit *after* me. They won't see a cent until I remarry or die, whichever comes first. It's the ultimate snub," she said glumly. "On our wedding night, he called them hypocrites because they scorned the origins of his wealth at the same time asking for handouts. The notion of them begging for money from me—a trollopy bastard, as he put it— must have amused him to no end."

"Your former husband was an ass," Andrew stated. "But whatever his motivations, he wanted you to have the money. Ergo, you've done nothing wrong."

"But I... I wasn't a real wife to him." Her fingers wove tightly in her lap.

"It's not your fault that he couldn't perform. Or that he cocked up his toes on your wedding night. The moment that marriage certificate was signed, the money was yours."

"I don't want it."

"Life doesn't always give us what we want, sweetheart."

"How can you be so blasé about the whole thing?"

"There are worse things than being handed a king's ransom. Your husband was using you to get at his relations: why should you feel responsible for that?" he said bluntly. "If you don't want the money for yourself, then use it to do good for others."

"Charitable work isn't my strength." Her expression turned dubious. "My sister Polly works with foundlings, but I never got the hang of it. Children are sticky, and I'm squeamish. I did try to volunteer my efforts at a madhouse once. I was scheduled to give a vocal performance—to cheer up the residents—and my singing was going over well, I thought... until a lunatic attacked me and held me at knifepoint." She wrinkled her nose. "After that, I gave up on altruistic endeavors."

He stared at her, torn between wrath over the danger she'd experienced... and the desire to laugh aloud at her harebrained account. Only Primrose could turn a charitable undertaking into a drama worthy of Drury Lane. He didn't know why he found that quality of hers endearing—and vastly entertaining—but, dammit, he did.

"You don't have to do charity work," he said. "Just donate funds to the cause in question."

"That *is* true—and a brilliant idea, actually. If I'm good at anything, it's spending money." Brightening, she touched his sleeve. "Thank you. I knew coming to you was the right thing to do."

"You're welcome. But you didn't come here to get advice about Daltry's money."

A pulse fluttered above the black lace at her throat. "Of course I did."

He captured her chin between finger and thumb. "Don't lie to me or yourself."

"Why else would I come?" She wetted her lips, her wide gaze fooling him not one bit.

"For this." He drew her close and sealed his mouth over hers.

Chapter Twenty-One

BOTHERATION. HE SAW through her ploy.

His advice was helpful, of course, but what she really wanted was *him*.

Luckily, he didn't seem to mind.

The slow burn of his kiss set fire to her senses, and she slid her hands into his tawny hair, relishing the rough silk texture between her fingers. She kissed him back with all the passion she felt for him: this man who was worldly and wise and treated her with care. Who didn't gloat or make her admit that he'd won... which made her want him even *more*.

She parted her lips, inviting him in, but his kiss remained gentle and coaxing, as if she needed to be courted. Didn't he know how desperately she wanted him?

She broke away, pleading, "Please, Andrew. I want you so much."

Satisfaction glittered in his eyes. Then he was pushing her back, his muscled length crushing her into the cushions. His mouth was no longer gentle but wild. His tongue thrust boldly between her lips, and she craved the thick glide, the flavor of whiskey and Andrew tingling over her taste buds. She sought out more, and when she tangled her tongue with his, he groaned, their mouths fusing as hunger flared out of control.

Her neck arched as he caught her earlobe between his teeth, licking, nipping. He worked his usual magic on her clothing, buttons and laces no match for his skill. He stripped her layer by layer, and she struggled to help him, to be freed from constriction, to be rid of anything that separated her from him.

When she lay naked before him, however, she felt suddenly shy. Unsure. Was she pleasing enough for him?

His pupils dilated, his nostrils flaring. "By God, you're a feast for the eyes."

Blushing yet emboldened, she fumbled with his cravat. "I want to see you too."

"Let me, love." He rose, tearing off the starchy linen, shrugging off his jacket and waistcoat. When he dragged his shirt over his head, a breath whooshed from her lips.

He was only the second man she'd seen unclothed, and his beauty was *stunning*. Worthy of being immortalized in marble. Taut, golden skin stretched over his wide shoulders, the defined slabs of his chest. She couldn't see an ounce of fat on his muscular torso, his abdomen rippled as a washboard. Bronze hair sprinkled his upper chest, narrowing into a trail that bisected his lean belly and disappeared into his trousers.

His hands on his waistband, he said, "On or off?"

"Off." Was that *her* voice, so sultry and breathless? "Take them off, please."

His lazy smile made her heart stutter. He dispensed with his boots, trousers, and all the rest of it. When he stood before her, his raw virility unveiled, a buffle-headed feeling stole over her.

Oh, my.

His mouth faintly curved, he let her look her fill—and, make no mistake, there was *a lot* to look at. His lower half was just as statue-worthy as the upper, his narrow hips girdled by a defined vee of muscle. His legs were sinewy and lean, and between them...

Her breath puffed out. Here, he veered from any Greek sculpture she'd seen. She couldn't help but stare at his manhood: its proportions were rather, well, *startling*. The big, thick shaft stood straight up from its bronze nest, the fat tip nudging his navel. Raised veins ran along the length, his heavy stones dangling at the base. When he took a step forward, his male equipment swayed like a ship's mast.

The thought inserted itself into her head: *Goodness, is that going to* fit?

As she fought to stay calm, he stood there, not arrogant (although he had ample reason to be) but comfortable in his own magnificent skin. Her gaze met his, and the message in his warm brown eyes flowed into her. *This desire between us is natural. There's nothing to be afraid of, nothing to hide.* His confidence eased some of her apprehension.

This was Andrew; he would not hurt her.

Before she lost her nerve, she held out her arms. "Come to me," she whispered.

He did, stretching over her, and at the first contact of skin on skin, she shivered. Sensations bombarded her: the heat and hardness of his body, his musk and spice scent, his turgid cock prodding her belly. It was overwhelming. A rash of heat spread over her insides, and she felt as if she might burst out of her skin.

"We're a perfect fit," he murmured. "Can you feel it?"

Could she. "It feels *too* good," she said, squirming restlessly.

"Sunshine,"—there was a smile in his voice—"it's about to get better."

He began kissing his way down her body, and she gave up resisting the pleasure. It was simply too much. Too powerful. Too good. 'Twas as if she'd been fighting against herself all her life, and now, finally, she had no choice but to surrender: to the decadent way he sucked her nipples, the velvet-soft lashes of his tongue over her ribs and belly.

He surprised her by turning her over. With her cheek pressed against the velvet cushion, she shuddered as his lips measured each dent of her spine, lingering at the dip. He pressed kisses on her bottom, the quicksilver flick of his tongue in between the mounds making her twitch in surprise. He seemed to know her body more intimately than she did, winnowing pleasure from every nook and cranny. Never would she have guessed that the backs of her knees were so sensitive nor the curves below her ankles nor the arches of her feet.

By the time he turned her over again, she was a wobbly mass of need. He leisurely nibbled his way up her legs, and, when he parted her thighs, she knew what was coming, but she couldn't bring herself to try to stop him. The first swipe of his tongue made her writhe in shameless delight.

"You're delicious all over and especially here." His voice was dark honey. "I want you to spend on my tongue, love. Can you do that for me?"

He gave her no choice. Not with the way he licked her, up and down, as if she were the sweetest treat. Not when he delved upward, teasing that hidden peak, praising her *pearl*, her *love-knot* for being so bold against his tongue. His thumb took over, rubbing that center of sensation until fragments of sound escaped her. *Yes. More. Please.*

"You're almost there, sweetheart," he urged. "Let me taste your ambrosia."

His tongue thrust into her opening, licking her *inside*— and she broke. Bliss shattered her into a thousand sparkling pieces. In the next instant, he moved over her, entering her in a swift thrust that startled a breath from her lips.

"All right, love?" His neck corded with tension, his brow glazed with sweat, he watched her face keenly. "It doesn't hurt, does it?"

His self-control and consideration filled her with tenderness—and a desire to please him as much as he pleased her. The truth was, despite his size, there was no pain. Or perhaps, on the heels of pleasure, she couldn't feel it. Whatever the case, he stretched her exquisitely to her limits. Filled her in a way that she was meant to be filled.

She touched his cheek, said wonderingly, "It feels… right."

"Yes." A wealth of emotion was conveyed in that single word, in his smoldering gaze.

He began moving, her breath stuttering as she skated the edge between pleasure and discomfort. His cock was huge, hard, each incursion opening her up to new sensations. When he withdrew, she felt relief followed by a strange ache; when he plunged, the ridges of his erection rubbed against nerve endings, setting off sparks of sensitivity and bliss.

It was too much; she wanted more.

"You're so tight," he rasped.

Sudden worry punctured her. "Am I doing something wrong?"

"God, no. I've never felt anything so fine." The glitter in his eyes told her he was telling the truth. "I want to fuck your tight pussy forever. I want to feel you squeezing my cock like you never want to let me go."

His wicked words, the slow roll of his hips made her gasp. Moisture gushed from her core, and before she could fret, he growled, "That's it, sweetheart. Drench my cock. Help me get deeper inside you."

He surged into her, deeper than he ever had before, her dew lubricating his penetration. Discomfort eased, pressure burgeoning into need, friction into consuming heat. When he hit some magical spot deep inside, embers of pleasure showered her insides. His hands cupped her bottom, tilting her up, and his next thrust pushed his name from her lips.

Her legs instinctively found purchase in the lean hollows of his hips, and she clung to him as his pace grew wilder, rougher. He shed his urbane mask—he was raw, animal in the pleasure he was giving to her and taking in return. The primal momentum swept her up, pushing her closer and closer to the fiery peak.

"Come for me," he growled.

At his command, her entire being seized. With his body rooted in hers, her release was more intense than any she'd experienced before. She cried out as she convulsed around him, her muscles milking pleasure from every thick inch.

As she tried to catch her breath, he suddenly withdrew. He rose onto his knees, cords leaping in his neck, his cock in his fist. He jerked on the engorged stalk with shocking force, his chest heaving, his gaze holding hers.

"Feel me, love," he groaned.

Moisture exploded from his cock, and she gasped when a hot splatter landed on her thigh. With a sensual growl, he directed more of it at her, warm rain falling on her ribs and breasts. One droplet clung to her nipple, and she cautiously caught it with her fingertip. Rubbing his slippery seed against the tight peak gave her a shivery thrill.

He collapsed onto the sofa with a groan, tucking her against him.

For a few moments, she was content listening to their hearts racing in unison.

Then she whispered into his chest, "So this is lovemaking. I never knew."

"Neither did I, sunshine." His deep voice was laced with triumph... and wonder. "With God as my witness, neither did I."

Chapter Twenty-Two

"ANDREW, WE OUGHT to talk."

In his experience, these words didn't bode well coming from a female. But with Primrose tucked against his chest, the carriage swaying in a lulling rhythm, he couldn't rouse the energy to get his guard up. The aftermath humming through his veins added to his satisfaction with life in general.

Making love to Primrose had been a revelation—and this was saying something given the extent of his carnal knowledge. In all the years of bedding women, not once had he felt anything close to what he'd shared with Primrose. With her, the act of desire had been transformed into something beyond the physical. Something beyond an exchange. Something... rare.

The image of her marked with his seed made his cock stir. God, he wanted to have her again, never mind that she'd made him come harder than he ever had just a half-hour ago. With Primrose, he was as randy as a greenling.

His arm tightened around her. "What do you wish to talk about?"

"There are things we should have discussed... before we made love." She tipped her head back to look at him. "I don't wish to mislead you."

Some of his contentment faded. He knew, of course, what she wanted to say. For a little while, he'd swept reality under the carpet and lost himself in the pleasure of the moment.

Then his sense of irony came to the rescue. The tables had

been turned, hadn't they? He couldn't count the number of times he'd said those exact same words to women who'd wanted more from him than just a casual tup.

"Tell me what you want," he said simply.

"I can't offer you more than what we just did." Her eyes searched his. "Having a position in Society is important to me. And I won't give it up. For anyone."

He hated that he couldn't give her the life she wanted. It was perhaps the closest he'd ever come to regretting the choices he'd made in life. But he was a realist.

"I understand," he said.

"You do?" Her brow pleated. "You're not... disappointed with me?"

"You've never lied about your priorities, sunshine. I respect that." He cupped her cheek, running his thumb along her lower lip. "And I'm willing to accommodate your needs— as long as you're willing to accommodate mine."

"What are your, um, needs?" The dimness didn't hide her blush.

"I plan to have you, Primrose," he said huskily, "as often and in as many creative ways as possible. We're going to explore this passion between us, and when we're together, I expect you to hold nothing back. You'll give yourself to me, and, in return, I'll show you pleasure you've never even dreamt of. All of this, I'll do with discretion."

A breath puffed from her lips, her pupils dilating. Hell, he could *see* how his words aroused her. His cockstand butted against his smalls.

"You'd do that for me?" she said.

"Upon my honor. And I should think I've earned your trust." He waggled his brows. "You'll recall I took pains to protect you from unwanted consequences tonight."

She looked confused. "By taking me home, you mean?"

Christ, it was easy to forget just how naïve she was. How

much she hid behind that willful, worldly façade of hers. How, underneath her self-proclaimed wickedness, lay an astonishingly innocent heart.

"That's not what I meant, but I'll explain later," he murmured. "In the meantime, you have my promise that I'll safeguard your well-being and your reputation."

"Thank you." Her voice was soft. "So we have an understanding? That it's, um, just sex between us?"

"I didn't say it's just sex for me," he said evenly. "I will have no expectations, however, when it comes to marriage."

"Oh." Emotions flashed across her exquisite features: fear and longing, a welter of others.

He leaned over to kiss her before her thinking confused matters unnecessarily.

Her palms pushed against his shoulders. "There's one more thing."

Give the chit an inch... He arched a brow.

"Given all my demands, I know I don't have a right to ask this too... but I'm going to anyway." She drew a breath. "During the course of our affair, I'd very much appreciate it if you didn't have any lovers. Other than me, that is."

Her request took him by surprise. Not the fact that she was possessive—he'd gleaned that early on and, indeed, relished it—but the fact that she thought an arrangement other than monogamy was possible between them. That she believed she would warrant anything less than his full commitment.

"I don't share what's mine," he said unequivocally. "I wouldn't expect you to either."

"I'm so glad." Relief shone in her eyes. "I feel very strongly about the issue."

"Primrose, the fact that circumstances rule out marriage doesn't lessen what is between us," he said, studying her intently. "When I say I intend for us to explore the desire between us, I'm not referring to a meaningless tumble. I expect you to share not just your body with me but your mind and spirit as well."

She hesitated. "And you'll give me the same in return?"

"I'm going to give you more than I've given any woman," he said huskily.

"Oh, that sounds lovely," she breathed.

His lips twitched. He chucked her beneath the chin. "Greedy chit."

"You don't mind." She dimpled at him. "When will I see you again?"

"I'll make the arrangements. You'll not risk your neck like you did tonight," he said sternly.

"No one saw—"

"It's more than that. My trade can be a dangerous one, and at present I'm at odds with a cutthroat. I don't want you caught in the crossfire. You'll wait until I can arrange a safe time and place for us to meet again."

"A *cutthroat*?" Her eyes rounded. "Never mind my safety, what about *yours*?"

"Fret not," he murmured, "I've survived worse than the likes of Malcolm Todd. But I'll rest easier knowing that you're not taking unnecessary risks."

She chewed on her lip. "I have a suggestion."

"While you've many talents, sweetheart, I doubt managing cutthroats is one of them."

"Not about that, silly. About where we could meet." Her gaze dropped to her hands, which were smoothing out her skirts. "In addition to the money, Daltry left me some properties, including a small house on Curzon Street. I was thinking of moving in—at least temporarily, until I figure out my future. I've been a burden on Polly and Revelstoke, and returning to my parents' house doesn't feel right either."

"You should do what is best for you," he said. "I'll arrange our rendezvous regardless—that you can count on."

"I think I'd prefer to be independent. I'm ready for the privacy of my own household."

"Then you should have it."

"I hope Mama and Papa agree with you. They still treat me as if I'm a little girl, incapable of making my own decisions. They'll think this is just another of my harebrained schemes."

She looked so disgruntled that he had to stifle a smile.

"Give them a chance to adjust to the change," he said solemnly. "Act with maturity, and they will see you in a different light."

Her gaze narrowed at him. "Are you saying I haven't been acting with maturity?"

He kept his expression bland.

She sighed. "I suppose you're right. Eloping with Daltry, avoiding Mama, and sneaking out of Polly's house aren't exactly the hallmarks of mature behavior, are they?" she said with wry candor. "It's high time I faced my problems rather than run from them."

Her insight surprised him—and yet didn't. Primrose was one of the cleverest, bravest, and most honest people he knew. When she let her defenses down, she was, in a word, breathtaking.

"You amaze me," he said.

Her smile was tremulous. "The feeling is mutual."

The carriage slowed; they'd arrived at the Revelstoke residence.

"I'm sorry the night has to end," she said, fiddling with a fold of his greatcoat.

"We'll have many more nights ahead, sunshine." He stole one last kiss. "Let's get you back inside before someone notices."

He opened the carriage door, vaulting down lightly. The moon slipped in and out of clouds, casting a ghostly light on the street lined with mansions. London was never quiet, but here in Mayfair the sounds were filtered by majestic trees and the intangible aura of wealth. Reaching up, he swung Primrose gently to the ground. He escorted her to the front door, and as he waited for her to dig the key out of her reticule, the staccato of hooves caught his attention.

He turned, glimpsed a dark figure approaching on horseback. The moon emerged, its cold light falling on the rider's scarf-covered face, glinting off the metal in his outstretched hand.

Andrew leapt forward, tackling Primrose.

A deafening blast drowned out her surprised cry. Pain seared his arm as they hit the ground. Covering her body with his own, he shouted at his groom Jem, who jumped off the driver's seat, firing shots after the vanishing rider.

Andrew rose, pulling Primrose up with him.

"Are you all right?" he demanded roughly.

"I—I think so." She pushed a curl out of her eyes. "Did someone *shoot* at us?"

"Yes." Seeing light beginning to flicker in surrounding windows, he issued terse commands to Jem to stand guard and hauled her toward the door.

"Goodness, your arm is bleeding! You've been shot," she gasped. "Did one of your enemies do this?"

He flashed back to the angle of the gun, the deadly aim.

A chill seized his gut, and he said grimly, "No—one of yours."

Chapter Twenty-Three

TWO DAYS LATER, Rosie perched on a chair on the premises of Kent and Associates. She'd always loved visiting her father's office located near Soho Square. Sandwiched between a bakery and a pianoforte maker's shop, the building had been remodeled due to a fire a few years back, and the understated elegance of the present suite with its oak paneling, studded leather seats, and stone fireplace suited her papa perfectly.

At present, no discordant sounds came from the piano maker's, but the tantalizing scent of fresh gingerbread wafted from the bakery. While the moist, spicy-sweet treat had been her favorite as a girl, as an adult her ubiquitous slimming plan curtailed such indulgences. At the moment, however, she would have given her eyeteeth for a slice. Knowing what was to take place this morning, she'd been too nervous to take more than a cup of tea at breakfast.

Next to her, Polly murmured, "You're fidgeting worse than Violet."

Botheration. Rosie stilled her tapping slipper. She slid a glance at Mama, who sat in a chair by Papa's desk, embroidering a handkerchief. This was not a good sign: Mama only did needlework when she was upset and needed distraction. As Rosie watched, her mother put in precise pink stitches that formed Sophie's initials, a complex garland surrounding them.

Since the attack, Mama had sewn a dozen of these

handkerchiefs.

She'd also had been glued to Rosie, the present danger dissipating the tension between them. For Rosie, reconciliation was a relief. While she didn't like that the other had kept the truth from her, she understood why. And she loved her mother too much to sustain the separation.

She'd decided to bury the hatchet—and the whole business of Coyner along with it. Nothing had happened, so what was the point in excavating such ugliness? Dwelling upon the horrid business would only lead to further friction with her mother.

No, she decided, she would not think about the matter ever again.

Anyway, she had more important things to contend with: Andrew would be arriving shortly.

Immediately after the attack, he'd apprised Polly and Revelstoke of the truth. Calm as could be, he'd told them that he'd been escorting Rosie home when they'd been shot at. He hadn't said what they'd been doing together (*thank goodness!*), but he also made no effort to hide the fact that, whatever it was, they'd been doing it alone and in the middle of the night.

Luckily for Rosie, Polly and Revelstoke had been more concerned about the attack on her life than her less than proper behavior. If they didn't ask, there was *no way* she was going to tell. Besides, being a widow, she had new freedoms, so perhaps she could just brazen the whole thing out.

When Andrew had announced his intention to alert Papa, however, she'd protested.

To no avail.

"Your life is in danger, and I'll do everything in my power to keep you safe," he'd said in a tone that brooked no refusal. "My guards will arrive directly, and you will stay here and under their protection until I've made arrangements with your father. Do you understand?"

She'd bristled at his high-handedness, but his hard expression had warned her against arguing. His aggression reminded her that he'd earned his success in one of London's darkest, most dangerous trades. Yet beneath his dictatorial manner, she sensed his fear for her, which had convinced her to comply.

That and the fact that he'd taken a bullet for her.

Luckily, the wound turned out to be a graze. Nonetheless, knowing that he'd risked his life for hers had melted her defenses. Thus, she'd said simply, "Yes, Andrew."

He'd given her a terse nod and walked out with Revelstoke. That had been at dawn yesterday. Since then, Rosie knew that Andrew had met with Papa, the two of them devising a plan to protect her and her reputation.

"I can't help fidgeting," Rosie whispered back to Polly. "This business has me all aflutter."

"Who wouldn't feel that way after being shot at?" Polly said sympathetically.

"Oh, I'm not aflutter over *that*. With Papa and Andrew on the case, I feel perfectly safe."

It was true. She had complete confidence in the two men. In fact, after the initial shock of the attack had worn off, she hadn't been so much afraid as she had been *infuriated*. Just when the clouds seemed to be clearing from the horizon, why did fortune have to shower her with more slings and arrows?

Polly blinked. "What *are* you worried about then?"

"Isn't it obvious?" she said under her breath. "Papa and Mama are about to be in the same room as Mr. Corbett."

Polly gave her hand a squeeze. After all, what could the other say about the awkward and fraught-with-peril situation of introducing one's lover to one's parents?

Why do these things always happen to me? Rosie was torn between mortification and worry. She prayed that her parents would treat Andrew with respect—and was prepared to rise to his defense if they didn't.

The door opened to reveal her father and his partners, Mr. McLeod, a brawny Scotsman, and Mr. Lugo, an equally imposing fellow who hailed from Africa. The two partners, who had known Rosie since she was a girl and were like uncles to her, nodded silent greetings and retreated to the back of the room. Andrew came in next, his gaze finding hers, and a curious thing happened.

Her anxieties eased; his mere presence anchored her.

He approached, bowing to her and Polly. "Good day, ladies."

While Polly smiled at him, Rosie tried to hide the fact that she felt as giddy as a schoolgirl. Andrew was a gentleman through and through, from his manner to his character to his impeccable looks. As always, his tailoring fit his virile form like a second skin.

She saw the bulge beneath the sleeve of his sage green jacket and blurted, "How is your arm?"

"'Twas but a scratch, my lady." His tone was formal, but the warmth in his eyes made her heart skip like a pebble across a pond. With seemly courtesy, he produced a small box from behind his back. "With my compliments for your full recovery."

"Oh. How kind." She smiled at him. "What is it?"

"Open it."

Untying the plain string, she lifted the lid. A petite loaf of gingerbread sat nestled in paper. Glazed with white icing and bejeweled with bits of candied lemon, it looked mouth-watering.

"How did you know that gingerbread is my favorite?" she said.

His eyes crinkled at the corners. "A lucky guess."

Before she could thank him, her mother's cultured voice cut in.

"Mr. Corbett, I have something I wish to say to you."
Mama approached Andrew, her demeanor somber as her grey
cashmere dress. Her slim shoulders were rigid.

Andrew inclined his head, the gesture polite and edged
with wariness. "Yes, ma'am?"

Rosie's breathing suspended. *Please be nice to him...*

"Thank you, sir. For helping to save my girl,"—Mama's
voice cracked—"again."

Seeing Mama's anguish, Rosie felt heat well behind her
own eyes. She would have gone to her mother, but Papa got
there first. He wrapped an arm around Mama's waist, and she
leaned into him the way a climbing bloom does a sturdy trellis.

"Think nothing of it," Andrew said quietly. "It is my
privilege, ma'am."

"We are in your debt, Corbett. I cannot, however,"—Papa
cast a severe glance in Rosie's direction—"approve of the
circumstances under which this recent rescue took place."

Rosie flushed, sneaking a peek at Andrew who remained
at the side of her chair. His expression was entirely neutral.
He said nothing, neither denied nor argued the charges. At
the same time, his manner conveyed that he was going to
continue doing as he damn well pleased.

How she wished she had his self-possession. His strength
and sophistication. Instead, her confidence was as fragile as
porcelain—and as for worldliness?

She was a girl who still collected dolls.

But you're not a girl any longer, you're a woman. For once,
the voice in her head championed her on. *You're a widow who
has the right to live an independent life.*

Act with maturity, and they will see you in a different light,
Andrew's deep tones advised.

Exhaling, she addressed the room at large. "It was
irresponsible of me to leave the house that night without
telling Polly and Revelstoke," she said candidly, "and for that

I apologize. I'm also truly sorry for having caused everyone worry in the past few weeks."

"Bit longer than that," Papa muttered.

"Let her finish, Ambrose," Mama murmured.

"I intend to turn over a new leaf," she told her parents. "From now on, I'll be honest with you and accountable for any decisions I make." She looked at Andrew, the approval in his eyes bolstering her courage. "While you may not approve of my decisions, I ask that you respect them. I am a grown woman—a widow, as a matter of fact."

"We'll discuss these decisions of yours later," Papa said. "For the time being, I suggest we focus on a plan to keep you safe."

She wondered if now was a good time to announce her intention to move into the house on Curzon Street. No assailant was going to stop her from carrying on with her life—and, more importantly, she refused to endanger the lives of her family. What if Polly or the earl had opened their front door during the shooting and got caught in the crossfire?

She shivered. No, she couldn't—*wouldn't*—allow that to happen.

Seeing her father's stern expression, however, she decided a Fabian strategy was in order. She'd wait for the right moment to spring the news.

"Yes, Papa," she said meekly.

Papa escorted Mama to a chair. He leaned against the front of his desk to address the room.

"Given the details Corbett provided us,"—he acknowledged Andrew with a nod—"my partners and I have devised a strategy for moving forward. Time is of essence here, so we've divided the tasks. McLeod will lead the search for the assailant."

The brown-haired Scot, who'd been leaning against the back wall, straightened.

"I've recovered the shot," McLeod said. "Two bullets were lodged in the Revelstokes' front door, so we're looking at a double-barreled firearm. No one got a good look at the shooter, but Corbett identified the horse as a bald-faced chestnut. Jem, his driver, got a couple shots off, and thinks he scored a hit in the assailant's left shoulder. So I've got men canvassing the rookery for an injured cove who rides a marked mount and uses a twin-barreled gun. Folk in the stews can be tight-lipped as clams, especially in the face of authority, but we won't give up until we find the villain."

"Thank you, Mr. McLeod," Rosie said gratefully.

The Scot's craggy features softened with a smile. "Rest easy we'll keep you safe, Miss Ros—I mean, my lady. And Annabelle sends her best."

Rosie adored Annabelle, Mr. McLeod's beloved auburn-haired wife. "Please give my regards to her and the girls."

"I was just thinking," Polly piped up, "that perhaps Revelstoke and I could help?"

The earl frowned. "In your condition, kitten, I hardly think—"

"I don't mean that *I* would search for the villain," Polly said hastily, "but we know those who are well equipped to do so. Who witness everything that goes on in the stews."

"Ah. The mudlarks," Revelstoke said.

Through her work at the foundling academy, Polly had befriended the mudlarks, children thus called because they made their living scavenging the banks of the Thames. And, during the course of his adventures, Revelstoke had once saved the life of the mudlarks' leader.

"The Larks would help. They have eyes and ears everywhere," Polly said earnestly.

"I'll talk to them after this," the earl said.

"Thank you both," Papa said. "In the meantime, Lugo and I have begun investigating the list of suspects, who fall in two categories: enemies of Corbett and,"—his amber gaze darkened—"those who might wish Rosie harm."

"The shooter was after Lady Daltry," Andrew said flatly. "The gun was aimed at her. And if perchance the killer was after me, I can handle my own enemies."

Papa's dark brows winged. "How many do you have, sir?"

"More than some, less than others," Andrew said blandly. "My point is that we must focus our energies on Lady Daltry's enemies—and God knows she's just inherited her share. There are six people with one hundred thousand reasons to want her dead."

"Peter Theale, Antonia and Alastair James, Lady Charlotte Daltry, and Misses Sybil and Eloisa Fossey." From the back of the room, Mr. Lugo rattled off the list in his distinctive bass. "All are potential suspects."

"Yesterday, Lugo and I met with Daltry's executor, Mr. Mayhew." Papa took up where his partner left off. "Mayhew confirmed that the money is Rosie's until death or remarriage. If either of those events occur, then the terms revert to those of Daltry's original will in which Peter Theale is the main beneficiary."

"Which makes Theale a prime suspect," Mr. McLeod commented.

"Yes, but shares of the wealth would also be disbursed to the other relatives—including Alastair James. Mr. James isn't a blood relation per se, but he cultivated a friendship with Daltry. Indeed, after Theale, James has the most to gain at five thousand pounds per annum. The ladies would each receive a yearly stipend of two thousand pounds."

"Kent and I will look into Theale and James first," Mr. Lugo noted.

"I've compiled financial information on both of them," Andrew said.

All heads swung in his direction.

"You have?" Papa looked surprised. "It's been a little over a day since the shooting, and such information takes time to track down."

"Information is part of my business," Andrew replied. "In my experience, following the money is the quickest way to find the culprit."

"A philosophy I happen to share." Papa cleared his throat. "Tell us what you know, sir."

"In a nutshell, both coves are in dun territory. Theale comes from a line of younger sons and inherits his poverty through natural bad luck. His attempts to gain a fortune at the gaming tables have not improved his situation, however. He's in five thousand quid to a moneylender at a rate that doubles that debt within six months."

"But Mr. Theale seems so nice," Rosie said in surprise.

Andrew's lips quirked. "Some of the nicest coves I know reside in the Marshalsea: debtor's prison doesn't discriminate. But I understand what you mean. Theale's gaming seems an act of desperation whereas Alastair James pursues his vices with the dedication of a true rakehell. He has his vowels scattered through every gaming hell, bawdy house, and tavern in Covent Garden. And earlier this month at White's, he placed a thousand pound bet with a crony over who could eat the most mincemeat pies."

She canted her head. "What was the result?"

"The sod emptied his accounts—in more ways than one," Andrew said derisively. "It's only a matter of time before he faces the music or makes a run for the Continent."

"Quite thorough, Corbett."

Papa sounded impressed—and Rosie knew he wasn't easily impressed. She, too, admired Andrew's prowess. His power and command of this (and any other) situation.

"Maybe we ought to hire him on, Kent," Mr. Lugo said. "Save us the shoe leather."

"Bloody hell, we can't afford the fellow." Beside Mr. Lugo, Mr. McLeod shook his shaggy head. "You ken the kind of blunt his club pulls in?"

"Maybe he'll work gratis." Mr. Lugo flashed straight white teeth. "On account of the family connection."

At Mr. McLeod's guffaw, Rosie blushed. She slid a look at Andrew, worried about how he might react to the men's good-natured jibing. Thankfully, he didn't look annoyed. In fact, he seemed… pleased?

"If the two of you are finished,"—Papa sent his partners a quelling look—"we'll move on with the plan. While McLeod searches for the shooter, Lugo and I will pay a visit to Theale and James. To my mind, the hiring of a cutthroat suggests that a male perpetrator is more likely, so we'll deal with the ladies after. At any rate, I have a feeling that Emma will want to handle the interrogation of the female suspects."

"Emma is coming all the way from Scotland?" Rosie said in surprise.

"We wrote the rest of the family about your troubles," Mama replied. "I predict Emma, Thea, *and* Violet will be arriving forthwith."

"Don't forget Harry," Papa said, referring to his younger brother, a scholar at Cambridge. "Lord knows we need all the help we can get. In the meantime, Rosie, you'll have a pair of guards assigned to you. You'll move back home, and you're not to go anywhere alone. In fact, you're not to go anywhere period until this case is concluded."

Rosie appreciated her father's concern, but there was no way on earth that she was going to endanger him, Mama, or her siblings. And she also wasn't about to be treated like a wayward girl. To be locked in her room while the adults made decisions for her.

She had plans of her own—and for once she didn't want to have to plead, pout, or charm to get her way. She wanted to address the matter head on, as a mature woman would.

"I appreciate everyone's help," she said earnestly, "but there's something I need to tell you."

"What is it?" Grooves of tension deepened around Papa's mouth.

You can't delay this forever. 'Tis now or never.

Her hands gripping in her lap, she declared, "I'm moving into my own residence."

Chapter Twenty-Four

"DID WE DO the right thing, Ambrose?" Marianne murmured later that evening.

Shucking his robe, Ambrose got into bed and gathered his wife against him. He stroked her silky hair, pensively watching the play of light and shadow on their bedchamber walls.

"I don't know," he admitted. "But short of locking Rosie in her room—an idea I'm not entirely opposed to—I don't know what else we could have done. You know what she's like when she's set her mind on a course."

"Of course I know. Where do you think she got that damnable tendency from?"

His lips twitched. "You mustn't blame yourself. If anything, I ought to have been firmer with her as a child."

In his mind, he saw Rosie as a small, bright-eyed poppet, and his chest tightened. How had time passed so quickly? In a blink of an eye, his little girl had grown into a woman... and now she was facing mortal danger.

"I was too lax when it came to discipline," he said heavily.

"You did your best, darling. Rosie always found some way to charm or cajole her way out of trouble." His wife sighed. "After we rescued her from that monster, we were both careful with her. Too careful, in retrospect, and me especially. I regret hiding the truth from her. I should have listened to you, Ambrose, and told her about Coyner's despicable plans much sooner."

"You wanted to protect her. You're a devoted mama and

always have been." He kissed her forehead. "We'll keep Rosie safe, I promise you. I'll have my best men posted on Curzon Street. It's but a five minute carriage ride away, and we can protect her there as well as here. And Corbett," he said after a moment, "insists on contributing to the watch. The truth is my men are stretched thin, and I could use the additional guards."

"What do you think is going on between Rosie and Corbett?" Marianne mused.

Ambrose didn't want to think about it. By nature, he preferred to face reality straight on, but the idea of his daughter engaged in illicit activity with a man—a brothel owner, no less—wasn't something he cared to contemplate, much less talk about.

His better half didn't seem to share his reluctance.

"They're lovers, aren't they?" she said quietly. "I've never seen Rosie look at any man in that way before. And Corbett—well, I'd say he's more than halfway in love with her."

Ambrose frowned. "Surely you're not condoning the behavior?"

His wife lifted her head from his chest, a hint of amusement in her emerald eyes. "I'm no prude, darling. If you'll recall, I was a widow myself and had a rather unconventional affair."

"That was different. I was a policeman, not a pimp," he pointed out. "Besides, it was only a matter of time before we got married. My intentions were always honorable."

"And you don't think Corbett feels the same way about Rosie?"

"Can a pimp be honorable?" That sounded priggish, even to his own ears. Heaving a sigh, he sat up against the pillows, drawing Marianne up with him.

"That was unfair," he acknowledged. "If I'm logical about the matter, I have no quarrel with what I know of Corbett's character. Other than his chosen trade, he has shown himself to be a man of principle. Years ago, he helped you to find Rosie. During the debacle with Revelstoke, he stood by his employee with uncommon integrity. Then there is all he's been apparently doing to protect Rosie."

With Ambrose, Corbett hadn't been exactly forthcoming, but he'd admitted that he'd watched over Rosie from afar. He'd said casually that he'd "called in a few favors" to quiet the talk and "negotiated an understanding" with Josiah Jenkins, the owner of the now defunct *Prattler*.

For his own piece of mind, Ambrose had hunted down Jenkins that afternoon.

"When I spoke to the owner of *The Prattler*," he said, "he told me that Corbett paid him a thousand pounds to shut his business down. *One thousand pounds* to quell that bloody poem. I don't know whether to shake Corbett's hand in gratitude or tell him to get his head checked. And what do you wish to wager that he'll refuse my offer to reimburse him?"

"And you still don't like him?" His wife's brows arched.

"Whether or not I like him isn't the issue. What kind of life will Rosie have, married to a man in his profession?"

"You're assuming they'll get married," Marianne said dryly.

His shoulders tensed. "If he intends to merely dally with our daughter, then by God—"

"Before you call Corbett out, I'd like to point out that the dallying is likely going the other way around."

Ambrose frowned. "What do you mean?"

"Darling, you know Rosie. You know how much having a position in Society means to her. Because she's a bastard,"— Marianne's voice quivered with the old guilt—"she's had to contend with the *ton*'s cruelty, and now she thinks she has what she wants. A title that will translate into respectability. I doubt she's willing to give that up—even if she has feelings for

Corbett."

"She can't think to have an affair *indefinitely*," he said hotly.

"Widows and married ladies do it all the time. Society turns a blind eye as long as everything is done with discretion. And Corbett is nothing if not discreet."

"I won't allow it. No daughter of mine, widow or not, is going to carry on in that disreputable fashion," he declared. "If she has feelings for him, then she damned well better do the right thing."

"So you do want Rosie to marry Corbett."

He opened his mouth—and shut it.

"Bloody hell," he muttered. "Am I truly considering a procurer for a son-in-law?"

"Better the devil you know. And you want to know the truth?"

He cocked a brow.

"I'd rather have Corbett in the family than Daltry any day," his wife said with feeling.

Ambrose couldn't argue with that. "So we're just going to... *accept* Rosie's carrying on with Corbett?"

"Precisely." A calculating gleam entered his spouse's gaze. "You know how Rosie is: if we try to stop her from seeing Corbett, she'll only want to do so more. Thus, we must stand back and allow her to make her own decisions. In other words—treat her like the adult she claims to be."

"*Claims* being the operative word." As much as he loved his daughter, he couldn't help but question her judgement. "How can we trust that she will act in her own best interests?"

"What choice do we have? She has her independence now." Marianne's tone turned contemplative. "And I begin to think that *not* trusting her may have been the root of this fiasco."

"How do you mean?"

"By being overprotective, I may have made Rosie doubt herself," she said slowly. "In retrospect, I think I've added to her insecurities by trying to shield her from the truth. By communicating to her—unintentionally—that I didn't believe in her ability to handle reality. Now she doubts her own instincts, and it is my fault."

"You cannot take responsibility for that," he said. "And I do not think Rosie suffers from an excess of self-doubt."

"Don't you?" Marianne's smile was edged with sadness. "She exudes confidence and charm, no doubt, but do you think a truly confident woman would care so much what the *ton* thinks? Would seek acceptance above all—even love?"

He hadn't considered the matter from this angle before. The idea that his bright, brave, and beautiful daughter might believe herself lacking in *any* way raised a welt on his heart.

"How can we help her?" he said tautly.

"We nudge her—gently—in the right direction. I think it would be in the best interests of everyone if you got to know Corbett better. Make sure that he is, indeed, a man of character and a suitable husband for Rosie. You wouldn't mind doing that, would you, darling?"

He rubbed the back of his neck, the muscles there fine-tuned to paternal stress. "I suppose not."

"Thank you." His wife's lips brushed his jaw. "I knew you would understand."

"I understand one thing for certain."

"What is that, my love?"

"I'm keeping Sophie under lock and key," he said darkly. "I've learned my lesson. No gentlemen are getting near our other daughter."

Marianne laughed. Apparently, she thought he was joking.

"I adore it when you get protective." Her hands wandered, and he felt himself responding, as ever, to her teasing touch. "You're my hero, Mr. Kent."

He rolled over her. "Don't you forget it, Mrs. Kent."

He kissed her smiling mouth with a need that had only grown deeper and fiercer with time. She responded with an ardor that always heated his blood. Together, they reaffirmed with their bodies and hearts the love that would see them through anything.

Chapter Twenty-Five

THE NEXT DAY, with Grier by his side, Andrew entered Will Nightingale's coffee house in the heart of the Seven Dials. Nightingale's was an ancient institution, a relic from another time when the public gathered in such venues to learn the news of the day and engage in the free exchange of ideas. Although the rising popularity of tea and private clubs had led to the demise of coffee houses, Nightingale's showed no acknowledgement of the times.

The interior hadn't changed much in the twenty-odd years since Andrew had first stepped foot into the place. It still had the same shaved wood floors and smoke-tinged air, the heads of bleary-eyed game serving as décor on the walls. He did notice a few new paintings: the amateurish watercolors sprang up like bizarre blooms in the field of furry trophies.

The place was bustling as always, serving boys dashing back and forth with silver pots, refilling the famous pitch-dark brew for the customers clustered around long tables. As potent as the coffee was, however, it wasn't the secret to Nightingale's longevity. That lay at the table set in a private alcove at the back of the room.

Andrew strode toward the alcove, Grier at his heels.

"Try not to kick the hornet's nest, will you?" the Scot said under his breath.

"Someone kicks first, I'm not backing away," Andrew said evenly.

He needed his full focus on protecting Primrose. This

meant he had to clean his own house. To end the feud with his nemesis Malcolm Todd, one way or another.

When he and Grier neared their destination, a pair of hulking guards blocked their access to the table, waiting for their master's decree.

Bartholomew Black, sitting on a throne-like chair, jerked his chin at Andrew. "Him only."

Grier cast Andrew a look of warning before being led off.

"Good morning, sir." Andrew bowed deeply—fitting when one was greeting the most powerful man in London.

Those who didn't know Black might mistake him for a doddering eccentric. He certainly dressed the part: from his lace-trimmed shirt to his embroidered puce waistcoat to his satin breeches, he looked as if he'd stumbled in from the previous century. Yet the dark eyes that looked out from beneath that ridiculous periwig were as sharp as a blade, and the beringed hands that were dumping sugar and cream into coffee could just as casually end a man's life.

Anyone who didn't respect the King of the Underworld was a fool.

Andrew was no fool.

Which was more than he could say about Black's son-in-law, Malcolm Todd. Todd occupied the seat *one down* from Black's right, a position rife with meaning. Black keeping the chair to his right empty was a subtle yet symbolic reflection of the state of affairs. Everyone knew Todd was chomping at the bit to inherit his father-in-law's power; Black, however, showed no signs of relinquishing the reins to his kingdom.

While Black commanded respect, Todd deserved nothing but contempt. A small, bald man with a round face and a vicious nature, Todd would stoop to any means to gain more power.

"Corbett," Todd said in his sneering manner.

Andrew calibrated his bow to his degree of respect.

"Todd."

"Hah." Black let out a bark of laughter, turning to his son-in-law. "Made a leg for me, didn't he, and a fine one, too. But you? Not as much as a bob o' the 'ead."

Todd's face reddened. "I don't give a rat's arse what the bugger—"

"And there's your problem. You don't care about doin' the pretty, but Corbett 'ere,"—Black jabbed a blunt finger in Andrew's direction—"'e does. Understands class, don't 'e, and *that's* the difference between 'im and you. Why 'is club draws all 'em fine coves with the fat purses while yours attracts the common riffraff."

"His blighted club is *not* better than mine—"

"God Almighty, shut your gob." Black aimed a squinty-eyed look at Todd, and the latter shut up. He turned his gaze to Andrew and gestured regally to the seat on his left. "Sit."

Andrew complied, and a serving boy rushed forward to place a dish of coffee in front of him. As he took a sip of the thick, fortifying brew, Black waved a hand, and the guards pulled a velvet curtain across the alcove, sealing them in privacy.

"Let's get down to business. Corbett,"—Black pinned him with a hard black stare—"Todd says you're violating the terms o' the accord and poaching on 'is territory. Is this true?"

"No, sir," Andrew said.

"That's a lie," Todd snarled at him from across the table. "You've opened a place, brazen as can be, a stone's throw away from my club."

"The Accord specifies that no one shall operate a competing business within another's territorial lines. As I've explained to you, I indeed own a property close to your club, but it is not a competing business. It's not a business at all."

"You got a 'ouse full 'o whores. What's that, if not a brothel?" Todd retorted.

"E's got you there." Black stirred his coffee. "Where there's smoke, there's usually a fire."

"All the wenches living in the Nursery House are with child," Andrew began.

"That so?" Black's bushy brows inched toward his wig. "No telling what gents fancy these days, eh?"

"The Nursery House is *not* a brothel," Andrew said with emphasis. "It's a place for my pregnant employees to have their babes and recover before returning to work."

"You expect us to believe that? That you're running some sort o' *charity*?" Todd jeered.

"I don't think of it as charity but innovation. A sound business practice." *How many times do I have to explain the facts to this idiot?* "If I look after my workers, I'll attract and retain the best. If I give them a safe place to go during pregnancy, they'll come back afterward, healthy and ready to work. In the end, it saves me time and money—and improves the lives of those who work for me."

"That's bloody preposterous!" Todd sprang up—not that he had far to go. Standing, the little tyrant was not much taller than Andrew was sitting. "Wench 'as a bun in the oven, you find a new one. Wench expires having a brat, you find a new one. Way o' the world. What you're doing is setting a bad example. Giving the whores *ideas*." He spat the word like an epithet. "Next thing you know they'll be wanting 'igher wages, a decent place to live, time off to spend with their brats. Your buggering Nursery is going to cause a mutiny—and I won't stand for it!"

Andrew decided now was not the time to disclose the second phase of his plan: to partner with a school to educate the whores' bastards.

Instead, he said levelly, "I don't tell you how to run your business, and you don't tell me how to run mine. That, Todd, is the way of *our* world."

"You uppity whoreson—"

"I am the son of a whore," Andrew acknowledged, "which explains why I view whores as human beings. Try that perspective, and you might find your business improves. What won't improve your business, however, is trying to intimidate me. Three nights ago, I was attacked."

He slid in the last fact—and watched for Todd's reaction.

He saw surprise... followed quickly by glee.

"Can't lay that at my door," Todd said smugly. "Can't say I'm shocked, though. Bastard like you is bound to 'ave more enemies than a dog 'as fleas."

"My enemies better know that I fight back. And when I do, I go for the throat."

"Is that a damned threat?"

"Enough. Both of you." Black's command cut through the tension. "Todd, sit your arse down."

Todd sat, his beady eyes aglitter.

"Way I see it, Corbett 'asn't violated the Accord," the King of the Underworld pronounced. "'E ain't operating a business that interferes with yours, Todd, so you got no bone to pick with 'im. Understand?"

"But—"

"Terms 'o the treaty are clear. The aggressor in any unwarranted conflict will answer to me."

Black's warning was unmistakable.

Todd gritted his teeth, remaining silent.

"As for you, Corbett,"—Black transferred a gimlet-eyed stare to him—"if I smell a whiff o' wrongdoing from that Nursery o' yours, it will be razed to the ground before you can blink twice. And you know from experience the fire of my wrath."

Even after all these years, the memory of the inferno that had been Kitty's club burned in Andrew's head.

"There will be no wrongdoing, sir," he said.

"Then we're done with business." Black's majestic nod ended the conversation. "Finish your coffee. Nightingale's makes the best in London."

Todd stood abruptly. "I 'ave matters that require my attention."

"You do indeed. You keeping an eye on that granddaughter o' mine?" Black demanded. "What's this I 'ear 'bout Tessie skipping lessons and carrying on like a hoyden?"

Todd looked annoyed. "I'm a busy man. I leave the domestic affairs to my wife."

"Well, your wife is my daughter, and we both know she ain't got the wherewithal to 'andle Tessie. So you'd best do your part, or you'll answer to me."

With a sullen jerk of the head, Todd departed through the curtain.

"God Almighty," Black muttered, "what kind o' man don't look after 'is own blood?"

Andrew wondered if he was expected to respond. He drank coffee instead.

"Tessie may not be my flesh and blood, but she might as well be. Girl takes after me. Got looks, brains, and deserves nothing but the best." Black pounded a fist to the table, making the cups jump in their saucers. "You understand, Corbett?"

"Er, yes. Of course."

"My Tessie's a fine lady." Black jabbed a finger at the framed paintings that lined the alcove walls. "Accomplished, ain't she?"

Andrew took in the cheerfully terrible watercolors. "She has... a unique talent."

"Exactly." Black sat back, slurped his coffee, fingers drumming on the table. After a moment, he declared, "I like you, Corbett. More since you finally cut ties with that blowsy bitch, Kitty Barnes. So this is why I'll spare you a word o' advice."

A chill permeated Andrew's gut. He shouldn't have been surprised that Black knew about his personal affairs; the other had an eye on most everything. His trepidation wasn't over Kitty but Primrose. Did the King know about her?

"What advice?" he said warily.

"You're a decent cove and rare man o' principle. That said, every man's got a weakness." Black's gaze held a shrewd glint. "Beware o' females, Corbett—they're yours."

Chapter Twenty-Six

"DO YOU THINK this gown is too much, Odette?" Rosie asked.

She was examining herself in the gilt-framed mirror on the wall of her new sitting room. She'd moved into the house on Curzon Street two days ago, and Andrew would be arriving shortly for a cozy midnight supper. In the reflection, her eyes sparkled with anticipation. She hadn't been alone with him since the shooting, and she couldn't wait to see him again.

Behind her, Odette paused in the act of arranging the flowers on the intimate table set for two. Rosie had been torn about whether to keep the maid on; she didn't like the fact that Odette had betrayed her trust by being a spy for Andrew. The maid was exceptional at her job, however... and an absolute *genius* with hair. Moreover, Odette had apologized, and Rosie couldn't stay angry at the other for helping Andrew to keep her safe.

Now the Frenchwoman inspected Rosie with the precision of a sergeant-at-arms scrutinizing a cadet. "Your ensemble—*c'est parfait*, my lady," was her verdict.

For tonight's special occasion, Odette had taken extra care with Rosie's toilette. Rosie wore a gown of violet taffeta so dark that it was nearly black, and it bared her shoulders, displaying the merest hint of her bosom. The bodice fit her torso like a second skin, ending in a point that was echoed in the cuffs of the full sleeves. The skirts were overlaid with black silk netting which caught the light and gleamed with her movements.

Odette had fashioned her hair into an Apollo's knot, violet ribbons woven into the complicated braids. Ringlets were left to frame Rosie's face. She'd kept her jewelry to a minimum: a cameo on a black ribbon nestled at the base of her throat.

She wanted to be beautiful for Andrew and hoped he would find her so.

Too restless to remain still, she went over to the table, inspecting the silver domed dishes on the cart beside it. "Do you think Mr. Corbett will like the menu?"

"*Mais oui*, my lady," the maid replied. "Cook has selected all of Mr. Corbett's favorites."

"And Cook would know his preferences," Rosie said dryly.

Cook—and the rest of Rosie's household staff—had been sent over the day before by Andrew. As the accompanying note had indicated, each of the servants had been personally vetted by him, having either worked in one of his clubs or private residences. If Rosie had found his actions a tad high-handed, his closing lines had dispersed her irritation like dandelion fluff in the wind.

Do this for your own good. And mine. For I won't rest easy until I know you are safe.
—*A*

How could she stay annoyed when he was so gallant?

The ormolu clock on the mantel chimed a whimsical tune, announcing the midnight hour. As if on cue, a rapping sounded on the door. Odette went to open it, and Andrew came in.

He looked as out of place in the peach and gold chamber as a lion prowling through a pet shop. He removed his hat, setting it down, his eyes smoldering in his godly face. Her heartbeat thundering in her ears, Rosie barely registered the maid's discreet exit.

Andrew came to her, his arms enfolding her, his mouth descending with crushing force.

She kissed him back with all the pent-up longing inside her.

When the kiss ended, he rasped, "Now there's a greeting for a man. Miss me, sunshine?"

Since her hands were fisted around the lapels of his greatcoat, she thought his might be a rhetorical question. She smoothed the thick wool back in place. "Perhaps a little."

"Well, I couldn't wait to see to you." He took her hands one by one, brushing his lips over her knuckles. "How ravishing you look."

Feeling unaccountably shy, she ducked her head. "Thank you for arranging to have your guards work tonight. A clandestine meeting would have been difficult had Papa's men been on duty."

"Kent's men might not be on duty, but I doubt we're pulling the wool over his eyes."

"Pardon?" she gasped.

Andrew's head canted. "Sweetheart, your father is a fine investigator. Your mama is known for her cleverness. I wouldn't be surprised if they knew I was here."

"Oh, no!" She panicked like a thief caught in the act. "What will we do? Should you go—"

"Primrose." His big hands framed her face. "Calm yourself."

"Calm? How can I be calm? It's one thing for Mama and Papa to *suspect* that we're lovers, but for them to actually *know* that you're here... " Hearing herself, she knew the distinction was ridiculous, yet she'd worked herself up into a state. Then another disastrous thought struck her. "Dear God, do you think Mr. McLeod and Mr. Lugo know as well?"

Andrew stared at her—and burst out laughing.

"What on earth is amusing?" she cried.

"You, love." Still smiling, he kissed her on the nose. "Some sophisticated widow you are. You so convincingly stated the case for your independence and living on your own that I forgot what an innocent you are."

"I'm not innocent. You took care of that—remember?" she said tartly.

"Every night, sweetheart. Every night." His wicked grin dissolved her pique.

Still, she bemoaned, "Just because I'm independent doesn't mean I want my parents knowing about our affair. What if they disapprove—"

"They know about us," he said, "and they're not standing in the way. Why do you think they allowed you to move into this house?"

She blinked as the truth sunk in. "You mean they approve... of us...?"

"*Approve* might be overstating the case," he said dryly. "I'd say they accept the circumstances for the time being and trust that I will keep you safe." He studied her. "Does their approval mean that much to you, then?"

"I want them to be proud of me," she said in a small voice.

The admission made her feel vulnerable, like the innocent he'd said she was, and sudden fear swirled in her. Andrew was a worldly and experienced man. What if he found her naiveté unappealing, what if he tired of her, wanted a more sophisticated lover—

"Your parents are proud of you. They love you." The tenderness in his brown eyes stemmed the flow of her anxiety. He kissed her forehead. "Now I hate to be rude, but I'm famished. Could we continue our conversation over supper?"

Feeling reassured, she nodded.

At the table, he seated her and then himself. He served them both from the covered dishes on the cart: partridge pie with a golden crust, sturgeon cooked with parsley and lemon, and a ragu of veal flavored with truffles.

"That's too much for me," she protested when he set the plate in front of her.

"Eat what you want to," he said.

Seeing him dig into his plate with gusto, she picked up her fork and took a bite of the sturgeon. *Mmm.* Warm and buttery, the fish melted in her mouth. She suddenly realized how hungry she was. Taking small bites of the delicious food and sipping the wine he poured for her, she savored the intimacy of having supper with her lover—of feeling like an adult.

Watching him polish off his plate, she marveled, "How can you eat like that and stay so fit?"

"I take regular exercise." He helped himself to more pie.

"What sort?"

"Boxing, mostly. I like to stay in fighting shape."

That explained his physique. Thinking of his hard, disciplined form, she had to squeeze her legs together to quell a wicked tingle. "Why do you have to stay in fighting shape?"

"Brawls, mainly. My customers may be fine gents but throw spirits and wenches into the mix…" He shrugged, as if no further explanation was necessary. "My guards generally keep the peace. I only step in when I have to."

She gnawed on her bottom lip. "What if you get injured?"

He paused, his fork halfway to his mouth. "You're worried about *me* getting hurt when you were shot at?"

"I have you and Papa to protect me. I'm perfectly safe," she said confidently. "You aren't, however, if you're wading into the thick of things."

He set down his fork and reached for her hand. "Thank you."

"For what?"

"Trusting me with your safety." His gaze was heated,

intense. "Caring about mine."

"You're welcome," she said softly.

"Speaking of your safety,"—he let go of her hand to pull something out of the greatcoat he'd slung over his chair—"I have something for you."

Brimming with curiosity, she took the white silk pouch from him. She untied the strings and pulled out the contents.

Her gaze bounced to his. "You brought me a *pistol*?"

"For added protection. It's a ladies piece, designed to fit in a purse or skirt pocket. Don't judge it by its size: while small, it shoots as well as any gun."

Fascinated by the petite weapon, she turned it over in her hands, admiring the fine craftsmanship. "What a darling mother-of-pearl handle. And are those flowers stamped in the metal?" she said in delight. "Why, this would look most fetching with my silver reticule…"

At the silence that greeted her, she looked up. Andrew had those crinkles around his eyes, the ones that made him look even more dashingly attractive.

"What is so amusing?" she said.

"You." His mouth twitched. "You do realize that the pistol is more than an accessory?"

"Well, yes. But it doesn't hurt if something looks pretty *and* has a sensible function, does it?" She gave the pistol a loving pat. "Thank you for the lovely and thoughtful gift."

"You're welcome." He smiled slowly. "I'll teach you how to shoot it, too."

After that, conversation turned to everyday topics. Andrew was easy to talk to and apparently interested in her mundane (compared to his) existence. As she told him about how she was settling into the house, she was reminded of a problem—one that she wanted to give him fair warning about.

How on earth do I bring this up… without sounding forward?

"I've been trying to decide what furnishings to keep and

what to have, um,"—her cheeks warmed as a specific item flashed in her mind—"... removed."

He glanced around the feminine sitting room. "This room is quite tasteful."

"To use Mr. Mayhew's discreet turn of phrase, Daltry used this house to entertain his *special friends*," she said dryly. "I do believe the previous occupant was one of his mistresses."

"Ah. Does that bother you?"

"Not at all. I'm just glad that, whoever she was, she had excellent taste. For the most part," she amended, thinking of the glaring exception in the bedchamber.

Andrew set down his napkin. "The meal was delicious."

"What can I say? Your cook is talented." Buying time, she said quickly, "There's dessert, if you want it."

"I do."

"The blancmange is on the bottom of the cart—" Her words ended in a gasp for he'd risen and swept her easily into his arms. "What are you doing?"

"Having dessert."

"There's something I ought to tell you," Primrose said.

"Let's talk in bed."

Andrew thought his a fair suggestion considering they were in her bedchamber, her clothing strewn in a trail behind them. He drank in the sight of Primrose: her golden tresses had fallen free of its fussy coiffure, her firm, pink-tipped tits giving a saucy bounce with each backward step she took. Six more, he judged, and she'd hit the edge of the bed—an oversized affair surrounded by gauzy white curtains that hung from the ceiling.

Five steps, four...

"I wanted to tell you this before," she persisted.

He stripped off his jacket, tossed it over a chair as he passed. "Tell me what, sweetheart?"

Her gaze landed on the prominent bulge in his trousers, and her bottom lip caught beneath her teeth. "It's about the bed."

"An apropos topic." His waistcoat went the way of his jacket, and he advanced another step.

She retreated accordingly.

...*three steps... two steps...*

The back of her knees hit the mattress; nowhere left for her to go.

"I didn't have time to have it changed," she blurted.

"I don't give a damn." He gave her a gentle push, and, with a little squeal, she tumbled backward onto the bed. He followed, careful to keep his weight from crushing her. He nuzzled her ear, inhaling her fragrance greedily. "In case you're worried, my servants are well trained. I'm certain they changed the sheets without your instruction."

"I wasn't referring to the sheets."

He raised his head, puzzled. Cheeks rosy, she wordlessly pointed upward.

He twisted his head around—and let out a bark of laughter. "Good God."

"I know. It's terribly wicked, isn't it?" Primrose said in a rush.

Her flushed cheeks and sultry eyes betrayed that she wasn't quite as scandalized as she wanted to be. He slanted another glance up at the enormous looking glass affixed to the ceiling. The image of their entwined bodies—hers nude, his clothed—magnified his lust.

Her eyes met his in the reflection, her lips parting. When she squirmed, his thigh nudged into the cove of her legs; he nearly groaned when her dew soaked his skin through the trousers. Despite her primness about certain matters,

Primrose was a firebrand in bed.

Recalling her reaction to the viewing holes in his club, he decided it was an excellent time to broaden her horizons. To show her that she didn't need to hide behind fashionable trappings and inhibitions. To guide her in the exploration of her desires.

"Who's to say what is wicked?" he murmured. "In the bedroom, there are no rules between us, sunshine, except what we choose."

"But you must admit a mirror above the bed is scandalous," she said in a muffled voice.

"Perhaps. Is it not also arousing?" Deliberately, he shifted onto his side, giving her a full view of herself in the mirror. Anticipation simmered as he saw her gaze transfixing upon the image. "Let's play a game, shall we? Keep your eyes on the mirror, and don't stop looking until I tell you to."

Chapter Twenty-Seven

"TELL ME WHAT you see, love," Andrew said.

As Rosie looked up at the image, she saw with growing horror that all her beautifying efforts had gone to waste. She had nary a stitch on, her carefully contrived ensemble scattered somewhere between the sitting room and the bed. And her coiffure—*Dear Lord*. The Apollo's knot had disintegrated, her hair tangled across the blue satin sheets in a messy riot of waves and braids. Unseemly color blotched her cheeks, and her breasts were surging, the tips brazenly erect.

When Andrew had made love to her in the past, she'd been so lost in the experience that she'd forgotten to care about her appearance. Now she was confronted with reality. The woman in the looking glass wasn't perfect or composed or ladylike.

She looked like a wicked trollop—like a flower that had been plucked.

Mortified, she tried to cover herself—only to find her hands pinned above her head, her wrists held in Andrew's large hand. Her gaze flew to his.

"Let me go," she said urgently. "I have to tidy myself. I'm—"

"Perfect."

"How can you say that? I'm at sixes and sevens." To her shame, her voice wobbled. "I don't want you to see me like this. Please, I have to get up."

"Primrose, you're always beautiful and never more so than

at this moment." He looked at her so intently that she squirmed. "Why would you doubt that?"

"Because everything I spent three hours perfecting is in shambles!" she cried. "Now I'm... I'm just..." *Me.* Fear welled from some deep place inside. "Please, let me go freshen up—"

"No."

At his firm reply, she blinked. "Pardon?"

"Whatever you mean to do is unnecessary," he stated. "You could spend another three hours fussing over your toilette, and it wouldn't make a difference. You couldn't be any more beautiful than you are right now."

Flabbergasted, she stared at him. "That... that isn't true."

"It is. Your beauty has nothing to do with your fancy gowns and coiffures. It has to do with *you.*" His knuckles brushed along her jaw, the warm authority in his gaze mesmerizing. "Your eyes alone could launch a thousand ships. Your body makes a man want to take on that entire fleet for the privilege of calling you his own. Add in your spirit, intelligence, and madcap tendencies,"—his lips quirked— "and, plainly put, sunshine: you're irresistible."

Was it *possible* that he believed what he was saying? She scrutinized his chiseled features and saw only earnestness. She recalled all the times he'd told her she was beautiful—that she had nothing to hide from him. His words sank into her like a balm, soothing her fears.

Flummoxed, a bit giddy, she blurted, "I'm not a madcap."

His smile reached his eyes. "You're a wee bit daft now and again; it's part of your charm. Now do you want to spend the evening arguing about this, or do you want me to make love to you?"

As much as she wanted to debate the finer points of her nature—she was definitely not daft in the *slightest*—there really was no contest.

"Make love to me," she breathed.

"With pleasure." His approval thrummed through her. "Keep your eyes on the mirror, darling."

She did, watching as Andrew's big hands cupped her breasts, his fingers skillfully teasing the rosy peaks. It *was* scandalous. And also... beautiful. From the outside looking in, there was nothing ugly or dirty about the lovers in the bed. As she witnessed the lovemaking unfold, her inhibitions loosened like a corset, and that first breath of freedom was heady.

Her back arched as his tongue worked lazily over her taut nipples.

"I love your tits," he murmured. "Do you like the way I'm touching you—licking you?"

Her gaze instinctively sought his. "Y-yes."

"Eyes on the glass, love," he ordered.

Aroused, curious, she obeyed. It was sinfully titillating to watch him, fully clothed, doing as he wished with her naked body. What he was doing was wicked... but it also made her feel worshipped. He gave her breasts one last lingering kiss before pressing his lips between her ribs, down the pale valley of her belly. She twisted restlessly, clutching the sheets; her nipples, still damp from his suckling, strained upward, wet and glistening.

"Do your breasts ache, sweeting?"

"Yes," she said quickly, hoping he would ease that sweet throbbing.

"Then touch them."

Her eyes widened in the reflection. "Pardon?"

"Pet your tits, love. Help me give you pleasure."

Her breath stuttered. She couldn't possibly... could she? Her hands seemed to have a mind of their own, moving toward the full mounds. Her trembling palms cupped the needy curves, pleasure tingling through her. What she was doing was depraved—and powerfully arousing.

"That's right, darling. Touch yourself for me," he encouraged in a guttural voice. "Play with those pretty nipples."

In the reflection, the woman shamelessly caressed her own breasts, rubbing the stiff pink tips between her fingers. Hot sparks danced from her nipples to her pussy. Knowing that Andrew was watching her, hearing the hunger in his growled praise, unspooled her remaining inhibitions. Pinching and playing, she abandoned herself to the pleasure that her body could give her.

Large hands clamped on her thighs, spreading them. Panting, she watched as he parted her blonde curls, exposing her vulnerable center. He ran a long finger along the slick seam, and her entire being shivered.

"Look at your beautiful cunny," he rasped. "Pink and wet with your cream. Can you see, love?"

Heavens, she could—and the fact made her even wetter. Need coiled in her belly. She was desperate for the relief he could give her.

"Look at me, Primrose."

Her gaze flew to his; the primal possessiveness in those dark depths made her pulse race.

"What do you want? Tell me, and it's yours," he commanded.

"Make love to me," she whispered.

"You can do better than that, sunshine." His thumb nudged upward, skirting around the peak of her bliss, teasing her. "Give me the words. The ones I taught you. The naughty ones running through your head right now."

Desire tore fear to shreds, tossing it to the winds.

"Put your cock in my pussy," she pleaded. "Please, Andrew."

Triumph burned in his eyes. "God, yes."

He tore off his shirt, and her mouth pooled at the sight of

his virile beauty, those carved slabs and ridges of muscle. His boots thumped onto the floor, his hands working on the waistband of his trousers. He stripped them off, baring his erection.

She couldn't help but gawk at the extent of his arousal: the thick, turgid shaft stood tall against his flat belly, the head engorged and glistening. He wrapped one hand around his member, the other taking something from his discarded trousers. Puzzled, she watched as he brought a white tube with dangling red strings toward his straining cock.

"What is that?" she said.

"A French letter." At her blank look, his lips curved. "It prevents conception, love. I promised to protect you, remember?"

As understanding dawned, her cheeks heated—and her belly did as well as she watched him don the sheath, which barely accommodated him. He deftly tied the strings and then he lunged over her. He pushed inside, and she gasped at the steady invasion, the unrelenting stretch of his cock opening her up. When he hilted fully inside her, she moaned, discomfort chased away by bliss. By having him where she needed him.

"Christ, that's good. The best bloody feeling in the world." His gaze smoldered into hers. "Being inside you, Primrose—there's no place I'd rather be."

The force of her emotions was almost too much to bear.

"I want you," she said achingly. "So much, Andrew."

"Then take me, love," he growled.

The rhythm of his hips whirled her senses. Gentle at first, then harder and harder, his thrusts pushed her toward that sparkling edge of abandon. Her mind blurred as he whispered hot, naughty words into her ear: how sweet her pussy was, how he loved its hungry kiss, loved feeding every inch of his prick into her tight little hole. She held on as best as she could as he pounded into her, grinding against her mound, making her see stars. The sound of smacking flesh mingled with her moans and his harsh breaths, and her gaze suddenly caught the reflection overhead.

Her slender limbs were wrapped all around Andrew. Her hands clutched his hard, flexing shoulders, her legs circling his lean hips as he rode her. The ropey muscles of his back rippled, his buttocks hollowing as he filled her again and again with throbbing joy.

The power of their mating surged through her. Their lovemaking was carnal, raw.

Beautiful.

Something broke inside her. She moaned his name as torrents of pleasure set her free, carrying her over the edge.

"*Yes*, Primrose," he groaned. "I can feel you coming."

Tremors of bliss shook her, yet he didn't stop. He continued to drive into her, his burning gaze her only anchor in the maelstrom. She absorbed the potent pummeling of his hips, the focused momentum of his thrusts, wanting to give him the same rapture he'd given her. Suddenly, he pushed her knees back, opening her further to his commanding incursions, and, incredibly, her spent nerves rekindled.

"So bloody beautiful," he growled. "This time, you're coming with me."

"But I just..." She gasped as his heavy stones slapped her sex, setting off new quakes.

"You can do it again." He leaned over and captured her right nipple between his lips. The hot, hard suckling caused her lower muscles to tighten, and he groaned, "Yes, squeeze me just like that. Stroke my cock with your sweet pussy until we both go over."

Molten pleasure rushed through her. She was so close... almost there...

He reached between their heaving bodies, strumming her

pearl as his cock drilled into her.

"Oh, Andrew—it's *happening*." Sensations overflowed, and, with a cry, she came again.

"Goddamn, it *is*." His head snapped back, the cords of his neck standing out in stark relief. He roared as he slammed into her again and again and again.

Finally he stilled, buried deep inside her. The rich satisfaction in his gaze curled her toes.

"Well, love?" he said huskily. "Have I scandalized you sufficiently?"

"No." She dimpled at him. "You're welcome to try even harder the next time."

Her reward was his laughter filling the room.

After Andrew disposed of the French letter and cleaned Primrose with a moist cloth, he returned to the bed. He doused the lamps and tucked her soft backside against his front. For the first time, he prepared to fall asleep with a partner after sex.

He'd made it a policy never to sleep with customers. If women wanted to fall asleep in his arms and paid to do so, he'd wait until they dozed off before leaving. With lovers, he either left after the act, or they did. He'd never even slept with Kitty: both of them had understood the limits of their intimacy.

For sleeping together was an intimate act. More intimate, in some ways, than sex itself. To be in that unguarded state with a woman, to hold her through dreams and nightmares, to wake tangled up in one another—it wasn't something he'd wanted to do... until now.

He cuddled Primrose closer. He felt mellow and satiated, his eyelids heavy.

"How does the French letter prevent conception?"

Primrose chirped.

He blinked away the beginnings of sleep. Then his lips curled. Her innocence and natural wantonness were a unique blend, to be sure, adding to her subtly off-kilter charm.

"It catches my seed. Prevents it from reaching your womb where it might take root and grow into a babe," he explained.

"Oh."

He could almost see the cogs turning in her head as she took this in. An image sprang into his own mind: of Primrose, her belly ripe with his child. The notion of siring a babe had never appealed to him before. For one, he wasn't certain what kind of father he'd make, having not known his own, and for another, he wouldn't get a woman with child unless she was his wife. And he'd never met a woman he'd wanted to marry.

Until Primrose. He shoved aside the thought, which was neither here nor there. Regardless of what he wanted, he knew marriage was not an option; she'd been perfectly clear on that, and he'd understood and accepted her terms.

Then why did the image of her, glowing and round with his babe, stir some unholy desire in him? Why did it make him want to mount her again, this time without the damned letter, and plow her until she was full of his seed? Until she was dripping with his essence...

"And the time before... when you, um, reached completion... *externally*, so to speak, was that also to prevent getting me with child?"

Despite his growing desire, he had to grin at her delicate wording. "Yes. Although," he said in the spirit of honesty, "it was also arousing to see my seed on your skin."

"Oh." This time the word had a breathy edge. "Is that a normal way of proceedings?"

"Perhaps not normal but also not unusual," he said judiciously. "When it comes to sex, there are many variations, and I'm of the mind that as long as the parties are agreeable and no one is harmed, there is no right or wrong." He stroked her shoulder, savoring its smoothness. "I meant what I said before: there are no rules in our bed except those we make. I want you to be free to explore your desires with me, Primrose. Tonight's experiment didn't turn out so badly, did it?"

"Not badly at all. In fact, I've grown rather attached to the looking glass."

Her sultry giggle dispersed wisps of heat through his blood. He'd never known a woman to be so chatty after intercourse. Primrose, however, seemed intent upon reviewing their sexual activities, and, instead of putting him to sleep, the conversation was having the opposite effect.

He'd climaxed vigorously not a quarter hour ago, and already he had a cockstand. Goddamn. Such recovery was exceptional, even for him.

"This is lovely, isn't it?" she said with a happy sigh. "I feel so free. I never thought having a lover would be *fun*."

His arm tightened around her waist. "Don't get any ideas. It's only fun with me."

She giggled again, turning to face him. Even in the dimness, he could see the gleam of mischief in her eyes. "Possessive, are you?"

"You're mine," he stated unequivocally. "In bed, you may play any games you want. Outside of bed—I won't tolerate it."

"You needn't be so serious." A pout entered her voice. "I was only teasing. I have no intention of taking other lovers."

"Good. Because I won't allow it."

"Come to think of it, isn't the pot calling the kettle black?" she said with a huff. "After all, you've had plenty of lovers."

"That was in the past."

There was a pause. "How long ago in the past?"

Damn, she'd caught him off guard. His jealousy had distracted him from the fact that her hand had crept slyly and directly onto the lid of Pandora's Box.

Apprehension prickled his nape, but he said dismissively, "It's been two years."

"Who was she?"

Christ. He couldn't bring himself to tell her. To bring into their bed a figure that ought to have disappeared from both their lives long ago. He couldn't allow the beauty blossoming between him and Primrose to be tainted by his weakness—by his sheer stupidity. Perhaps later he'd tell her; there was no reason to do so now. Not when they were just finding their balance in what had been a tempestuous journey.

"I don't discuss my past lovers," he said. "You'll have to take my word for it that what you and I have are different."

"How is it different?" she persisted. "How am I different from all your other lovers?"

You're different because... I love you. Goddamnit.

Aye, he was in love with Primrose. There was no denying it. As a girl, she'd had a piece of his heart; as a woman, she'd owned the whole bloody thing from the moment their paths had crossed again at the masquerade.

He loved Primrose—and he also understood her. She wasn't ready to hear those words from him. She was skittish about their affair as it was. Besides, experience had taught him that love didn't necessarily change anything. He couldn't help loving Primrose, but he also knew better than to expect anything in return.

"You're different because you're you." He traced the contours of her face, framing its delicate strength. "Unique, captivating—and a saucy little baggage. You need a man like me to take you on."

"I'm not a baggage," she retorted. "And I don't *need* any man."

"Don't you?" In an easy motion, he rolled onto his back, hoisting her on top so that she straddled him, her knees bracketing his hips. He felt her shiver, the moist kiss of her cunny against his abdomen, and his erection reared against her bottom. "Could have fooled me."

"Wretch." She sighed it.

"You're right, however. It's not *any* man you need—it's me."

Gripping his prick with one hand, he ran the engorged head along her dewy slit.

"You're mine, Primrose. Say it," he instructed.

"I'm yours," she said breathlessly.

Triumph blazed through him. "Bloody right, you are."

He hauled her higher, positioning her sex over his mouth. He ate her until she climaxed, her sleek thighs shaking around his face, her lips chanting his name. Only then did he don another sheath and bring them both to ecstasy once more, laying his claim on her the surest way he knew how.

Chapter Twenty-Eight

BY THE NEXT day, Papa's siblings had arrived in London, and the family convened at the Kent residence. Rosie received squishy kisses and hugs from her aunts' offspring—an adorable and ever expanding lot—before the children toddled off with their nannies. The adults took advantage of the momentary peace to have tea in the drawing room.

Papa's siblings were actually half-siblings, their mama having married Papa's widowed father. While they were technically Rosie's aunts and uncle, they felt more like siblings to her due to their closeness in age. Emma, the eldest sister, was only eight years older than Rosie. She and the rest of the family—Thea, Harry, Violet, and Polly—were now crowded around the refreshment-laden coffee table, listening as Rosie gave an abridged version of her adventures.

"We're so sorry we didn't make it here sooner," Thea, the Marchioness of Tremont said. The gentlest of the Kents, she was an angel with golden brown hair and soft hazel eyes. "We couldn't travel until Freddy was feeling better."

Frederick, Thea's beloved stepson, was a robust adolescent who suffered from occasional bouts of a chronic ailment.

With concern, Rosie said, "He's fully recovered, I hope?"

"Despite Thea's fretting, Freddy just had a head cold." This came from Thea's husband, who stood behind her chair. Tremont was a stoic fellow whose cool grey eyes warmed whenever they were upon his lady. "Right now, he's out in the garden with Edward."

Being the same age, Freddy and Rosie's brother were best cronies and usually up to some kind of mischief.

"Harry brought them a new toy. They're *experimenting*," Tremont added wryly.

A loud bang came from the back of the house, followed by gleeful shouts.

"Thunder 'n turf, what did you give them, Harry?" Violet, a lithe brunette, exclaimed from the settee that she shared with her husband, Viscount Carlisle. At the explosive sound, Carlisle, a strapping sportsman, had thrown a protective arm around her.

Papa aimed an alarmed look at his younger brother. "It wasn't gunpowder, was it, lad?"

"Of course not," Harry said, continuing to stack sandwiches onto his plate.

At eight-and-twenty, he was tall and darkly handsome like Papa. His spectacles hinted at his scholarly bent while his rangy, muscular build showed his love of sporting. Harry spent most of his time at the university, and Rosie was surprised at how much he'd changed since his last visit. There was a new brooding quality to him—one that tempered his good-naturedness and gave him a harder and more jaded air.

Has something happened to Harry? she wondered. She thought about asking—and decided against it. Despite his easygoing ways, Harry was notoriously private. Having grown up with five sisters, he knew how to keep feminine inquisitiveness at bay.

"I'd never give them a saltpeter mixture; it's too unstable." He popped a ham and watercress triangle into his mouth, chewed, and swallowed. "They have a sample of a new compound I've been working on. All bang and no blast, I assure you."

A small explosion rattled the windows. Worried looks

were exchanged around the room... followed by shrugs. By now, they were all accustomed to Harry's experiments.

"Well, then, let's get on with the critical business: that of finding Rosie's attacker," Em said in her usual brisk manner. "Ambrose, will you brief us on the case?"

A petite and buxom brunette, Em had an active interest in sleuthing. At one time, she'd wanted to join Papa's firm, and it was during her first case that she'd met the Duke of Strathaven. Despite being a duchess and mama now, Em still liked to keep up her investigative skills, and His Grace indulged her in this hobby as he did everything else.

Papa gave a summary of the facts, making note of Andrew's contributions. He did so in a neutral manner, not commenting on the nature of Rosie's relationship with Andrew. Relieved at the lack of censure, Rosie couldn't help but think about her lover. When he left her bed this morning, he'd promised to have a special surprise for her tonight. She wondered giddily what he had planned. Who knew that having an affair would be so exciting and delightful?

It wasn't just the lovemaking—her belly fluttered at the memory of those steamy hours—but how *free* she felt in his presence. When he'd made her look in the mirror, she'd seen herself clearly for the first time. In the reflection, she hadn't been wicked or bad. Andrew was teaching her to accept herself as she was.

He'd given her so much... and what did she have to give him in return?

The imbalance niggled at her. Looking around the room, she wished she had some special quality the way each of her family members did. She wished she had Em's practicality or Thea's gentleness, Vi's agility or Polly's goodness. All she possessed was beauty and passion, and, if Andrew were to be believed, certain madcap tendencies.

What sort of offering was that to a man like Andrew? A

man who was so worldly, powerful, and self-contained. What could *she* give to *him*?

She couldn't even offer marriage—if, indeed, he even wanted to marry her…

She gave herself a mental shake. Why was she thinking about marriage? She had everything she wanted: a passionate relationship with a devastatingly attractive man *and* a position in Society… why rock the boat? Her journey was finally smooth sailing—with the exception of someone wanting her dead. Being targeted for murder did cause some choppiness in the waters.

The reminder made her focus back on Papa, who'd just finished recounting the events.

"Crumpets," Violet said, her caramel-colored eyes wide. "I thought I was the hoyden of the family, but Rosie has me beat!"

"That's debatable," Carlisle muttered.

When his viscountess responded by elbowing him in the side, his rugged face creased in a grin.

"Wasn't Andrew Corbett the one who accused Revelstoke of that ghastly business last year?" Emma asked. She'd aided Papa in the investigation that had cleared Polly's husband of any wrongdoing. "Why has he gone to such lengths to protect Rosie?"

Before Rosie could muster up an explanation, Mama said, "As it happens, Corbett is an old friend."

Em's brows knitted together. "Why haven't you mentioned that before, Marianne?"

"Corbett is part of a past I'd wanted to forget. He assisted me during those dark times when I was searching for Rosie." Reaching up, Mama squeezed the hand that Papa had placed on her shoulder. "Corbett knew Rosie when she was a child, and he was a friend to her then." Mama's eyes met Rosie's, and the maternal understanding in those emerald depths clogged her throat. "He still is."

"Any friend of Rosie's is a friend of the Kents," Em declared. "Given his integral involvement in the case, why didn't we invite him today?"

Seated next to her, Strathaven, a darkly elegant man, murmured, "Discretion is in order, pet."

Em canted her head at her husband, her expression puzzled.

That was the charming thing about Em—about all of the Kents, Rosie thought. Growing up in an unconventional, middling class household, none of them gave a farthing about things like status or social acceptance. How she wished she could be more like them.

"Mama is right. Mr. Corbett has been a good friend to me," she said quietly, "and a true gentleman, despite his profession. I owe him more than I can ever repay."

"How lovely that you've found a champion." Emma beamed. "Speaking of which—what can we do to help, Ambrose?"

Going to the hearth, Papa faced them all, his eyes somber. "Thanks to Polly and Revelstoke's friends, the mudlarks, we've had several sightings of a man who could be the shooter within St. Giles. He's evaded capture thus far, but we'll have him soon." Papa's jaw tightened. "Which is a good thing because we've made little progress with Alastair James and Peter Theale."

"They've denied involvement?" Em inquired.

"Vehemently. James was blasé about it, but his sort appears blasé about everything. Even last year, when he nearly killed a man in a drunken duel—a little known fact that Lugo dug up. So we now know James has a history of committing violence." Papa's fingers drummed on the mantel. "Theale, on the other hand, was all nerves. His hands were shaking like he'd been struck by palsy."

"Do you think this Theale fellow is the guilty one?" Harry said.

"I don't know that he'd have the nerve to hire a cutthroat," Papa said, "but he, of all the suspects, is the one who stands to gain the most. And not just in terms of money. I delved further into the financial information Corbett provided. It appears that Theale recently received a large loan from Mr. Albert Brace, a tea merchant."

"Tea merchants have joined the usury business now?" Harry's brows rose.

"It's not money that Brace is after but the social connection," Papa replied. "He has a daughter who he's apparently been trying to marry off for years. Her main attraction, according to sources, is her dowry. Apparently, Theale has been dragging his heels for months, and Brace's loan is part of ongoing negotiations."

"So we have one man with a history of violence and another desperate enough for money to consider an unwanted match," Emma mused. "What do we know about the female suspects?"

Mama spoke up. "On that subject, I've made a few inquiries of my own. According to the drawing room talk, Antonia James' husband has recently lost a fortune to bad investments, and they are in dire financial straits. Lady Charlotte Daltry, the dowager countess, has a modest stipend exceeded, at times, by her expenses. Her wards, Sybil and Eloisa Fossey, are both penniless. Thus, for any of the four, two thousand pounds per annum might be sufficient incentive for murder."

Em hopped to her feet. "Since female suspects are my specialty, I'll go interview them straightaway."

"It is past calling hours, pet." His Grace's large hand circled his wife's slender wrist. "Send a note requesting a visit tomorrow. And frame it as your desire to meet Rosie's new family rather than your desire to hunt down a murderer."

"I suppose you've got a point." Em plopped back onto the cushions. "Tomorrow, then."

"I'll come," Thea said.

"Me, too," Vi and Polly chimed in.

"I'd like to meet with the ladies as well," Rosie said quickly.

Not only did she want to aid in the capture of the villain, she needed to start her campaign for social acceptance. She needed to get into the good graces of Mrs. James and the dowager—assuming they weren't the ones who wanted her dead, of course.

"Rosie should stay at home where it's safe," Papa said, frowning.

"Actually, I think having Rosie there would be useful." Em tapped her chin. "We'll be able to monitor the suspects for any tell-tale signs of guilt in her presence. And safety won't be a problem—Strathaven will accompany us."

"As will I." The words boomed through the room: they'd been uttered simultaneously by the other husbands.

"Excellent. It's decided then." A smile of satisfaction tucked into Em's cheeks. "With all of us working together, we'll capture the villain in no time."

Chapter Twenty-Nine

T AKING THE ARM he offered, Primrose alighted gracefully from the carriage.

"We're at your club?" Her veil didn't dampen the excitement in her voice. "Is this my surprise?"

Andrew hid a smile. "If I told you, it wouldn't be a surprise, would it?"

Steering her past his guards, he led her through his private entrance at the back of the club. She'd pestered him about her surprise the entirety of the ride over. When that hadn't worked, she'd playfully attempted to seduce it out of him. She'd peppered his face with kisses, her bottom wriggling enticingly in his lap—and she'd done this knowing that a coterie of his men had been right outside, riding along for protection.

Something had definitely changed in her since their lovemaking last night, he mused. Perhaps that mirror had helped her to see how beautiful and sensual she was, peeling away another layer of her inhibitions. He couldn't wait to see what else lay beneath. His little minx was taking to sexual exploration like a duck to water, and anticipation simmered in him as he thought of the games ahead.

"I need to fetch something from my office, and then we'll be off," he told her.

"Off to where?" she said immediately.

"That's for me to know, you impatient wench."

Although she pretended to pout, she took the hand he

held out to her, and they traversed the hidden corridor, sounds of the club filtering through the walls. Past midnight, the festivities were just getting underway.

"I can't stay out too late." She'd pinned up her veil, her eyes luminous in the dimness. "I have plans on the morrow. I'm paying a visit to—"

"Mrs. James and the dowager countess. Yes, I know." He aimed a wicked look at her. "I'll try not to tire you overmuch."

"How did you know about my plans?"

"Kent told me."

"Papa?" She blinked owlishly. "You spoke with him today?"

"Most every day, sunshine. To coordinate your protection."

He stopped, opening the panel that led into his office. As he led her into the room, she was uncommonly quiet. Pensive. He recalled her initial resistance to him contacting her father, his buoyant spirits deflating. He couldn't blame her for wanting to minimize her family's exposure to him. He wondered if she was embarrassed about having an ex-prostitute as her lover, and his gut balled.

"The meetings are brief and address only the plans for your safety," he said in clipped tones. "Your father and I discuss nothing personal. I have no wish for an appointment with him at dawn."

"I trust you." Her voice was quiet as she removed her bonnet and veil, placing her woolen cape over the back of a sofa.

"Then why are you disquieted?" Opening a drawer of his desk, he searched for the key he needed with studied carelessness.

"I'm not disquieted; I'm surprised. Papa didn't mention that he was meeting with you. Actually, I am glad that you and he are getting to know one another."

He gave her a swift look. "Are you?"

"Yes. I imagine the two of you get along. Being so alike."

"You think your *father* and I are alike?" he said incredulously.

Ambrose Kent was a gentleman, one who commanded respect due to his honorable character and pursuit of justice. Andrew was a bastard and a pimp.

"Well, yes." Primrose faced him across the desk, running a gloved finger over the polished edge. "You're both men of honor. Both protective of those you care about." She wrinkled her nose. "And you both like to tell me what to do."

Her words flooded him like sunlight, reaching into his darkest corners and chasing away shadows—ghosts that he hadn't realized still lurked. Out of nowhere, Bartholomew Black's voice emerged. *Every man's got a weakness. Beware o' females, Corbett—they're yours.*

Andrew couldn't deny that he'd been used by women in the past. By Kitty, his customers, even his former employee, Nicoletta, who'd manipulated him as part of her nefarious plot against the Earl of Revelstoke. He had ample reason to be cynical, hardened toward the opposite sex.

Yet with Primrose, he couldn't form any sort of callus over his emotions. With her, he felt everything. She was different from other females: she didn't just take from him... she gave.

Rounding the desk corner, he caught her by the waist.

"The difference is that you like doing what *I* tell you to do," he said. "Admit it."

She looped her arms around his neck. With her dimples peeping out, she looked so adorable that his heart stuttered. "Perhaps I don't mind that dictatorial side of you *too* much."

"Then kiss me," he challenged.

Her lashes fluttered. Then she rose on tiptoe. The soft brush of her mouth set fire to his blood. When she lapped at the seam of his lips like an inquisitive kitten, he let her in. The kiss grew hotter, and, before he knew it, he'd planted her arse on the desk, her skirts ruched in his fist—

A banging pierced his haze of lust.

"Corbett? Are you in there?" Fanny's insistent tones filtered through the door. "I need to speak with you."

With an oath, he set Primrose on her feet and instructed, "Wait here."

He stalked to the door, cracked it open. Fanny stood there, fist raised to knock again.

"I'm busy," he said shortly.

"You've been busy for the past week. We need to talk about the Nursery—"

"What nursery?" Primrose's voice emerged from behind him.

Fanny's gaze darted over his shoulder. "What're you doing here?"

"I'm here with Andrew," Primrose shot back.

Christ. "Fanny, I'll talk to you tomorrow," he said impatiently.

"But I have a new list of items that need to be approved for the Nursery—"

"What *is* this nursery she's talking about?" Primrose demanded.

Before he could answer, Fanny drawled, "A milk-fed miss like yourself wouldn't understand. Then again, there's a lot you don't understand about Corbett here, isn't there?"

"I know him better than you do," Primrose snapped. "You're nothing but his employee. A bumptious old *bawd*."

"Better a bawd who knows how to *really* please a man,"— Fanny's hand slapped onto one out-thrust hip—"than some green chit who thinks lying on her back is all it takes. Really, Corbett, don't you get tired of showing her around the bedchamber by her leading strings?"

"Shut your mouth, Fanny," he growled, "and be on your

way."

The menace in his tone finally sunk in; his employee flounced off.

The minute he closed the door, Primrose rounded on him. "Are you sleeping with her?"

"I've already told you the answer to that," he said curtly.

"*Have* you slept with her?"

"For Christ's sake, no." Striving for patience, he raked a hand through his hair. "I do not have sexual affairs with my employees. Ever."

"What is this nursery, then?"

Seeing the suspicion in her eyes, he realized there'd be no peace until she had her answers. Stubborn chit.

"Although I encourage the use of contraceptive measures in the club, accidents still happen. The Nursery House is a new initiative of mine, a place where wenches can go to deliver their babes safely. Fanny is helping me with the project."

"Oh." Primrose's lashes fanned. "So that is all you and Fanny are doing together—working?"

"Yes. Now I've explained the situation to you, and I expect you to let it alone."

She drew in a breath, and he prepared for further argument.

What he didn't do was brace himself for her to rush pell-mell into him. His torso rocked back as he absorbed the shock of her embrace. Her arms locked around his waist.

"I'm sorry." Her voice was muffled against his waistcoat. "I don't mean to act like a jealous fishwife. I just don't want you wanting anyone but me."

His arms closed around her. "I only want you, Primrose."

She tipped her head back, and he was startled to see the moisture gleaming in her eyes. "Truly?" Her voice hitched. "Even though I'm petty and shallow and act without thinking?"

"Sweetheart, you're not petty or shallow, but you do have to learn to trust me."

"I *do* trust you." Vulnerability shadowed her fine features. "I just don't understand why you like *me*. When you're so handsome and worldly and,"—her bottom lip caught beneath her teeth—"you could have someone far more experienced. Who knows how to please you."

That was what she believed? Her thinking mystified him. At the same time, his heart tumbled helplessly, bruising his chest with tenderness.

"You please me, love." He tucked a curl behind her ear. "More than anyone I've been with."

"Even if I'm a… green chit in the bedchamber?" Her gaze searched his.

"I like that you're inexperienced," he said quietly, "that I'm the only one who has the privilege of making love to you. I get to explore your desires with you. Me—and no one else. I've never had that before, never felt possessive over anyone before you." He trailed his thumbs down her neck, loving her shiver of awareness, loving everything that she gave him. "You belong to me completely, Primrose, and that is the finest gift any woman has ever given me."

"I'm so glad." Her eyes shimmered. "Because you have given me so much."

He was tempted to kiss her again. But if he started, he wouldn't want to stop—and he didn't want to spoil what he had planned for her.

"Since that's settled," he murmured, "let's get to your surprise, shall we?"

She blinked, as if she'd forgotten all about it. Then she wrinkled her nose. "You mean that delightful exchange with Fanny wasn't it?"

"Minx. You're going to enjoy what I have planned far more." He took her hand, his blood quickening. "We both are."

Rosie's hand trembled in Andrew's large one as they ascended a private stairway to the top of the club. Her excitement mounted with each step, her nipples puckering against the silk robe he'd provided for her. She was nude beneath the fine gold fabric embroidered with peonies, as was he beneath his black robe, a silver dragon breathing fire across his broad back. The fact that they were traipsing through a pleasure house practically naked was undoubtedly wanton—and yet there was something strangely right about it too.

She couldn't quite put her finger on it, but it had to do with having her hand in his. With seeking out adventure together. With Andrew by her side, she felt brave and strong, like an explorer ready to chart a new world.

They arrived at the top of the steps, where a closed door waited.

Andrew unlocked it. "Ladies first," he murmured.

She stepped inside, her eyes widening at the sumptuous chamber, her slippers sinking into the thick ruby Aubusson. The walls were papered in soft gold silk, a gilt and crystal chandelier showering sparkles through the intimate dimness. A large tester bed occupied the back of the room, a wide red divan the front. Oddly positioned, the divan faced a blank wall.

Andrew came up behind her. His warm breath caressed her ear. "Like it?"

Desire tremored through her. "It's very luxurious," she managed.

He led her over to the divan, sitting first and pulling her onto his lap. With only the thin silk between them, the granite ridge of his cock pressed against her, making her squirm.

A smile lurked in his eyes. "One of these days, love, I'll teach you the pleasures of waiting."

"I *have* been patient. And I adore my surprise," she said, playing with the lapel of his robe, "so can't we *please* get on with things?"

"Sweetheart, you haven't even seen your surprise."

She canted her head. "I haven't?"

He reached over to the wall, sliding open a panel that had been camouflaged by the pattern of the wallpaper. A pair of viewing holes appeared, and the sudden swell of sound caused goose-pimples to prickle over Rosie's skin.

"Here's your surprise. Go on," he said huskily. "Have a look."

Leaning forward, she did.

Her eyes widened at the sight of men and women—a dozen, maybe more—frolicking inside a circular arena decorated in a style reminiscent of the Near East. Blue arabesque tiles covered the walls, gauzy material flowing in the white plaster archways. Thick rugs and large jewel-colored cushions covered the floor, upon which people were engaging in astonishing sexual acts.

Rosie's gaze landed on a blonde, whose breasts bounced as she gyrated *atop* a man reclined on pillows. Her eyes migrated over to a redhead kneeling in front of another male. His scarlet member pointed at her like a lance, and she wrapped her hand around it, dragging her fist up and down…

Nearby, a dark-haired fellow was rutting a brunette, who was positioned on her hands and knees—like a farmyard animal! When a blond man approached, she winked at him… then took his cock *in her mouth*. Her voluptuous body jiggled as she was jousted between her partners, one at each end…

Reeling at the vibrant debauchery, Rosie turned to Andrew. His eyes had a wicked, seductive gleam. Her breasts tingled, her pussy moistening in a hot rush.

Chapter Thirty

A$_{\text{S}}$ THE SOUNDS of boisterous fucking filled the room, Andrew reflected that he was right about his naughty minx. She liked to watch.

He'd observed her titillated response the last time she was at his club, when he'd mentioned the viewing holes. Then there'd been her delightfully wanton response to the looking glass above her bed. Thus, he'd thought to give her the ultimate voyeuristic experience: observing the play in the Sultan's Seraglio.

As she perched on his lap, her cheeks were flushed, her tits surging, the tight tips visible beneath the gold silk. Her arousal was a potent aphrodisiac. Against her arse, his prick was steel-hard and throbbing with a heartbeat of its own.

"Do they know they're being observed?" she whispered.

"Yes. It's part of the allure." He nuzzled her ear, feeling her shiver all the way in his bollocks. "Those who seek out the Sultan's Seraglio enjoy being watched during sex. And for those who want to only observe, there are five other private viewing rooms like this one."

"But what we're doing—isn't it terribly wicked?" She bit her lip.

"No rules but what we make, remember? You're safe to explore your desires with me." He caressed her shoulder. "I want to know what arouses you. I want *you* to know what arouses you."

Her gaze veered back to the viewing hole, and he saw what

caught her attention: Jilly, one of his lustiest and most sought-after wenches, was entertaining two of the customers simultaneously. The brunette's skills were on full display as she took a ramming from the rear while performing fellatio with genuine enthusiasm.

Primrose suddenly tensed, and Andrew's gaze shot to her face. Seeing her lips tremble, he wondered if he'd made a miscalculation. What went on in the orgy room was as common as bread and butter for him—but for her? While naturally sensual, she was recently a virgin and a well-bred one at that. Modesty was as ingrained in her as depravity was in him.

He silently cursed himself for his stupidity. For forgetting the differences between the two of them—for taking her too far into the darkness of his world. As an apology surfaced on his lips, she suddenly ducked her head, tucking it into the crook of his neck.

Her words were whisper-soft against his throat. "I find watching quite... titillating."

That she had the courage to own her desires humbled him. And the fact that she trusted him—*Christ*, it was a feeling like no other. Pride expanded his chest.

"It's a natural reaction, love." He stroked her cheek. "And you're a passionate woman."

"I feel all awash," she said in a soft rush.

She was trembling with need, with the arousal that she hadn't yet learned to control.

Tenderness and lust surged through him. "I'll take care of you. Trust me, sweetheart..."

He claimed her mouth, drinking in her sweetness while he untied her robe, pushing the silk off her shoulders. He cupped her breast, pinching the bold tip, and she moaned against his lips. Hell, they'd hardly begun, and she was about to go off like a Roman candle. Reaching between her thighs, he groaned at her lushness. He rubbed the heel of his palm against her pearl and drove two fingers into her tight sheath—and that was all it took.

Her cry of release made his cock jerk, pre-spend dampening the tip. He growled with pleasure as her cunny milked his fingers. When she was done, he brought his hand to his mouth, and, holding her passion-dazed eyes, licked her honey from his fingers.

"Goddamn, you're sweet," he said thickly.

Cheeks pink, she said, "But I… it was over so quickly."

"It's not over." He took her mouth, sharing her delectable flavor with her, smiling when she quivered. "Sunshine, we're just beginning."

"Oh, I can't. Not again."

Except for her pout, Primrose made the perfect Lady Godiva, he thought. In fact, he wanted to have her immortalized in paint, a portrait for his eyes only. He wanted to view Primrose this way whenever he wished: sitting astride him, her supple curves playing peek-a-boo through the shining curtain of her hair, her milky skin flushed and dewy from their lovemaking.

After her first incandescent climax, he'd taken her on the divan, first on her back and then, when she seemed ready for something more adventurous, he'd positioned her on all fours. She'd gotten over her shock quickly, purring when he entered her from behind. Her snug, eager pussy had tested the limits of his endurance. Through sheer force of will, he'd made sure that she came again before he did. And while he recovered, he'd fingered and licked her until she creamed upon his tongue once more.

Thus, he had ample evidence to support the fact that not

only could Primrose come again, she *would*. And she was so full of passion that it wouldn't take much. Christ, she was his match in every way—and he was one lucky bastard.

Now they were on the bed, he sitting against the headboard, she atop him.

"You can," he told her.

To prove his point, he fisted his cock, running the burgeoned head against her damp and swollen petals until she sighed. Quickly donning a fresh French letter, he fitted his prick to her hole, yanking her down as he thrust up. They both moaned. Gripping her soft hips, he guided her up and down on his rod, her quim flowering around him, slathering him with slick honey.

"It's too much," she gasped.

"Ride me. You saw how it's done." Deliberately, he reminded her of what she'd glimpsed through the viewing hole... and groaned when his ploy worked, her pussy constricting helplessly. "Goddamn, you're milking me like a *fist*."

"That feels so... I can't..." Panting, she strained to reach her summit.

He grabbed one of her hands, brought it to where their bodies joined.

"Rub your pearl, love." He guided the motion with their twined fingers. "Make it nice and slick while you ride me."

Whimpering, she did as he instructed, and, God, she was stunning. Her jade gaze swirling with gold, her slim fingers diddling herself as she impaled herself on his cock, she was desire incarnate. He couldn't take his eyes off of her. She absorbed him completely, like no one else ever had or would. When she took him into her body, she took all of him—his cock, his mind... his heart.

Raw need pumped through him, pushing a spurt of pre-seed into the sheath. In that instant, he wanted to tear the bloody thing off, to have nothing between him and Primrose, to take her and take her until they came together. Until she was plowed full of his seed, dripping with it. Gritting his teeth, he held onto his sanity. He palmed her shoulder blades, pulling her toward him, altering the angle so that his cock drilled against her pearl.

Her entire body tautened... and then—*bloody fuck*. Her cunny convulsed around him, lightning-quick spasms that sucked the seed from his balls, forcing it up his shaft. He roared in ecstasy, his hips bucking as he shot stream after stream of hot spend into the sheep-gut barrier.

She collapsed atop him, boneless as a kitten. He held her close, his fingers tangling in her silken tresses. Unspoken words pounded in his heart, and he smothered them against her lips.

"Andrew, are you awake?" Rosie whispered.

"Hmm." His voice rumbled beneath her ear; he definitely sounded drowsy.

After the exertions of the evening, she probably ought to let him rest. Cuddled atop his chest, watching the flickering fire in the hearth, she basked in the aftermath. Being with Andrew innervated her—made her feel content and limitless at the same time.

She rubbed her cheek against him, enjoying the light scratch of chest hair over hard, warm muscle. "Thank you for showing me this chamber."

"Hmm hmm."

"And for showing me that there's nothing wrong with me or my desires."

His hand ran lightly over her hair. "You're a naturally sensual woman, Primrose—everything a man could desire.

Why would you think there's anything wrong with you?"

In her present relaxed state, it was so easy to share with him. "Because of the gossip about me. According to the *ton*, I'm a trollop."

"The *ton* is made up of idiots and hypocrites."

"Even if I'm not a trollop, I *am* a bastard. Even worse than that, I was…" She caught herself, just barely, a frisson of fear sizzling through her. Heavens, had she been about to blurt out a thought she hadn't even allowed herself to think? Since Mama's ugly revelation, she'd blocked the matter from her mind; she hadn't permitted herself to consciously dwell upon it.

"What, love?" His hand continued its soothing stroke. "You can tell me."

Could she? Could she trust him with the vile reality?

He gave her hair a gentle tug, and she lifted her head to meet his eyes.

"Tell me," he said.

"Mama told me why Coyner took me as his ward." The words tumbled from her lips. "It wasn't because he wanted a daughter. He wanted… he wanted me for…"

She couldn't make herself finish. Even if she could, she wouldn't have been able to—for Andrew's arms had tightened like steel bands around her, crushing her against him.

"It's not your fault." His voice vibrated with suppressed fury. "Whatever happened, it's not your fault."

"Nothing happened. According to Mama, Coyner meant to eventually make me his child bride, but she and Papa rescued me before that. Coyner died fighting Papa—died because he refused to let me go." Her cheek pressed against Andrew's hammering heart, Rosie fought to unearth the rest. "I do have memories of that time, and I don't remember Coyner ever… harming me. In any way."

She was rolled over. Made to look into Andrew's intense

gaze.

"Then what distresses you?" he said.

She inhaled deeply. "Even though he didn't abuse me in any way, the fact that he *meant* to…" Nausea hit the back of her throat, but Andrew's steadiness urged her on. Gave her the strength to untangle the jumbled skeins of her thoughts and feelings.

"I remember how he cossetted me, called me his *Little Flower*. When I pleased him, he would buy me anything I wanted." Her insides roiled. "So I tried to please him, to be his good girl, and for what? Some frock, some stupid doll. Remembering what I did,"—she swallowed against the rising bile—"*disgusts* me."

Until that moment, she hadn't realized just how much. How dirty and unclean the truth made her feel. Before Mama's revelation, she'd just been a bastard—now she was a bastard who'd been bought to satisfy a lecher's perversions. No wonder the *ton* rejected her. They'd sensed that she was damaged goods.

"You were just a girl. You didn't know Coyner's true intentions. It was only natural that you should want to gain your guardian's approval."

"But the fact that I was willing to sing him a song to get a music box, dance for him for a new pair of slippers," she said bitterly, "that makes me no better than a…"

She trailed off, suddenly realizing what she'd been about to say. And to whom.

"Whore?" Andrew's tone was free of inflection.

"That was thoughtless of me," she said in a small voice. "I'm sorry."

"Don't be sorry. I'm not."

Despite her tumultuous state, questions deluged her. She'd been curious about his past, of course, but she'd never felt quite right asking about it. The truth was they'd spent most of the time focusing on *her* troubles. Andrew's primary concern was always her welfare and, as a consequence, she realized, he talked very little about his own.

He was so in command of himself, so self-possessed that it seemed he had no need to confide in another. Nonetheless, *she* wanted to know him. To give him the same attention and care he'd shown her, even if he didn't need it.

"You're not sorry that you... sold your, um, services for money?"

"I used my body and my mind to survive," he said flatly. "There's no shame in that."

As she looked up at his stark, beautiful face, her throat clenched. He was right, of course. His self-acceptance, his ability to see past what others might think of him, humbled her. Heightened her desire to understand this strong, tender, and complex man who was her lover.

"No, there isn't," she agreed. "But how did you end up in that trade?"

He studied her a moment before answering. "One could say I carried on the family tradition. Although my mother was an actress, her talent lay more in the bedchamber than on the boards. She began a career as a courtesan, and I was the result of it."

Recalling what her mama had said about Andrew's parentage, she said tentatively, "Is it true that you have royal blood?" At his startled look, she mumbled, "Mama told me."

"Ah. The old rumors." His lips twisted. "Yes, it's possible. My mother was the Prince Regent's mistress for a brief time, but neither of them were the faithful sort. By the time she realized she was with child, Prinny had already lost interest in her. So she was left pregnant and without resources to care for herself or her unborn bastard."

"How dreadful," Rosie whispered.

"My mother nearly died bringing me into the world, but

somehow she survived. She continued selling her wares to support the two of us. By the time I was eight, drink had taken over her life,"—a muscle shifted in his cheek—"and, one by one, she lost her money, beauty, and health."

His emotionless recounting of his childhood chilled Rosie—made her want to gather him in her arms and hold him tight. Something in his expression warned her not to.

Swallowing, she said, "You were so young. How did you survive?"

"I had quick and sticky fingers, so I got us by. When I turned fourteen, my mother introduced me to a bawd who catered to female clientele."

Rosie couldn't stop herself from recoiling. "Your mother sold you into prostitution?"

"She didn't sell me. It was my choice." A banked fire flared in his eyes. "I wanted to put food on our table, to have a roof over our heads, and fucking was an easier way to do it than thieving or running with cutthroats."

"But you were only fourteen!"

Incredibly, his broad shoulders flexed in a shrug. "I was large for my age. The bawd taught me the essentials of pleasing a woman, and anything she left out, I figured out quickly on my own. Don't make my life into a Cheltenham Tragedy. The last thing I want or need is your pity."

The steely edge in his voice told her that he meant it.

Then another thought hit her. "Was this bawd Kitty Barnes?"

"No, I met her a year later."

By the way his eyes shuttered, she could tell that he wouldn't say more about it. And a part of her didn't want to know. Wanted to keep that ugliness buried where it belonged.

"What happened to your mama?" she ventured.

"She died when I was sixteen."

"Did you forgive her?"

"For what?"

"Um, for all of it?" She blinked at him. "Turning to drink. Depending on you to take care of her." *Forcing you to make a choice no child should have to make.* "Weren't you angry at her?"

"None of it was her fault," came his startling reply. "She was a victim of her circumstance, and she did the best she could with what she had. She taught me to do the same. So, no, I wasn't angry at her. I loved her."

Listening to his matter-of-fact accounting, Rosie felt a shift inside her. An undertow of understanding that challenged her perceptions. For so long, she'd raged at being a victim: of her birth, of Draven, of Coyner... even of the *ton*. Life had been unfair to her—yet how much worse had things been for Andrew?

Despite that, he didn't rail at fate. He didn't wallow in self-pity. He didn't act out in reckless desperation.

No, *he* had loved and taken care of the mama who'd failed him. He'd defied all odds to become one of the most successful businessmen in all of London. And he'd gone to extraordinary lengths to protect Rosie.

Her throat swelled. She needed time to sort the chaotic thoughts in her head, the lessons to be gleaned by new insights. But she did know one thing.

She smoothed a bronze lock from his forehead. "You're a strong man, Andrew Corbett—and a good one. I'm so lucky that you're my lover."

His gaze heated. "I'm the lucky one, sweetheart."

"Thank you for tonight." She smiled tremulously at him. "For trusting me with the truth and being honest with me. For teaching me to be honest with myself."

He responded with a kiss. One simmering with passion and deep undercurrents of emotion. By the time he raised his head, she was panting for him.

"Again?" he murmured, his thumb tracing the slope of her

cheekbone.

Her pussy fluttered. As did her heart. How she *craved* this man.

"Yes, please," she whispered.

A corner of his mouth kicked up. "You're going to kill me, you know."

"Can you think of a better way to greet the hereafter?" With great daring, she ran her hands over the bulging muscles of his shoulders, down the marble-hard ridges of his backside and was rewarded by the fierce rise of his erection against her thigh.

"By all means," he said huskily, "let us find *le petit mort* together."

Chapter Thirty-One

Rosie awoke the next morning to find herself alone. After the decadent night of lovemaking, Andrew had escorted her home in the wee hours, carried her to her bedchamber, and tucked her into bed. She had immediately fallen into a deep sleep and wasn't sure if he'd stayed. Rolling over to see if she could sniff out his delicious scent on the sheets, she saw a note and box on the pillow next to hers. Sitting up, she unfolded the paper.

Sunshine (the note read),
I'm sorry I couldn't stay. In lieu, I've left you a small memento. I hope you will think of me, as my thoughts will undoubtedly be of you. Until tonight. —A.

Dreamily, Rosie pressed the letter to her bosom. Andrew made her feel like the most special lady in all the world. She picked up the blue velvet box, wondering what he'd gotten her this time. She smiled to herself. Thus far, his unconventional gifts had included gingerbread and a pistol; what would he surprise her with now?

She lifted the lid—and her breath lodged in her throat. *Goodness.*

The necklace was the most exquisite she'd ever seen. Cast in white gold, it took the shape of flowing vines and delicate leaves, all of it encrusted with brilliant diamonds. The centerpiece was a cluster of blooming flowers, their shape

unmistakably those of primroses. Three large diamonds, over
a carat each, were suspended from the blossoms like sparkling
dewdrops.

When her lover had a mind to give a gift, he *truly* gave a
gift. She ran a fingertip over the stunning piece; she couldn't
wait for her period of mourning to be over so that she could
wear it.

As much as she wanted to stay in bed and gawk over the
necklace, she had a busy day ahead of her. She glanced at the
bedside clock—and gave a little shriek. Heavens, she only had
two hours to get ready for the meeting with Lady Charlotte!
She hurtled out of bed, ringing for Odette.

Thanks to her maid's efficiency, she was suitably groomed
by the time Emma came to pick her up. Her hair was parted
in the middle, curls upswept, a few left to frame her face. She'd
worn a stylish black taffeta with a V-shaped neckline, leg-o'-
mutton sleeves, and full skirts.

Rosie and her entourage soon arrived at the dowager's
house, a modest abode on the fringes of Mayfair. She waited
patiently as her sisters negotiated with their husbands. The
men wanted to escort them inside; the ladies said a male
presence would hamper the interview (Rosie had to agree).
Finally, after whispered back-and-forth negotiations, the men
agreed to wait outside on one condition: if their wives didn't
emerge in an hour, they would personally go in and *carry* them
out.

"Let's hurry," Emma muttered, casting a backward glance
at her large spouse, who stood next to the carriage with his
arms crossed, his pale green gaze tracking her every move. "I
wouldn't put it past His Grace to carry out his troglodytic
threat."

Her sisters looked back at *their* looming husbands, and all
of them hastened to the front door.

Once inside, they were ushered by an ancient butler into

a sitting room. The space was dated, the dark and faded brocade fashionable several decades ago. Flanked by the Misses Fossey, the dowager countess came over to greet them. In the background, Mrs. James rose but kept her distance.

Introductions and greetings were exchanged.

"Please make yourselves comfortable." The dowager waved them toward the seating area. "And do call me Charlotte: we are family after all. Indeed, the girls and I had planned to call upon you, Lady Daltry,"—she cast a flustered glance at Rosie—"but we did not wish to intrude upon your privacy."

Looking into Lady Charlotte's plump, pleasant features, framed by silver curls and a lace cap, Rosie could not imagine that this mother hen would want to harm her.

So she smiled and said, "You are welcome to visit any time, Lady Charlotte. And please call me Rosie."

"Rosie, then." Clearly relieved, Lady Charlotte smiled back at her.

"It is a pleasure to see you again," Miss Sybil ventured shyly from beside her aunt.

"And you as well," Rosie said warmly.

Sybil flushed to the roots of her dull blonde hair. Rosie thought the girl could be pretty if she chose more flattering clothes (the loose-fitting grey gown did nothing for the other's figure) and a more stylish coiffure than the scraped-back topknot. As Rosie was wondering how she might subtly dispense some fashion advice, Sybil's younger sister pushed forward.

"May I say how much I adore your ensemble, Rosie?" Miss Eloisa gushed. "Your widow's weeds put the most fashionable gowns to shame. The work of Madame Rousseau, I believe?"

"Why, yes, it is." Although Rosie was surprised by the turnabout in Miss Eloisa's manner, she wasn't about to look a gift horse in the mouth.

"Madame is a favorite of mine as well." Eloisa linked arms with her, drawing her toward the sitting area. "You must sit by me for I'm certain we have *so* much in common to discuss."

The countess and Miss Sybil followed behind, as did Emma and the clan.

When everyone was settled and tea had been poured, Mrs. James spoke up.

"As charming as this is," she said—truly, she'd be an attractive woman if not for her sneer, as unsightly as a mustache would be on her face—"I'd prefer we get to the point. Why was I summoned here today?"

"Now, Antonia, you were not *summoned*," Lady Charlotte said hastily. "The duchess merely wrote that she hoped to meet with all the ladies in our family during her visit today."

"I don't have your appetite for niceties," Mrs. James retorted. "I call a spade a spade."

"I, too, prefer directness," Emma said. "The truth is, we are here on an urgent matter."

"Oh?" Lady Charlotte's forehead pleated beneath her frilly lace cap.

"A week ago, someone tried to murder Rosie."

At Emma's declaration, Rosie observed the reactions of her new relatives. Papa had warned Mr. Theale and Mr. James not to speak of the matter for their own good, and apparently the men had taken his caution to heart. The ladies appeared shocked by the news. The dowager and Miss Eloisa gasped, Miss Sybil's hand flew to her mouth, and Mrs. James' face drained of color.

"Goodness," Lady Charlotte whispered. "You are unharmed, I hope?"

Having rehearsed the story with her papa, Rosie knew what to say. "I was fortunate that my driver chased off the attacker."

"How brave you are!" Miss Eloisa's sapphire eyes were

unblinkingly wide. "I'm certain I wouldn't have half your composure under such circumstances."

"She wouldn't need the composure if she'd practiced more caution." Recovering from her shock, Mrs. James said with cold hauteur, "A lady has no business traipsing about at night. She's lucky the groom chased the shooter away."

"Hold up." This came from Violet, whose tawny gaze had honed in upon Mrs. James' face. "How did you know this happened at night? No one has mentioned when the attack occurred."

Tell-tale red appeared on Mrs. James' sharp cheekbones. "I… I just assumed… that is, don't most attacks happen in the evening?"

"And how did you know I was shot at?" Rosie said. "I didn't specify the method of attack."

Mrs. James' tongue touched her upper lip. "I just thought that cutthroats used firearms…"

"I find the accuracy of your assumptions fascinating," Emma said.

Drawing herself up, Mrs. James glared at the room at large. "Are you accusing *me* of trying to harm Lady Daltry?"

"No, ma'am," Thea said in her gentle yet resolute way, "but in order to protect Rosie, we must talk to all those who would benefit from her death."

"Well, I *never*." Mrs. James shot up, the jet beads on her bodice quivering. "I refuse to stay and be subjected to these insults!"

"We are merely discussing facts." Emma's eyes had a shrewd gleam. "If you know about the attack from another source—for instance, your stepson, who my brother has also interviewed—then you need only say so. While my brother asked Mr. James to keep the details private, it wouldn't be a crime if your stepson shared them with you."

"Why would Alastair share a private matter with me?"

Mrs. James' gaze shifted left and right. "As I said, my assumptions were guesses, nothing more. I had nothing to do with the attack on Lady Daltry. Good day."

She swept out, leaving the room in silence.

"Well, *that* was awkward." Miss Eloisa tittered. "The lady doth protest, as they say. You don't suppose Aunt Antonia is involved in any way?"

"Hush, Eloisa," Lady Charlotte said, a handkerchief knotted in her hands. "Now is not the time for your wit. This is a serious matter, and we must put our heads together to help Rosie."

"But, Aunt Charlotte... aren't we suspects too?" Miss Sybil said timorously.

"Oh, dear." The dowager's gaze went to Rosie. "I suppose you are right."

Rosie didn't want to lose the newly won goodwill. Besides, now that the ladies had warmed toward her, she thought they were rather nice. And they were her new relations, after all.

She glanced at Em, who lifted her chin slightly as if to say, *We'll follow your lead.*

Rosie made her decision. "We mean no insult, Lady Charlotte. We're merely trying to get to the bottom of this situation."

"I quite understand," the dowager said. "And I wish to help."

"In that case, can you think of anything that might point us to a particular suspect?"

Lady Charlotte clenched her handkerchief, her expression torn.

"I'll say it since no one else will. Peter has the most to gain," Eloisa declared. "He's forever short of funds, and now with the estate on his hands, he's sunk unless he gets the inheritance."

"That's unfair," Sybil protested. "Peter is no murderer.

He's a kind and gentle man."

"You're far too charitable." Snorting, Eloisa turned to Rosie. "Peter has cried on all of our shoulders, and Sybil's the only one who feels sorry for him. Then again, she's a soft touch for hopeless cases."

Her older sister flushed. "I am not."

"All your life, you've collected strays. Remember our old butler? You were forever making those herbal poultices for his bad leg." Eloisa rolled her eyes. "Then there's your spinster friend Miss What's-Her-Name, who constantly summons you to her deathbed. Peter is more of the same."

"He is *not*." Sybil bit her lip. "Besides, if anyone needs money, it's Alastair. Remember how he showed up that time, deep in his cups, demanding that Aunt Charlotte lend him funds?"

"Girls, that is enough," the dowager said. "These are members of our family you're casting aspersions at. Family is everything; haven't I taught you that?"

Sybil looked chastened, Eloisa sulky.

Sensing that the interview had come to an end, Rosie didn't want to push her luck.

"Thank you for your time." On impulse, she added, "And on the topic of family, if I can be of assistance in any way, please let me know. I'm certain my late husband would want his generosity to be shared with his kin."

That was a lie, of course. Just because Daltry had been a tight-fisted miser with his relatives, however, didn't mean that *she* had to be.

The lines on Lady Charlotte's face eased. Her eyes warmed. "How kind of you. Your support is appreciated, my dear."

"And if there's anything that *we* can do for you," Miss Eloisa chimed in, "please let us know."

"Anything at all," Miss Sybil said diffidently.

It was an opening that Rosie hadn't expected. Yet the three seemed in earnest, and she knew she couldn't let the opportunity pass her by.

"Since you asked," she said with thudding hope, "I do have a favor to ask."

Chapter Thirty-Two

TWO NIGHTS LATER, Andrew found himself in the not altogether comfortable position of riding in a carriage with his lover's father and uncle, both of whom were armed to the gills. He'd just arrived at Kent's office for a briefing when the news arrived that the mudlarks had located the shooter's hideout. He'd insisted on accompanying the mission as had Harry Kent, who'd happened to be at his brother's office. Now Kent's partners were in a carriage behind them, their small caravan winding through the dark, twisting streets of St. Giles.

The older Kent looked out one window, his gloved fingers drumming on his knee whilst the younger looked out the other. Conversation during the ride had been stilted. The one thing Andrew had in common with the other two— Primrose—was a topic he didn't want to delve too deeply into. For reasons he couldn't quite fathom, the Kents were tolerating his presence in Primrose's life, and he didn't want to push his luck.

Andrew knew Primrose deserved better than him; he also knew that every moment they spent together made it more difficult for him to contemplate ever letting her go. With their every encounter, he discovered more to adore: her passion, theatrics… even the fact that she could be, on occasion, a wee bit daft. And, Christ, when she opened to him like a flower, exposing her vulnerable core—there wasn't anything he wouldn't do for her.

He loved every enchanting iota of who she was.

He knew his feelings but hadn't shared them with her.
The time wasn't right. There was mayhem and murder to deal
with and, besides, she'd been clear that she wanted an affair
with no strings attached. Especially now, when her efforts to
gain social approval were bearing fruit.

In bed last night, she'd told him about her success with
Lady Charlotte. He wasn't surprised; Primrose could charm
birds from their leafy perches if she wished. In this instance,
she'd convinced the respected dowager and her charges to put
in a good word for her in the right circles. Her new relations
had done more than that: they'd sung her praises. Now
tongues were wagging about Primrose's kindness to her new
family and her grace in the face of tragedy.

"I'm on the path to respectability once more!" Primrose
had said happily.

He was glad for her—glad that she was finally getting
what she wanted. But it made him even more reticent to
declare his love. The last thing he wanted was to pressure or
burden her with the feelings he had no right to have.

Thus, he forced himself to take their affair day by day, to
enjoy every moment that she was his—and it wasn't difficult.
His nights had become an orgy of pleasure. She, a novice, was
teaching *him* about desire. Her natural sensuality astounded
and entranced him, and she was growing bolder by the
minute.

Last night, when she'd thanked him prettily for the
diamond necklace, her hands had wandered farther and
farther south. When her fingers had circled his cock, his
breath had hissed through his teeth. It had been her first
attempt at frigging him, and the way she'd explored his
erection with feather-light caresses had nearly driven him out
of his mind...

With a touch—hell, a *smile*—she brought him more
pleasure than any of his previous lovers had. She was showing

him that sex could be more than a physical exchange. His gut knotted as he thought of Kitty, of the years he'd spent tangled in her web. It shamed him more than ever that he'd once mistaken his feelings toward her for love.

Love didn't take without giving. Love didn't leave you feeling dirty and used.

Love didn't make a whore of you.

It had taken him a long time—too long—to understand this. He couldn't bring himself to tell Primrose about his stupidity. His weakness. He'd broken things off with Kitty too many times to count, and yet she would turn up like a bad penny after months or even years and somehow worm her way back into his bed. She'd never stayed long, only until she'd gotten whatever it was that she'd wanted. Money, usually.

It sickened him to think of how he'd allowed himself to be used. He almost wished that it had just been about the sex, which had been depraved yet never satisfying. But his addiction to Kitty had been more insidious: she'd treated him like a whore, and he'd believed that he deserved it.

He'd finally come to his senses two years ago—and Primrose had played a part in that, too. Around that time, her plight had come to his attention, and he'd begun to keep a watch on her from afar. He couldn't explain it exactly, but witnessing her spirited struggle to overcome her origins had triggered a shift in him. Primrose's bright determination had made him long to step out of the darkness. He'd ended his relationship with Kitty for good.

Was it any wonder that he didn't want to expose this ugliness to Primrose? Guilt churning, he told himself that it was for the best to protect her from the darkness that Kitty had brought into both their lives. His gut clenched as he recalled Primrose's revelations about Coyner—he hadn't known the truth of her history until she'd told him.

He'd been aware that Primrose was reunited with her

mama at age eight, but the circumstances surrounding that reunion had been shadowed in secrecy. When Kitty had re-entered his life sometime after that, she'd said that she'd dealt with a solicitor, had never known the identity of the man she'd sold Primrose to—only that he was some upstanding gent who'd promised to treat the girl like his own.

I did right by Primrose, Kitty had claimed.

Andrew hadn't pressed her for details; a part of him hadn't wanted to know. All that had mattered was that Primrose was back in the loving bosom of her family, and, by all accounts, a happy, carefree child.

Hearing from Primrose about this bastard Coyner and his vile plans... it had made Andrew want to punch something. Himself, for starters. As relieved as he was that nothing had happened to her, he hated that he'd failed her. Hated that he'd allowed her to be exposed to such risk.

"We're almost there."

Kent's words refocused him. Looking out the window, he saw they were deep in the heart of the rookery, on a street crammed with flash houses, taverns, and pawnshops. Gangs of ruffians eyed their passing carriage, spitting on the ground.

"I cannot wait to get my hands on the bastard who shot at Rosie," Harry said grimly.

The words echoed Andrew's own thoughts. He was surprised to see a bloodthirsty gleam behind the other's spectacles. Apparently a vein of ferocity ran beneath that scholarly mien.

Maybe he and Harry had more in common than he realized.

"You'll have to get in queue," Andrew said.

Harry looked at him—and grinned.

"Let's keep the bloodshed to a minimum, shall we?" Kent muttered as the carriage rolled to a stop. "Although, from the looks of it, there may be plenty to go around."

Vaulting from the carriage, Andrew could see what the other meant. A pack of brutes milled in front of their destination, a decrepit tenement. At a glance, he counted a dozen men.

"Welcoming party, I see." The comment came from McLeod, who along with Lugo and three additional guards, had joined them from the other carriage.

"Twelve to our eight," was Lugo's laconic reply.

"I like those odds," Andrew said.

The partners looked at him—and grinned.

Shaking his head, Kent led their group toward the tenement. They hadn't made it within ten feet of the entrance when a hulking, whiskered fellow in the rough-woven uniform of the stews blocked their path.

"Wot's yer business 'ere, eh?" he demanded.

"We're here to see someone," Kent said calmly. "Step aside, if you please."

"Ye 'ear that? The guv's 'ere to *see* someone." Turning to his snickering companions, the man said, "Any o' ye expectin' such fine company?"

"Not me," a gap-toothed fellow called out. "Already 'ad me tea wif the King yesterday."

More guffaws came from the group.

"Step aside," Kent repeated. "I will not ask again."

"And I'll not take orders on me turf from some nob." A knife flashed in the leader's grip. "Be gone, or I'll gut ye like a fish."

When Kent didn't budge, the brute charged. The investigator moved quickly for a man of his size, neatly sidestepping his attacker at the same time grabbing hold of the other's arm, wrenching away the weapon with efficient force. The man yowled with pain, his knife clattering to the stones.

Pandemonium erupted.

A cutthroat came at Andrew, swinging for his head. He

ducked the blow and went in low, plowing his fists into the
other's gut. The other staggered back a few steps, then came
again. Andrew feigned to the right, catching his attacker off
balance and landing a right hook to the jaw. Bone cracked
against bone, the impact searing down Andrew's arm. The
other collapsed to the ground in a heap.

His blood fired up, Andrew took stock of the situation:
Lugo and McLeod were fighting in tandem, fallen cutthroats
piling around them. Kent and the guards were also holding
their own. He spotted Harry being circled by three villains.
As he sprinted over, he saw Harry's powerful hook and jab
combination, and his brows rose.

Andrew grabbed the scruff of one of Harry's foes, plowing
a fist into the bastard's face. He threw the moaning man to the
ground and went to Harry's side.

"You're monopolizing the action, Kent," he said.

Harry swiped at a bleeding cut on his cheek. "There's
plenty to go around."

More cutthroats had joined the fray, five of them forming
a ring around Andrew and Harry.

Anticipation simmered in Andrew's veins. "Excellent."

The ne'er-do-wells rushed all at once. Back to back,
Andrew and Harry fought them off. Andrew traded punches
with one burly cutthroat, at the last instant dodging the
other's blow—which swerved into the jaw of another villain,
who groaned, crumpling to the ground. Andrew defeated his
remaining opponent with well-aimed jabs to the gut. Pivoting,
he saw that Harry had taken care of two more of the bounders.
The remaining one stared at Andrew... and then turned and
ran, his tail between his legs.

Kent jogged up, followed by his partners.

"Let's find that shooter before we have to take on the
whole damned rookery." From his greatcoat, he produced
whistles and passed them out to each man. "There are four

floors to the tenement, so we'll split up in pairs and each take one. If you find our suspect, sound the alarm."

Andrew and Harry were assigned the ground floor. Inside, the building was even more dilapidated than the exterior. The cesspit of human misery felt eerily familiar to the dwellings of Andrew's childhood. He'd lived in more than his share of such places where sewage festered in the open and vermin invaded every crevice. Wailing babes and shouting adults sounded through the paper-thin walls.

Andrew caught a movement up ahead: at the end of the corridor, a woman stood against the wall, her skirts raised, a man rutting between her legs.

Her face was turned to the side as her customer took his pleasure, grunting, and even from a distance, Andrew could see her flat expression. It knotted his insides. Reminded him too keenly of his own mother and the resignation that had led her to drink away her cares... and her life.

Until Primrose had asked about his mother, he'd never spoken of her. It had been strange bringing those memories into the light. Strange... but not unwelcome.

"I count at least twenty doors, so we'd best start knocking," Harry said.

"Wait." Andrew saw that the whore had finished with her customer. The man buttoned up his trousers, deposited coins in the woman's palm, and disappeared around the corner. "Let's speak to her first."

He approached her as she was pulling her patched skirts into place. "Miss?"

The woman's head snapped in his direction. She was young, yet life had aged her prematurely, her eyes filled with weariness.

Still, she looked him and Harry up and down, working up enough sauce to say, "Lookin' for some fun, me fine gents? I can show ye a good time, anything ye want—"

"It's information we're after," Andrew said.

Her eyes shuttered. "Ain't got none o' that."

First rule of the rookery: no one knew anything.

"We're looking for a man. Big fellow, rides a bald-faced chestnut. Has an injured shoulder." Andrew removed a bag of coins, dangling it, letting the clink of guineas get her attention. "This goes to the first person who points us in the right direction."

Second rule (which trumped the first): anything was available for a price.

She licked her lips, her gaze scanning the empty corridor. "I might know 'im. But ye didn't 'ear it from me—agreed?"

"Agreed."

Glancing around once more, she said in a low voice, "Cove in the first room 'round the corner 'as a bandage on 'is shoulder. Been wearin' it fer 'bout a week."

The timing fit with the attack on Rosie.

Pulse quickening, Andrew said, "Have you seen him tonight?"

The woman nodded. "Came in 'bout an hour ago, carrying a bottle o' spirits. It weren't rotgut but the fine stuff the nobs like. Cove must 'ave nicked it. Reckon wif posh drink like that, 'e's still in there toasting 'imself."

"Thank you." He handed her the coin bag.

As he and Harry set off, he heard the woman gasp behind them. The twenty pounds he'd given her was more than she'd make in a year of selling her wares.

Turning the corner, he and Harry found the room. He took out his pistol and positioned himself in front of the door while Harry went to the side, his back to the wall, firearm drawn. Andrew knocked on the peeling wood. No reply—and no sound of scuffling from the other side.

A sense of foreboding prickled his nape.

"I don't hear any noise inside," Harry said in low tones.

"Do you think he came and left?"

"Only one way to find out." Taking a step back, Andrew slammed his boot into the door.

The flimsy barrier burst open, and he charged inside. At a glance, he saw a single room… and a man slumped over the table at its center. The fellow's head was turned away from them, the tallow candle next to him sputtering, emitting smoky light. As Andrew approached, the smell of vomit grew stronger, and he saw rats feasting on a pool of detritus on the floor. A half-finished bottle of cognac sat on the table.

"Is he three sheets to the wind?" Harry kept his gun trained on the unmoving figure.

Going to the other side, Andrew saw the man's unblinking gaze. To be certain, he removed his glove and touched the man's neck. No pulse beneath the cooling skin.

"The bastard's found another kind of oblivion," he said grimly.

Reaching for his whistle, he signaled the end of the hunt.

Chapter Thirty-Three

PACING IN HER father's office, Rosie said, "Are you certain they will come, Papa?"

"I'm certain." Papa stood by the window behind his desk, his keen gaze surveying the street below. "There's still a quarter hour before the appointed time, so be patient."

"You'll try not to alienate Lady Charlotte and the Misses Fossey, won't you? They've been so kind to me of late—"

"If they are innocent of the crime, then they'll have no reason to be offended, dearest." This came from Mama, who sat in one of the chairs that had been arranged to face the desk. She was dressed for battle in a stylish navy dress embellished *à la militaire*. "At any rate, your safety is more important than the *ton*'s approval."

Rosie bit her lip. Her mother was right, of course. Yet her new friends were doing wonders for her reputation. Their glowing accounts filled the gossip rags: the *beau monde* was eating up the tragic tale of the Young Beautiful Widow, and she was the Plucked Rose no more. She'd begun to receive notes of condolence from ladies (even some sticklers) and bouquets from gentlemen (these she promptly dispatched to the rubbish bin).

The *ton* was now courting her; the acceptance she'd fought so long for was finally hers.

Now she just had to live long enough to enjoy it.

"What if no one confesses?" she said.

"We don't expect anyone to," Emma said from her chair

by the desk. "But even alibis can provide clues."

"We'll sift the truth from the lies." Mr. Lugo's deep bass joined the conversation.

He was the final member of the group who would be conducting the interview. For propriety's sake, Andrew couldn't be present, and Mr. McLeod had left for Gretna to hunt for clues. For a lot had happened since the discovery of the dead cutthroat two nights ago.

Papa had brought in Dr. Abernathy, a brilliant Scottish physician, to examine the corpse. Yesterday afternoon, the doctor had presented his findings to the family and Andrew.

"I believe the cause of death was poisoning," Dr. Abernathy had said in his strong burr. "The man was otherwise healthy, the wound on his shoulder nearly healed. Most telling, I found several dead rats by the pool of his vomitus. I tested some of the remaining cognac on other rats: all of them died."

According to Dr. Abernathy, foxglove was the likely toxin as it was fast-acting, symptoms occurring within half an hour of administration. Foxglove often went undetected for it mimicked the signs of a heart ailment, accompanied by slurred speech and flushing of the skin. At the physician's description, Rosie had had a sudden, jolting memory: the smell of vomit on Daltry's breath, his garbled speech and red face on their wedding night. She'd attributed it to his drinking—but what if it he'd been poisoned?

What if Daltry had been *murdered*?

She recalled that he'd been absent for two hours before coming to her room. What if he'd met with the murderer then and been given the poisoned beverage? When she'd blurted her suspicions, the energy in the room had grown even darker.

"That makes sense," Andrew had said, his jaw hard. "Whoever murdered Daltry did so expecting to get their hands on his money. When instead Primrose inherited everything, the murderer then tried to eliminate her as well."

"We're back to Daltry's relatives," Papa had said. "But which one—or ones?"

"Poison, as they say, is a woman's weapon." Em grimaced. "I can vouch for that personally."

Strathaven's arm circled his wife's waist. "So we focus on the female suspects?"

Papa shook his head. "We cannot deny that Theale has the most to gain financially. We must continue pursuing all leads. Whoever the villain is, he or she is damned clever. I've had the suspects followed on a few occasions, but none of them have done anything of note."

"He or she is being careful," Emma mused, "now that they know they're under suspicion."

"Shall I make a trip to Gretna?" This had come from McLeod. "Maybe the innkeep or staff saw Daltry with someone."

"Thank you, McLeod. An excellent suggestion." Stroking his chin, Papa had said, "In the meantime, we'll interrogate the suspects as a group and get their alibis for the time of Daltry's murder. With the others present, it'll be more difficult for the culprit to get away with lies."

Everyone had agreed to the plan. Which brought them to the present.

The clock on the mantel struck three.

"Here they come," Papa said, his eyes on the street below.

Minutes later, Papa's clerk ushered the visitors into the office. Rosie exchanged warm greetings with Lady Daltry, the Fossey sisters, and Mr. Theale. She returned Mr. James flirtatious smile with a reserved one of her own and kept her distance from his stepmama, who seemed no friendlier today than she'd been at their prior meeting.

"What's this about, then?" Mrs. James announced imperiously the instant everyone had taken a seat. "I have prior engagements. Indeed, I would not have responded to these presumptuous summons had Alastair not convinced me that it was in the best interests of the family."

"My stepmama is *all* about duty," Alastair James said in an undertone to Rosie and winked.

The glare Mrs. James trained upon her stepson ought to have melted the skin from his bones.

"I apologize for the inconvenience," Papa said from behind his desk, "but we have come upon some new evidence."

"Evidence?" The dowager countess looked faintly alarmed. "Concerning what?"

"We now have reason to believe that the former Earl of Daltry was poisoned."

If the surprise Rosie saw in the office was feigned, she couldn't tell. Mrs. James paled and exchanged horrified looks with the dowager. Alastair James blinked, then his eyes narrowed at Mr. Theale. The latter, in turn, was looking in the direction of the Fossey sisters, who were sitting side by side on the leather sofa, their hands clutched.

"George was poisoned?" The dowager was the first to regain her voice. "But... why?"

"The answer's obvious, don't you think?" Mr. James drawled. "Which one of us benefits the most from his death?"

Mr. Theale jumped to his feet, his mask of amiability slipping. "How *dare* you accuse me, you bastard. I should call you out, sirrah!"

"Name the time and place." Mr. James smirked. "I'm not afraid of you."

"Alastair," Mrs. James said sharply.

"That's right—I forgot. Of course the *great* Alastair James isn't afraid of a duel." Mr. Theale's fists clenched at his sides. "After all, you've killed before."

Mr. James rose. "That was a goddamned accident!"

"Once a murderer always a murderer," Mr. Theale shot back.

"Please," Sybil said, her timid blue gaze skittering between the two men, "fighting doesn't help matters."

"Sit—both of you," the dowager said. "And finish listening to what Mr. Kent has to say."

The pair sat, anger and resentment sizzling between them.

"To clear up the matter, I wish to know your whereabouts, what you were doing and with whom, on the day Daltry was killed," Papa said evenly. "You should also know that my colleague is, at this moment, en route to Gretna, where he will question the innkeep and others to track down the killer. One way or another, the truth will come out."

"This is outrageous." Mrs. James' voice lacked its normal conviction.

Papa opened a notebook and picked up his pen. "Who would like to go first?"

"I will. I have nothing to hide," Mr. Theale declared. "I was in Brighton."

As Papa jotted this down, Mr. Lugo said, "With whom?"

"I was staying at the home of Mr. Albert Brace." Mr. Theale flushed, his gaze trained on the carpet. "His daughter, Miss Bertha Brace, was also present."

"I was at a house party," Mr. James said quickly, as if he didn't want to be outdone. "At a crony's country seat in Kent."

Papa's pen poised above the page. "And this crony's name?"

"Viscount Cranston."

"Mrs. James?" Emma prompted, going along the circle of seats.

"I was in Ashford," she said with clear reluctance. "I fancied some solitude so I did not bring a maid."

"Am I to understand that both you and your stepson were in Kent that day?" Papa said.

"It was a coincidence." She wetted her lips. "Kent is a large county. We did not see each other."

"Aunt Charlotte and I were in Town," Eloisa chimed in. "I cannot recall for the life of me what we were doing, however."

"We visited the haberdasher's that day," Lady Charlotte replied, "because you wanted new ribbons for the St. Clare affair that night, remember?"

"Quite right," Eloisa agreed. "And we saw oodles of people there."

"Were you with them, Miss Fossey?" Emma turned to Sybil.

"No, I was visiting a friend in Lancashire. I didn't have a maid with me either since my friend lives in a tiny cottage," Sybil said apologetically. "You see—"

"As I've mentioned, my older sister has a charitable nature." Eloisa's sapphire eyes were mocking. "She befriends outcasts wherever she goes."

"Miss Bunbury is not an outcast," Sybil protested.

"She's an invalid spinster with no connections to speak of." With a sniff, Eloisa confided to Rosie, "Miss Bunbury is my sister's old schoolmistress and forever on her deathbed. Don't you think Sybil could make better use of her time?"

"I think Miss Sybil's loyalty speaks well of her," Rosie said.

Sybil sent her a grateful smile.

"Are we done?" Mrs. James said abruptly.

"I have a final question." Mama's emerald eyes circled the group. "How would each of you describe your relationship with the former earl?"

Tension blanketed the room.

Alastair James spoke first. "I'll say what everyone is thinking: George was a mushroom. The pushy merchant relation that none of us wanted anything to do with until the title fell into his lap."

"Speak ill of yourself if you wish," Eloisa said heatedly, "but not of the rest of us. Aunt Charlotte generously entertained Cousin George in our home for years. *Long* before he became the earl. And Sybil and I were always nice to him."

"Quite right. And George always made a point of telling me how much he enjoyed his visits," Lady Charlotte agreed.

"He reeked of trade," Mr. James said with a sneer.

"Alastair," Mrs. James said faintly, "don't be unkind. You were George's favorite."

"George had only one favorite: himself. He didn't give a damn about anyone else. Did you know he used to make fun of you all when he was in his cups?" Mr. James' derisive glance swept around the room, pausing on each of his relations in turn. "He called you a whiny milksop, Peter."

Theale's shoulders stiffened.

"And you, Charlotte, a fat old hen who couldn't lay eggs."

Lady Charlotte's hands pressed to her bosom, her lips trembling.

"He thought Eloisa was pretty," Mr. James went on. "And a conniving bitch."

Eloisa's nostrils flared. "How *dare* you."

"As for Sybil," Mr. James said, his eyes gleaming with malice, "George said she was like cut-rate goods that a shop couldn't get off its shelf."

Tears shimmered in Sybil's pale blue gaze.

Peter Theale surged to his feet. "Stop picking on her, you bastard!"

"Really, Alastair." Even his stepmama looked uncomfortable. "Is this necessary?"

"Mrs. Kent asked about our relationships with George; I'm answering her question." Alastair aimed a sardonic look at Mama. "George also thought that my stepmother was a grasping termagant and I a toadying fool who was after his money. There you have it: our splendid family portrait. Now are we done?"

A chilling awareness swept over Rosie. Her dead husband had had enemies—and not just because of his money. Hostility crackled in the room.

"We're done." Papa closed his notebook. "For the time being."

One by one, Daltry's stony-faced relatives filed out.

As they passed her, Rosie shivered. *Which one of you killed Daltry? Which one of you wants me dead?*

Chapter Thirty-Four

ROSIE AWOKE, A scream crowding her throat.

Disoriented, breathing heavily, she waited until the tentacles of the nightmare receded. She must have dozed off in the wingchair whilst waiting for Andrew's arrival. Rising, she went to check the ormolu clock on the mantel: it was nearing *midnight?* Andrew had said he'd be here by ten o'clock so that she could fill him in on the outcome of the interviews today.

Where is he? Although she told herself that her panic was due to the bad dream, she couldn't stem the feeling of dread. An icy fear that something had happened to Andrew.

She pulled the bell.

When Odette appeared, Rosie blurted, "Have you heard anything from Mr. Corbett?"

"Yes, my lady. You were asleep when his messenger arrived, so I didn't disturb you."

"What was the message?"

"Mr. Corbett apologizes, but he will not be coming this evening. He was detained by a problem at the Nursery House."

Rosie's relief dwindled. "What kind of a problem?"

"He did not provide specifics, my lady."

Agitation thrummed in Rosie. She couldn't shake off the sense of impending peril, and she didn't like the idea of Andrew facing some trouble alone. Or, worse yet, *not* alone. Wasn't the Nursery House the project that he and Fanny

Argent were working on together? The notion of him being alone with that woman and *at night…*

A milk-fed miss like yourself wouldn't understand, Fanny's voice taunted her. *Then again, there's a lot you don't understand about Corbett here, isn't there?*

Her shoulders tensing, Rosie came to an instant decision. Andrew was *her* lover. If anyone was going to help him with a problem, it should be *her*. God knew that she'd leaned on him enough. She wanted to return the favor—and to show that bloody Mrs. Argent that she was no useless miss.

"Fetch my cloak, please," she said.

"Your cloak?" The maid frowned. "It is late, my lady, and not safe to go out—"

"I'll take the guards with me. Go on."

After Odette left, Rosie took out the pistol that Andrew had given her. True to his word, he'd taught her to shoot it a few nights ago, and she tucked it into her reticule for added security.

When Rosie went downstairs, she had a skirmish with Andrew's guards, which she ended by saying, "If you don't take me, I'll hail a hackney and go on my own." Ten minutes later, she was in a carriage headed for the Nursery House, accompanied by an armed retinue.

They arrived in a part of town Rosie had never been before. Here, the streets were narrow and winding, alleyways branching off like dark veins. Crowds flooded the street, a motley mix of locals, brightly painted prostitutes, and even a few well-to-do gentlemen out to sample the debauchery of the stews. Pickpockets darted through the sea of bodies like hungry minnows.

The carriage turned into a back lane, stopping at black iron gates. Rosie's escorts conferred with the men standing guard, and the gate was opened, the conveyance pulling into a courtyard which abutted the back of a squat brick building.

"Stay 'ere, my lady," one of the guards instructed.

A few minutes later, she heard footsteps, and the carriage door was yanked open. Andrew stood there, glowering at her. He was in his shirtsleeves, the white linen over his chest covered in... *blood*? Rosie's heart jammed in her throat.

"What the devil are you doing here?" he thundered.

Panicked, she reached out to pat his chest. "Are you hurt? Why are you bleeding—"

"The blood's not mine." He seized both her hands in one of his. "I repeat: why are you here?"

His anger sank in. Recognizing that her decision to seek him out might not have been the most prudent, she squirmed in her seat. Her jealousy over Fanny had fueled her recklessness, and one glimpse at Andrew's foreboding expression told her there was no way she could share that.

"I had a bad dream," she mumbled (which was true). "When I woke up, you weren't there, and I had a dreadful feeling that something had happened to you."

"I sent you a message."

"I know. And I thought... I might be able to help." She took a breath and went to the heart of the matter. The truth that went deeper than her stupid jealousy. "You're always dealing with my troubles, and for once I wanted to reciprocate."

He stared at her. "You thought you could help me?"

He made it sound as if the likelihood of her being of use was slightly less than the possibility of teaching a pig to fly. And that *hurt*. While she was used to the *ton* thinking of her as a shallow flirt, she didn't expect it of Andrew. He'd helped her to regain confidence in herself, to accept her own desires and the foibles of her nature. He'd protected her and, at the same time, he'd respected her independence in a way that no one—not even her family—had before.

Now, confronted with his incredulity, she couldn't help

but wonder if she'd been blinded by her feelings for him. The voice in her head that had always whispered that he was too good for her—too good to be true—now declared, *Didn't I tell you, you ninny? You're merely a pretty ornament, one to share a bed with. Did you think you had more to offer him?*

Pain spread like cracks through porcelain. "Do you think so little of me?"

"That has nothing to do with it." His brows snapped together. "You shouldn't be here. You're risking not only your neck but your reputation—"

"Corbett, where the blooming 'ell are you?" Fanny Argent appeared behind Andrew, her gaze fixing on Rosie. "Mary's tits, what's *she* doing here? We 'ave enough on our 'ands without—"

"Shut up, Fanny." Any glee that Rosie might have felt at Andrew's clipped words to his employee evaporated at his next words. "She's leaving."

"Good riddance," Fanny said with a sniff.

I don't think so. Rage spilled inside Rosie, distracting from her heartache. *If that… that crone thinks she can get away with dismissing me…*

Pulling down her veil to shield her face, Rosie pushed both hands into Andrew's chest. Andrew staggered back a step, obviously unprepared for her actions—probably because he thought she would be a good little girl and go home like he ordered—and she used that opportunity to hop down from the carriage, her half-boots hitting the ground.

Facing Fanny, she said, "I'm not going anywhere. Whatever problem Andrew is dealing with, I can help him with it as well as you."

"You think so?" The bawd's smirk was visible even through the filter of Rosie's veil. "'Ow many brats 'ave you pulled into the world with yer lily-white 'ands, eh?"

That was what Andrew and Fanny were doing… assisting

in a childbirth?

Rosie had never attended a birthing, seeing as she'd been an unmarried miss until recently *and* she was squeamish by nature. Her belly gave an uneasy flutter, but she lifted her chin. There was no way she was backing down to Fanny.

"I can follow the physician's orders as well as anybody." She prayed this would be limited to fetching things like hot water, towels, and whatnot—errands that would keep her out of the birthing chamber as much as possible.

"*Physician?*" Fanny's laugh was like a slap to the face. "Do you think Corbett and I would be elbow deep in blood and guts if we 'ad a quack around to 'elp?"

Blood... and *guts? Eww.*

Bile hit her throat, yet Rosie stood her ground. "Well, you have someone to help now. Me."

Fanny opened her mouth, Andrew silencing her with a glare. "Go inside, Fanny." His tone was so lethal that the bawd did as she was told. Then he turned to Rosie. "As for you—"

"I'm staying." If he thought he could order her about like some employee, then he had better think twice. "If Fanny can help, then I can too. I *want* to."

"Damnit, this isn't for you," he growled.

"Why—because you think I'm a useless, milk-fed chit who isn't good for anything but looking pretty?" The words burst from her like fester from a boil.

"Where in blazes did you get that insane idea?" He raked a hand through his tawny mane, a gesture of supreme male impatience. "I never said that."

"You *think* it." Her voice trembled with accusation. "That's why you don't want me here. That's why you're always helping me while I'm never allowed to reciprocate. That's why you let Fanny stay but not me—your *lover.* You told me once that you expect me to share not just my body but my mind and spirit as well. For your edification, I expect the same,"—she poked a finger into his chest—"of *you*."

He stared at her as if she were a candidate for Bedlam. Then his gaze rose upward, as if searching for divine intervention. *Then* his hand clamped around her arm, dragging her unceremoniously toward the building.

Her feet and mind struggled to keep up. "Where are we going?"

He didn't look back at her, just kept going. "You wanted to be part of this."

Hope percolated through her. "You're letting me stay?"

"Not only are you staying, you're helping." Opening the door, he pulled her through. "An enemy of mine has seen fit to threaten or pay off all the available midwives and quacks in the vicinity. Now I find myself with three women all on the verge of delivering their babes—and there's me, Fanny, and a maid who just fainted at the sight of blood to handle it. Luckily,"—he sent her a sardonic look—"I now have an extra pair of hands."

Swallowing nervously, Rosie didn't dare say a word as he led her through a kitchen, up some stairs, and into a long hallway. Rooms branched off on either side, the layout suggesting the place's prior use as an inn or boarding house.

A scream came from a room on the right. Rosie jerked—then jerked again when a long wail followed, this time from a room on the left. A string of unladylike curses came from some other room up ahead.

Fanny's head poked out from the nearest room, her brown curls plastered to her forehead.

"Babe's coming and not easily," she said tersely to Andrew. "I need you in here."

He rolled his sleeves as he strode over.

Rosie couldn't seem to get her feet to move. "I'll, um, fetch some hot water," she said feebly.

Fanny managed to get off a snide look before she

disappeared into the room with Andrew.

Sighing, Rosie deposited her cloak and bonnet on a bench and headed back to the kitchen, where she'd seen a large pot boiling on the stove. She filled a pail and lugged it back up the steps. Inhaling deeply, she entered the room where Andrew and Fanny had gone.

"I've brought the water..." A light-headed sensation hit her. A woman was groaning and writhing on the bed, her knees up, blood soaking the sheets beneath her swollen body...

"Leave it by the door," Andrew instructed.

Gladly. Rosie dropped the bucket and dashed out.

In the hallway, she pressed her clammy hands to her cheeks, fighting back nausea. *For goodness sake, don't cast your accounts. You have to show Andrew that you're equal to the task.*

What if you're not? Her inner voice mocked her. *What if you are just a useless chit...?*

"Please. Someone 'elp me."

The labored voice diverted Rosie from her inner debate. It came again, and, warily, she followed it into a room to her left. A redheaded woman around Rosie's age lay upon a cot. She wore a shift, a sheet draped over her burgeoned belly, her pretty freckled face twisted in pain.

"'Oo are you?" she gasped.

"Oh, hello there. I'm, um, a friend of Mr. Corbett's." Relieved at the lack of any visible bodily fluids, Rosie said, "Is there anything I can do for you?"

"More w-water." The woman gestured to the empty glass on the bedside table.

Spotting a pitcher on the washstand, Rosie went to refill the glass. She returned, helping the woman to sit up. "Have some sips." She held the glass to the other's lips. "Easy does it."

After drinking, the other sank back against the pillows.

"Thank ye, miss. The pain comes in waves, but it's passed fer now."

"I'm glad. And, please, call me Rosie. You are...?"

"Name's Sally, miss."

"A pleasure to make your acquaintance, Sally." She went back to the washstand, returning with a wet towel, which she placed on the other's sweaty forehead. "Is that better?"

"Yes, and 'aving company 'elps, Wish me ma were 'ere, but she passed." Sally's hazel eyes turned rueful. "Though she might turn in 'er grave if she knew I were in this pickle."

Knowing a thing or two about maternal disapproval, Rosie squeezed the other's hand in silent empathy.

Apparently eager to chat, Sally went on, "'Ave you known our Mr. Corbett long?"

"Most of my life," Rosie said honestly.

"Fine gent, ain't he?"

"Yes, he is."

"And the best employer I ever 'ad. I didn't catch this,"— she pointed to her sheet-covered belly—"from Corbett's, you know. It were from another establishment. The minute they found out me condition, I was shown the door. Found myself in dire straits, I did, and it were a miracle Mr. Corbett took me in. 'E wanted to put me in the kitchens, but I told 'im, *Scrubbin' pots ain't fer me. I got other talents.*" She winked. "Turns out some coves'll pay extra for a wench *wif* extra, if ye catch me meaning."

"Oh... well." Flummoxed at how to respond to that, Rosie changed the subject. "So, um, if your mama were here, what would she do for you?"

"She'd sing. Whene'er me or one o' my brothers or sisters were ill, she'd give us a tune, and it'd make things—*ooh.*" Her grip on Rosie's hand tightened like a vise. "Oh, Lord, it's comin' again."

"Shall I fetch someone?" Rosie said quickly.

"*No*, don't leave me." Sally broke off, her face contorting.

Screams came from across the hall, and Rosie knew that Andrew had his hands full. Desperation filled her as she looked at the woman groaning in the bed, the hand clutching hers. What could she do to help?

Impulse took over; she sang the first lines that came to her:

What's this dull town to me
When Robin's not near
What was't I wish'd to see
What wish'd to hear

When she paused, Sally panted, "That's pretty, miss. Give us another verse, then."

So she did. When she finished the ballad, Sally asked for more, so she sang a Scottish air. Then another song. Her recital was accompanied by Sally's heavy breaths and occasional groans. She'd gone through half her repertoire and was starting to feel like Scheherazade when Sally bit out, "Ye got to get 'old of the babe now."

"Pardon?" Rosie squeaked.

"Grab the babe—it's comin' out." Sally grimaced, shoving off the sheet and revealing her shift-clad body. "Me water came a few songs back, and I've been pushing since. The babe's *ready*."

The last word came out in a howl, propelling Rosie to her feet. "I'll go get Mr. Corbett—"

"Ain't no time," Sally yelled. "Get it *now*."

Panicked, Rosie dashed to the end of the bed. *Dear Lord.*

The baby *was* coming out of Sally. There was no time to faint, to do anything but act. She reached out and caught the wet slippery head as it slipped out.

"I've got the head," she managed.

Sally grunted, her heels digging into the mattress.

"Can you push a bit harder?" Sweat glazed Rosie's brow. "The shoulders seem to be stuck…"

Sally gnashed her teeth and bore down. Without warning, the babe popped out on a wave of liquid. With a shriek of surprise, Rosie caught the little body. Heart thumping, she stared at the breathing, tiny human she held in her hands.

"Is it…?"

The babe let out a high-pitched wail.

"A girl." Rosie placed the babe in Sally's arms, taking care not to tangle the purplish cord that still connected the two. "Oh, Sally, you have a beautiful daughter."

"She is a sight, ain't she?" Sally breathed.

"Sally, are you all right? I heard…"

Rosie whirled around to see Andrew rushing into the room. He stopped short as Sally, sweaty and beaming with pride, announced, "I 'ave a daughter, Mr. Corbett."

He blinked. "I see that."

"And I'm going to name 'er Rose—after Miss Rosie 'ere who brought 'er into the world," Sally added.

Andrew's gaze went to Rosie. His brows inched upward.

"I helped a little." Modestly, Rosie looked down at her hands.

Which was a mistake.

She saw the blood—and *other* bodily secretions—covering her skin. Her stomach lurched as she also became aware of the slime oozing between her fingers and the smells…

A buffle-headed feeling stole over her, and the floor rushed up.

Chapter Thirty-Five

"RISE AND SHINE, sleepyhead," Andrew murmured.

"Mmm grmph."

Smiling at Primrose's grumbled reply, he swept her golden tresses back and kissed her shoulder. They were in her bed, her back nestled against his front, the same position they'd fallen asleep in. He *loved* sleeping with her. His body craved the closeness of hers during slumber, and if she moved during the night, even asleep, he pulled her back into his arms. He found it a singular joy to wake up entangled with her.

He traced a finger down her arm, and her sleepy shiver hit him straight in the groin. He was already hard, his morning cockstand nestled between the plush curves of her derriere. He hadn't made love to her last night; they'd arrived back at her house just before dawn, both of them exhausted. After a quick wash, they'd gone straight to bed.

Although he hadn't slept more than a few hours, he felt invigorated. A burden had eased. True, he still had Todd to deal with—and, make no mistake, he would have his retribution—but all three wenches had delivered their babes safely last night.

And Primrose had played an unexpected role in that.

While he'd always known that she was brave and strong, her actions last night had surpassed even his expectations. She'd allowed her brightness and natural warmth to shine. Sally couldn't stop singing her praises, and even Fanny expressed grudging respect.

Primrose had awed him. And she'd made him laugh.

He'd caught her when she swooned. The episode hadn't lasted more than a minute, but her chagrin had been bloody adorable. He'd teased her for fainting *after* the fact.

Her pout had been priceless.

Even more precious was the fact that she'd gone to the Nursery House because she'd wanted to help him. She'd made it clear that she wanted him to share his mind, body, and spirit with her. Was it possible that this was more than an affair to her—that she might one day return his feelings?

The thought filled him with hope.

It also made him randier than the devil.

Beneath the coverlet, he slid his hand over her firm breast, the tip stiffening at his touch. As he stroked her nipple, she sighed, her bottom wriggling against his cock. With his top leg, he pulled back hers, trapping it and shifting them both so that he was on his back and she lying half on his chest. With one hand, he played with her tits while the other skimmed over her silken rib cage and soft belly to her cunny.

"Christ, you're dripping," he rasped against her ear. "I love how wet you get for me."

"It feels so good when you touch me." Her newly awakened voice was sultry.

He adored her honesty and the fact that she responded so readily to him. He didn't mind working for her pleasure—indeed, he enjoyed it—but, God's teeth, he counted it a blessing that he could make his lover spend multiple times and with ease. He'd never met another woman whose appetites so perfectly matched his own. He sucked her earlobe while he diddled her pearl. Her hips moved to the rhythm of his fingers, her thighs squeezing his hand as she came.

He eased from beneath her, rolling onto his side so that he could look at her. Her cheeks were flushed, her jade-colored eyes drowsy and sated.

"You're so bloody beautiful," he said reverently.

He brought his fingers, still wet from her climax, to her breasts and painted the tips with her own dew. His nostrils flared at his handiwork: her nipples glistened like honey-glazed berries. He bent his head, arousal pounding in his veins as he licked her taste from her tits. Soon, he craved more, wanted to drink from the source. He kissed his way downward—and was surprised when her fingers slid into his hair, stopping him.

"What's the matter, sweetheart?" he said.

"I want to do something different." Her cheeks were pink, her eyes determined.

He quirked a brow. "You have complaints about how I make love to you?"

"You know I don't. But I want to try something. Will you let me?"

He wondered what was going on in that gorgeous head of hers, and a hot flame of anticipation licked his gut. "Be my guest."

"Then will you please lie back against the pillows?"

He acquiesced, tucking his hands behind his head. "How's that?"

"Splendid." Her feminine excitement made his balls throb. "Keep your hands right there."

She clambered gracefully atop him, her damp cunny nestling against his rock-hard abdomen. He stifled a groan, his cock prodding her arse like a poker. She leaned in to kiss him, tangling her tongue sweetly with his, and then peppering kisses over his jaw. She licked his earlobe, gnawing delicately at the tendon of his neck.

He realized that she was making love to him the way he'd made love to her. Up until now, Primrose had seemed content to let him direct their lovemaking, and although he didn't quite understand her sudden desire to take charge, he wasn't about to look a gift horse in the mouth.

When her lips closed around his right nipple, he groaned with pleasure.

"Are you sensitive here?" Her eyes held his, her finger circling the hard, flat nub.

"Yes, sunshine," he said huskily.

She licked his other nipple, and the graze of her teeth made his hips buck, his cock sliding against the luxurious crease of her arse. She teased him some more before kissing her way down his body. His muscles flexed and quivered beneath her sensual assault, his brain turning molten as he considered where she was headed. He'd never pushed her in this regard, wanting her to explore at her own pace: she was a lady, after all.

She made a place for herself between his thighs, and her ladylike fingers wrapped around his cock. His gentlemanly consideration flew out the window. *Christ*, he liked her hands on him.

"You're rather a handful," she said breathily.

She wasn't wrong. He was so burgeoned that her fingers didn't reach all the way around his girth, and watching her carefully pet his veined beast aroused him even more. His prick swelled, testing the limits of her grip.

"It's all for you. Help yourself," he invited.

She dimpled. Her gentle frigging was a unique brand of torture, and he wasn't complaining. She slid her fist down his shaft, moving the supple skin over the rigid core. Squeezing his thick root, she made her way back up to the tip, rubbing the slit with her index finger. His chest heaved as she drew a circle, spreading pre-seed over his sensitive crown.

"Does that feel good?" she whispered.

"How does it feel when I rub your pearl, make it wet with your cream?"

Golden lust sparkled in her eyes. "Arousing beyond

words."

"That's how it feels for me."

"So *everything* you've done to me—I can do the same to you?"

Hell, yes.

"There are no rules in our bed, remember?" He couldn't resist reaching out to tuck a silken tress behind her ear. "If I don't like something, I'll tell you. Otherwise, have at it."

"I've always liked the idea of *carte blanche*," she said with a flirty grin.

The sensual mischief in her eyes ratcheted up his desire to near perilous proportions. His stones pulsed, steamy pressure building in his shaft. Another bead of moisture formed on his cockhead, and his heart thudded as Primrose stared intently at the pearly droplet. Would she...?

She leaned forward and licked it off.

Christ Almighty.

He instantly spurted more seed, and she licked him again. A breathless grunt left him as he watched her little pink tongue flick back and forth over his swollen dome. She did this while frigging him with a feather-light touch. Prolonging the pleasure, building it this way was usually the act of someone who'd mastered the love arts, and the irony didn't escape him that Primrose, in her innocence, was keeping him right there on the razor's edge.

Then she fitted her lips over the tip of his cock and gave a light, awkward suck. She did it again, and he didn't know whether to laugh or groan at the exquisite torment of being treated to inexperienced fellatio. On her third attempt, his fingers tangled in her hair, bringing her head up.

She looked adorably befuddled. "Am I doing this right?"

"If your aim is to torture me," he said, amused, "then definitely. If you want me to come—"

"I want you to come." Her sweet, earnest reply nearly

brought about her wish. "Won't you please show me how?"

In a heartbeat, he had her in his arms, carrying her to the blazing hearth.

"Why did we leave the bed?" she said breathlessly.

He sat in the wingchair, settling her on the carpet between his legs. He ran a thumb along her cheekbone. "It's easier for you to suck my cock in this position, love."

"Oh." A sultry awareness entered her eyes. She raised herself on her knees, her hands falling lightly on his corded thighs. "What should I, um, do?"

He fisted his prick, adoring her feminine hunger, the way her gaze followed the movement of his hand as he frigged himself slowly. "Take as much in your mouth as you can—the deeper the better. Try relaxing your jaw and breathing through your nose. Lastly, be careful with your teeth. Any questions?"

She shook her head.

He slid his free hand into her hair, holding her head steady while he carefully fed her the first few inches of his cock. Fire blazed down his spine as his shaft disappeared between her pure pink lips. *Bloody heaven*. He tried to control the pace, to not demand too much of her during her first foray into oral play. It soon became clear, however, that she was a quick study.

Her hair draping over his thighs in pale streamers, she took him deeper and deeper into her hot, wet hole. She sucked his rod with a dainty fervor that filled him with lust and wonder. No one had ever dedicated herself to his pleasure this completely. No one had ever cared about pleasing him the way she did. No one had ever made him feel this *wanted*. When she swatted his hand off his cock so she could take him deeper still, he nearly blew his seed. Then and there.

He gripped the arms of the chair as she tested his resolve, cramming more and more of his prick into her mouth. When he nudged the end of her throat, she coughed, the reflexive squeeze making his neck arch in bliss. God, it was too much. With an oath, he wrenched himself from her generous kiss.

"Why did you do that? I'm not finished," she pouted.

This close to exploding, he gritted out, "I was about to come."

Her brow furrowed. "So?"

"So it's not polite to spend in a lady's mouth." With wenches, the privilege cost extra.

Her cheeks turned rosy. "But don't I, um… do that… in yours?"

Hell, he was going to spend then and there if this conversation continued. "I like it when you do, sweetheart,"—understatement of the century—"but you might not feel the same way."

"I *want* to taste your pleasure," she whispered, "the same way you do mine."

Which meant—conversation *over*.

In a blink, he had them both on the carpet. He lay on his back, positioning a startled Primrose on her hands and knees over him, her knees straddling his head, her mouth lining up with his cock. He wasted no time, yanking her hips down and burying his face in her luscious cunny. At the same time, he reached down, pressing between her shoulder blades, and he knew she understood when, an instant later, his cock was engulfed in wet heat.

Bloody. Fucking. *Heaven*.

While she sucked him, he ate her pussy like a man starved. Fucking her with two fingers, he sucked on her bold nub until her thighs tautened around his head, and he tasted the first gush of her honey. She moaned around his cock as she came, the reverberations taking him over the edge. He bellowed, his hips bucking as his release shot from him like a geyser. He jetted again and again, and she didn't move away, taking all of it—of him—into her keeping.

Afterward, he had just enough energy to get them both back into bed. He tucked her against his side, her head nestling in the crook of his shoulder. He was fully prepared to fall asleep again when he heard her giggle.

He twisted his head to look at her, and his mouth twitched. She looked exceedingly pleased with herself. "You look like the cat that got the cream."

Her eyes sparkled. "Well, I did, didn't I?"

"You certainly did." Laughing softly, he kissed her nose. "Then again, so did I."

"I liked doing that with you. Liked being… your equal."

Surprised, he took in her earnest expression. "You are my equal, sunshine."

"All this time, you've protected me—from gossip and my own mistakes and even an attempt on my life." Her gaze followed her finger, which was tracing a circle on his chest. "You've also shown me pleasure I never knew existed… and you've taught me to accept and embrace myself and my desires. You've given me all that,"—her troubled eyes lifted to his—"and what have I given you in return?"

He couldn't hold back the words.

"You," he said tenderly. "I love you, Primrose."

"Oh, Andrew, I—"

"I know you only want an affair, and this doesn't change anything between us. I just wanted you to know that no one has ever given me what you have—passion, sweetness, joy. I don't deserve it, but you make me feel like a different man. My heart is yours, Primrose. As a girl, you owned a piece of it; as a woman, you've claimed the rest."

"You're so good to me." A tear trickled down her cheek. "I don't deserve you."

He thumbed the moisture away, and wanting to bring back her smile, he teased, "I think you just proved otherwise, hmm?"

His ploy worked; her lips curved.

"If *that* is all it takes," she said tremulously, "then we'll have to repeat the experience. Practice makes perfect, you know."

Goddamn. Despite the fact that he'd come just minutes ago, his cock stirred. People might say that a way to a man's heart was through his stomach—and they'd be wrong.

"Andrew?"

Hastily, he tucked away the image of her mouth on his cock. "Yes, love?"

"My parents are having a supper party tomorrow night." She paused and said rather shyly, "Would you come as my guest?"

Thus far, his interactions with her family had been strictly related to the business of protecting her. It was one thing for her kin to tolerate him for the sake of her safety... and quite another for them to see him by her side on a social occasion. He was grateful that they hadn't interfered with his and Primrose's relationship thus far; he didn't want to rock the boat.

"It sounds like a family affair," he said with care.

"It is. So will you please come?"

Her smile dazzled him, and what he saw in her eyes made his heart pound with hope.

Chapter Thirty-Six

As THE EVENING unfolded, Rosie's trepidation over inviting her lover to a family gathering faded. Despite the nature of her relationship with Andrew and the fact that he was engaged in a less than reputable trade, one thing was clear: her family liked him. She'd been less concerned about the ladies and more about the men, who tended to be overprotective. Yet Papa and Andrew conversed readily enough over the twelve-course supper, the two of a like mind when it came to social issues. With his knowledge of business and sports, Andrew also fit right in with the husbands.

He even managed to draw Harry into the conversation. Harry had been quiet and preoccupied all evening; in fact, Rosie had never seen him in such a brooding state before. When Emma asked him about it, he cut her off with a firm, "Nothing is the matter. Leave it alone, Em."

An awkward silence ensued. Everyone knew how private Harry was and not to push him. But Emma, being Emma, was about to pursue the subject further, despite everyone's warning looks.

Luckily, Andrew cut in. "Where do you box, Harry?" he said easily. "I've never seen a jab-hook combination like yours."

After a moment, the lines around Harry's mouth eased. "I trained myself. It's physics, really."

This launched an in-depth discussion of boxing principles, one that drew in all the men and cleared away the remaining tension. At the meal's conclusion, the ladies exited to the drawing room, leaving the males to their cigars and brandy. Rosie sat next to Mama, who held a grumpy Sophie. The babe was going through a colicky patch, and Mama had taken her from Libby, the nursemaid, to see if she could calm her.

Sophie's red face scrunched up, and she wailed, her little fists waving.

"I was up with her half the night. Nothing seems to calm her." Rarely did Mama appear flustered, but lines of worry fanned from her eyes.

"Perhaps she is teething?" Emma said. "Livy was a terror during those months. I gave her a sachet of herbs to chew on, and that seemed to help."

"We used cloth dipped in brandy with our little ones," Thea suggested.

"Libby tried both to no avail," Mama said.

Violet trotted over to peer at the babe. "Whenever Jamie got fussy, I strapped him to me and took him for a ride. The bouncing quieted him."

Everyone stared at her. Sophie let out another squeal of displeasure.

Mama sighed. "I'd best take her upstairs."

"Let me take her for a bit," Rosie offered.

"You wouldn't mind?" Mama said.

Rosie scooped up her sister. While Sophie squawked in protest, Rosie walked around the room, rocking her gently and singing a lullaby. Sophie eventually quieted, her brown eyes wide, rosebud mouth puckering.

"You're a pretty thing, aren't you?" Rosie said. "Maybe you just wanted some attention."

The babe cooed in reply.

"Well, I understand. I'm a bit dramatic myself," Rosie confided.

Sophie belched—and Rosie didn't even flinch. Perhaps

the Nursery House had cured her of her squeamishness.

"Was that what was bothering you?" She adjusted Sophie to an upright position, rubbing the babe's back. "You let it all out. I won't tell anyone, I promise."

She strolled and hummed, feeling Sophie's soft weight, smelling her sweet baby smell.

The door opened, and the men entered.

"Shh, I've just rung for the nursemaid," Mama said in a hushed voice. "Rosie managed to get Sophie to fall asleep."

"You've worked a miracle, poppet," Papa said.

Rosie's insides warmed at her father's approval. Then the sight of Andrew made her breath catch. He was staring at her holding Sophie, the longing in his dark eyes raw and undisguised. At that moment, it was clear to her what he wanted... because, she realized in a flash, she wanted it too.

Love. Marriage. The family that she and Andrew could create together.

I love you, Primrose.

He'd given her his heart, and she knew it was the most precious thing anyone had given her. At the time, something had stopped her from saying the words back—fear, a mistrust that something this good would last. Did she have the courage to give him her love, to relinquish the safety she'd found? All day she'd mulled over it, and the insight hit her now: safety wasn't about protecting her heart. It wasn't about sealing it like a doll inside a locked cabinet.

Safety was about giving her heart to the right man, the one who would protect her and love her and accept her for who she was. Safety was passion and laughter. Safety was Andrew.

The man she loved.

The revelation washed through her, leaving nerves and giddiness in its wake.

Tonight, after the party, I'll tell him how I feel.

Libby arrived, and Rosie gently transferred her sleepy

sister to the nursemaid. She went over to Andrew, who was standing by the pianoforte. He smiled at her, his tawny hair gleaming, his eyes warm. He was so virile and handsome in his stark evening attire that her heart hiccupped. Later on tonight, after she told him she loved him, she looked forward to removing his garments, piece by well-tailored piece. Her nipples budded beneath her black velvet bodice, her pussy dampening.

Flustered, she hid her response behind a bright smile. "Enjoying yourself?"

"Evidently not as much as I'm going to later," he murmured, "when I take you home."

As usual, he saw straight through her.

Her cheeks warmed; the crinkles around his eyes deepened.

Before she could come up with some rejoinder, Edward and Frederick, the Tremonts' eldest, ambled over. How quickly the two of them were growing out of their boyhood. Their lean, gangly frames were starting to fill out, and both adolescents bore the stamp of their handsome fathers. And, goodness, was that a shadow of a mustache on Freddy's upper lip?

"I have a question for Corbett," Edward said without preamble.

Oh, Lord. Precocious as a child, Edward had blossomed into a full-blown genius who could converse freely on any number of intellectual topics. Despite his undeniable intelligence, he could be oblivious to basic social niceties. To Rosie's exasperation, he was often too direct and intellectual in polite company... and he could never manage to keep his cravat straight. She itched to straighten his crooked Four-in-Hand at the same time that she braced for his question, which could be about anything from the history of the cosmos to mathematical theorems to crop rotation.

"I'm at your disposal," Andrew said gravely.

Edward looked him in the eye. "Are you courting my sister?"

Rosie's jaw slackened.

"I want to know as well." Freddy drew himself up, his light hair gleaming and grey eyes serious. "No one will tell Edward and me anything."

Andrew cleared his throat. "That is a matter between your sister and me."

"Since my sister has shown questionable judgement of late," Edward said stiffly, "I must insist that you answer the question, sir."

Rosie's surprise at her brother's newfound protectiveness evaporated in an instant.

She crossed her arms over her bosom. "My *questionable* judgement?"

Edward turned an acute green gaze upon her. "You eloped with a fellow who was murdered on your wedding night. You've been shot at."

"And you need to have guards accompanying you for protection," Freddy added.

Botheration. They had a point.

Loftily, she said, "This is an adult matter."

"I am not a child, Rosie." Edward's hands balled at his sides. "When I ask Mama and Papa, they tell me to mind my own business. But you are my sister, and therefore it *is* my business to protect you if need be."

Two facts astonished her: the first was that her parents were defending her right to privacy and the second that her little brother was worried about her and wanted to defend her honor. She and Edward loved each other unconditionally, of course, but their interactions had historically consisted of bickering and annoying one another, mostly on purpose. This was a side of Edward she hadn't encountered before, and his care for her warmed her insides like mulled cider.

"Thank you, Edward," she said softly. "And you too, Freddy. But you don't need to protect me from Mr. Corbett. He's been my champion. I don't know what I would have done without him."

Edward gave Andrew another once-over. Andrew, to his credit, kept his expression neutral while being sized up by the adolescent.

"Do you play *vingt-et-un*?" Edward said abruptly.

Now *this* was the brother she knew. All his life, Edward had been prone to non sequiturs. Mama said it was because his brain worked too quickly for most to follow.

Andrew's brows raised slightly. "Yes."

"Fancy a game? Freddy will deal."

Rosie didn't trust the smug look exchanged between the adolescent pair.

"Why not?" Andrew said.

As the boys headed toward the card table, Rosie placed a staying hand on Andrew's arm.

"My brother is an expert at counting cards," she said under her breath. "He's fleeced everyone in the family."

Andrew looked unconcerned.

After a few rounds, it became obvious why. Andrew won the entire pile of chips, and Edward and Freddy were looking at him as if he'd just pranced across the Thames. Even Harry stopped brooding long enough to look thoroughly impressed.

"Where did you learn to play like that, Corbett?" he asked.

"Practice." Andrew shuffled the cards, the showy arc making Edward and Freddy whoop with delight. "This is how I got the stake to buy my first club."

This was news to Rosie, yet another fascinating facet of Andrew. He was a man of hidden talents and depths, and she wanted to spend the rest of her life discovering all that she could about him... and he wanted the same, didn't he? The discordant thought hit her: he'd said he loved her, but he hadn't mentioned marriage. In fact, he'd never pushed it once during their affair.

Was that because of what he believed to be her wishes? Or did he, himself, have no desire to marry her? As insecurities pulled at her like invisible strings, she refused to be swayed by them. She knew in her heart that she and Andrew were meant to be together. Thus, tonight when they were alone, she would tell him she loved him and ask him what he wanted.

The butler came in, handing Papa a note. Rosie's nape stirred; from her father's alert expression, she could tell he'd received important news.

"Can you teach me your method?" Edward was saying eagerly to Andrew. "Do you use a particular algorithm for calculating the odds or—"

"Lesson's over, lads," Papa announced. "The adults have something to discuss."

"I'm an adult," Edward said.

"Me too," Freddy chimed in.

"Off you go." Papa's tone brooked no refusal, and, grumbling, the boys shuffled off.

"What is it, Papa?" Rosie said. "Did you receive news?"

He closed the door. Facing everyone, he held up the note.

"This is from Lugo. He's in Kent and he's spoken to Lord Cranston, the friend of Alastair James. Cranston confirmed that James was indeed at his house party. He didn't recall seeing James on the day that Daltry died, but he said his guests came and went as they pleased. Certainly James was never gone long enough to get himself to Gretna and back. So his alibi holds."

"What about Mrs. James?" Rosie said. "Has Mr. Lugo confirmed that she was also in Kent?"

Papa frowned. "That is the strange thing. As it happens,

Ashford is only an hour away from the Cranston estate, and Lugo went there to inquire at the inn where she claimed she was staying. There is no record of her being a guest, nor do any of the staff remember her. Lugo plans to canvass the area to see if anyone recalls seeing her."

"My gut tells me she's hiding something," Emma said. "Which is why I interviewed one of her maids today."

"How did you manage that?" Rosie was surprised that Mrs. James would agree to any invasion of privacy.

"Her Grace is quite inventive when she sets her mind upon a thing," the Duke of Strathaven drawled. "She convinced me to stalk the servants' entrance of the James residence with her."

"As if you mind a little adventure," his duchess retorted.

"I don't—when I get to reap its sweet rewards," he murmured.

Blushing, Em went on, "On the condition of anonymity, the maid told me that her mistress has a habit of disappearing and for blocks of time. Apparently, Antonia James' husband is a jealous man, and she's bribed the servants into telling him that she's at this charitable function or that—but no one knows where she really went."

"Good work, Em," Papa said. "So Antonia James stays on the list of suspects, while Alastair James goes off… along with Lady Charlotte and Miss Eloisa, whose alibis we were able to verify. We still need to hear back about Peter Theale and Miss Sybil. I've sent a man to Bristol to speak to Albert Brace, Theale's alibi. And McLeod will stop in Lancashire on the way back from Gretna to pay a visit to Miss Bunbury, Miss Sybil's friend."

"We're making progress," Emma said. "Soon we'll have the villain behind bars."

"That time can't come soon enough," Rosie said with feeling.

Chapter Thirty-Seven

AFTER THE PARTY, Andrew escorted Rosie home in his carriage. Tucked against his hard strength, her head on his shoulder, she felt cherished and protected. Soon the murderer would be captured, and she would be free to pursue the life she wanted—with the man she loved.

Knowing that she would soon expose her heart to him, she felt a thrill of anticipation mingled with fear. To steady her nerves, she looked through the slit in the curtains—and frowned. "The driver's headed in the opposite direction of Curzon Street."

"We're not going to your house."

"Where are we going then?" She tilted her head to look at him.

"To mine."

Although the prospect of another adventure at his club made her tingle, at present she craved intimacy more than sexual exploration. She wanted to tell Andrew that she loved him, that she wanted to share the rest of her life with him— and then she wanted to make love in the cozy privacy of her bedchamber. Afterward, she wanted to fall asleep in his arms and wake up there, too.

Hesitating, she said, "If you don't mind, I'd rather visit the club another time. It's late and—"

"The club's not where I live, silly chit." The chiseled planes of his face reflected his amusement. "I'm taking you to one of my residences."

She had the faint recollection that he'd mentioned owning some properties.

"One?" She raised her brows. "How many do you own?"

"In London?"

She blinked. Nodded.

"A dozen, give or take. Two I reserve for personal use, the rest are commercial holdings. In fact, the majority of my income these days derives from rents and other investments."

"Then why do you still operate..." She bit her lip, realizing how judgmental she might sound.

"Corbett's? My other bawdy houses?"

Afraid that she'd insulted him, she gave a wary nod.

"It's what I do. What I've always done in some form or another." He looked pensive rather than affronted. With a self-deprecating shrug, he said, "We all have to be good at something, and I suppose I'm a good pimp."

She couldn't stand for him to diminish himself in any way.

"You're more than that. You're an employer who treats his workers with dignity and kindness. You're a keen and hard-working businessman who has earned every bit of his success. You're a good, honorable man who protects those he cares about and acts with integrity..." She caught herself; heavens, she was babbling like an idiot. "Well, I could go on," she finished lamely.

Andrew was staring at her. The raw longing in his eyes melted her insides, summoning up more words, the ones she'd held back for too long. Before she could utter them, a knock sounded on the carriage door.

"We've arrived, sir," one of the guards said.

She'd been so caught up in her defense of him that she hadn't noticed the carriage stopping. The door opened, and she saw that they were still in Mayfair, in the gated courtyard of a stately Palladian mansion. Andrew exited first, then swung her down.

"For safety, we'll go in through the back," he said.

They entered through the kitchens, a vast and spotless space, the walls lined with glass jars of dried herbs and spices, gleaming pots hanging from hooks. Despite the scent and warmth of recent use, the room was empty.

"Where are the servants?" she said curiously.

"They're gone for the night. I thought privacy would be best." He led her up the steps. "If you need a ladies maid, I could be persuaded to volunteer my services."

She smiled back at him, partly in response to his flirtation, but more so because of his thoughtfulness. Everything he did reflected his concern for her, how attuned he was to her needs and moods. The way he took care of her made her want to do the same for him. To give him... everything.

They arrived on the main floor of the townhouse, as grand as any she'd been in. The grey-veined marble of the foyer gleamed beneath her slippers, a tiered chandelier dripping light from three floors above. The double wings of the mahogany stairwell soared with majestic grace.

"Your home is beautiful," she breathed.

"I'm glad it meets with your approval. Would you like a tour now, or are you ready to retire?"

She met his gaze, and the simmering heat in those coffee-dark eyes made her heart thump.

"I'd like to retire," she said.

His slow smile rewarded her boldness. Then she was swept off her feet, and they were headed up the stairwell.

Her arms circling his neck, she dimpled at him. "You don't have to carry me, you know. I'm more than willing to get myself to your bedchamber."

"Don't deny me the pleasure of having you in my arms, sunshine," he murmured.

Since he did seem to enjoy it, and she *knew* she did, she snuggled closer, resting her head in the crook of his neck.

Arriving on the next floor, he strode down the corridor and through the double doors at the end. The suite, like everything she'd seen thus far, was tastefully appointed. They passed a sitting room decorated in shades of blue and maize and entered the bedchamber.

Crossing the threshold of his inner sanctum, she felt a secret thrill. A white marble hearth flickered along one wall, the firelight gleaming off the heavy masculine furnishings and the posters of a huge bed which lay in shadows just beyond.

Catching a movement in that bed, Primrose blinked.

Andrew's muscles turned to rock around her.

An instant later, a female voice emerged from the dark. "Corby, love, what took you so long?"

What on earth?

Before Rosie could gather her wits, Andrew set her on her feet, pushing her none too gently behind him. "How the devil did you get in here?" he growled.

This question wasn't directed at her but at the woman who'd emerged from the bed—*from Andrew's bed*. Pressure built in Rosie's chest as she took in the other's voluptuous form, the ripe curves barely covered by a scanty negligee of flesh-colored satin. The woman's auburn hair tumbled lushly around her classical features, framing eyes that were an arresting shade of grey. She was older than Rosie, somewhere in her forties, with fine-grained skin and handsome features that suited her aura of worldly sophistication.

"How did I get in?" The woman gave a husky laugh. "Why, with the key you gave me, lover."

"Andrew, who is she?" Rosie's voice trembled along with the rest of her.

"You don't remember me?" The curve of the woman's red lips stirred a sense of recognition, frost spreading over Rosie's insides. "Ah, but I remember you. How my little flower has blossomed."

"Don't speak to her." Menace dripped from Andrew's voice. "Get out. Now."

"Is that any way to treat an old friend?"

Smirking, the woman came even closer, ran a finger down Andrew's lapel.

He caught her wrist, shoving her hand aside. "We're not friends."

The woman clucked her tongue. "In the two years since I last *saw* you,"—her emphasis on the verb implied that she and Andrew had done a lot more than look at each other—"it seems you've forgotten your pretty manners. The manners that I taught you. Clearly, you need your Kitty to take care of you."

Primrose's heart knocked against her ribs. "You... you're Kitty Barnes?"

Kitty's eyes gleamed. "Recognized me at last have you, Primrose?"

In her imaginings, Rosie had pictured Kitty as a witch of a woman. One whose exterior matched up with the dark and ugly emotions Rosie associated with her. Far from being a dried-up old hag, Kitty brimmed with vibrant sensuality.

In a flash, Andrew moved, his hand closing like a vise around the redhead's arm. "I'm bloody tossing you out."

"No need. I can see that I'm not wanted... at the moment."

Already reeling, Rosie took in the knowing curve of Kitty's full mouth, and her insides twisted into a knot so tight that she could scarcely breathe.

"I'll come back when you're not busy, lover," Kitty drawled, "and we'll pick up where we left off. Like we always do."

"Shut up, you damned bitch—"

"Andrew, what does she mean?" Rosie's shock faded, replaced by a suffocating awareness. "Are the two of you...

still lovers?"

He swung to face her, his face ravaged. "Primrose, I can explain—"

"Corby and I have been lovers since you were in leading strings, dear." Kitty's smile condescended and gloated at the same time. "We've had our ups and downs, but he always comes back to my bed."

Pain ripped through Rosie, hopes and dreams bleeding from her.

"It's done between Kitty and me," Andrew said in a gritty voice. "Whatever we had, it was *nothing* like what we share, Primrose—"

"How long has it been since you've shared her bed?"

His turbulent gaze held hers. "I love you. I've loved you since—"

"*How long?*"

His chest heaved. "Two years."

Two years. It's only been two years since he made love to that woman—that witch who sold *me* to a monster. Rosie's chest burned, fire rising to the back of her eyes.

"It ought to have been over long before that," Andrew said hoarsely. "I knew it wasn't right; it never was. I tried to end it. I wouldn't see her for years, but then she would show up and I… I don't know why I let her back in. If you'd let me explain—"

"I don't want to hear any more of your lies!" The words left her in a shout.

"That's probably wise, dear," Kitty drawled, "since it seems Corby here hasn't been entirely disclosing to you. Did he mention, for instance, that he knew that I planned to sell you to the highest bidder—that he could have prevented it… but instead he ran off and took up with another bawd? Well, I suppose one can't blame him for his survival tactics. As they say—once a whore, always a whore."

If Rosie had thought her life couldn't shatter any further, this was proof that she was wrong. The shards of her dreams rained upon her, slicing the heart she'd exposed into a thousand foolish pieces.

"Primrose, please listen to me—"

She backed away from Andrew's outstretched hand, his tormented eyes. "Stay away from me. You're disgusting... *you disgust me*. I never want to see you again!"

Whirling around, she ran from the room.

With leaden steps, Andrew ascended the stairs to his chamber. Inside he was cold—colder than he ever remembered being. He'd watched the woman he loved run from him... and he was powerless to stop it.

He didn't know how he would fix things with Primrose. Didn't know if he could or deserved to. He did know that there was nothing he could do about it tonight. So he'd let her go. He'd instructed his guards to take her back to her parents, waiting for confirmation that she was safe.

Now it was time to deal with Kitty.

He entered the bedchamber, not surprised to see her fully dressed, sitting by the fire. She hadn't come for sex—of that he was certain. For Kitty, pleasure had always come second to her desire for gain: for money or power or whatever it was she wanted.

During their association, he'd accepted her cold, calculating nature. She was who she was... just as he was who he was. Survival had made them both hard, immune to life's venom. But his time with Primrose had changed him. Her sweetness and generosity had shown him a relationship he'd never imagined he could have. One full of laughter, passion, and love.

Seeing Kitty in his wingchair—in his house where she had no business being—he felt her poison seeping into his bloodstream. And it made him cold with rage.

He stood in front of her chair. "Who put you up to this?"

"Maybe I missed you, lover, and wanted to fuck for old time's sake."

"You have a minute to answer me before I throttle it out of you."

"You'd never lay hands on a woman, Corby. You and I both know that."

Her bravado faded when his stare didn't waver, his knuckles cracking as his hands fisted.

"At any rate," she said hastily, "I did you a favor. What were you thinking, letting that milk-fed chit wind you around her little finger?"

He slammed his palms onto the wingchair's arms with enough force to make Kitty jolt.

"Who. Paid. *You?*" he roared.

"T-Todd," she stammered. "It was Malcolm Todd."

Just as he thought. Twice now, Todd had crossed him. The bastard was going to *pay*.

Straightening, Andrew stalked to the mantelpiece and clipped out, "Tell me everything."

"Todd approached me. Apparently, he has some beef with you," Kitty said warily. "He discovered that you were having an affair, and since it's no secret that you and I have a past, he wanted me to cause trouble for you. Between you and your new lover." She swallowed, her throat bobbing. "I had no choice, Corby. I owe Todd money. I've played too deeply at his tables, and you know what he does to those who don't pay their debts. This was the only way I could save myself. I *had* to do this."

He looked into her pleading grey eyes—and felt nothing.

"Get out," he said.

Instead of leaving, she came to him. "I... I've missed you. I've thought about what you said the last time, about wanting more than fucking, and I realize that—"

"I don't want more from you. I don't want anything." He didn't know who disgusted him more: her or himself. "Fucking's all we ever did, Kitty, and it wasn't even good."

Her eyes flashed, but she said in a wheedling tone, "I've changed—"

"I don't give a damn," he said flatly. "Your poison stopped working on me long ago."

That was what Kitty had fed him for all those years: her own brand of toxicity. What she'd labelled as necessary for survival had been a recipe for his self-doubt and self-hatred— the better for her to manipulate him with. He'd realized this when he'd ended things with her; now he *felt* it in the depths of his soul. The soul that had been awakened by joy and love— because of Primrose.

Pain bled through his icy control. How could he make things right with her? How could he—when the truth was she deserved better than him?

"You think that high-kick chit is better than me?" Kitty scoffed.

"I know she is."

"She's a bastard," Kitty spat, "same as you and me."

"She's a lady, and it has nothing to do with her birth. It's something you'll never understand. Now get out," he said in glacial tones. "If you breathe word of this, if I see you again— you will regret it."

Fear darkened her eyes—then again, she'd always been a coward. She'd bullied and used those weaker than her. She'd called it survival, but in truth she was nothing more than a predator.

She headed for the doorway, where she, being who she was, couldn't resist a parting shot. "What lady would want a pimp for a husband?" she sneered before flouncing off.

It wasn't Kitty's words that stayed with him but Primrose's.

You disgust me. I never want to see you again.

A spasm hit his chest. *I don't blame you, sunshine.*

Going to his bedside table, he opened the drawer. The rag doll looked out at him with lifeless eyes. He sank onto the mattress, his elbows bracing his thighs, and dropped his head into his hands.

Chapter Thirty-Eight

IN HER OLD bedchamber, Rosie opened the cabinet that contained her dolls. She'd left them here when she'd moved into Curzon Street; at the time, she'd thought of it as a symbolic letting go of her childhood. Now she found herself holding Calliope once more, looking at the doll's composed porcelain face, her fingers curling into the folds of the doll's perfect ballgown.

"Why did he lie to me?" she whispered.

Calliope stared back at her blankly.

"I don't understand it. I thought Andrew loved me—he said he did," she said, her throat swelling. "Why would he go to such lengths to protect me, only to betray me in the end?"

She'd been asking herself that question for the past two days. Well, that wasn't precisely true. The day after Kitty's shocking revelations Rosie had spent weeping. She'd cried and cried and cried. When her parents and even Edward had come to check in on her, she'd told them, "Go away." She hadn't been ready to talk; the last thing her misery wanted was company.

That had been yesterday. Today, she felt as dry as bone. But now that her emotions were sapped, fresh questions whirled in her mind.

Why did Andrew lie to me about Kitty?

Now that she was calmer, she had to admit that he hadn't lied, not exactly. His sin had been one of omission. He simply hadn't told her when he'd ended things with Kitty, and, to be fair, she hadn't asked. She'd just assumed that it had been longer than *two years*.

As her belly churned, she tried to think rationally. Two years were two years. It was not as if he'd been unfaithful to her.... then why did she *feel* as if he had?

It was because of Kitty. The cold, calculating bitch who had sold her to a disgusting lecher.

Rosie's fingers clenched the doll's satin skirts. Why hadn't Andrew fought to save her back then? Why had he abandoned her to those *monsters*?

With a cry of rage, she threw the doll across the room. She watched, bosom heaving, as it flew through the air and smashed against a wall, pieces scattering on the ground.

Slowly, she went over. She crouched and picked up the largest piece—the doll's face: still white, still pretty, still composed. She turned it over in her palm, and her breath jammed at the discovery.

The inside of the figurine wasn't white, pretty, or composed. Here, the unglazed clay was dark and rough. Before being hardened by fire, the pliable material had been deeply scored, slashed with random marks.

All this time... her beautiful companion had been scarred on the inside.

Scarred on the inside.

Scars on the inside.

Out of nowhere, memories pelted her.

I thought you came to me because of what I used to do, and I didn't like that.... She didn't sell me. It was my choice. I wanted to put food on our table and fucking was an easier way to do it than thieving or running with cutthroats.... We all have to be good at something, and I'm a good pimp.... No one has ever given me what you have—passion, sweetness, joy. I don't deserve it, but you make me feel like a different man.

Awareness prickled through her like sensation through an

awakening limb.

"Rosie, are you all right?" Mama entered in a swish of forest green velvet, a sleeping Sophie in her arms. "I thought I heard something…" Her gaze went to the fragments on the floor.

Rosie stood, swallowing thickly. "I think I broke something, Mama. And I—I'm not sure how to fix it."

"Are you ready to talk about it?" her mother said quietly.

"May I hold Sophie while we do?"

Cuddling her sleeping sister close, she sat next to her mama on the window seat and told the other about Kitty Barnes—about everything.

"I was so hurt, Mama, that I just ran away. I didn't give Andrew a chance to explain," she said miserably. "Now that I've had a chance to think, I suspect there's more to the story than I realized. More to *his* story."

"Don't be too hard on yourself," Mama murmured. "Given your own history, it's no wonder you'd react that way. And I think you're right about Corbett. He's a complex fellow. I realized that when I met him all those years ago."

"What was he like then?" she couldn't help but ask.

"Charming, confident… and young." Mama hesitated. "Despite what he must have seen of the world, he wasn't as jaded as one would expect. His sense of honor was still intact, and there was a tenderness in him that life hadn't managed to extinguish. It was those two qualities, I think, that prompted him to aid in my quest to find you."

"Andrew *is* honorable and tender," Rosie said, her voice scratchy, "and he's been through so much. More than you know. His mother was addicted to drink, and she brought him into the trade when he was only…" She bit her lip, not wanting to betray her lover's confidences. "The point is, he had every reason to resent his mama. But he didn't. He loved her. And despite the fact that he's a pimp, he's a good man—

just ask anyone who works for him. He's generous and strong and caring."

Mama regarded her with compassionate eyes. "You love him."

"I do." Rosie's voice hitched. "I'm so confused!"

"Because he hasn't told you he loves you?"

"No, he did. In fact, *I'm* the one who hasn't said the words. I was going to the night that Kitty appeared. Now I don't know what to do." Belly clenching, she recognized the crux of her dilemma. "How can I love a man who'd love a woman like Kitty? Who'd leave me with her, knowing what she intended to do?"

"First things first. What makes you think Corbett loved Kitty Barnes?"

"He told me he started sleeping with her when he was fifteen. He didn't end the affair until two years ago. Why would he consort with her for that long—even if it was on and off—if not for love?"

"How old was Kitty when the affair began?"

Mama's question made Rosie blink. Her heart began to thud. "I... don't know."

"Well, I met that woman fourteen years ago, and I'd give her more than a decade on Corbett," Mama said bluntly. "Which means that she was at least twenty-five when she began an affair with a fifteen-year-old. A boy only months older than your brother is now. So you tell me: do you think love is the true explanation for why he got tangled in her web?"

The realization slammed into Rosie—and made her *ill*. She hadn't even thought of the age difference between Kitty and Andrew at the start of their relationship. Of how vulnerable he must have been back then. How easily he could have been preyed upon by an experienced bawd. One who'd not only taken him to her bed but *sold his services* to others.

His words suddenly surfaced from two nights ago. *I knew it wasn't right... it never was... I tried to end it... I don't know why I let her back in...*

Rosie's heart splintered. Because *she* knew why he'd let Kitty back.

It was the same reason she'd tried to win the *ton's* approval. The same reason she'd made all those stupid mistakes over and over again and made the worst of one of all by marrying Daltry. The same reason she'd been *afraid* of falling in love with Andrew—the best thing that had ever happened to her.

She doubted her own self-worth... as Andrew doubted his.

"Andrew couldn't rid himself of Kitty," she said in a pained whisper, "because he didn't think he deserved any better."

"Knowing what I do of that woman," Mama said, her eyes hard, "I am certain she had tactics for keeping him under her thumb. For taking advantage of his good character."

It killed Rosie to think that Kitty had gotten her claws into Andrew. And it killed her even more to realize that she hadn't seen it. How similar she and Andrew were. How, beneath his powerful self-possession and all his success, he harbored his own insecurities... even as he'd worked toward curing hers. He'd made her feel cherished, beautiful—never dirty or damaged. And what had she given him in return?

With throbbing remorse, she realized that she, in her own way, had also taken advantage of Andrew's noble nature. After all he'd done for her, protecting her, *loving* her, she hadn't even given him a chance to explain. Instead, she'd doubted him, blamed him for not rescuing her from Kitty—when he'd, in truth, been little more than a boy himself. A victim of the circumstances just as she'd been.

She understood that now.

"Oh, Mama," she said fitfully, "I've treated Andrew so shabbily!"

"Your reaction is understandable." Mama's eyes were overly bright. "Because of the mistakes I made, you didn't have security or love for the first eight years of your life. Is it any wonder that Kitty's appearance would trigger your fears of abandonment—of being betrayed?"

"The past is not your fault, Mama." Keeping her sister in the crook of her arm, Rosie reached for her mother's hand and squeezed it. "You always did your best by me, and you've taught me to be strong. I couldn't have wished for a better mother," she said sincerely. "I love you, and I'm sorry I don't say it often enough."

"Dearest." A tear trickled down Mama's cheek.

"And thank you for helping me figure out what I need to do next."

"What is that?"

"I have to apologize to Andrew—and listen to what he has to say." Rosie swallowed. "But I think... I think the past doesn't matter any longer. Because I love him, Mama. If he can forgive me for all my mistakes, then surely I can do the same for him."

"My little girl, all grown up." Mama laid a hand on her cheek.

Sophie chose that moment to wake up, her rosebud mouth puckering into a howl.

"Good thing you still have another," Rosie said ruefully.

She rose, rocking her sister and humming a tune. The crying turned to gentle cooing.

"You're a natural with her, you know." Mama's smile had an edge of wistfulness. "Soon you'll be ready for a child of your own."

The thought of having a babe—Andrew's babe—made Rosie's heart thump but not with panic. For the first time, the idea of motherhood seemed almost... desirable.

Cuddling her sister, she said with feeling, "Andrew and I have a lot to iron out before that."

"The important thing is that you know you love him. I didn't realize what your papa meant to me until it was almost too late."

"So that is why my ears are burning," came Papa's voice.

He entered the sitting room, Edward following behind. Both were attired in fashionable garb that set off their lean, lanky figures and handsome dark looks—though Edward's cravat was, as always, slightly askew. Papa's amber gaze went to Rosie; yesterday, he'd given her a wide berth, and she knew he was trying to gauge her present state.

She gave him a tremulous smile. "Mama was just telling me what you mean to her."

His watchful gaze remained on her for another moment and then the grooves around his mouth eased. "Is that right, poppet? And what did your mother say?"

"Well, she hadn't actually said it *yet*," she said impishly.

"I'll say it now," Mama declared. "Your papa means *everything* to me."

Papa's eyes flashed, and he crossed over to Mama, bending to kiss her cheek and murmur something in her ear. Edward sauntered up to Primrose.

"Well, now you've done it. They're at it again," he muttered. "We'll never make it to the luncheon in time."

"I'm surprised you want to go." Rosie lifted Sophie into the air, the babe gurgling in delight. "Don't these sorts of affairs bore you?"

She knew her brother would prefer a visit to a museum over a charity luncheon any day. He was only going because the event was being hosted by the Hunts, dear friends of the family. Being in mourning prevented Rosie from participating in the public event—which was just as well. She had to plan her reunion with Andrew.

What would she say? What would she *wear*?

"Uncle Harry is going to be there," Edward replied. "And he promised to show me and Frederick another of his inventions."

Good Lord. *That* explained her brother's willingness to go.

"If you want company, however," he added gruffly, "I could stay."

"Thank you, I'll be fine. And Edward?"

"Yes?"

"I love you, dear."

Edward's face reddened. "Good God, not you too. Is this excess of sentimentality catching?"

"You'd best watch out." She grinned at him. "By the by, your cravat is crooked."

Her parents came over. Mama took Sophie, and Papa cleared his throat.

"Your mother tells me you've decided to patch things up with Corbett."

Rosie couldn't tell from her father's expression whether he approved of her decision or not.

"I'm going to try," she said earnestly.

"You're certain this is the future you want?" Her father's eyes searched her face. "Certain that you wish to give up your title and money for this fellow?"

"Yes, Papa." She'd never been more certain of anything.

"Then, whenever you are ready, I'll invite Corbett over to supper." Papa's expression was stern, but his eyes smiled at her. "We'll do this thing properly from here on in."

"Thank you, Papa." Gladness flooded her, and she rose on tiptoe to kiss her father's lean cheek. "I only hope Andrew will forgive me."

Papa snorted. "Poor chap doesn't stand a chance."

A knock sounded on the door, and Libby entered. Curtsying, she said to Mama, "It's time for Miss Sophie's daily outing. I thought I'd take her to see the aviary at the Pantheon."

"I'm sure she will enjoy that." Mama kissed Sophie before handing her over to the maid.

"We should be back by mid-afternoon," Papa told Rosie. "Stay put, and if you need anything, Caster's the guard on duty today. I won't rest easy until we get to the bottom of this."

"I'll be fine." Rosie smiled at her family. "Have a lovely time, and send my best to the Hunts."

A short while later, Rosie was sitting at her old escritoire, trying to compose a letter to Andrew, when she was interrupted by Susie, one of the newer housemaids.

Susie curtsied, holding out a vibrant, paper-wrapped bouquet. "These just came for ye, miss."

Heart racing, Rosie thanked the maid and took the fragrant flowers. She set them on the desk, rummaging through the foliage to find the note. It was sealed, her name boldly inked on the front. Hands trembling, she broke the wax.

Shock jolted her.

I have your sister and her maid. If you wish to see them alive, you will meet me at No. 3 Bulstrode Street in half an hour. I have eyes everywhere, so come alone—or your sister and the maid will die.

P.S. Enclosed is a memento from Sophie.

Rosie looked at the handkerchief: the initials SK were embroidered in pink silk, entwined with a garland of flowers.

Mama's handiwork was unmistakable. Proof that the villain—whoever he or she was—did indeed have Sophie.

What should I do?

Wings of panic beat in Rosie's chest. She couldn't risk Sophie coming to harm; she had to do something—and she couldn't alert Caster. The kidnapper had been clear that she was to come alone: any wrong move on her part could result in Sophie's demise.

I can't let that happen. I won't.

Resolve set her into action. There was no time to waste. To arrive at the given address on time, she would need to sneak out from the house and hail a hackney immediately.

But she wouldn't go into the situation unarmed.

She grabbed her reticule, feeling the welcome weight of the pistol Andrew had given her. For added insurance, she paused to dash off a quick note, sealing it. She summoned Susie, instructing the other to give the note to Caster in exactly half an hour.

After the maid left, Rosie waited until the hallway was empty. She descended the steps, her heart measuring out the frantic rhythm of her mission.

Wait for me, Sophie—I'm coming.

Chapter Thirty-Nine

ROSIE ARRIVED AT her destination just shy of the appointed time. Bulstrode Street was located north of Mayfair, a relatively quiet lane off High Street in Marylebone. Number Three was a modest terraced townhouse with a plain brick front and an entryway recessed beneath a crumbling stone arch.

Passing through, Rosie approached the front door—saw that it was ajar. She took a breath and pushed it open. She found herself in a cramped foyer, a closed door to the right, stairs ascending to the upper floor, and a dark, narrow corridor leading to the back of the house. As she cautiously crossed the worn threshold, heavy gloom and stillness shrouded her, the hairs on her nape shivering.

"H-hello?" she called out.

She strained to hear any sounds that might betray Sophie's presence—and heard only the click of the door closing behind her, blown shut by some ghostly gust. The outside world grew distant as she ventured forward into the tomb-like space, the floorboards squeaking beneath her. She paused at the closed door; before she could decide whether to knock, it suddenly opened.

She stood face to face with Sybil Fossey.

Sybil appeared her usual diffident, mousy self, the only difference being that this time she held a pistol in her gloved hand, aiming it at Rosie's heart.

"Hand over your reticule," Sybil said.

Rosie gripped her bag. "Sybil, let us talk—"

"Give it to me, or I will put a hole through you and then your sister."

At Sybil's calm, measured tones, fear snaked down Rosie's spine. She did as the other asked, and Sybil took the reticule, flinging it into the room behind her where it landed with a thump. Then she gestured at Rosie with the pistol.

"Turn around and walk toward the hallway. I will be behind you. Make one false move, and I will shoot. Now go."

Heart pounding, Rosie started down the corridor. "Where is my sister?"

"Be quiet and walk. Or she's dead."

Did Sybil have accomplices? Were they holding Sophie and Libby somewhere in the house? Swallowing, Rosie obeyed Sybil's commands. When they reached the last room at the end of the hall, Sybil said, "Go inside."

Rosie went into the small study. It was sparsely furnished with a sagging couch covered in moth-eaten pillows and a table flanked by two chairs and set with a tea service. The room had no windows, a single lamp the only relief from the gloom.

Here, at the back of the house, the outside world had vanished completely. In here, anything could happen and no one would be the wiser. Fear washed over Rosie as Sybil closed the door.

"Where is Sophie?" Rosie said.

"Sit." Sybil waved the gun at one of the chairs. "We'll get to your sister in a moment."

She sat, her mind working furiously. "Why are you doing this?"

Sybil took the opposite chair. Keeping the pistol aimed at Rosie, she picked up the tea pot, pouring liquid into the cups in front of them. Tendrils of steam curled upward.

"Have some tea," she said politely—as if this were a social

gathering.

Enough is enough.

"I'm not doing another dashed thing you say until you tell me where Sophie is," Rosie said.

"I suppose it doesn't matter now. Very well." Sybil held the pistol steady. "By my estimation, your sister will be on her way home from her outing with her maid."

"Pardon?" Rosie whispered.

"It was a ruse," the other explained. "Since you came into Daltry's money, I've been watching you. One can learn a lot from simply observing household routines—such as the fact that your sister's nursemaid takes her for an outing at the same time each day. It was easy to compose a note saying that I'd taken her."

"But you had the handkerchief—"

"I followed the nursemaid to the park one day and pretended to admire the babe. Whilst I did this, I filched the handkerchief. Simple, really."

Sybil smiled complacently, and Rosie's relief that Sophie and Libby were safe faded to the awareness that she'd walked right into this deranged woman's trap. She had two options: use the pistol she'd secreted in the pocket of her skirts—or keep Sybil talking, delaying until Caster got her note and sent in reinforcements.

Eyeing Sybil's steady grip on the firearm, Rosie decided that delaying was a better choice. By the time she had her pistol in hand and ready to shoot, she might already have a hole through her.

"So you were behind everything?" she said, trying to buy time. "You poisoned Daltry, hired a cutthroat to kill me?"

Sybil inclined her head.

"Was it all for the money?"

"Money was part of it. Not all."

"Why, then?" In an effort to draw the other in, Rosie kept

her tone conversational. "Why would you, a well-bred lady, go to such lengths for two thousand pounds per annum?"

"Don't you listen? I said it was not just because of the money." Rage entered Sybil's voice.

"Then what made you resort to murder?"

"I hated Daltry." Sybil's expression was arctic. "He *owed* me for what he did to me."

A new chill permeated Rosie's insides. "What did he do?"

"He forced me to have relations with him." Ice glittered in the other's pale blue eyes. "For years, I had no choice but to endure his advances."

Rosie stared at her. "Why… why didn't you tell someone? Surely your aunt—"

"Would have disowned me if she knew the truth. Daltry was blackmailing me, you see. Five years ago, he discovered my indiscretion with my aunt's butler. I was in love; my lover was older than me and lower in rank, yet I was planning to run off with him. Daltry found out and paid my lover to leave me. Soon thereafter, I discovered I was with child." Bleakness deadened Sybil's voice, and, despite everything, empathy surged in Rosie. "I would have been ruined had Daltry not offered me a way out. He brought me to a midwife who took care of my 'problem.' And he vowed never to tell anyone of the sordid truth—as long as I went to his bed and did whatever he wanted. And so I did. For five long years, I did."

To think she'd been married, even briefly, to that monster made Rosie nauseous.

"I'm sorry, Sybil," she said, her throat tight. "No one should have to endure such things."

Sybil's eyes flashed. "I don't need your pity. I got something better: *revenge*. Before Daltry eloped with you, he paid me a final visit. Here in this shabby apartment that he used for our rendezvous. He crowed about finding a pretty young thing to breed his heirs—and that was when I knew I had to act."

"Because you didn't want his fortune to go to his heirs?"

"Because if he married you and had heirs, then Peter wouldn't inherit."

"Peter... you mean Mr. Theale?" Rosie said in surprise. "Is he involved?"

"Peter knows nothing of what I've done. We are in love, and he is a good man, but he cannot marry me because of his debts. He has been forced to consider offering for a merchant's daughter—and I couldn't let it happen." Sybil's lips pressed together. "I couldn't allow Daltry to stand in the way of my happiness again. So I made the trip to Gretna and surprised him."

More pieces fell into place. "He was with you... before our wedding night?"

Sybil gave a grim nod. "It didn't take much to entice him. Daltry was nothing if not a lecher and a vain one to boot. He actually believed my Banbury Tale that I'd followed him like a lovesick fool, not wanting to let him go. We tupped, and afterward, we toasted, and he drank the wine I'd laced with foxglove. Then he went back to you, and the rest, as they say, is history."

Seeing the demented gleam in Sybil's eyes, Rosie prayed that Caster had received her note. *I have to keep Sybil talking until he arrives.*

"But it isn't quite," she said. "Because after you killed Daltry, you also tried to kill me."

"I do regret that." Sybil stood. "Again, the blame lies at Daltry's door. He was the one who altered the terms of the will, leaving his fortune to you instead of Peter. This left Peter in direr straits than ever—unless you remarried or met an early demise. I couldn't wait for the former to happen: Peter was too close to offering for that tea merchant's girl. So I had to get rid of you."

Get rid *of me—as if that were nothing more than tossing out an old slipper!*

Rosie quelled a shudder. "Did you hire the cutthroat to assassinate me? Did you kill him too?"

"When I learned the contents of Daltry's will, I panicked. Given that I'd poisoned Daltry, I didn't want to poison you for fear of rousing suspicion. So I hired the cutthroat. It turned out to be a mistake for he demanded full payment despite his failure to complete his task. Since I couldn't trust him not to talk, I had to take care of him too." Sybil shrugged. "All it took was a bottle of cognac laced with foxglove."

Shaking her head, Rosie said, "Do you think Mr. Theale will want to be with you knowing what you've done?"

"Peter will never find out the cost for our happiness. Being with him and having my freedom are worth any price." Sybil's face blazed with righteous conviction. "Daltry deserved what he got for making me suffer. Finally, I will have my happy ending."

"I'm sorry for your suffering," Rosie said quietly, "but that does not give you the right to cause suffering to others. I've done nothing to you."

Sybil's lips pressed together, and Rosie felt a spark of hope—which was snuffed out when the other came closer, waving the gun at her. "Time to drink your tea."

What kind of fool does she think I am?

"I'll not drink your poison," Rosie declared.

"You'd rather die with a bullet in your brain?" The gun's cold muzzle dug into Rosie's left temple. "Because those are your choices."

She had a third choice—and now was the time to act upon it. If Sybil truly meant to shoot her, she'd have done so already. No, the other *wanted* her to die from poisoning: a cleaner method of murder and one that would be more difficult to prove.

Over my dead body. Hopefully, not literally.

"All right," she said quickly. "I'll drink the tea. But I can't very well do so with a pistol embedded in my head."

While the pressure on her temple eased, Sybil remained at her side, keeping the weapon trained on her. "Be quick about it."

Rosie reached for the tea cup with one hand, the other slipping beneath the table, into the hidden pocket of her skirts. She gripped the handle of the loaded pistol.

She paused, the cup's rim inches from her lips. "May I have some sugar? I like my tea sweet."

"Stop stalling," Sybil snapped, "or I'll just shoot you and be done with it."

Rosie whipped out her pistol, had a moment to aim for Sybil's shoulder before squeezing the trigger. The blast and Sybil's scream filled the room. Rosie stumbled backward from the table, clutching the gun.

The door flew open. At the sight of the large figure filling the doorway, a dizzying wave of relief crashed through her.

"Andrew," she breathed.

The next instant, her knees crumpled. Strong arms caught her. She found herself looking up into her beloved's face, his blazing eyes.

"Are you hurt?" he demanded.

"No." She shook her head, a bit woozy. "I shot *her*."

The fire slowly banked in his eyes. His lips quirked. "Then there's no use fainting after the fact, sunshine."

"Did I... is Sybil...?"

"She's alive, my lady. 'Tis just a flesh wound." She turned her head at Jem's voice; she hadn't noticed the groom's presence—or the other men's. He and two guards surrounded Sybil, who remained lying on the ground, her chest rising and falling in shallow surges.

"We'll staunch the bleeding," Jem went on, "and she'll

live to see justice served."

With a nod, Rosie turned back to Andrew. "How did you find me?"

"I had a guard watching you. He saw you leave the house alone and sensed something was amiss. So he followed you here, sent word to me."

"Thank you for protecting me," she said softly.

"Don't thank me." His expression was stark. "I've done a shoddy job of keeping you safe. You protected yourself."

"You gave me the pistol, remember?"

"I didn't think you'd actually have to *use* it."

He sounded so disgruntled that she was tempted to smile. Instead, all the feelings she had for this strong, beautiful man pushed to the surface.

"I love you," she blurted. "And I'm so sorry I didn't let you explain about Kitty."

His pupils flared. Before he could say anything, footsteps pounded down the hallway. The next instant Papa stormed in, Harry and Caster on his heels.

Ashen-faced, her father said, "Poppet, are you—"

"I'm fine." Exhaling, she smiled shakily at him, then at Andrew. "My troubles are finally behind me."

Chapter Forty

THE NEXT EVENING, Rosie sat with the ladies of her family in her drawing room. Mama and Aunt Helena shared the settee next to Rosie's chaise whilst Emma, Thea, and Polly occupied curricle chairs. Violet, never one to sit still, wandered around the room munching on bonbons and fiddling with things.

"It is such a relief for the business to be over," Mama was saying.

"Indeed. Sybil Fossey was more cunning than I'd given her credit for." A notch formed between Emma's brows. "Thank heavens she is safe behind bars at Newgate."

"According to Ambrose, she might end up in Bedlam eventually," Mama said.

"I think an insane asylum is a fitting place for Sybil. Then again, it wasn't me she tried to murder." Canting her head, Em said, "How do you feel about it, Rosie?"

Despite Sybil's evil intentions, Rosie had a degree of empathy for the other, who'd suffered greatly at Daltry's hands. It didn't excuse Sybil's actions, but it did make them more understandable.

"Bedlam's no stroll in the park," she said quietly. "And I think it'll be easier for the rest of her family to have her in a hospital rather than in gaol... or worse. As it is, Lady Charlotte and Eloisa are beside themselves."

"They truly had no idea that Daltry had been blackmailing Sybil all these years?" Polly's aquamarine eyes shone with sympathy.

Rosie shook her head. "They didn't know about her affair with the butler, her terminated pregnancy, or her forced relations with Daltry. Whenever she needed to get away, she would use the excuse of visiting her friend Miss Bunbury. When Mr. McLeod stopped in Lancashire, he discovered that Miss Bunbury had, in fact, died many years ago."

Shuddering, Polly said, "How is Peter Theale taking the news?"

"He's distressed, naturally," Rosie said, "and shocked to discover that the woman he loves is capable of murder."

"Thunder 'n turf, I'd be shocked too," Violet exclaimed. "But what shocks me *more* is that Mrs. James was carrying on with her own stepson! Remember how hoity-toity she was toward us? Someone ought to tell her about glass houses."

In his investigation in Kent, Mr. Lugo had found several shopkeepers who did indeed recognize Mrs. James; all of them had put her in the company of a younger fellow who seemed like an "intimate friend"—and who fit the description of Alastair James. When confronted, the Jameses had confessed to their affair; Mrs. James also admitted that she'd first learned the details of the shooting from her lover. She'd begged to have their affair kept under wraps in order to avoid a ruinous scandal.

Rosie, knowing the hurt that gossip could inflict, had assured the other that she would say nothing. A grateful Mrs. James promised to repay the favor by throwing her considerable social weight behind Rosie, and her support, along with the Lady Charlotte's, would cement Rosie's position in the upper echelons.

The irony was supreme: now that Rosie had everything she'd once wanted, she realized it meant nothing. Respectability, acceptance—none of it meant a thing without Andrew.

Her heart clenched. *Why hasn't he come to me?*

"Glass houses aside, I, for one, prefer to have Mrs. James as a friend to Rosie rather than an enemy," Mama said. "My daughter has been through enough peril for a lifetime. And I have done enough embroidery to last *two* lifetimes."

Now that the threat to her life was over, Rosie found herself confronting an even larger catastrophe. Unable to stand it any longer, she burst out, "Why hasn't Andrew called upon me? It's been an entire *day*."

Glances skated around the room.

Polly spoke first. "Perhaps because he wanted to give you time to recover? You've been through a lot, dearest."

"Would Revelstoke stay away if you'd been held at gunpoint by a madwoman?" Rosie said.

Looking chagrinned, Polly shook her head.

"Maybe he doesn't want to compromise your newly restored reputation," Thea put in.

"But he could have come to me privately last night..." Rosie stopped short, casting a wary glance at her mama and Aunt Helena.

The two ladies looked at each other.

"Why is it," Mama mused to her best friend, "that the younger generation believes they invented scandalous behavior?"

Aunt Helena's brunette brows rose. "Because you and I are such paragons of propriety?"

The pair erupted into gales of laughter.

Rosie's gaze veered heavenward. "Now that you're done amusing yourselves, may we *please* focus on the situation at hand? That of my future happiness?"

Sobering, Mama said, "Of course, dearest."

"What *do* you want for your future?" Emma said.

"Isn't it obvious?" Rosie threw her hands out in exasperation. "I'm in love with Andrew. I want to marry him."

"Perhaps it is obvious to *you*," Polly said reasonably, "but up until recently your goal was to be respectable at any cost. Does Mr. Corbett know of your change of heart?"

"Yes. That is, I think so." Rosie bit her lip. "When he rescued me, I told him that I loved him. How much clearer could I be?"

Fear welled. Although she'd confessed her true feelings and apologized for not giving him a chance to explain about Kitty, he was keeping his distance. He hadn't even responded to Papa's invitation to supper. The behavior was unlike Andrew unless... unless he'd changed his mind about her? Had her shameful treatment of him driven him away?

"Love and marriage don't always go hand in hand," Mama said patiently, "and Corbett is a sophisticated man who understands that. While you may have told him that you feel the former for him, it seems to me that you've said nothing of the latter. Corbett has a sense of honor as strong as your father's. Knowing his character, I'd wager he's keeping his distance because he thinks it's in *your* best interests. That you deserve better than what he has to offer you."

The realization plunged like an arrow into Rosie's heart.

"I'm the biggest ninny who ever *lived*," she said in horror.

"Falling in love can do that to one." A grin tucked into Em's cheeks. "Don't feel too badly. It's happened to all of us."

"Speak for yourself." Vi plopped onto the chaise next to Rosie. "I retained my wits entirely during my courtship with Carlisle."

"So says the lady who pushed her future husband into a fountain," Em retorted.

"It was an accident." Vi's grin was reminiscent rather than repentant. "Besides, Carlisle didn't mind. In fact, one time he got even by—"

"Dear heaven, spare us the intimate details," Em muttered.

"We ought to focus on Rosie's dilemma," Thea agreed. "Now, Rosie dear, are you certain you wish to marry Mr. Corbett? Even if it means giving up your hard-won respectability—not to mention your title and fortune?"

"All I want is Andrew," she said simply.

With aching remorse, she recognized that while Andrew had always put her needs first—had protected her, *loved* her through it all—she'd not done the same for him. She'd only recently confessed her feelings... and apparently not as clearly as she ought to have.

"Then you must talk to Mr. Corbett," Thea said with her gentle smile.

Rosie nodded absently. A plan was already formulating in her head. Andrew deserved more than mere words: he deserved to be shown in no uncertain terms just how much he meant to her.

"We'll finalize the details in the upcoming weeks." Andrew pushed the contract across the desk. "For now, I've had my solicitor draw this up."

Across the desk, his new partners looked at him.

"You're certain you want to do this?" Grier said gruffly. "It's your life's work—"

"And you're signing it away for a song." Sitting next to Grier, Fanny frowned in concern. "You nicked in the nob, Corbett?"

He wasn't. For the first time, his head was on straight, and he was thinking clearly. He saw now that, somewhere along the way, his life had turned in the wrong direction. He wasn't the man he wanted to be. Needed to be—in order to be deserving of Primrose.

I love you... I'm so sorry I didn't let you explain about Kitty.

The words wrought an exquisite pain, tightening his throat. One day, he hoped that he would have an adequate explanation to give Primrose. That he would be worthy of her love. But right now it wouldn't be fair to ask her to give up her bright future—her title, place in society, and wealth—for a man who had abandoned her so unforgivably. Who didn't even know where he was headed next.

It had taken all his willpower not to go to her. The last two days had been hell, and he didn't know how many more he could endure, with the temptation of her so close. Maybe he ought to go travel. See the world. He had money, time, and, for the first time in his life, freedom to do what he wanted.

The problem was that the only thing he wanted was Primrose. Wherever he went, for as long as he lived, he would never forget her. He would hoard his memories of their time together, warm himself with them in the cold, lonely nights that stretched ahead.

"You're doing me a favor," he said quietly. "It makes it easier to walk away knowing that I'm leaving Corbett's and the other clubs in good hands."

He'd spelled it all out in the contract. He would give ownership of his brothels to Fanny and Grier in exchange for a cut of the profits. The pair would uphold all the benefits he extended to his employees—and offer a new one.

"This new profit-sharing idea of yours is bound to rile up Todd," Grier said dourly.

Rewarding workers with a small percentage of the revenues was an idea that had been percolating for some time. It would be Andrew's final legacy to the business.

The fact that his plan would irk Todd was just a bonus.

"You don't have to worry about Todd," he said. "I've spoken to Bartholomew Black. He knows what's what. If Todd makes a move, he'll step in."

"And that's it? That's your revenge on Todd?" Fanny planted her hands on the desk, her expression indignant. "After all the trouble's he caused?"

"Lord, woman," Grier muttered. "Leave it be."

"Oh no, you don't, Horace Grier. Just because we're to be partners doesn't mean you can order me about," Fanny warned.

It's going to be a beautiful partnership, Andrew thought with a touch of satisfaction.

Aloud, he said, "Doing what I want—what I believe to be right—is the best revenge."

And it was.

A knock sounded on the door, and Grier left to answer it.

Fanny eyed him. "You're doing this for the chit, aren't you?"

His chest tightened. "I'm doing it for myself."

"You can't fool me, Corbett." The bawd snorted. "Why don't you just marry her and be done with it?"

Because she deserves better. Because I want her to have the best. Because I love her... and always will.

Grier returned, announcing, "We've got a problem."

"What sort of problem?" Andrew said.

The Scot shook his head. "It's best you see for yourself."

That didn't bode well.

Getting to his feet, he shrugged into his jacket. "Lead the way."

He and Grier hadn't even made it to the front salon when he heard the brouhaha, the excited swell of chatter. He frowned. *What the bloody hell is going on?* The salon was packed with bodies. Men were craning their necks to see over one another, their attention centered on something... by the pianoforte? He couldn't see through the throng, couldn't guess what would captivate this raucous bunch. Surely not a musical performance—unless one of the wenches was doing it naked.

While that did happen occasionally, it never created a stir like this one.

Andrew pushed through to the front of the crowd—and stopped short.

His disbelieving eyes took in *Primrose* standing by the pianoforte. No longer dressed in widow's weeds, she wore a vibrant yellow gown the color of her namesake. The diamond necklace he'd given her sparkled like dew around her throat. She was so beautiful that he ached just looking at her. Her eyes met his, and the expression in those jade orbs jammed his breath.

She said to Sally, who was seated at the piano (fully dressed—thank God), "I'm ready."

Sally played the opening bars of a ballad.

Primrose began to sing, and the room fell silent as her voice floated into the air.

What's this dull town to me
When you're not near....
Where all the joy and mirth
Made this town heaven on earth
Oh, they're all fled with thee
My own true love...

His throat clogged as she sang the words to him, her gaze never leaving his. He couldn't believe that she was doing this. Couldn't believe what she was sacrificing in doing so. All she'd ever wanted was respectability and now—

A part of him knew he should put a stop to this, salvage whatever part of her reputation he could... but he couldn't move. Couldn't fight his love for her any more. This glorious woman whose song reached his soul, chasing away the darkness and filling it with her own bright, unique light.

His Primrose. His love. *His.*

What when the play was o'er
What made my heart so sore
Oh, it was parting with
My own true love...

She devastated his self-control, and for once he didn't care if the world knew what he was feeling. He saw the answering love on her face, and the rest of the room disappeared. It was just the two of them, the way it had always been and was meant to be.

But now thou'rt cold to me
My own true love
Yet he I loved so well
Still in my heart shall dwell
Oh, I can ne'er forget my own true love

The last note lingered in the air. An instant later, thunderous applause broke out. Amidst the shouts, whistles, and foot stomping, he went to Primrose. Her arms looped around his neck as he carried her away from the mayhem—and past Grier and Fanny, who stood side by side, grinning.

In the privacy of the hidden corridor, he said hoarsely, "I wasn't being cold to you. I wanted you to have a better man than me."

"Oh, Andrew, don't you know?" Her eyes glimmered. "There *is* no better man than you."

"Even though... I didn't tell you about Kitty?" He swallowed over the razors in his throat. "I wanted to, but I was ashamed. It was never good, never right. I tried to end it—"

"I understand." The tenderness in her expression told him that somehow, miraculously, she did. "You were just a boy when you got tangled in her web. And, trust me, I know a thing or two about repeating mistakes. I won't judge your past any more than you judge mine."

"What about the fact that I left you with her?" he said with roiling self-recrimination. "I wanted to take you, but I didn't have the money. Or the courage."

"Andrew, you were scarcely more than a boy yourself. How could you be expected to take care of another child?" The compassion in her eyes made his own heat. "It was wrong of me to blame you, and I'm so, so sorry that I did. But don't you dare question your own courage. You've survived more than I can even imagine, and I admire you more than I can say. I *love* you so much."

"I love you," he said fiercely. "It's been hell without you."

Her dimples peeped out. "Does that mean you're going to marry me?"

"I'll challenge any man who dares to stop me." He paused. "Er, unless that man happens to be your father. Or another of your kin."

"My family adores you," she said.

He was certain she was lying, and he didn't even care. He would win her family over. With her by his side, he knew he could do anything... but did she feel the same way about him? Was it fair of him to ask her to give up everything to be his wife?

He forced himself to remind her of the consequences.

"If you marry me, you won't be marrying a gentleman. You'll lose your position, title, and fortune," he said. "Are you certain that's what you want?"

"You *are* a gentleman, Andrew Corbett." Her hands clenched his lapels in emphasis. "And none of the rest matters. I don't want anything but you."

He strode into his suite, didn't stop until he had her in his bed. He followed her down, her soft curves swamping him with pleasure. With love and lust and joy beyond imagining. Looking into her precious face, he knew there was one last thing he needed to say.

"Thank you for the song, sunshine," he murmured. "It is a gift I'll treasure forever."

"You know my fondness for the dramatic." She touched his jaw, her eyes smiling at him. "I hope you don't mind a lifetime of this."

"A lifetime with you won't nearly be enough," he said, "but I'll take what I can get."

He sealed his vow with a kiss. Then again—with his body, heart, and soul.

Epilogue

Seven months later

THAT NIGHT, LYING in bed, Rosie watched her husband enter their bedchamber.

Despite her dark mood—or perhaps *because* of it—she noted how absurdly attractive he was. One wouldn't think it possible, yet during their year of marriage, he'd grown even *more* handsome. He smiled more. He looked more relaxed, his face tanned and hair gilded from the wedding trip they'd taken abroad. He engaged in daily physical pursuits—riding or boxing at his club—and his black silk dressing gown showcased his honed virility.

The man she adored looked happy and healthy, and her heart swelled with gladness. When he'd first told her about his plans to give up Corbett's and his other clubs, she'd had mixed feelings. She hadn't wanted him to change for her. Wanted him to know that she loved him unconditionally.

"Don't do it for me," she'd said resolutely. "Do whatever makes *you* happy."

His eyes had grown serious.

"I've worked all my life, in one form or another," he'd said quietly. "I'm done with it. Now all I want is to enjoy being married. I want to spend time with my beautiful wife, who I've waited for all my life. I want to travel with her, show her exotic places, and share adventures with her… especially in bed."

That had been that.

He'd done all the things he'd wanted—and not necessarily in that order.

They'd gone on a glorious, extended wedding trip. They'd toured the vineyards of France, the villas of Italy, and the breathtaking islands of Greece. Exploring foreign lands with the love of her life had been an exhilarating time of adventure and discovery... and, near the end of it, Rosie had received another surprise.

Not that it ought to have been a surprise, she thought dryly. Since their wedding night, Andrew had stopped using the sheaths, and given the frequency of their lovemaking, it had only been a matter of time before she got with child. When he found out about her pregnancy, Andrew had arranged their immediate return to London.

Since arriving home, she'd divided her time between lying nauseated in bed, casting her accounts in a chamber pot, and bursting into tears for no reason. She felt worn, frayed, and ugly—like the little rag doll that Andrew kept in his bedside cabinet. The fact that he'd kept a memento of her all those years was achingly sweet... but she didn't want him to think that she *resembled* the pitiful thing.

And she feared that he did. No, she didn't just fear it, she *knew* it. Knew that he was losing interest in her. His behavior proved it: her passionate, exciting lover—who'd made love to her during a gondola ride in Venice, on a secluded beach in Crete, and on a balcony overlooking Paris—hadn't touched her for weeks.

Panic thrummed as the subject of her brooding came over to her. Tucking a curl behind her ear, he murmured, "How are you feeling, sunshine?"

"Fine." She was *not* fine. How could she be when the man she loved no longer found her attractive?

"Good." He paused. "Can I get you anything?"

Over the past few weeks, she'd learned to resent that

solicitous tone. The unfailingly gentle manner in which he treated her—as if she were an invalid.

"No," she said shortly.

He went to his side of the bed. She watched as he removed his dressing robe—and, Dear God, she couldn't stem the longing that flooded her at the sight of her husband's naked form. She couldn't stop her eyes from devouring his powerfully hewn chest with its light furring of hair, the rippling ridges of his flat belly. And between his muscular thighs...

Her mouth pooled. His cock hung big and thick, semi-erect.

Her pulse racing, she raised her eyes to his and saw the frown carved between his brows. As if he were disgusted... at *her*? Her heart seized. A moment later, he doused the lights and got into bed. He put an arm around her but did nothing else. They lay next to one another in the darkness, still and stiff and awkward as two corpses.

He doesn't want me. He doesn't love me...

In an act of pure desperation, Rosie turned and put a hand on her husband's chest.

His hoarse voice came at her like a blade through the darkness. "Sunshine, perhaps it would be better if I slept in the dressing room tonight."

Her heart lodged in her throat. In all the time that they'd been married, he'd *never* slept apart from her. In fact, he'd told her that she was the first woman he'd ever spent the entire night with, and she loved how he never let go of her, how they always woke tangled up together.

Now she said in a choked voice, "You can't even stand to share a bed with me anymore? I disgust you *that* much?"

The mattress shifted, and the lamp flared to life.

Andrew was sitting up in bed, staring at her. "What the devil?"

She struggled up against the pillows. "I know I'm ugly and fat, but I'm still your wife! You're supposed to love me no matter what. You *promised*."

He looked... mystified? "First of all, you're gorgeous. Second, you're not fat—you're expecting. And third..."

"Third, what?" she challenged.

He opened his mouth—and closed it. "Third, this conversation is so insane that I've forgotten what I was going to say," he muttered.

"I'm not insane! You haven't touched me for *weeks*. You used to *all the time*,"—her voice broke—"but now you can't even stand the sight of me. I'm so revolting you want to sleep in a different *bed*."

She burst into tears. When he put a hand on her shoulder, she shrugged him off and, burying her face in her hands, began weeping in earnest.

"Christ. This is mad." Through her tears, she saw him rake a hand through his hair. "How could you think that you revolt me? The opposite is true. You're beautiful, and I want you... but I don't want to hurt you."

"You're lying," she wailed, "just to make me feel better."

Sobs shook her. She felt hurt, agitated, and, truth be told... a teensy bit daft. A part of her knew she was being irrational, but she couldn't seem to help herself. These days, emotions rolled over her in sudden, overwhelming waves, and she struggled to find her equilibrium.

"Twenty-seven days."

At his non sequitur, she stopped crying long enough to say, "Pardon?"

"Twenty-seven days."

"I heard you the first time, but I don't know what you mean," she said, sniffling.

"It's been twenty-seven days since I last made love to you," he clarified.

His meaning hit her like a face full of sunshine.

"You've been *counting*?" she breathed.

"Days, hours, sometimes even the damned minutes," he said ruefully. "Why did you think I offered to sleep in the dressing room just now? You'd tempt a saint, and I'm trying to be a considerate husband. One who doesn't make demands on his wife when she's not feeling well. Christ, Primrose, I'll *always* want you—and knowing you have my babe inside you, seeing you glow with new life… you've never been more beautiful or desirable to me."

Once again, emotions swept over her. Only this time, they were waves of relief and joy.

"Oh, Andrew," she said tremulously, "I'm so glad you think so. To be honest, I haven't been glowing with life; I've been perspiring in the most unmentionable fashion."

"Minx." His mouth twitched. "I know you haven't been comfortable. Why do you think I've left you alone?"

"It was all… for me?" She felt ridiculous and swoony at the same time.

He nodded.

"You're the most considerate, most wonderful, most loving husband in the *world*," she blurted.

Lines crinkled around his eyes. "Is that all?"

"I'm, um, sorry if I've been acting a bit daft."

"At least you seem to be feeling better."

"I am," she said brightly. The storm had passed; she felt better than she had in weeks.

"Excellent." His slow, sensual smile stirred a different sort of turbulence in her. "Then you can make it up to me. Your considerate, wonderful, and—might I add—randy husband."

He swept aside the coverlet, revealing his magnificent erection.

Rosie giggled. "You *did* miss me."

"Wretch. You know you have this effect on me."

"Shall I kiss it better?"

His coffee-dark gaze turned steamy. "I always love it when you do."

She made a space for herself between his legs. Taking firm hold of his cock in both her hands, she brought her lips to the burgeoned head and gave it a generous lick. His chest heaved, and on the second swipe of her tongue, she tasted his essence: salty, male, and infinitely arousing. Eagerly, she took more of him, reveling in the sounds he made, the way his hands clenched in her hair when he hit the end of her throat.

"Christ, your *mouth*," he growled. "You make me feel so bloody good."

She answered by bobbing up and down on his cock, wanting to make him feel even *better*. Wanting to give her beloved all the joy and bliss that he gave her every single day, just by being himself. She released him with a popping sound that made him groan (she knew it would). Continuing to frig him firmly the way he liked, she traced her tongue down one of the raised veins of his mighty shaft. Reaching the base, she kissed the soft, supple sac of his stones—then she mouthed them, sucking gently.

"Bloody *fuck*." His neck arched, the tendons stretched taut.

She returned to the tip, taking him as deep as she could, savoring his hot spurts of pleasure.

The next thing she knew, her chemise was whipped off, and she was flat on her back, her husband's mouth between her legs. It wasn't long before she was crying out his name, her climax rippling over her. And it wasn't long after that—in fact, it was less than a minute because her climax was still rippling—when he surged inside her, vital, essential, filling her completely.

He took, and she took, and both of them gave and gave.

They came together, face to face, heart to heart, their

hands linked on the mattress.

Afterward, they lay on their sides, tucked together like spoons. Content and drowsy with love, she snuggled against him. "I did warn you that I can be a bit dramatic."

"Be as dramatic as you want, love." His voice was a wicked whisper against her ear. "I look forward to a lifetime of your apologies."

Quite a few years later

Andrew entered the heart of mayhem.

Given that it was his own home, however, he was used to it. Children—his and Primrose's as well as those belonging to her family—were everywhere: laughing and playing and generally carrying on like wild animals that had been cooped up too long. He didn't blame them. The opening ceremony of the new hospital had dragged on for hours, taking place out in the hot summer sun, and, through it all, the bantlings had looked and behaved like little angels.

Now his children and their cousins were making the most of their freedom. The adults sat around the drawing room chatting, enjoying the respite; like him, they knew it wouldn't last. The children always got on like a house on fire... until they didn't.

"Papa!" On cue, Miranda, his eldest, dashed over to where he was standing, her beautiful jade eyes full of pique. "Oliver is being a pest again!"

He placed a hand on her sunny curls. "What did he do now, little chick?"

"He's waving his sword about like a *maniac*. I told him to stop, but he wouldn't listen to me. Look,"—she pointed accusingly at a tiny tear in her puffed white sleeve—"he's *ruined* my new dress!"

"Oliver." Andrew crooked his finger at his brown-haired middle child.

Oliver toddled over, lugging his wooden sword with him. "Yes, Papa?" he said, all innocence.

"What did I tell you about playing with your sword indoors? Now apologize to your sister for ruining her dress."

"But I didn't do anything," Oliver protested.

"Liar," his sister hissed.

"Tattle-tale," he shot back.

"That's enough from both of you," Andrew said sternly. "Oliver, when you do something wrong, you take responsibility for it. That is what gentlemen do."

"But I didn't *mean* to ruin Miranda's dress." Oliver's brown gaze widened. "I was trying to give her an aclade with the sword—the same way Her Majesty gave one to you, Papa."

"That's an ac*co*lade, dummy," his sister said.

"Miranda, a lady doesn't engage in name-calling." Crouching, Andrew looked into his children's adorable faces; from experience, he knew not to give into those pleading eyes. "Now apologize to one another—and mean it."

"I'm sorry for putting a hole in your dress," Oliver muttered.

"I'm sorry for calling you a dummy," Miranda muttered back.

"Good. Now go play with your cousins."

Peace temporarily restored, the two scampered off, Miranda going to her bosom chum Sophie and Oliver to the pack that included the Carlisle boys, Revelstoke's eldest, and Harry Kent's son.

Awareness tingled on Andrew's nape, and he turned to see his wife entering the room. Even after all the years of marriage, the sight of her never failed to move him. She looked like a dream in her pink frock, and when she came over, he put an arm around her waist, tucking her close.

"Is Lily asleep?" he said.

Primrose gave a rueful nod. "Poor thing went out like a light. I left her with Nanny."

"The day has been too much for her. For all of us."

"Nonsense." His wife smiled at him. "Today was a tribute to you, my darling, and you earned every minute of it."

"I still can't believe Her Majesty conferred the honor on a man like me," he mused.

Of all the things he'd never expected to find, respectability was near the top of the list.

Right under love.

"After all your charitable contributions to society, you deserve no less. Why, Nursery House has become a model of care for women and children, and the hospitals you've built, including the new one, help so many in need. You've created 'innovations in social welfare'—and those aren't my words but those of His Royal Highness."

His lips twitched at her zealous defense of his achievements. "I had to do something. Idle hands and all that."

"Your hands haven't been idle a day in your life." Her grin turned flirty. "I can attest for that."

Before he could give her a proper answer, the butler entered with a cart of iced champagne for the adults and cold lemonade for the children. Glasses were passed around, and everyone, young and old, gathered in a circle. Even Horace and Fanny Grier were there. Andrew's throat felt oddly scratchy as he took in the beaming faces of his friends—and of the family Primrose had given him.

"A toast." Ambrose Kent raised a glass. "To Sir Andrew Corbett."

"And Lady Corbett," Marianne Kent added with a smile.

"To Sir and Lady Corbett," everyone chorused.

They all drank to that.

Leaning over, Primrose whispered, "See? I always knew I married a gentleman."

Lifting his lady's hand, Andrew kissed it tenderly. "So you did, sunshine. A gentleman who loves you."

**Please enjoy a peek at
Grace's other books...**

The *Heart of Enquiry* series

Prequel Novella: *The Widow Vanishes*
Fate throws beautiful widow Annabel Foster into the arms of William McLeod, her enemy's most ruthless soldier. When an unexpected and explosive night of passion ensues, she must decide: should she run for her life—or stay for her heart?

Book 1: *The Duke Who Knew Too Much*
When Miss Emma Kent witnesses a depraved encounter involving the wicked Duke of Strathaven, her honor compels her to do the right thing. But steamy desire challenges her quest for justice, and she and Strathaven must work together to unravel a dangerous mystery... before it's too late.

Book 2: *M is for Marquess*
With her frail constitution improving, Miss Dorothea Kent yearns to live a full and passionate life. Desire blooms between her and Gabriel Ridgley, the Marquess of Tremont, an enigmatic widower with a disabled son. But the road to love proves treacherous as Gabriel's past as a spy emerges to threaten them both... and they must defeat a dangerous enemy lying in wait.

Book 3: *The Lady Who Came in from the Cold*
Former spy Pandora Hudson gave up espionage for love. Twelve years later, her dark secret rises to threaten her blissful marriage to Marcus, Marquess of Blackwood, and she must face her most challenging mission yet: winning back the heart of the only man she's ever loved.

Book 4: *The Viscount Always Knocks Twice*
Sparks fly when feisty hoyden Violet Kent and proper gentleman Richard Murray, Viscount Carlisle, meet at a house party. Yet their forbidden passion and blossoming romance are not the only adventures afoot. For a guest is soon discovered dead—and Violet and Richard must join forces to solve the mystery and protect their

loved ones… before the murderer strikes again.

Book 5: *Never Say Never to an Earl*
Despite their outer differences, shy wallflower Polly Kent and wild rake Sinjin Pelham, the Earl of Revelstoke, have secrets to hide—and both desperately fear exposing their true selves. Yet the attraction between them is too strong to deny, and they become entangled in a passionate adventure. Both will have to face their greatest fear in order to win the love of a lifetime… and to survive the machinations of the enemy who lies in wait.

The *Mayhem in Mayfair* series

Book 1: *Her Husband's Harlot*
How far will a wallflower go to win her husband's love? When her disguise as a courtesan backfires, Lady Helena finds herself entangled in a game of deception and desire with her husband Nicholas, the Marquess of Harteford… and discovers that he has dark secrets of his own.

Book 2: *Her Wanton Wager*
To what lengths will a feisty miss go to save her family from ruin? Miss Persephone Fines takes on a wager of seduction with notorious gaming hell owner Gavin Hunt and discovers that love is the most dangerous risk of all.

Book 3: *Her Protector's Pleasure*
Wealthy widow Lady Marianne Draven will stop at nothing to find her kidnapped daughter. Having suffered betrayal in the past, she trusts no man—and especially not Thames River Policeman Ambrose Kent, who has a few secrets of his own. Yet fiery passion ignites between the unlikely pair as they battle a shadowy foe. Can they work together to save Marianne's daughter? And will nights of pleasure turn into a love for all time?

Book 4: *Her Prodigal Passion*

Sensible Miss Charity Sparkler has been in love with Paul Fines, her best friend's brother, for years. When he accidentally compromises her, they find themselves wed in haste. Can an ugly duckling recognize her own beauty and a reformed rake his own value? As secrets of the past lead to present dangers, will this marriage of convenience transform into one of love?

The *Chronicles of Abigail Jones* series

Book 1: *Abigail Jones*
When destiny brings shy Victorian maid Abigail Jones into the home of the brooding and enigmatic Earl of Huxton, she discovers forbidden passion ... and a dangerous world of supernatural forces.

About the Author

National & International Bestselling Author Grace Callaway writes steamy historical romances set in the Regency and Victorian eras. Her debut book, *Her Husband's Harlot*, was a Romance Writers of America® Golden Heart® Finalist and a #1 Kindle Regency Bestseller. Her subsequent books have hit Top 100 Bestselling lists on Amazon, iBooks, and Barnes & Noble, and she's a finalist for the National Reader's Choice Awards® and the Daphne du Maurier Award® for Excellence in Mystery/ Suspense.

As a child growing up on the Canadian prairies, Grace could often be found with her nose in a book—and not much has changed since. She set aside her favorite romance novels long enough to get her doctorate from the University of Michigan. A practicing clinical psychologist, she lives with her family in California, where their adventures include remodeling a ramshackle house, exploring the great outdoors, and sampling local artisanal goodies.

Grace loves to hear from her readers and can be reached at grace@gracecallaway.com.

Other ways to connect:

Newsletter: www.gracecallaway.com/newsletter
Facebook: www.facebook.com/GraceCallawayBooks
Website: www.gracecallaway.com